About the Editors

LIZ GRZYB was born in the middle of a thunderstorm in Perth, Western Australia. She is the editor of acclaimed paranormal romance anthologies *Scary Kisses* and *More Scary Kisses*, and the website ticon4.com. Liz is also the fantasy editor for *The Year's Best Australian Fantasy and Horror* anthologies from Ticonderoga Publications.

AMANDA PILLAR is an award-winning editor and speculative fiction author who lives in Victoria, Australia, with her partner and two children, Saxon and Lilith (Burmese cats). Amanda has had numerous short stories published and is the Editor-in-Chief for Morrigan Books. She has co-edited the fiction anthologies *Voices* (2008), *Grants Pass* (2009), *The Phantom Queen Awakes* (2010), *Scenes from the Second Storey* (2010) and *Ishtar* (2011). She is also working on the *Bloodstones* anthology, due out in 2012. In her 'free time', she works as an archaeologist.

Damnation and Dames

Also edited by LIZ GRZYB

Scary Kisses
More Scary Kisses
The Year's Best Australian Fantasy & Horror 2010 (with Talie Helene)
The Year's Best Australian Fantasy & Horror 2011* (with Talie Helene)

Also edited by AMANDA PILLAR

Voices (with Mark S. Deniz)
Grants Pass (with Jennifer Brozek)
Scenes from the Second Storey (with Pete Kempshall)
The Phantom Queen Awakes (with Mark S. Deniz)
Ishtar (with K.V. Taylor)
Bloodstones*

**forthcoming from Ticonderoga Publications*

DAMNATION
AND
DAMES

EDITED BY
LIZ GRZYB AND
AMANDA PILLAR

Ticonderoga
publications

*To those who fight the good fight.
You are our heroes, no matter the outcome.*

Damnation and Dames edited by Liz Grzyb & Amanda Pillar

Published by Ticonderoga Publications

Copyright © 2012 Liz Grzyb & Amanda Pillar

All rights reserved. Without limiting the rights under copyright reserved above, no part of this publication may be reproduced, stored in or introduced into a retrieval system, or transmitted in any form or by any means (electronic, mechanical, recording or otherwise) without the express prior written permission of the copyright holder concerned. Page 303 constitutes an extension of this copyright page.

Introduction copyright © 2012 Liz Grzyb & Amanda Pillar

Designed and edited by Russell B. Farr

Typeset in Sabon and Electro Gothic

A Cataloging-in-Publications entry for this title is available from The National Library of Australia.

ISBN   978-1-921857-03-4 (trade paperback)
           978-1-921857-04-1 (ebook)

Ticonderoga Publications
PO Box 29 Greenwood
Western Australia 6924

www.ticonderogapublications.com

10 9 8 7 6 5 4 3 2 1

ACKNOWLEDGEMENTS

The editors would like to thank Lindsy Anderson, Chris Bauer, Alan Baxter, Jay Caselberg, M.L.D. Curelas, Karen Dent, Felicity Dowker, Dirk Flinthart, Lisa L. Hannett, Donna Maree Hanson, Robert Hood, Joseph L. Kellogg, Pete Kempshall, Chris Large, Penelope Love, Nicole Murphy, Brian G. Ross, Angela Slatter, Marianne de Pierres, Kim Wilkins, Russell B. Farr, and Hilary Donraadt.

Liz would like to thank Amanda Pillar, Angela Challis, Shane Cummings, Kate Dunbar-Smith, Kate Williams, Andrew Williams, Debbie Wilson, Jacinta Rosielle, Ambre Hillier, Michael Hillier, Tasmar Dixon, Mel Donald, Phil Ward, Helen Grzyb, the English Department, and the girls at Mystique.

Amanda would like to thank Liz Grzyb, Tom Bicknell, Judi Jaensch, Boris Dzuris, Sue Bicknell, David Bicknell, and Sarah Goldfarb.

Contents

INTRODUCTION	13
BLIND PIG	15
Jay Caselberg	
A CASE TO DIE FOR	25
Karen Dent	
SOUND AND FURY	47
Pete Kempshall	
BURNING, ALWAYS BURNING	65
Alan Baxter and Felicity Dowker	
THE BLACK STAR KILLER	75
Nicole Murphy	
HARD BOILED	89
Brian G. Ross	
SILVER COMES THE NIGHT	107
M.L.D. Curelas	
OUTLINES	123
Dirk Flinthart	
SANGUE DELLA NOTTE	141
Donna Maree Hanson	
THE AWAKENED ADVENTURE OF RICK CANDLE	155
Joseph L. Kellogg	
THIRD CIRCLE	175
Lindsy Anderson	
THREE QUESTIONS AND ONE TROLL	193
Chris Bauer	
BE GOOD, SWEET MAID	213
Penelope Love	
WALKING THE DEAD BEAT	229
Robert Hood	
ONE NIGHT AT THE CHERRY	257
Chris Large	
PROHIBITION BLUES	271
Lisa L. Hannett and Angela Slatter	
ABOUT THE CONTRIBUTORS	299

INTRODUCTION

The idea for *Damnation & Dames* was spawned while we were working at the Ticonderoga Publications' table during Worldcon 2010, Melbourne. Liz was in the throes of reading for her second paranormal romance anthology, and Amanda had just finished working on a horror anthology. While the streams of readers and writers fanned past the table, we began swapping war stories; soon after that, it was decided that we should work on a collection together. It was dealer room madness, clearly.

The genre blending of paranormal and noir seemed an obvious choice. (Or as Alan Baxter and Felicity Dowker called it, "paranoirmal".)

We both love reading paranormal stories: vampires, werewolves, ghosts, zombies, and angels; they're all awesome. And when it comes down to it, they're superheroes for adult readers. There's the superhuman strength, the ability to walk through walls, the casting of spells and even the chance to fly. Ideal reading for those searching for that elusive sense of escapism.

Then we have noir. It has a real sense of mystique: magnetic elements like the smoky bars, the glamour, the sizzling attraction between the *femme fatale* and her love interest. There's also the current fascination with the fashion of the 1920s, 30s, 40s and 50s (your editors are not immune here, dear reader) and we are left with an alluring genre with which to blend, mix and play.

The combination of paranormal and noir seemed like a relatively untapped market; it had some logical and interesting links that we wanted to explore—ghostly fog and cigarette smoke, dangerously compelling women, stoic detectives dealing with mysteries that aren't always as they seem...and of course, twists on that theme.

When we put out the call for stories, we were looking for tales that were addictive from the start. We wanted sizzle, allure and a plot to make us think. Strong male characters balanced by an outstanding femme fatale; female leads with the cunning and smarts that meant *they* solved their *own* problems. Ultimately, we wanted the traditional boundaries of noir to be blurred by the wonders of the paranormal.

The quality and range of the stories submitted for the anthology were outstanding and some very difficult decisions were made in the selection of the sixteen sensational stories you will find between these covers.

In the end, we decided on a collection of stories that run the gamut between saucy and thrilling, serious and fun, and vintage and fantastical. We hope you love this collection. We certainly do.

LIZ GRZYB AND AMANDA PILLAR
APRIL 2012

BLIND PIG

Jay Caselberg

Word on the street was out. Blood simply wasn't blood any more. It wasn't what it used to be, wasn't any good. Me? It didn't matter a hill of beans to me, but the Vamps, well, they weren't too happy about it. Don't get me wrong; there are vamps and there are Vamps. I'm talking about the second type, the ones with the big teeth. I'd heard the mutterings on the street, of course—the shine guy was the one who told me first—but I didn't expect the subject of the scuttlebutt to walk right into my office on a pair of spiked heels and a tight black dress, not too long after sunset.

Sunset comes early in the city anyways. It has to do with the buildings. I don't quite understand it, and I guess it's a technicality, but once the sun is gone, it's set. City like ours, it's the ideal place for Vamps; the buildings are taller. Maybe that's why they passed the Vladimir Act in the first place. Folks, quite naturally, were getting kind of unsettled with all the public and open consumption. Sure, we understand it, and me, I was kinda queasy too. It was blood, after all. The more Vamps, the more ruby stained lips, the unavoidable viscous pools. You know, no matter how much you try to ignore it, it's hard to look away. The colour draws you in like a tarnished dream reminding you of your mortality.

The place had changed since the turn of the century. Chicago, the great melting pot. It was the yards really—the great Stockyards. Give them work and they'll come. It was no surprise that the Vamps were drawn to the place. It was their heritage too, the old Eastern European influence, the old Eastern European flavour. And there, in the Back of the Yards, amongst the 475 acres of old swamp, the 50 miles of road and the 130 miles of rail track, they lived and loved and died. Problem was, some of them didn't really stay dead.

Before that night, I wasn't too worried about any of that. The Yards were there, sitting in the back of my consciousness like a grey smudge, and when it came down to it, I was more content wrapping myself around the contents of a bourbon bottle. The day had been pretty slow. A divorce, a missing person, both of them leading to nothing. I was halfway through my first glass when she sashayed in and fixed me with that look. You know the one. She had that accent too—full of 'v's and 'z's.

"You are Walker?"

It took me a moment or two to free up my throat, despite the burn at the back of my mouth.

"Um, yeah. That's me."

"You came recommended."

Who the hell would be recommending me to the likes of her didn't pass my thoughts right then. My mind was on other things.

"So what can I do for you?" I cleared my throat and took another swallow.

"There is a problem among... our kind. We need you to investigate. That is what you do, no? Investigate."

"Yeah. Charlie Walker, Private Investigator. That's what I do. Just like it says on the sign. Take a seat." I waved her in the direction of the pair of hard-backed chairs sitting in front of my desk. I watched her all the way. If she hadn't have been what she was, I mighta been dizzy for this dame. Instead, I pulled another glass from the desk and slid it her way, but she didn't even look at it.

"So what can I do for you, Miss...?"

"You can call me Jirina."

"Okay, so how can I help? Why did you come to me?"

She fixed me with that look again and I reached for my glass. I couldn't help myself.

"It has to be someone outside. One of your kind. We cannot move as you can." She glanced out the window at the gloom outside. The look was almost wistful.

I got it then. There was something going on that needed freedom of movement in daylight.

"So, what is it?"

"Someone is targeting our kind, Mr Walker. We need to find out who."

"Targeting, how?"

"You have to see." She gave a wry laugh then.

I started to talk about fees, but she simply waved her hand and instead slipped a piece of paper across the desk.

"Be there at midnight," she said.

It was an address not too far from the Palace Theatre. I sort of knew the place, but I wasn't too comfortable with the midnight thing. I kept my eyes on the address.

"Do not worry, Mr Walker. We will make sure you are all right. You need to see."

"Uh huh," I said, and met her gaze.

"Good," she said and pushed back the chair.

I wasn't too sure it was good, or what I was getting into, but I guess I was hooked, not that I couldn't do with the extra dough. I watched her as she glided out of the office and reached for my glass again.

• • •

I turned up on West Randolph about 11:15, suitably fortified and ready for anything... well, less worried about what I was going to find. I stayed back in the shadows and settled down to watch before the appointed time. Force of habit. The shadows weren't going to make a difference to them. I was probably standing there glowing like an engine light, but I didn't really know how they saw things.

The place was set close to the sidewalk, downstairs with a no-name door announcing to no one what it was. There were a lot of these places since the Vladimir Act. I observed a couple of clients arrive in succession—the usual get up, the dark clothes, the plush red, the boots. I never worked out whether it was a peculiar fashion sense or a carryover from some past age.

About twenty minutes later, my vigil was rewarded: a couple approached the discreet doorway, one leading the other. The one who was being led seemed to be having difficulty seeing his way; he stumbled on the steps, ended up in the arms of his companion, who then led him to the door and rapped. The small slide opened, checking them out and then the door swung open, granting them access. I'd never seen Vamps walk like that. Maybe zombies, sure, but they were a whole different ball game.

It was getting close to the time. Swallowing hard, I checked either way making sure there were no surprises and headed down to the simple doorway. Taking a real big breath, I knocked. I knew what I was expecting—it was just another Vamp juice joint after all, but I can't say I was real easy about it.

The small peephole slid open and a pair of eyes fixed me with that look. There was a moment's hesitation, the panel slid back into place and then nothing. I thought I was going to be stuck out there looking like a chump, standing in the dark and shaking in my shoes, but finally the door swung open. Nervously, I slid inside.

The place was full of Vamps. They looked pretty much alike; the black, the red, the slick pale look and those particular gazes that almost had me fixed right where I was. I needn't have worried though; the one called Jirina was standing there in a huddle and she beckoned me over.

"Mr Walker," she said. Again with the 'v'.

"So, why here?" I asked, glancing nervously around. There was something funny going on, all right. Some of them were draped over the bar, slumped. Another was holding his head. A low muttering circulated through the narrow space. I thought it mighta been me, but they didn't seem to be interested at all.

"You can see," she said.

"I don't get it, sister," I said, taking another quick look around. One of them looked over at me and then looked away, not even giving me the gaze. I turned my attention back to Jirina.

"Someone is sabotaging us, Mr Walker. Whatever they are doing, it is robbing us of our night vision. What good are we when we cannot see any better than your kind? Blind at night and unable to move in the daylight. You can see, around you. We believe the source of the problem is here, but we are powerless. We need you to find out what is happening and we need you to stop it."

I'd seen this sort of thing before. There'd been word on the street about the normal juice joints. People tampering with the product, that sort of thing, coffin varnish. Torrio and The Big Fellow had put a stop to most of that in our joints. Over on the bar, there were glasses, full of red. I hadn't even registered them, but I got an eyeful of them then.

I looked at her and frowned. "Well, it's pretty clear," I told her. "Why do you need me?"

She sighed then and fixed me with the look. "We have spoken among ourselves. Our source is reliable. We know that. What is being done is being done somewhere else. We suspect it is in the Yards. It is not safe for us to be there, and since the Act, our movements there are restricted. Most of what happens there is in the day. So . . ."

"So you want me to go to the Yards and find out."

"If we cannot rely on our sources anymore," she said slowly, pausing, letting the message sink in, "Then we will have to find other ways."

I thought it through and saw what she was saying. The picture in my mind was one I didn't want. Not where I was standing right then. I swallowed and I nodded.

"So you will do it?" she asked.

"You got yourself a gumshoe," I said.

It had been quite a while since I was as happy as I was to get out of a place and back onto the street. I was even happier by the time I got out of the neighbourhood and back to my small apartment. The bottle there waiting for me was new. It was about half empty when I finally hit the sack.

. . .

I headed down to the Stockyards armed with nothing more than my gun and a name: Karnecki. He was a Pole, like thousands of others who worked around the Yards. If he'd worked up a line in supplying the Vamps, then he wasn't likely to be threatening it, I thought. That meant there had to be some other connection. Most sane people made it a habit to stay pretty clear of the Union Stock Yards. The working conditions for the thousands employed there were pretty bad. Those who worked on the killing floors had to do so amidst stench and shrieks of animals being slaughtered while they stood on blood-soaked floors. Ten to twelve hours a day in temperatures exceeding 100 degrees was not unusual. Wages were low and that was it, but the immigrant workers were desperate to earn a living. Those guys could get away with murder. Perhaps someone was trying to return the favour, but it wasn't the Vamps who were to blame, so that just didn't add up.

I asked around, but it wasn't so easy. A lot of them down there looked at me with suspicion or simply couldn't understand. English just wasn't their natural way of talking, after all. They tended to stick to themselves as well. Ukraine with Ukraine, Pole with Pole and so on. Finally, I found someone who pointed me in the direction of the Poles and I picked my way through rail cars and sleepers, sheds and trucks in that general direction. All the way, I kept one hand on my gat. It wasn't the safest place to be. When you're scraping for a dime, there're all sorts of ways to make ends meet, and I didn't particularly want to end up being one of them.

By the time I found who I was looking for, I was wishing I was somewhere else. It makes you edgy, a place like that.

Karnecki was a stocky man, a ring of white stubble above a round balding pate. He had a couple of days of white growth on his cheeks and chin as well. When I asked him if he was the guy, he peered at me suspiciously with ice-blue eyes, sizing me up.

"Who are you? What you want?" he said.

His suspicion was natural, especially if he was involved in any sort of business. I could have easily been someone from any one of the local families looking for a rake off.

"Relax, Karnecki," I told him. "I'm here on behalf of a—" I paused. "A woman . . . called Jirina. My name is Walker. She has a little problem that needs fixing."

His eyes shifted, glancing to the other side, behind me, then back over his shoulder. "You'd better come inside," he said, gesturing to the door of some sort of cobbled together shack behind him. I was happy enough to follow him into the gloom; the sights and sounds and smells out there were starting to get on more than my nerves.

"So what do you want?" he asked. Straight to the point.

There didn't seem to be any reason to do otherwise. "Someone is tampering with your supplies," I said.

"But that is not possible. You are mistaken."

"I can assure you, I'm not. I've seen what's out there," I said. "It wouldn't be hard, would it, Karnecki? There's plenty of stuff out there on the floors. Just a bit here. Just a bit there."

He had his back pressed hard against the tin and wooden door, and it creaked with his weight as he shook his head and frowned. "No. It is not possible."

"Why do you say that?" I said. "Where do you get your, um, product?"

He looked me straight in the eye. "It is all from the community. They are volunteers. Of course they get a little extra income, and I am happy to help out. These are my people, Mr Walker. Why would I do this?"

"I dunno. That's what I am trying to find out."

Karnecki was being straight with me. I had the feeling in my gut that told me so. And what he said was making sense. Why would he tamper with his income stream? Conditions were hard enough down here. And his people . . . they all stuck together, looked after their own. It was the sort of thing they'd do together.

"So who? Is there someone who wishes you harm? Maybe one of the Families? Another community?"

He held his hands wide and shrugged. "We keep to our own. We do not interfere."

I was drawing a blank.

"When are you due to make your next delivery?"

"Tomorrow night."

"And the product?"

"It takes place nearby."

"Well, you're going to have to show me. We have to see what happens. I need to see who comes and goes, need to see if there's anyone."

He was frowning again. "These are my people, Mr Walker. Why would *they* do this?"

"That's what we have to find out."

Karnecki looked troubled, chewing on what I was suggesting as if it were something bad, but he agreed to help. He didn't really have much choice.

. . .

The following afternoon, I watched them all file in, in groups, in ones and twos, individually. Families, single men, girls together, there must have been fifty of them all told. All of them wore work clothes of one form or another. They were either from the slaughterhouse floors, or the packing lines. One thing they had in common, apart from the particular look that bound them together, was that they all wore long sleeves, despite the sweltering heat of the day. There wasn't much chat, and they were pale. They disappeared inside the small building on the edges of the rail yards, and then they appeared again, perhaps looking even paler than when they entered. Finally, Karnecki appeared, wearing a stained apron, rubbing his hands as if trying to clean them of something, and then wiping them on the back of his overalls. He glanced towards my place of concealment, but apart from that, gave no sign that he knew I was there.

I waited until dark, but there was nothing. Eventually, after a few hours, after the sun had set, Karnecki reappeared in the company of two others. They were of the same stock, heavy set men, dressed in the clothing of the workers, one of them wearing a cloth cap, another, bare headed, his balding head shining in the darkness. The younger of the two companions stood outside the shack looking up and down, keeping watch, while the other two slipped inside, and then reappeared, rolling a large barrel between them. They loaded it onto a nearby cart, and then all together, pulled and guided it across some tracks and away, further into the darkening rail yards.

Still, I waited for about another hour, but there was nothing. Another blind alley. Feeling exposed, I quit my place and also headed across the tracks and back out of the Yards and home. If something didn't turn up soon, I was going to run out of ideas and I'd have to go back to their place empty-handed.

Three more times, each a couple of days apart, I held the vigil. Three more times I came up with nothing. I thought that even Karnecki was getting tired of seeing my face.

On the fourth night, I hit pay dirt, but not in a way I expected.

I was close to giving up, tired, my mouth dry and my mind wandering to the bottle sitting lonely on the desk in my office, when there was movement near the makeshift shack. I had watched the afternoon procession long enough to recognise a couple of the earlier visitors. An older man and a woman, straining with the weight of a wooden container between them. I kept still, waiting, biding my time. Sure enough, they reached for the door and went inside.

Quietly, carefully, I stepped across to the door, my gun already out and ready. I eased the door open and entered.

They had the large barrel open between them, the contents black in the gloom. Together, they were straining, lifting the container between them.

"What are you doing?" I said.

The woman looked up and gasped, fumbled, lost her grip. The container slipped from her grasp and thumped to the ground, its contents slopping out and pooling and then seeping, dark into the loose earth floor. That smell filled the small space. You know the one.

"What do you think you're doing?" I said again.

The woman stood with her mouth still open, looking at me, then the gun, then at the man she was with. He looked only at the gun.

"What we must," he said haltingly. "We are doing our duty."

I tilted my head to one side, asking a question.

"Giving them what they deserve," said the woman. "They deserve this," she said, pointing at the dark patch on the floor. "They deserve only what is left from pigs. They are pigs."

I didn't get it straight away. This wasn't an attempt to do anything to Karnecki, as I had first suspected. They were after the Vamps themselves.

"But why?" I said. "I saw you today. You were with the rest of them."

The old man cleared his throat and spoke in a quiet voice. "We understand what Cyryl is doing. He tries to help us. They come to him, because they know he comes from our old home. He tries to help us all. But he doesn't remember like we do. Back home, back in Krakau, they took my father. They took my wife's sister, too. We have seen. We can understand what Cyryl does, but we can have some vengeance, too. They should pay for what they have done."

Finally, he lifted his gaze to mine and met my eyes. His expression was almost pleading. I kinda felt sorry for the guy.

"But these Vamps weren't responsible," I said. "Or even if they were, how could you know?"

"It doesn't matter," he said. "We come from the same place. We honour the memories of our families."

I bit my lip and sighed. Me, I didn't have a family, not anymore, but I could understand what the old guy was saying. "Listen," I said. "I'm not going to argue about why you're doing it, but you have to understand. What you're doing is hurting you, me, your people: all of us."

He frowned and glanced at the old woman, who looked back at him, seeking some sort of explanation. I continued. "The Vladimir Act keeps them regulated, controlled. If they can't get what they need, they'll just go back to the old ways. We can't get rid of them, we know that. So, we gotta live together. What you're doing here, is spoiling what they need. It makes them sick. It makes them blind. Well, not blind like you or I would be, but blind all the same from the way they see things. If this goes on, they're going to stop drinking what they're given, what they're getting from people like Karnecki, and they'll go and get their own. Think about it. Think about the way things were."

As the message started to sink in, the old woman's eyes widened.

I took pity on the both of them. "Yeah," I said. "Now, get out of here."

I waited for them to leave, and then I followed, closing the door carefully behind me.

...

I didn't get back in touch with Karnecki. I figured the empty container and the stain on the floor in the old shack would be enough. Maybe he'd be more vigilant in future.

I went back to the Vamp juice joint though, and I relayed what I'd found to Jirina. When her fury subsided and she'd got a hold of herself, she reluctantly accepted what I'd told her. She paid my fee, and that was that. I didn't think I'd be seeing them again. Well, not by choice.

The last thing I did was ask her where she was from.

When she told me Krakau, well, I guess I didn't like thinking about that too much.

A CASE TO DIE FOR

Karen Dent

Looking in the mirror, I took in the damage to my face. Three steri-strips stared back. I was lucky. It could have been ten. And they could have been on my neck, holding my head back on.

Playing rough was taking its toll; and I was tired.

I shrugged out of my bloody shirt and washed up in my tiny office bathroom. Its cracked grey tiles and peeling paint were long past their prime. Just like me. Gerry Macklevoy. My clients call me GM or Gerry. My mother, well, she likes to piss me off and string out my whole name. Geraldine Helaine Macklevoy. I hate that.

I limped back into my luxurious suite, an 8x15 shoebox I referred to as my home-away-from-home and grabbed a rumpled black T-shirt from the pile on the floor. I yanked it on and winced. Don't let anyone kid you. Shoving a dislocated shoulder back into place hurts before, during and after.

I plopped down in Betsy, who squeaked and threatened to tip over. I ignored her. Rummaging through my desk, I came up with my old friend, Jack, and set it next to the jelly jar. I stared at the amber liquid as the afternoon's memory flooded back. Like the bloated body of my partner, Riley, it stank of a set-up; but I hadn't listened then, either.

My current client had come to pay his fee. We'd lifted glasses, even clinked. If Betsey's broken leg hadn't dipped when it did, I'd have been a goner. And my client would have been 5K richer.

I hate lots of things, but one thing really gets me: a client who tries to pull a double-cross. He won't be doing that again. Not for a long time.

I smiled, but it hurt, so I poured and pondered my future. It wasn't pretty. An inherited PI business, a dead partner and ten long years of bruises and mementos cut into flesh and ego. Riley's and my grandiose plans of getting better cases and moving to a decent office had turned to squat.

Just like my life.

Being a freak growing up hadn't helped. Talking to inanimate objects and having them answer back made people think you were nuts. My mother, grandmother, her grandmother's mother. All had the Talk. The big T. 'Course, it came in handy as a PI and Riley hadn't objected. He had been pretty freaky, too. He'd seen dead people. And once the murdered ones knew, well, they were relentless in wanting to hire him.

But Riley hadn't minded. Actually, neither had I. We re-opened more cold and missing person cases than the cops. And, I might add, solved more, too.

The cops hadn't liked it, but we wised up, told a few doozies to the papers: like, if it wasn't for the cooperation of our fine police force working closely with us, blah blah. Made it easier for us to get information and polished a few apples along the way. No skin off our noses. Our clients didn't care, but they put a real literal slant to the word 'deadbeat'. So we'd squeeze the family to pay up their posted 'reward leading to any information . . . ', in order to scrounge something. It hadn't helped our finances when one of them turned out to be the perpetrator. They got real nasty about paying up. But we managed. And we were a pretty good team. I took a swig and let the alcohol warm me—good until Riley had got himself killed.

I rocked back in Betsy and stroked her arm, promising to oil her joints and add a good polish. I owed her. She'd seen the gun my client had pulled out under the table and had tossed me on my arse before the bastard could drill me.

But the polish would have to wait for tomorrow. Tonight, I had other plans.

I pulled over the stack of police reports relating to Riley's murder. His would be my last case in Boston. Too many bad memories in this lousy town.

I could still hear his enthusiasm: "Gerry, this one's a slam dunk. We'll be able to head West like we planned. Hollywood. Glam jobs with lots of dough and beautiful dames."

"Nothing's ever that easy and you know it." I hadn't liked the case from the beginning. Something just didn't feel right. And there'd been no body. Well, except the ethereal one that kept telling Riley he was dead, with no idea how it had happened or even where his corpse was.

All we had to go on was that the dead john had been asking a kid some questions, and he'd gotten blackjacked for an answer.

And then there were the client's progeny. Shifty-eyed, haunted little shits, who threw more mud at their step-mother than I'd seen in a watering hole wrestling match. There had also been his missing daughter. She was the runaway the dead guy had been looking for before he ended pushing up daisies somewhere.

But that wasn't all of it. There'd also been Detective Manning. Grey eyes with a hard face that told nothing.

I poured myself another glass of Jack and swallowed it down. Felt good. Especially while I reflected on Detective Manning. He was a closed book and I was pretty sure his eyes were the same colour as his soul. Grey.

The police in Beantown were soaked in the treacle of IOUs. And I'd heard Manning had come from a long line of cops with connections.

I don't like people I can't trust.

A whisper from the outer hallway warned me I had a visitor. The threadbare carpet and wooden stairs gave me enough warning to strap my snub nose to my ankle. I checked the bullets in my spare, and pointed it at the door. At the last minute, I put the bottle back in the drawer. No sense in wasting good liquor if things got ugly.

A broad shouldered shape showed in the half-glass of my front door and took off his slouch hat before opening it.

"Detective Manning. I was just thinking about you."

Manning walked in. His eyes swivelled and took in my décor. The bullet holes in the outside wall behind me whistled in appreciation. *Mmmm,* I agreed.

"Windy in here." He nodded at the holes. "Nice air-conditioning."

"What can I do for you?" I lifted out the Jack, got another Yabadaba-Doo glass from my stellar collection and poured him one.

"I'm working," he told me.

"Me too," I lifted my glass. "Cheers." I drank.

He took his time, but finally walked over, got rid of the books on the chair opposite me and sat. He lifted his glass and tossed its contents down.

I was surprised. And wary. Detective Manning had never come to my office for a drink before. Something was up.

We sat there, watching each other for a while. Not that I was complaining. He was damn nice to look at. Chiselled chin, dark with shadow, black curly hair that refused to stay gelled in place. And those eyes. Piercing, intelligent, thoughtful.

I stared back and wondered what he saw. Not much tonight, that was for sure. My dark brown hair was pulled away from a battered face with large amber eyes that Nanna used to call lion-yellow. My arched brows and stubborn chin completed the picture. Nothing to write home about. I sighed inwardly. More than likely he saw me as some pain-in-the-arse rookie who'd hooked up with a wannabe Sam Spade.

I cleared my throat in the lengthening silence. "Shall we head to the bathroom and see who can piss the farthest? You have an unfair advantage, but I bet I last the longest." I smiled my smart-mouth challenge and instantly regretted it. Damn bruised lip.

"Nice. You kiss your mother with that mouth, Geraldine?"

I put the bottle away and slammed the drawer. "What do you want?"

"That's better." He grinned and showed even white teeth and a dimple.

I'd never seen that dimple before. I liked it.

He reached into his coat pocket and tossed me an ice bag. "For your lip. Or your cheek. Or your shoulder. Whatever."

I caught the instant ice bag and activated it. "Gosh, I didn't think you cared." I placed it on my lip and sighed at the immediate relief.

"I came to get your statement. Your ex-client is screaming brutality and unwarranted violence. I need your side." He looked at the bullet holes. "Those his?"

"Bastard thought it best not to pay me. I thought different and used his face to prove my point."

"Let's not forget his broken wrist and leg," he added.

"Oh yeah, those. Well, he wouldn't let go of the gun." I smiled again and this time it didn't hurt. Much.

Manning smiled back and that dimple peeped out again. Damn if he wasn't cute.

I hardened my expression. I'd been down that road before. Two serious relationships broken when they found out about my big T. No way was I ever doing that again. Now I stuck to casual sex, but not with anyone I was actually interested in. Or liked. Too risky.

I shuffled the papers on my desk. "I'm kinda busy right now." I pointed to a small camera placed in a shadowed corner of the room. "If you want proof he started it, you can have the tape. I made my statement at the hospital. It'll jive." I got up to retrieve the recording and instantly regretted it.

He saw me wince and quickly stood. "I'll get it." He walked over, reached up and took the camera down.

I got a nice view of his rear and sat back down. Six-four, fluid muscles, well-toned. Hey, I wasn't going to get involved, but that didn't mean I couldn't look.

He wrote out a receipt and put it on my desk. "If you want to press charges, I'll make sure the tape doesn't disappear."

"Now I know we're engaged." He snorted and I kicked myself. No banter, I reminded myself. Strictly business. "If I prosecute my own client, I'll be a pariah."

He headed out. "Don't need to. You gave a warning to future assholes. Thanks for the drink."

"Hey," I called after him. "If you can squeeze another grand out of him for damages, I'd appreciate it."

The wall whistled softly as he walked out. "My sentiments exactly," I agreed.

Two days later, Manning walked back into my less-than luxurious office with a stunning blonde. She had long, smooth legs, which were tanned and tapered to expensive stilettos. Her hair was swept up and over one eye, gracefully falling in a bounce just above her shoulders, sparkling like real gold.

I put on my curious face, sat back in Betsey and watched Blondie look around and assess my office. I'd cleaned it up a bit, but the inspection made me feel judged. Another thing I hate. I also don't like drop-ins without a call first. So I waited.

She looked at Manning, a sculpted eyebrow raised and I watched the unspoken question flutter between them.

Definitely didn't like Blondie.

"Darling, are you sure?" Her voice was cultured, smooth like silk.

I couldn't help a snarky, "Yes, darling. Are you?" And we both beaded him with a cold stare.

He removed his arm from hers and turned to me. "I've brought you a client." Manning led Blondie over to the chair before my desk. "Have a seat and talk."

I held up my hand. "No, don't. I've already made plans to get out of Dodge in less than a month. My bills and rent's paid up, boxes are filled. I don't have time to start another case."

She deflated right before my eyes. The air whooshed from her lungs and she sagged into ol' Earl like she was cooked pasta.

Manning patted her shoulder and glared at me. "Lying doesn't suit you, GM."

"First, I'm not lying. Second, I don't take every case that comes my way. And third," I tapped my pencil impatiently, "I'm busy with my last case." I was annoyed. Seeing Manning with this rich, beautiful Grace Kelly of woman-flesh really put me in a bad mood.

Insultingly, I let my lazy gaze wander up from her manicured, French-tipped nails to her flawless skin. Her eyes were deepened with smoky grey shadows, which emphasised the steely blue glittering back at me. Good. She was pissed off, too.

I tucked a stray wisp of my hair back into the messy bun I'd jerked it into that morning. She mirrored my insult by moving her eyes down from my bruised, naked face to my short unvarnished nails. *Right back atcha, bitch.*

I gave her kudos for match point: *Well-played.*

Manning glared at me. "GM, she's a paying client and might have some information that will help with your last case." He looked pointedly at the photos of Riley on my desk and turned to Blondie. "Jess, she's got," he paused, as if to choose the right word. "Talents that go beyond what we can do at the station."

I tensed and wondered how much he knew about me, so I countered with "Flattery will get you zippo, Manning. Why me and what's the catch?"

"You're good and this case is right up your alley."

"Like I said: what's the catch?"

Jessica Rabbit—my new name for Blondie—took a deep breath. "Ever heard of Christian Dempsey?"

I sat back. "Who hasn't? Big Poobah of The World Order, who, besides spreading the Word of God as they see it, has also been accused of targeting the progeny of the exclusively rich and brainwashing them into donating their mega millions to his cause." I lifted my fist. "Power to the Lord, Amen."

The Rabbit stared at me stone-faced.

I looked at both of them and crossed my arms. "So? One of your kind got snagged and you want to liberate them. There are plenty of snatch-and-run experts out there." I looked at Manning accusingly; "At the very least, it's a two person job and in case you forgot, I'm down one."

Manning glanced at the boxes stacked against my wall and frowned. "You're really leaving?"

"Yeah. Going West like Riley and I planned. Time for a change."

"Yes," Jessica's silky voice sliced in. "But about me?" She rose and started to pace while I tried to figure out what Manning's face was telling me. He seemed disturbed. He seemed confused. He seemed—upset?

I half-listened to the rolling Rs and clipped sentences as the Rabbit told her story, while the other half of my brain tried to interpret what I was picking up from Manning. Surely he wasn't interested in me. And, I thought resentfully, so what? I'd promised myself not to be a sucker again.

I became aware of the practised vulnerable quiver in Rabbit's voice and watched her eyes plead to be helped.

Of course, she was eyeballing Manning, not me. Her beam of helpless female had locked onto him as she sashayed over and buried her face in his chest.

Wow, I thought, *she's good. I bet you couldn't fit a thin mint between them.*

Gently he pushed her away, her fingers clinging like a gecko's suction cups. "Jess, GM can help, I'm sure of it." He led her back to the chair and she reluctantly sat down.

Manning looked at me over her head and smiled.

Love that dimple.

Despite myself, I smiled back.

Manning broke the silence. "I have a possible location, and I can set up a safe perimeter for us to view the area and a possible cover if we can get in to look around."

The Rabbit wheedled, "I still don't understand why you can't do this yourself, darling."

"Yes, sweetheart," I quipped. "Why can't you?"

This time, the Rabbit dropped her mask and startled me with her naked ferociousness. I got a scary idea of what she looked like alone, in front of a mirror, thinking unguarded Evil Queen thoughts.

"Miss Macklevoy, this is no joke," she snapped. "As we speak, my brother is being brainwashed by this group. The money is irrelevant. No one who survives 'the process' has ever been normal again." At this point, she brought out her handkerchief and dabbed at the corners of her eyes.

I didn't see any moisture, but maybe I missed it. I looked up at Manning and he was frowning at me. For a micro-moment, I felt guilty.

I glanced the Rabbit's way and wondered what her scheme was. Was she using her brother's disappearance to get Manning into bed? Or was she covering her arse after doing something ugly? Both scenarios seemed viable, but then, I'm the suspicious type.

Manning was still frowning, so I said, "I apologise, but I doubt if I can actually do anything substantial on your case since I'll be gone in a few weeks. You have the money, why don't you storm the gates?"

"I have the address of one of their compounds, which is near here; but they have many. Unfortunately we don't know which one he's being held at," Manning admitted. "And we'd be shut down before the ink dried on the storming papers."

"When you do find him, snatch him back and re-brainwash him," I offered helpfully.

He cleared his throat, "There's something very odd about the people that get taken. The ones who actually leave the enclave usually end up dead; either by an OD or a more direct method of suicide, like leaping off a bridge."

The Rabbit let out a well-placed whimper and Manning squeezed her shoulder in comfort. I, on the other hand, watched her blue eyes glitter.

Manning continued, "Despite efforts of the families, they disintegrate and wind up dead."

I wanted to know how this was connected to Riley. Sure, he'd been permanently and forever changed; but not by being tricked, forced or otherwise coerced into eating his own gun. He was murdered, plain and simple. "And this figures in with Riley's death, how?"

Manning looked startled. "You don't know?"

I gave him my best Marcel Marceau look of dripping sarcasm. He looked embarrassed.

"Apparently the report you have in front of you still doesn't contain one interesting fact: Riley was tailing one of our MLCs."

"Speak English."

"Some of the patrols began noticing the usual street people vanishing. At first, they thought they'd voluntarily moved to another locality, but it was too big an exodus."

"Since when do the coppers care?"

"When they go missing for no damn good reason. We tagged them as Missing Links by Counties because we noticed the same thing happening in other bright lights/big city districts."

I settled back in Betsey and felt the small hairs on my neck rise. All of a sudden, this case felt real hinky.

"Like the same neighbourhoods where Christian Demspey has a following," Manning added. "Usually around whatever large fortress he and his son call home at the time."

"What tweaked you to the MLCs in the first place?" I asked, wondering if he was ever going to get to the part where Riley fit in.

He looked uncomfortable, but ploughed on; "Beat cops patrol the same basic area at night. After a while, they get to recognise faces."

The Rabbit shifted restlessly. "Get to the point, Charles." I watched Manning stiffen while she languidly got up and walked to the door. "I'll meet you downstairs." Her seductive smile launched itself like a three-pronged fishhook as she said, "See what you can do," before swaying out the door and leaving the delicate smell of lilacs behind.

I decided that if I ever wore perfume, it wouldn't be lilac.

Manning and I stared at each other while Jess clicked down the two flights of wooden stairs. He wasn't a sap, so I tried to figure out his relationship to the blonde succubus.

"The patrols talked to the few street people left and the buzz was that they were picked up by a large black van, no plates," he explained. "The cops weren't aware of any clean-up programme, so they stationed O'Leary as a lookout." He looked away. "Riley must have gotten careless. He was seen asking questions down there and . . . "

Clarity made my eyes blaze as I realised what he was saying. "Freakin' stupid cops! I could have been all over this and maybe even solved my partner's murder by now!"

"I know," he said. "I didn't agree with keeping it on the downlow, especially from you, but the order came from above."

I pushed my chair back and stomped around my small office, finally kicking the innocent piles of newspapers stacked at my door. They let out a soft squeal of joy. Papers enjoy being scattered.

I took a deep breath, turned and walked back to Betsey, and sat. She gave a sympathetic squeak and I felt better. Riley had probably been asking about the missing daughter his dead guy had been looking for. She must have been one of the MLCs.

I looked at Manning and gave him a tight smile. "Please explain the machinations of your illustrious police force."

"The boys were investigating the disappearances, but were told to let it go. The mayor laid it out for them: no one important had gone missing, just the Boston bum population which, he insisted, the department needed to view as a good thing. Until . . . "

"Riley." I said.

He shrugged. "We'd launched our own quiet investigation, but Riley got spotted nosing around the disappearances and got himself bumped off. His death turned everything upside down."

"You mean the Big Boys couldn't ignore the convenient clean-up anymore."

"Riley's death connects him to the disappearances and has now opened up a possible crime investigation. Nobody, but nobody, is happy about that."

"Least of all his widow," I interjected.

He gave me a hard stare then took a deep breath. "Let me know if you're in on this case." He sat down, put his feet up on a corner of my desk and waited.

I had to confess: in my opinion, a man willing to wait for a decision not of his making, is a very sexy man. I sat back, hooked my feet up beside his and slouched. I opened myself up to hearing the opinions around me.

Graystone, the desk, had been particularly fond of Riley, who used to faithfully polish him once a week and was gung-ho about finding his killer. The Phone, Rug and Window were more concerned about what would happen to them, once I left. But Graystone, Wall, Earl and Betsey all wanted justice for Riley.

All in favour of taking the job said aye. That included me, but I didn't tell Manning right away. It was real nice to smell his aftershave and see him all comfy not two feet away.

I sighed. *Down girl,* I told myself. *Enjoy the view, but remember, California is a blink away.*

• • •

One week later, Manning and I met for a drink at The Flight Deck, a small, drinking man's pub with only one TV stuck in a dark forgotten corner.

Manning was there when I arrived. "One of The World Order's holdings is in Topsfield," he said as I joined him. "A big, sprawling twenty acre parcel of land with a large Victorian mansion smack in the middle."

"Topsfield?" I repeated, surprised at the choice of such a depressed area.

He shrugged. "It fits Dempsey's most important criteria: it's big and secluded."

I watched his eyes darken. "I gather this guy's been on your radar for a while."

"Yep. So," he took a swig of beer. "Ask me what you want to know and if I can, I'll spill. Then we go to work."

"Okay," I said. "So who exactly is Blondie and why do you trust her?"

He looked at me and started to laugh. I don't like people laughing at me, but I stayed seated and 'accidentally' kicked him when I crossed my legs.

"Sorry," he coughed, and moved out of my leg-line of fire. "Jess is an old childhood friend." He glanced at me. A cautious look sprang into his eyes. "Her father practically raised me before I went off to college."

"What happened to your family?"

"My father died in a plane crash. Mr Montova was my father's best friend and took me in when my mother did the world tour and forgot she had a son."

I couldn't help but note the bitterness underneath the glib description of his early life. I guess everyone's got their demons.

But I was confused. Montova was Money with a capital M. So when did he and Manning's father become BFFs? The polo pony stables? Mucker and muckee?

Manning watched me try to figure it out before adding, "My last name isn't Manning. It's Sperling. Actually Sperling Jr. Legally changed to Manning."

"Why?"

"I had my reasons."

"So you're rich like . . . " I tried to think in zillions and couldn't quite grasp the right comparison.

"Yes. Now that we've gotten past my pedigree, let's get back to the case."

"Fine," I agreed. People have secrets and I was never one to pick at old wounds. After all, I had a few of my own.

He spread out a map, gave me a list and a bag containing an Orkin Pest Control uniform.

"We're going in as the poison squad? You know, I've got sensitive nasal cavities," I whined.

He ignored me. "The good news for us is that they're overrun with termites. We go in, you snoop, I'll spray. Easy peasy."

I sighed and thought: *Doesn't he know by now that nothing is ever as easy as peasy?*

. . .

The guards patted us down and led us to the backyard. The liquid Manning had pressurised in his spray can was actually some kind of knock-out gas. Once we were cleared by the front gate crew and were brought out back, we could begin our master plan: spray the faces of our 'bodyguards', knock 'em out and be guaranteed at least 90 minutes of uninterrupted snooping. Then, case the inner sanctum, find out what we could, and *vamoose*.

Except life's full of 'Fuck your big plans'.

Unbeknownst to us, as well as the guards outside, there were extra guards posted inside; to eyeball the ones outside.

Whatever happened to trust?

Our tour-guards stuck to us like Velcro while we poked rotted wood and said inspector type things like, "Ooo, That's bad," and "mmm, look at this." We finally got enough elbow room to whirl and dose them. They collapsed face down, bug-eyed with surprise. I snuck through a window into the house not realising I had less than five minutes to snoop around. But the second my sneakered foot stepped on one of the old floorboards, I knew we'd made a mistake.

The soft, pitiful wail from the threadbare carpet combined in a horrible duet with the flat discordant screeching from the faded wallpaper. I froze mid-step. I'm not faint-hearted, but nothing good can come from entering a house that suffers The Shrieks.

As the sound intensified, my hackles rose. *Time to leave!* I reversed and began to climb right back out the window when a whisper from down the hall stopped me. "You. Hey you."

With one leg dangling over the window ledge, I turned and peered into the gloom. Suddenly the house went silent, which creeped me out even more.

"Come here. Quickly, over here."

Against my better judgment, I slipped back inside, reassuring myself with, *bad idea, bad idea,* and darted over to Sophie, The Guarding Door. Large steel plates a battering ram couldn't dent stretched across her chest. Somebody didn't want something to get out of the basement.

Great.

What Sophie told me made my sweat, sweat. In perfect synchronicity, I did the twenty-three skiddoo toward the window just as the howling resumed. I was climbing back out when some big yahoo steroid-user crashed out of the hallway, snagged my collar, and yanked. Hard. I wind-milled backwards across the floor. Luckily for me, free Tai Chi classes at my gym helped turn a potential bone break into several graceful somersaults. Landing on my feet, I had just enough time to register his meaty paw power housing toward my face. I ducked and kicked his knee hard. I heard a pop as he went down and I tried to leap over him to get to the window. Stupid. Adrenalin is not always your friend. It floods your brain with *escape at all costs* commands which can make you reckless. On my leap up and over, the guard's hand shot out, grabbed my ankle, twisted and pulled. It felt like bungy jumping with an iron chain. First, I was flying up and over, the next I was yanked back so hard I almost dislocated my hip bone. I landed on top of him, staring into some really pissed eyes. By this time, reinforcements had arrived and another guard picked me up and bundled my complaining arse into a room to face the powers that be.

Manning was already there, cursing and blustering to Mr Dempsey's son, Junior, and six muscle-heads, who were all flexing their stubby fingers around dangerous weapons pointed his way. "Here's a flash for you idiots," Manning shouted, "Important People know we're here. In fact, if they don't hear from us in thirty minutes, you'll be in deep shit."

"Yeah!" I piped up and used my best glare while I massaged my hip. "*You're* the ones in trouble, right Crippen?"

"Right," he agreed.

I got instantly cold. *Uh oh*. I turned and looked at him. He's bluffing!

Shit!

Goosebumps marched down my arms. *He must have told someone*, I thought, and prayed it wasn't Blondie.

Junior laughed "I'm not stupid or without informative friends, Mr . . . Crippen, is it? I specifically asked Orkin for photo IDs of the crew they were sending today. Surprise surprise, no crew expected and your name tag doesn't square with your employee picture, either." He turned to me. "Ms Macklevoy, you're smaller in person than in your photos."

I stiffened. "Photos? Why the hell were you taking photos of me?"

He chuckled and my fingers itched to slap him upside his head. But then I've been told I've got anger issues.

I could tell Junior wanted kudos for his cleverness. It certainly couldn't hurt to have him tell his tale. The longer he yapped, the longer we had to escape or be saved. Or so my theory went.

I simpered a bit. "Actually, I really would like to know why you were interested in me." I chose not to include the 'lil ol', but did bat my eyelashes. Manning gave me a strange look. *Hey*, I thought, *you use what you got*; and so far, it looked like it was working. Junior was definitely itching for some back-slapping praise.

If I got close enough to one of the guns, I'd do more than slap his back.

"No sense in keeping it secret now," Junior snickered. "After one of my staff killed your partner, we had you followed to make sure you didn't get too nosey or close."

That hurt. I always know when I'm being tailed. Or so I'd thought. I turned to Manning, "Shadowed and not know? Shoot me."

Junior smiled, showing teeth, but his eyes were dead orbs of soullessness. Daddy's genes had obviously gone over to the dark side when they created his mini-me.

"Shoot you?" Junior said. "No, I have better plans for the two of you." He licked his lips as he studied me. "A shame, really. You alone could be put to much better use."

"You flatterer," I said and quirked my lips in what I hoped was a saucy way. "Perhaps we could negotiate a better plan?"

"No," he said regretfully, "too bad you didn't leave your partner's death alone." He looked at Manning, "Or you copper—what? Thought I didn't know you were snooping around?—it's on your head what happens next. Your fault the doll's not worth more than a tasty tidbit."

My stomach dropped and I regretted those French fries I ate earlier. *Not the basement*, I prayed. Please *not the basement.*

Junior smirked, then laughed like a hyena.

Manning and I exchanged looks.

Crap! No one would know what happened to us if what Sophie, The Guarding Door, said was true.

And I had a baaaad feeling she didn't lie.

In short order, we were lobbed down the laundry chute and landed in our very own Stephen King horror story. The air was full of white wisps that looked and felt like strings of cotton candy. Thin tendrils floated languidly in the cement room, along the walls, becoming progressively thicker further down the dark corridor. I swiped at a few wisps floating in the air near my face. The sticky strands clung to my fingers and wouldn't shake off.

I whirled on Manning. "While I realise logically why you had to keep this a covert operation, please tell me you peeped to a pal." He shook his head and my voice rose an octave; "*No one* knows we're here?"

"One civilian was told. If what we were doing was leaked, we'd be facing some serious charges."

"Could that one civilian possibly be your gal pal, otherwise known as Junior's informative friend?"

He ignored me. I knew it must hurt him, to realise that Blondie had probably set us up for her own nefarious purposes. I tried to figure out her angle.

It was always either money or power, and my vote was power. According to the grapevine, Mr Montova was away on business, and Rabbit must have known Manning would be suspicious if she didn't ask him for help with her 'missing' brother. But, with her brother out of the way—say, conveniently trapped in a cult—Rabbit would control the family business, not to mention having all of Daddy's love for herself. Two obstacles removed with one clean shot. Nice.

Manning studied our surroundings, absentmindedly pulling bits of cotton candy fluff from his face. "Come on," Manning insisted. "We've got to get out of here."

"No shit, Sherlock, but I'm not going near that opening."

"Look, there are no windows, no doors, except that one." He grabbed my arm and tried pulling me toward the apex of Hell.

I'm small, but strong and my point of gravity was lower than his. I didn't budge.

"Come on," he whispered. "The schematics showed there's another door leading to the outside, ten feet down that corridor."

"Yes, there is. The door with the white light at the end of the tunnel and dead friends all saying hi. Don't you wonder what made all these strands?" He started to tug and I wrenched my arm free. "Sophie the Door told me this old house belonged to some crazy genetic scientist who discovered a way to enlarge and combine insects. He was . . . "

"Sophie the door?" he asked, swiping at the annoying and insistent strands that curled around arms and legs as he approached the corridor. "What were you saying about insects?" He cursed, trying to pull off the tacky threads.

Hell, I decided, *we're going to die anyway, who cares if he thinks I'm nuts.* "Sophie, the Guarding Door, told me they have a giant termite/spider *thing* down here that—" I broke off and screamed as a large, dead-black shape appeared in the doorframe. Sixteen enormous, hairy legs sidled up the doorway, eight on each side, effectively plugging up our getaway hole. The stiff black fur waved curiously toward us like a pointer dog, sensing our presence.

Manning and I froze. Before I could suck in another breath to yell again, the creature skittered forward, spitting out tough gluey filaments that mummified our legs and arms together, binding them to our bodies.

We screamed.

The spider-thing opened its ugly mouth in reply. The inside of its gaping maw was coated with razor-sharp black and red spikes. It inched toward us, its multi-faceted eyes reeling crazily.

A high-pitched moan escaped my lips as I watched a twelve inch, needle-thin protuberance emerge from its throat tissue. The protrusion dripped a viscous green slime and vibrated like a tuning fork right above Manning's temple. Manning moved frantically, but the creature's pincers grabbed his head, steadying his movements. It twisted its greedy face to the side, ready to insert its venom.

A long strand of white that trailed from the monster's swollen, bloated belly was softly tugged. The creature whirled and with a look I recognised as proprietary, stared down the corridor. Then it turned back and beaded us with a malevolent red glare before scurrying away, apparently satisfied its hog-tied prey wasn't going anywhere. Whatever food that momentarily escaped had my biggest thanks and deepest sympathy.

To give him credit, Manning didn't say jack about Sophie. He just grunted and said, "You knew this was waiting for us before we got lobbed down here?"

"I was hoping Sophie exaggerated."

"You should have told me anyway. I might have . . . "

"Turned into Superman? Hey Clark, did you forget they were packing 9mm kryptonite?" He gave me a black look and I guess I couldn't blame him. We struggled against our bonds, but they tightened against our flesh, like a Chinese finger puzzle. While I didn't want to ruin his last seconds on earth, I had to ask. "You figured out the set up yet?"

He stopped struggling. "Yeah, I should have known. Jess was always a jealous, greedy kid and lately she'd looked," he stopped, thought, then added, "dull."

Weird way to put it, but I added my two cents. "Yeah, I've noticed murderous, conniving, sneaky plans can really wreak havoc on a girl's complexion."

Manning just shook his head before taking a deep breath and looking at me. "Geraldine, I want to say something and while it's not the best timing in the world . . . "

"Geraldine!" I exclaimed. "Are you kidding? You're still ticked off I didn't tell you what Sophie said? Get your priorities in order, Manning. Say some prayers. 'Cause in case you didn't notice, we're going to die! And, in a horrible, icky, freakazoid way."

"Shut up," he shouted. Then, more quietly, "I like you."

I shut up.

I have to admit, I felt kinda happy, despite the fact that I knew death was only sixteen hairy, literal feet away.

Then I saw them.

"Hold that thought, Manning; I need to concentrate." Now was not the time to hide my skills under any bushel. I looked at the two sticks of wood I'd just noticed lying on the floor, right behind me. "Hey, you two."

Manning's face glowed with hope as he frantically twisted his head around to see who I was talking to.

"Hey, Frick and Frack, I'm talking to you."

Surprised, the wooden sticks answered. Then they started to tell me their life story, while Manning's shoulders drooped, thinking I'd lost it. I didn't have time to explain, so I launched into my big T.

"Sorry, I don't mean to be rude, but I'm pressed for time. I need you two to cuddle up to each other, vibrate and well, explode with passion."

I looked at Manning and mouthed, "Fire."

He looked at the sticks that had agreeably begun their friction dance and watched as they burst into flames.

"Please avoid the flesh, but burn the web," I instructed.

As the twin flames followed orders and freed us from our bonds, Manning continued watching with an inscrutable expression.

I heard the scratching of sixteen needle-like nails skitter toward our room.

"Quickly," I begged. "Follow the strands to its source, and," I raised my voice, "feed upon the scourge of this temple."

Sometimes it's worth going all biblical when you ask for self-sacrifice.

The flames leapt up, full of self-importance, and rocketed away from us, down the fine webs and into the corridor. Screeches of pain and fury echoed through the basement, while the flames licked the ceiling and up the walls.

Surprised, we heard fire engines and the tramp of crashing boots above us.

That was fast.

It turned out that good ol' Sophie, thrilled with having someone listen to her, had communicated with the floorboards, who had asked the phone to ask the hardwired alarm system to send a FireAlert to the protection agency, even before we were thrown down into Hell.

Before the firemen made it downstairs, Manning grabbed me and kissed me. Hard. I kissed him back, just as fiercely. Near death experiences can affect you like that.

Chaos reigned around us, though I couldn't tell if it was internal or external.

. . .

After the fire department rescue, Manning and I continued our appreciation of life back at my place and well into the next morning. When I woke, sore from lovemaking, Manning was nowhere to be found. No scribbled note. No text message. No nothing.

Okay, I thought. *That's fine. No biggie.* No awkward goodbyes.

The papers and TV were full of The World Order's bizarre financial scheme and the horror show that went along with it. The story was that upon purchasing the original house, Dempsey stumbled upon the weird giant arachnid after it attacked one of his crew. Rescuing the guy after the brain injection, but before the monster consumed him, they discovered the power of its bite.

A sting from the monster to the head re-fused the brain's circuitry, rendering the victim susceptible to suggestion. Dempsey had been reportedly thrilled. Once he realised he could force people to give him their money, and make it impossible for them to squeal on him, his master plan to become the richest man in the world went into hyper drive. The biggest problem was a constant need for fresh meat, which their new pet needed to survive. The homeless population provided a handy supermarket.

The newspapers, newscasters and radio announcers had a field day, and somewhere in all that news, Riley was mentioned. Thanks to Manning's connections, the papers hailed Riley a hero after the police department gave him credit for being one of the first in suspecting foul play by The World Order. Ol' Riley would have liked that.

I was glad to see his murderers were finally going to be punished. Poor guy had stumbled on the wrong case at the wrong time.

That night, I still hadn't heard from Manning. I broke down and called his cell, which went straight to voicemail. I called his work and got the "nope, not here". I started to get a little irked. Realising I was being given the brush-off, survival mode kicked in with a vengeance. I made to leave on the red-eye. It was a week earlier than I planned and involved a costly upgrade, but I didn't care. This town held nothing for me.

...

The airport was unusually busy; people were jostling, planes took off and landed, and I was miserable.

I thought about how I'd let my guard down and gotten screwed in more ways than one. Why couldn't I find someone sexy and *sympatico*? Someone willing to overlook my idiosyncrasies? No one's perfect. I saved his freakin' life. That should count for something.

I felt a tap on my shoulder and when I turned, there were those dimples. I caught my breath. "What do you want?" While I suppose I could have chosen a more polite greeting, I was feeling rather testy.

"I heard you could use another partner," he said, choosing to ignore my furrowed brow and cranky comment.

I had to hand it to him, he was good.

"I also heard LA is the number one place to relocate."

I didn't want to spoil the mood, but needed to get some things out in the open. "What about my ability to talk to pretty much every inanimate object in existence?"

"Very helpful."

I looked at my carry-on luggage who insisted I ask the question. I sighed. "Okay. Where'd you go this morning?"

"I needed to tie up loose ends."

I tried not to sound needy. "You left no note."

"Yes, I did."

"Hey, I would have noticed." I felt hurt shine through my eyes, despised my weakness and looked away. But damn, I thought, we shared some serious emotion between those sheets. I had thought he felt as much as I did.

He looked puzzled. "I didn't want to wake you: you looked so cute and peaceful." He grinned rather lasciviously. "So I left an elaborate message taped to your bathroom mirror." He looked at me. "You didn't see it?"

"You picked the one object that hates me. Evil Mary never understood why I wouldn't play beauty salon in front of her. She's such a diva."

"So," he tried to understand. "She somehow . . ."

"Managed to get rid of the note. How'd you know I was here?"

"I have my ways."

I gave him the hairy eyeball and he laughed.

"Sam monitors the airport red flags. Your name popped up, changing flights like that."

"Speaking of red flags, what's going to happen to your Machiavellian *femme fatale*?" I was hoping for two consecutive life sentences, but would settle for a good thirty years without parole. "After all, she willingly brought her brother to Dempsey's door and suckered us both into being delicacies on an appetiser tray."

"I know." He looked pained.

"You do realise it was just dumb luck that we managed to survive without a lobotomy?"

"Luck and your talents." He took a deep breath. "Family pulled strings. She's being treated in Switzerland for 'emotional issues'."

"It pays to know people." He looked away and I felt bad. "Not to change the subject, but let's get back to the part where you're not freaked out by my 'abilities' and you elaborate on how cute I looked sleeping."

"I'll sketch out the details on the plane." He looked nervous. "That is, if you'll consider another partner?"

My flight was announced and I stood. "That depends. What's your full name and how come you want to change jobs?"

"I'm not changing professions, but segueing into another aspect of the biz."

"Biz?" I cocked an eyebrow.

"My full name is Lewis Bernard Sperling, Jr."

"Oh crap. Please don't make me say 'Louie; this could be the beginning of a beautiful friendship'."

"Why not? Could be. You know, I have a bulging roster of good connections."

"Bulging roster?" I complained. "Double crap, Manning. No self-respecting PI says stuff like that." He leered at me and I blushed. "Oh."

We spent the next six hours on the flight setting boundaries on what our partnership would entail.

And I found out Manning was a bit on the freaky side himself.

But that's another story.

SOUND AND FURY

Pete Kempshall

The woman in front of him was a wreck: her wet, phlegmy cough had marked her out as a risk even before she'd stepped off the boat. She'd tried to conceal it, to control the hacking, rasping expectoration, but it hadn't taken long for an immigration officer to pull her out of the line, a belated precaution against infecting everyone else. Once she was clear, the guard made an apathetic swipe across her shoulder with his hand. The resulting white chalk mark on the sick woman's coat was what everyone arriving at Ellis Island feared: branded for deportation, she was shuffled away to the dorm area where she could infect only those people who had already ceased to matter.

The human jetsam flowed on through the maze of fences and gates. The waist-high metal barricades directed the new arrivals through a series of switchbacks; every twenty feet or so the queue would turn on itself, a meandering course of unwashed desperation.

Roman let the press of bodies carry him. A number of other immigrants were talking in nervous voices, a mélange of tongues: some he recognised, most he didn't. They sought companionship and consolation; kindred spirits with whom to share their hopes, their fears as they stumbled towards judgment. He didn't feel the need to join in, there was a good chance any friendships he struck with these strangers would be broken by the immigration men at the end of the queue, men who had few qualms about splitting mothers from their children, if quotas dictated they do so. But even if that hadn't been the case, he'd still have stayed silent.

The line ahead of him doubled back, and he found himself staring at the couple again. He'd first noticed them on the quayside, his curiosity piqued by the woman's face. She was a beauty, no doubt, but that beauty was marred. Spoiled. Even the most desperate in the line had some spark of hope burning inside, some belief that this was it, the land of opportunity, and that at last their ship had come in. Literally.

With her downcast eyes and sagging shoulders, this woman looked so thoroughly . . . beaten.

Of course, Roman had worked out why soon enough, when he'd seen her husband.

While the woman was slim and carried herself with a certain defeated grace, her spouse was wide, weight-lifter broad and with the flattened, hard face of a pugilist. He kept his thick fingers wrapped around her bicep, clamped tight. The same white-knuckled fists could be seen up and down the line, clutched around the handles of the cardboard suitcases, all proclaiming the same thing.

This is my property. God help you if you try to take it from me.

"Listen up! Pipe down, people!"

At the head of the line, an officer had climbed atop a packing crate, and surveyed the crowd. "You musta seen it's late, we ain't got no choice but to suspend processing 'til morning. Alla you will be assigned a bed in the dorms until such a time as we start up again."

Groans erupted throughout the line: confusion from those with insufficient English to understand, consternation from those who did. The dorms had a bad reputation, dirty, ill-maintained. Only potential deportees ended up there, the illiterate, the infirm, the criminal. Potential burdens on the State.

As the men and women were separated out into lines for their segregated accommodation, Roman looked across at the couple again. There was no mistaking it. Shepherded away from her husband, to spend the night in cramped, noisy squalor, the only emotion on the woman's face was relief.

• • •

The cot next to the heavy-set man was empty, so Roman took it. Curiosity, perhaps.

He removed his hat and tilted his head at his new neighbour. Hands pillowed behind his head, the man didn't react in the slightest, just kept staring up at the bottom of the bunk above. For everyone else in the large but cramped room, the night ahead would be a trial—but this guy? This guy looked smug.

Roman bent to stow his case beneath the bunk. When he stood up again, the big man had turned on his thin mattress to face him.

"You come far?" he asked.

"Brighton."

"All the way from Dublin, me," said the man, the revelation made somewhat redundant by his lilting voice. He paused, looked thoughtful. "I liked Brighton. Took me ma there on holiday once." He propped himself up on an elbow. "What the hell ye doin' coming here from Brighton?"

"Getting away."

"Chatty, ain't ye?" The man regarded him for a second, then, catching something behind Roman's eyes, suddenly understood. "Where was ye stationed?"

"Ypres."

"Aye, well this'll be far enough away for ye and no mistake. Colm," he said, proffering a hand like a meaty spade. Roman took it, felt his knuckles give slightly as the Irishman squeezed.

"Roman. You alone?"

Colm smirked. "Not on yer life, son. Got me someone over in the other dorm there."

"Wife?"

"In a manner o' speaking."

Roman held the man's gaze, maintaining a fixed expression of confusion and curiosity until at last Colm cracked.

"All right, just between you and me, right?"

"Right."

"Let's just say her da owed me, and I called in the debt."
Roman said nothing.
"Oh don't start with me, son. She's as willing to come as he was willing to send her. Best for everyone. And what of yerself?"
"Pardon me?"
"No one with ye? Good looking lad like you?"
"No," Roman murmured. "It'th jutht me."

• • •

He couldn't sleep that night. Snores mixed with tears, mixed with groans, mixed with pleas and lamentations in every language under the sun, and all of it kept Roman from rest as surely as the guards on the doors kept him from leaving.

And then there was the woman. Thoughts assailed him, of her, of the life she'd be forced to lead once she and her husband-to-be—her owner—left Ellis. She'd be better off getting straight back on the boat.

Roman turned over, tried to get comfortable. Perhaps he'd read. There was just enough light from the corridor, and he had a book in his case. Take his mind off things . . .

Reaching under the bunk, his fingers brushed something small, unfamiliar. Snagging it, he picked it up. It must have been dropped by a guard, kicked away by the press of humanity and forgotten.

And looking at it in the palm of his hand, Roman knew exactly what to do with it.

• • •

The guards woke everyone early, no doubt hoping to process the crowd before the next boat came in and the logjam grew worse. They separated the bleary, exhausted cattle into lines. Roman found himself hustled into the queue for assessment—there'd be a medical and the twenty-nine questions he'd need to answer to the satisfaction of the authorities if he wanted to stay in the country. He dismissed any notion that his condition would stop him—they'd have seen far worse cases of shellshock, and a lisp hardly qualified him as a burden on society. No, he'd pass both tests and then never look back.

• • •

Behind him, he could hear Colm grumbling his way towards the door.

"What do you think you're doing, then?"

Roman looked over his shoulder to see a guard blocking Colm's way with a long wooden baton. The Irishman's face was a mask of irritation.

"I'm getting out of here, aren't I? Got me tests this morning."

The guard shot a look at his partner, who shook his head in a blend of disbelief and amusement. "Oh, is that right? Think I was born yesterday?"

"Listen to me, sonny; I came in last night—"

"And got yerself one of them," the guard interrupted, indicating with his truncheon. "Which means you're staying right here."

Colm looked down at his shoulder. A white slash of chalk marked the dark material of his coat. "Now wait a goddamn—"

The guard pushed him back with the stick. "Listen to me, you bloody mick. You ain't got the sense to even try rubbing it off last night, you deserve what you get." He prodded Colm again. "Back. In. Now."

Colm seemed to inflate, redden as the violence rose inside him. And then he sank back, nodded. Roman could tell he'd worked it out—starting a fight would get him deported faster than he could blink.

"Right ye are," he said, flashing a grin at the guard. "Worth a try though, right?"

The entire room seemed to have stopped to watch the drama, but it was Roman's eyes that Colm met. He winked at Roman, a gesture entirely without warmth, and turned his back on him.

• • •

She was waiting outside, the early morning sun flaring on her red hair. She clutched her battered case in both hands and looked lost, so very lost. He put his hand in his pocket, touched the gritty white stick, like somehow it would bring him luck, and he walked towards her.

"Excuthe me, can I help you? My name'th Roman."

She gathered herself together, burying any sign of concern and looked directly at him. And in the moment she met his gaze, Roman knew. He'd be with this woman forever, take care of her forever. No matter what.

• • •

Roman continued to stare at the screen long after the pictures stopped, the white rectangle strobing as the loose end of the film flick-flick-flicked through the spool. The plushness of the seat seemed to suck him down like quicksand, and he let it, no longer caring if he ever emerged from it again.

"Jethuth Critht," he murmured.

Up in the booth, the projectionist stopped the reels and raised the lights in the private theatre, but still Roman couldn't bear to look at the man beside him. From the corner of his eye, he could see Art raising a cigarette to his lips and dredging his pockets for a light. A sharp hiss and the faint reek of sulphur snaked up Roman's nose as smoke billowed in his peripheral view. At last, Roman turned, looked at his agent as he drew on the crackling tobacco.

"Son," Art said, exhaling a voluminous cloud. "You're history."

• • •

He had little memory of the walk to the car, just that he had to get to it, to the hidden compartment in the back seat. It wasn't much of a hiding place—Roman knew that if the cops ever pulled him over they'd find the liquor in a flash—but it was worth the risk precisely for times like these, when 'want' became 'need'. Besides, he'd not met an officer yet who wasn't prepared to look the other way for some folded green and an autograph.

Glugging the deep-brown liquid into the heavy crystal glass he also kept in the hidey-hole, Roman wondered how long that privilege would extend.

His driver, Jimmy, was on borrowed time, that was for sure. Once the studio realised Roman's star was dimming, they'd reclaim the chauffeur-cum-bodyguard without a second thought. No bones about it, Jimmy was a great guy: discreet, loyal so far as it went, but he knew on which side his bread was buttered. He'd driven Arbuckle for a while, held his tongue while the fat man's life went to shit and then got out while the going was good. Yeah, once he was done with Roman he'd move on to the next job and never look back.

"Where to, Mr Landry?" He met Roman's eyes in the rear-view mirror, one brow raised expectantly. Roman swigged at the rotgut. It seared and coated his throat, like drinking turpentine, which he probably was. He drained the glass, said nothing, turned his gaze to the window.

Jimmy read the look on Roman's face and, without another word, swung the car out into the traffic.

. . .

Thelma straddled him, one hand each side of his head, rubbed herself up and down along his crotch. "Well, if this ain't what you wanted, honey, why'd you come?"

A slender chain swung between her breasts, a small golden box dangling from it, tickling Roman's chest hair. They were all the rage now in certain circles, a way for women to keep a small sniff of powder somewhere convenient, as well as a big fat middle finger to the more puritanical elements of LA society. It was inevitable Thelma would end up with one. But who was Roman to judge, with his own small box of white powder in his jacket, the one he told everyone was cocaine, like hers?

"I jutht want to talk," he said.

She giggled. Roman was prepared to bet good money that her little gold box was already empty. "Yeah. You and everyone else in the biz."

Roman clapped his hands on her shoulders and pushed her off him, dumping her onto the rumpled sheets she'd stewed in for most of the day. He swung his legs off the bed and reached for his pants. "Fuck you."

"I should be so lucky," she purred. She shifted her weight on the mattress behind him, slid her arms around his waist. "Or ith that thomething elth you can't manage?"

"Ith jutht thome damn joke to you, ithn't it?" Roman spat. Flinging aside his pants, he grabbed her by the arm and hauled her from the bed, dragging her to the door and out onto the landing beyond. He let her go, and she slumped to her knees in front of him, eyeing him like a sulky child.

"You thee that?" he barked, jabbing a finger towards the picture hanging at the head of the stairs.

The framed one-sheet's primary colours depicted Roman and Thelma in full costume—she the doe-eyed maiden, easy prey to pirates, he the dashing buccaneer who'd save her, fall for her and wed her by the final reel. *Doubloons of Desire*, their first picture together.

Thelma pouted at his feet. "That," he growled. "That'th all gone. That thon of a bitch Jolthon and that fucking *Jath Thinger*, he'th killed it."

"Jolson's a putz. And he ain't nearly as handsome as you."

"It doethn't matter how good I look! You think anyone'th going to want to thee a hero who thpeaks like a theven-year-old in a candythtore?"

She gazed up at him, anger flaring in her cat-like eyes. "Don't be a sap. You think I'd let all this slip away? I need you, Roman, honey. We're royalty. You and me, it ain't going to be long before we're bigger than Fairbanks and Pickford."

"How'th that going to happen?"

"This is Hollywood, you get to meet all sorts. Powerful people, baby."

"And I thuppothe you can jutht click your fingerth and they'll fix my voith like magic?"

She stroked the inside of his leg, her travelling fingers sending shivers up him. "Oh, I know all about magic, baby. Magic like you wouldn't believe."

And taking hold of his hips, she moved her mouth over him. Roman's ire evaporated as she went to work. Hollywood was about as debauched a place as you'd find, especially for someone with his money, but this was about as filthy as it got. No one else ever did this for him. No one.

Not even his wife.

...

She'd been drinking again.

Roman could smell the fumes the moment he walked through the door, like she'd doused the whole house in ethanol and wandered off to look for a match.

At least she wouldn't smell Thelma on him.

He hung his hat on the polished wooden stand just inside the doorway and slipped across the foyer. With luck, he could get to bed without a confrontation.

But then there she was, weaving her way out from the drawing room to stand between him and the stairs. Ice tinkled in a glass so full it slopped.

"I waited up for you, honey," she drawled. "I missed you."

"I had a meeting with Art at the thtudio."

"Oh baby," she dragged her feet towards him, trailing a rotgut miasma. "It don't matter anymore."

"We'll lothe it. All thith."

"You can just..." Her eyes lost focus for a moment, and she twisted her lip to blow a strand of deep red hair out of her face. "You can just retire. Then I can have you. Only ever wanted..." She stopped, the words eluding her.

"I'm tired," Roman said. "I'd like to go to bed."

"Thass a good idea," his wife slurred. "I'll come with you."

She held out an arm, crooked at the elbow, and Roman steadied her, steered her up the staircase. By the top he was taking her whole weight and several steps later, he was carrying her. She snored as he placed her on the bed and he kissed her, once, on the forehead.

"Night, Elaine."

He watched her for a while, the most peaceful he'd seen her in weeks. He could save her. He'd done it once, he could do it again. He just had to let go—of the money, the fame—and just *be* with her. If ever there was a right time...

Slipping into the bathroom, he ran a faucet and splashed water on his face, over and over. When he stopped, his cheeks still burned.

• • •

The stairs down to the basement were putrid, clogged with trash from the alley and stinking of piss. As Roman picked his way down them, it occurred to him that it was probably the best cover the place could have. No one in their right mind would be seen dead here.

He hadn't wanted to go crawling back to Thelma, but what else could he do? He'd been in the business too long, grown to love the money, the prestige, and yes, the sex. He lived like a god. The talkies would take it all away, leaving him with nothing but a wife who'd spent the last six years paying the emotional toll for his success.

He'd told Thelma he was willing to try anything.

Shivering in the cool air, he put a hand in his jacket pocket, allowed his fingers to touch the small box of powder inside, then raised his fist to the solid metal door and knocked, two quick, one long, two quick, just as Thelma had instructed. She got her coke here, she'd said, but Rick, the guy with the juice, he could fix Roman's problem, too. "Special services," she'd said.

A small square panel popped open in the door, and a pair of eyes set just a little too close together glared out at Roman.

"Whatcha want?"

Roman shifted, uncomfortable, glancing back up at the top of the stairs. "I'm looking for Thilath."

"Wuh?"

"Thilath!" Roman lisped. When Thelma had told him the codeword, he'd thought she was joking.

"Hey, ain't you—?" The doorman's single eyebrow rose in recognition. One advantage of being a movie star, Roman thought to himself—no way will anyone believe you're working for the law.

"You sound like a girl." The ape of a man threw back the bolts and cracked open the door. "I'd never have picked it."

"Thcrew you," Roman muttered. "I want to thee Rick."

The doorman shot him a poisonous look, then opened the inner door. Cigarette smoke, chatter and music billowed out. He gestured through it. "Out back, past the stage."

"Thank you."

Beyond the door, the main room was set up with dozens of wooden tables, the circumference of each packed with chairs, the chairs packed with revellers. Men in expensive suits balanced inebriated women on their knees, barked with laughter and swilled drinks. One or two of the ladies had started early, dancing on tables to sporadic roars of approval. At the far end of the room, a small stage groaned under the weight of a nine-foot Steinway, at which a sweating pianist hammered out Jelly Roll Morton. Besides the dancers, no one seemed to be listening.

Roman skirted the edge of the room, keeping his hat on and his head down. Tomorrow, the doorman would be telling everyone he had been in, but for tonight, Roman didn't want to be recognised. He just wanted to do his deal and get out.

A brick wall of a man stood in front of the door behind the stage, but as soon as he saw Roman he stepped aside. He rapped on the wood with a huge fist, eyes never leaving the new arrival. At once, the door opened and the brick man nodded for Roman to enter.

The door closed behind him, muffling the majority of the din from the floor. The room beyond was large, lined with bookshelves and what looked to Roman's untrained eye like fine art. Nothing about it said 'Bootleggers' Hideout'.

A huge pot plant sat in one corner, and in an armchair under it, a dark-skinned man in a well-cut suit smoked a thin cigarette, the smoke more aromatic than the fug in the main room. Roman had never indulged, but had been to enough tea parties to know the difference.

"Rick?"

The man shook his head, slow, as if every degree of movement was the result of immense force of will.

"Ith Rick here?"

Nod.

"Where?"

The negro grinned. Roman sensed movement behind him: one of the bookshelves swung open, a concealed door.

"Roman. Long time, no see."

Rick sauntered over to the desk, pulled out a chair and slumped into it. Without looking, he reached down to the drawers, pulled one open and removed a bottle. A broad smile split his flattened, hard face, no less cruel than it had been a decade ago. "Drink?"

"*You're* Rick?

"One and the same. Had to change me name to get in the country, didn't I? Second time of asking and all. So. Drink?"

Roman backed towards the door. "I don't think tho."

"What, you don't want to talk about your little problem?" Rick poured three fingers of dark liquid into a tumbler and downed it in a single swallow. The second the glass was back on the desk, he was refreshing it. "Thelma told me you needed a hand with something, ye shell-shocked wee cunt."

"I don't want anything from you."

"Not like last time, eh?" Rick laughed.

Roman turned to the door, only to find the brick man from outside had stepped into the room and barred the way.

"Oh come on now, sit yerself down," Rick called out. "I think I've got just what you're looking for."

Roman turned back to the desk and sat.

"So, I understand you're concerned about your career there." Rick raised his glass again, sipped this time. "Talkies and that." Roman held his gaze, said nothing. Rick shrugged. "Well, what if I could change the way ye speak? Fix it for ye."

"Impothible."

Rick snorted. "No such thing, sonny, no such thing. You've met Josiah, yes?" He indicated the smoker, still silent in the corner.

"Not long up from N'Orlins," he drawled in a passable mockery of the accent. "They know some damn strange stuff down there, let me tell you.

"Now Josiah there, he can fix your problem. Give the man a wee sample, Josiah."

Josiah rose in a slow, languid motion, looked straight at Roman and closed his eyes.

Roman felt the air around him change, the way air changed when thunder was coming. Josiah opened his eyes, and Roman recoiled to see that the orbs in the man's head were brilliant white, all sign of humanity gone.

"Ye feel that?" Rick chuckled.

"Yes."

"What's that, son, I can't hear you?"

"*Yes!*"

"Well, there you go, then."

A short, hard punch of realisation.

Across from Roman, Josiah's eyelids snapped shut, then opened, restored to normal. Gradually the disturbance in the air subsided.

"That's—I—I don't—"

Rick grinned. "Don't tell me you got a stutter as well. Jaysus, one problem at a time!"

Roman fought to control the shaking in his limbs, the increased tempo of his heartbeat. So fast, all of this, he couldn't come to grips . . . "How?"

"Old Josiah here can do all manner o' things, for the right price." Rick sat back in his seat, drummed his fingers on the desk. "Which o'course brings us to remuneration."

"Remuneration." Roman stumbled over the word. His tongue felt different, strange. Wrong.

"Oh come on now, ye don't expect to get that for free, do ye? Big thing like that. I just guaranteed yer future there, Roman. Bit of respect."

"How much do you want?" Roman reached into his pocket and pulled out a billfold. His fingers fumbled, scattering notes on the carpeted floor.

"Put yer money away, it's no good here. Not when we're such old pals."

"So, what then?"

Rick leaned forward. "Well, normally I'd be asking ye for the cash and something ... personal. See, to make Josiah's magic permanent, like, he'd need something, a token if ye like. Something precious, freely given. Ain't that right, Big J?"

Back in his marijuana fug, Josiah nodded.

"It channels his, what ye call it, mystic power. So yeh, money and something precious. Normally. But for you, Roman, me old mate, I just want something precious."

Roman took a second to put it together. "Not a chance."

"Ah, now see I thought ye'd say that. Ye know what I do for a living now, don't ye?"

"Bootlegging."

"Aye, that too. I provide certain substances to people that wants them. 'S how Thelma knows me, right? And ye see, there's ways to do that kind of business. What ye do, right, ye give people a taste, and when they know yer product's good, they come back to ye for more, see?

"What ye've got there, that new voice o' yers, that's just a taster. Twelve hours' time—" Rick held up a fist, threw the fingers wide in a sudden bursting motion, "—it's gone. Ye want a proper voice—for good and all, mind—ye got to pay.

"So what's it to be? Fame, money and power, or a wife ye don't even love anymore?"

Roman bristled. "I do love her."

"Bollocks ye do. Hammering away at that Thelma, that's loving yer wife, is it?" Rick examined a well-trimmed fingernail. "In fact, the way I see it, I'd be doing ye a favour by taking Elaine off yer hands. Can you imagine what yer public would think if they found out ye were shagging someone else? It's not like ye can get a divorce."

"Fairbanks and Pickford did, the public forgave them."

Rick slammed a fist onto the desk. "Ye ain't Dougie Fairbanks and that slut of yers ain't no Mary Pickford. Ye leave your wife for her, yer career's done, voice or no." His voice wavered, temper subsiding. "But if ye can say Elaine left ye ... for a bootlegger ... "

Roman eyed the Irishman. "Your man there, what's to stop him just taking Elaine?"

"You're not listening, are ye, son?" Rick rolled his eyes. "Needs a token, doesn't he? But ye're right, even if he didn't ... I want to see her face when ye bring her here and hand her over to me. Willingly."

"She'll never love you."

"Oh, I don't want her to," Rick said. "I want her to hate me. Hate me," he continued, gesturing at Josiah, "but still do anything I want her to do. Ye get me?"

Roman stared hard at the ground. Nodded.

"Good." Rick stood and walked back to the hidden room. "Run along then. I'll be seeing ye later." He stopped and shot a sly glance back at Roman. "Tell ye what, though, why not stick around out front a while, try the new voice out on the ladies. It's very sexy. Fuck, if I was that way inclined, I would."

. . .

Roman trudged up the steps to the house. His tongue felt thick in his mouth, and he hadn't uttered a word since leaving the speakeasy. Before he could reach out and turn the handle, the front door swung open and Thelma rushed out to meet him.

"Did it work?" she panted, bouncing around him like an eager puppy.

"Yes."

She squealed and threw her arms around him, standing on tiptoe to press her lips to his. With a gentle but firm motion, Roman pushed her away. He felt hot, constrained.

"Jeez, babe, you're sweating like a pig." Thelma removed his hat and started to peel off his jacket. He shrugged himself out of it, handed it to her without thinking and she slung it on a seat. His shirt was plastered to his skin.

"What's up?" she whined. "It worked! Say something else. Say 'Sasquatch'!"

"It's temporary," Roman explained, sliding past her and into the foyer. "Got about six hours left."

Thelma stared daggers at him. "Whaddya mean, temporary?"

"If I want it permanently, it's going to cost."

"So pay the man!"

"He wants Elaine."

Thelma's brow creased, considering the request. "So give her to him."

"No."

"What?"

Roman slumped into an armchair, looked up at her, filled with a sudden and abiding loathing. "If I give him Elaine, he'll torture her until her gets bored, then she'll disappear. Forever."

Thelma put her hands on her hips. "I ain't seeing a downside here, honey."

"No," Roman sighed. "You wouldn't."

"Listen, baby," she said, mollifying her tone and hitching her skirt up to straddle him on the seat. "She's holding you back, always has done. With her out of the picture, we could rule this town, no question. You get to keep your voice; we become the most famous couple in the world . . . Pay the man."

Roman lifted her off and set her down on her feet. "I'm sorry. I just thought I should tell you myself."

"Bullshit," Thelma spat. "You really wanna be a silent movie star the rest of your life? When you could have all this?"

"I really do." He made his way out, stooping to pick up his hat and coat. "Good luck to you, Thelma. I mean that."

And she was on him, slapping, clawing, raging, her fury driving him back, taking him off balance. He threw up his hands, tried to fend her off, but her nails caught him on the neck, a stinging cut opening in the flesh below his jaw. Dazed and thinking only of escape, he threw open the door and tumbled into the night. With a last, ear-rending shriek, Thelma slammed the door behind him. From the other side, he could hear things breaking.

Shivering in the night air, he thought about going back for his hat and coat, but decided the cold would be more forgiving.

· · ·

"Wasn't expecting you," Elaine said. Her voice was weary and her shoulders slumped. In all likelihood she'd fallen asleep in her chair by the fire. Roman had spotted an open bottle in the drawing room, but she didn't look to have got too deep into it.

Christ, Roman thought, what have I done to you?

"Well, I'm back," he smiled. "Back for good."

Puzzlement flashed across her face. "What do you mean?"

"I'm done with it. Movieth." He'd muttered to himself the whole way home, forcing his tongue back into its old lisp. He still had a few hours left, but he hadn't wanted to upset her.

"I don't—"

"I've had my time. Betht I get out now before they fire me, right?"

"You really mean it?"

"I really do." Light dawned across her face, the likes of which he hadn't seen in years, the very same light he'd fallen in love with at Ellis Island. "Firtht thing in the morning, I'm going to tell them."

...

Roman flipped open the secret compartment in the car seat and took out the bottle. Sure, he'd been confident enough last night, but in the cold light of day, heading out to the studio to tell them where to shove their job . . . He'd be needing a stiff belt or two before the trip was over.

The scratch on his neck stung. He'd dressed it after he got home, convinced Elaine it was nothing, but God, it felt like it was on fire. He poured another drink, swallowed it, refilled the glass.

He was two more large glasses in before he realised Jimmy had stopped the car.

Roman looked out of the window, knew they were still in the Hollywood Hills somewhere, but more than that . . .

"Jimmy? What'th the deal?"

"Change of plan, Mr Landry. No need to get hot under the collar or nothin'. Just gotta stop for someone."

Three of the car's doors popped open. On Roman's right, the torpedo from the night before hopped in, the side of the car sagging with his weight. Up front, Josiah climbed in next to Jimmy, cigarette dangling from lips bent into something that may have been a smile. And while Roman stared at the magician, Rick slipped in the back on the other side, hemming the actor in.

"Well if it isn't himself. How ye doin', Roman me man?"

Roman ignored him. "Jimmy?"

"Sorry, Mr Landry. Just looking out for myself. Unnerstand my job's gone, come tomorrow."

"Why don't ye go and have a little smoke, Jimmy," Rick suggested. "Ye look like ye could use a break."

Jimmy opened his door, unfolded himself from his seat and started walking. As far as Roman could see through the window, his driver didn't look back.

"What'th thith all about?" he said. "I don't need your bloody magic trickth now. I'm quitting the bithness."

Rick's eyebrows raised in comic disbelief. "Well now, that's a big call, isn't it? Are ye sure that's how ye want to play it?"

"Pith off, Colm. I'm done."

Rick exhaled a long loud breath. "Well, to be fair I'm relieved. Josiah there gets awful tired when he has to work his—what you call it?"

"Mojo," Josiah drawled.

"Aye, mojo. Ye see, that's why we wanted to see ye. We've just this morning had another commission," Rick smiled. "So, all for the best really."

Roman lunged across Rick, grasping for the door handle, but all too quickly the enforcer to his right seized his arms, pulled him back.

"Now then, that's enough of that." Rick wagged an admonishing finger at the pinioned Roman.

"Let me go, you fucker!"

Rick sighed. "Let's keep it civil, shall we? Like me old ma used to say, 'If you can't think of anything nice to say . . .'"

In the front seat, Josiah chuckled.

• • •

The young couple took one look at him and accelerated away. You heard such stories about the things that happened in the Hills—thieves who'd beat you to within an inch of your life, just to get your car, kidnappers looking to snatch wealthy heiresses as they drove home. Murderers.

No, no one was going to stop for a filthy, wild-eyed figure, lurching up the road in the dark.

If anyone had stopped, they wouldn't have recognised him. Given the bruising around the man's face and neck, given the dirt and the ragged state of his clothes, given all that, no one would have picked him for Roman Landry, star of *Doubloons of Desire*. Sure, he could have told them, could have revealed himself and asked for help, except Roman Landry hadn't stopped screaming in hours.

But then, no one noticed that either, given no noise was coming out.

• • •

"What do I owe you?" Thelma said, tilting her head forward so that Rick could do up the clasp on her chain.

"On the house," he said. "Couldn't have done it without ye. One thing, though."

"What's that?"

"Don't ever open it. Don't let anyone else open it or he's back where he started."

"Oh, don't you worry about that," she answered, her fingers rising to touch the small gold box around her neck. "This box's staying put, pal. Say," she added, an idea dawning at the back of her mind, "since I can't use mine for . . . powder any more, what say you let me have that one back?"

Rick shook his head. "Sorry, my dear." He walked around the desk to where the box she had taken from Roman's jacket pocket now rested. "I believe I'll be keeping this one."

She shrugged. "See ya around."

Rick said nothing as she sashayed out, instead popping open Roman's box and dipping his fingers into the powder within. For a second or two he rubbed the gritty white dust between his fingertips—all that remained of a stick of chalk from oh-so-long-ago—and then gently closed the lid.

BURNING, ALWAYS BURNING

Alan Baxter and Felicity Dowker

I sat in my shabby office, working hard at my full-time occupation of drinking the memories away. Street cars rattled outside, a zeppelin droned past, and the dame sashayed in. She had a double espresso, a crooked smile, and a figure to make men weep. Blonde curls exploded like a starburst from under her bowler hat. Her right eye was heavily kohled and surrounded with a thick ring of false lashes, while her left was bare. I figured right off the bat this broad was gonna be trouble. Weren't they all?

She slid into the chair on the other side of my desk, her white braces straining over her breasts as she moved, and said, "I'm not bad. You have to understand that."

What I understood was that her sitting there telling me she was a good girl didn't cut much mustard, given the way she tongued her cigarette and flashed one stockinged leg right up to the garter as she downed her coffee. My heart raced my brain to my mouth, and that was always a one-sided competition. I knew this was a mistake, but it's one I've made before, and I'll make it again. And again. And again.

"What is it you're after?" I asked.

She leant forward, the very embodiment of an intimate secret about to be shared. "That all depends on what you can offer." When she spoke, smoke tumbled from her mouth. She was an explosion poured into a tight white shirt.

"What I can offer," I said, all casual-like, "is pretty much anything you need. The real question is; can you afford me?" I took a deep breath and tasted expensive perfume. Oh yeah, she could pay, all right.

She held my gaze as she reached into the pocket of her short black skirt. Her hand emerged stuffed with paper bills. She threw them on my desk, affecting carelessness, but I noticed the tremble in her hand before she withdrew it.

"Question answered, babyface," she said, lighting another cigarette off the smouldering butt of the first and settling back in the chair with a rustle of silk. "Now, as to what I need . . . "

She let the words hang in the air with the curtain of smoke.

I stared at the bills on the desk and the little girl in her eyes and knew this was about love. I also knew it was going to involve me taking a liberal interpretation of the law—but that's what I'm here for. If she could've gone to the police, she would've; probably already had, and got laughed out of the station. So she found her way to my unmarked door, all cashed up, with a score that needed settling. And here I sat, waiting for her. Ol' babyface; always underestimated, always okay with that.

I watched the cigarette smoke curl between her wild locks, wishing it was my fingers. I gave her my own crooked smile.

"I'm Sam," I told her.

"I know," she said. "I'm Esme."

I was playing with fire, but I kinda liked to get burned.

• • •

I stood outside the rowdy gin joint, feeling just a little ridiculous. It was the goddamn necklace Esme had insisted I wear tonight—a huge thing dangling with amethysts and peacock and swallow feathers. I couldn't hide it under my shirt, couldn't cover it with my tie. I looked like some kinda confused witchdoctor in a baggy suit and fedora.

But it smelt like her, and that was something. That girl had got under my skin quicker than a hungry tick.

"You can't go in there without it," she'd said back in my office, leaning in real close to drape the thing around my neck, allowing me a perfect view of her perfect breasts. "You won't come out alive if you do. Or worse, you won't come out *you*." Her lips had touched my ear as she whispered into it, her tongue flicking the lobe so faintly I could've imagined it. I shivered, remembering.

Women.

I dropped my cigar onto the rain-slick ground and rapped on the door, three times fast, twice slow, twice fast, just like Esme had told me. A small panel slid open at eye level. I squinted, but couldn't see anything but murk and smoke. God, smoke everywhere, all the time, like this whole filthy city was permanently ablaze. Or maybe it was just me burning.

"Password," a voice said from within.

"Dashiell Chandler's red harvest is the big sleep," I recited. Esme had made me repeat it over and over back in my office, the words at first nonsensical, then later, eerie in some way I couldn't place. I didn't like saying them out loud, here in this dark alley. But Esme could pay, and I needed the money, and I *wanted* her. I also wanted a drink, but that would have to wait.

The panel slammed shut and the door opened. A woman stepped out, pulled me in, and smiled at me as she shut the door behind us.

It was *her*. Esme. Standing right in front of me in that same crazy get-up she'd worn this morning at my office.

"What do you see?" she said, her voice just like Esme's, except it was too eager, too hungry. The necklace I wore felt heavy, a dead albatross around my neck, smelling now not of Esme, but of the grave. A drop of sweat traced its way down my spine; it was cold.

"My mother," I lied. You don't live this long in my line of work without sharp instincts and quick wits.

The woman laughed, shrugged her shoulders, and in the time it took for me to blink, became something else; not *my* sexy, troubled dame, just another woman, in a red dress and chunky boots, pocketknife tucked behind her ear, clipboard in her hands.

"Oedipus was right," she said, and waved me forward.

"Not as right as Electra," I told her as I passed, enjoying her raised eyebrow and the startled tilt of her head. I doffed my hat, ran my fingers through my short, oiled hair, and stepped through the saloon-like inner gin-joint doors into another world.

"Ask for Doc Starlight," Esme had told me. "Tell him you're on the case for me. He needs to know I'm trying to sort this out."

"Sort what out?" I'd asked, the hairs on the back of my neck tickling with trepidation.

"He'll explain," she'd said, smoke pouring over red lips.

I'd dragged a hand across my neck and brushed away the warning I usually listened to.

This joint was like so many others, but it had a vibe I couldn't place. Strawberry and sandalwood odours soaked the air, twisting with the smoke and grinding jazzcore. There were punters like Esme, kohled eyes and bowlers, but other styles too, like strutting peacocks with their tails fanned out to the world. So much competition, so little confidence.

Something else, too. Something bad.

I went to the bar, ordered a cold beer. I leaned on one elbow and watched the crowd as I drank, trying to get a grip on the place. My unease was like the flavoured smoke, impossible to grasp. Shrugging it off, mentally filing it under *Be Careful*, I turned to the barmaid, crooking one finger to attract her attention.

She looked annoyed to be bothered. "Something wrong with the beer?"

"Only that I'm drinking it alone." I winked as I spoke.

She just looked bored. Cold bitch. I let the moment hang until it got uncomfortable, but this icy nut wasn't for cracking.

"I'm here to see Doc Starlight," I said.

The barmaid's eyes lit up at last. "What for?" she asked.

"Kinda private."

Her momentary interest turned to disdain in an instant. She jerked her thumb towards the back of the joint and walked away. A guy stood at a studded red leather door, his arms like sides of ham crossed over a barrel chest. His dark skin made his eyes hard to see under a serious brow.

I approached the door, trying to observe everything at once. There was a distinct lack of exits and bolt-holes in the wide open joint.

The big dude raised his chin.

"Doc Starlight in?" I asked.

For such a big guy, standing tall over me, he managed to keep his chin up and look down at me simultaneously. Intimidating. I was impressed. When he said nothing, I felt like I needed to elaborate.

"I'm here for Esme," I said, fingering the ridiculous necklace.

The door opened without him touching it. Creepy. I squeezed past him into a corridor that was cold and smoke-free, a sudden and disconcerting change. The bouncer's strong cologne tickled my nose for a second, then the door closed with a heavy thud. I paused, something niggling at my mind, until I realised the pounding jazzcore outside wasn't just muffled, but silenced. I pressed my ear to the door, but couldn't hear a sound.

Twenty yards ahead was another door, a standard wooden thing like you'd find anywhere. One hand still fingering the necklace, the hard, empowering metal of a revolver reassuring under my left arm, I walked to the door and knocked. Nothing happened. As I raised my hand to knock again, it swung silently in.

The room beyond swam in red and ochre silk, cushions strewn everywhere. Feathered fetishes and instruments of kinky extravagance adorned the walls—whips, chains, masks, cuffs. People lounged, semi-naked men and women, smiling at me like they'd just shared a joke at my expense. Perhaps they had.

Doc Starlight was obvious, his skin slick with oil, hair a crazy cloud of wiry darkness, eyes shining electric blue. I wondered if that was due to contact lenses or something more arcane. His eyes roamed up and down, paused at my crazy necklace, and something like a smile touched his lips. Then he seemed to look closer, deeper, right down to my core, and the smile wavered. Did he *see* me?

"So, you're here for Esme?" he asked, his voice deeper than an ocean trench.

A part of me cursed Esme, but another part remembered those curves, and my anxiety was carried away on the memory of perfect cleavage. Screw my nerves. I'm not a naturally fraught person. Some would call me stupid; I prefer heroic. "Esme told me to come and tell you she's trying to sort this out."

"With you?" He seemed amused. That irritated the hell out of me.

"Yeah. With me. So how about we stop all this fucking around and you tell me what I need to do to make Esme's problems go away."

Doc Starlight grinned, his teeth altogether too white, too wide. The grin rumbled into a laugh and he tipped his head back, sending his mirth to the heavens. I jumped when he snapped his eyes back to me, locking on to my soul. "Can you die for her, Private Eye?" he asked, so quietly I almost couldn't hear him.

"Yes," I said.

I didn't know I was going to say it until the word had left my mouth. Whaddya know? I meant it, too.

"Then we can do business," Doc Starlight said. The others in the room began to silently pour out, by some invisible signal, until we were alone. "Here is what you need to know . . ."

. . .

When I returned to my sad excuse for an office, Esme seemed almost surprised, but she was grateful, and she wanted me to know it. And after what Doc Starlight had told me—what he'd said I would do—y'know, I figured I'd just about earned all the gratitude she was inclined to give. I didn't want that crazy Doc to be right.

Candles burned, cheap grubby tealights from a dime store, but the thought counted. She'd sprayed her perfume everywhere and it made me feel drunk. A record played, something with a woman singing huskily above a thrumming beat, and after the jazzcore at the gin joint, it was like salve to an open wound.

"All sorted out?" she asked, innocence and sultry vamp combined.

"You could say that," I said, nerves tickling the base of my spine.

She narrowed her eyes at me, tipped her head like she was weighing odds, then shrugged. "Nothing ventured, nothing gained," she purred and slipped her braces down each shoulder. She peeled off the tight shirt, stepped out of the little black skirt, and my heart tangoed all the way into my throat.

She perched on the edge of my desk, legs apart, one stilettoed heel resting on the arm of the guest chair, the other planted on the threadbare carpet like she was staking a claim. Which, I guess, she was. She wore stockings, garter belt, bowler hat and make-up, and nothing else.

Oh, Lordy.

"Come here," she said, and I obeyed.

She took off my ridiculous necklace and laid it reverently on the floor, like it still meant something; like it ever had. Beautiful liar. My fedora she lifted from my head and tossed into a corner. She traced a lacquered fingernail down the lapel of my jacket and looked up at me with those eyes, one aggressive with black kohl, the other naked and vulnerable. She flicked one of my buttons and, taking her hint, I slid off my jacket.

Her fingers stroked my cheek, and for the briefest moment, her lips brushed mine.

Then she lay back on my desk, staring at me between the valley of her breasts. Her bowler finally fell from her head and her curls tumbled free.

"Come here," she repeated, and once again, I followed orders.

. . .

That was a sweet moment. The thing about sweet moments is they end all too soon and are too easily overpowered by all the bitterness that follows. I've always tried to remember her like that, all warm and soft and spread out on my desk, smiling, but it's futile.

I remember the blood and the screaming, and what she *became*. It'd been about love all right, her coming to me, but not in the way I'd thought. Doc Starlight had walked over to me in that back room of his, flicked the necklace hanging down my chest and said, "Esme gift-wrapped you for me. She always does."

I looked at him crooked and he said, "But she fucked up. She killed my favourite lover boy; did you know that, *Sam*? She thinks gifts will work on me now? So desperate to escape my wrath, she can't see what's right before her eyes. But I can, *Sam*. My tastes are quite particular. You're not my type."

"She killed your lover boy?" I asked him and he laughed that deep rumble again.

"This isn't something she can make right, not something that can be atoned for. She doesn't understand love, you see, except as a lure. And as for you—this all started because she paid well, yes?"

That made me angry and I snarled at him. "It's more than that!"

And still he laughed. "Sure it is, now. That's her magic. But she paid well. You know, I can pay better. You're in a . . . *unique* position to tie up this loose end for me. But you have to see her true form to do it. And show her yours."

I clenched my fist so I didn't crack him across the jaw.

Unabashed, he rummaged in a drawer and handed me a small, strange dagger. It sparkled with arcane light. "You'll need this," he told me.

And explained things I refused to believe . . . then.

• • •

There Esme lay, so beautiful, so desirable. I ground my teeth, still refusing to believe.

Can you die for her, Private Eye?

I crawled up on the desk, letting my fingers trace her soft thigh, the shallow valley inside her hip, her smooth stomach and the curve of her breast. I leaned forward, dusting kisses across her hard nipples, as my heart pounded against my ribs so powerfully I thought my chest would split open. The weight of the dagger in my back pocket dragged at my soul.

She gasped, shuddered. She lifted her head and buried her lips in the crook of my neck and I lifted my chin to let her in.

Can you die for her, Sam?

I felt her form shift underneath me and I cursed Doc Starlight aloud as her teeth split the skin at my throat and my blood spilled over her lips. I cursed him for being right, and Esme for being what she was, and myself for falling for all this bullshit.

But then, she'd fallen for my bullshit, too.

Esme gasped again and drew back from me, her face harsh and angular, eyes narrow, black and deep. Her body, serpent coils from the waist down, curled around me. *Lamia*, Doc Starlight had said. *Monster* would've done just fine for the thing that was trying to kill me. "What the fuck are you?" she hissed, and ripped my shirt from my body.

She stared at my breasts—small, but unmistakably feminine—and the realisation swirled in her obsidian eyes. I remembered my mother's words, *You have to decide on one or the other.* And I'd screamed, *WHY?*

Esme's hand, wizened and sharply taloned, swept up to take out my throat. I thrust one hand out to stop her as my other drew the dagger from my pocket and slammed it down into her cold, shrivelled heart.

"No!" she screamed, but I couldn't hear her over my own sobs of anguish. I could barely see her through my tears.

That's the problem with people underestimating me: *everyone* suffers. I felt the magic flood through the dagger, just like Doc Starlight had said it would.

Your own life will power this to end hers. Be careful you don't give your true self away before you get the chance to kill her.

Esme wailed as her skin blackened and stretched taut. Fire burst from her throat and her eyes melted from the inside and trickled down her cheeks. With a furnace burst of heat, she exploded beneath me in a shower of ash and I fell to the burned desk, empty and drained, and wept.

. . .

It was a long time before I finally pulled myself up and dusted myself off. I was still reluctant to accept what had happened, but the scorch marks on me and my cheap furniture told the truth of the tale.

Well, like I said, I kinda liked to get burnt. Here's the thing about fire, though: it spreads. Often, it consumes the one who ignited it in the first place. Esme had set me to burn, but she was just a lick of flame, blown my way by an ill wind. She was what she was, and I doubt she ever had much choice in that. Like me, in a way. Doc Starlight, though. He was something else. He was the one who lit the match. He played us both like a couple of pawns and he was the only one who got what he wanted out of the whole sorry game.

Revenge . . . well, that has a way of coming back on people. I'd get my own revenge; for me, for Esme, for all of us monsters. I'd reduce Doc Starlight's empire-between-worlds to ashes, spit in them, and call it a good day's work.

And if I failed? If, instead, it was me who went up in flames?

Well, what the hell. I was already burning.

Always burning.

THE BLACK STAR KILLER

Nicole Murphy

Sinéad waved her hand over the candles and flames sparked to life. She smiled—the table looked perfect. The glass glimmered, the silverware gleamed and the red napkins provided a passionate splash of colour against the crisp white tablecloth.

Combined with the enticing smells wafting from the kitchen and the sultry jazz floating in the air, it added up to the perfect setting in which to welcome Dylan back home.

Her husband had been gone for two weeks—part of his role as the Heasimir, giving gadda worldwide their annual health check. She understood the dedication, just as he did when she was summoned away to deal with an errant incantation, but still she missed him.

A chime rang—someone was trying to contact her. Stifling a sigh, Sinéad walked through the loungeroom into her office.

A glowing orb hung over her desk. She touched it with a finger and it peeled open.

"Sabhamir? This is John O'Connor, from Boston. There is some reported trouble in Chicago that I think you should know about."

Sinéad took hold of her power and smiled as its warmth spread through her. Then she mentally contacted John.

"John, this is the Sabhamir. What is the problem?"

"I have been reading some newspaper reports of a murderer the police are chasing in Chicago. He has been leaving a calling-card, and it looks to me like the Star of Gulagh."

Sinéad frowned. The six-pointed star, with a heart at the centre, had been decreed the symbol of the gadda centuries ago. How could a human know about it?

"Can I come to see you?"

"Of course."

Sinéad broke the contact. She looked down at her silk evening gown and sighed, then flicked her wrist. The gown changed into the neck-to-ankle black robe of the Sabhamir. Her red hair cascaded over her shoulders. Mentally, she sought the pinpoint of essence that was her husband's. "Dylan?"

"Just a few more moments, my love. I do like your impatience to see me again."

Sinéad smiled. "It is not that. I have been summoned."

"Of course you have." She could picture his twisted smile. "I hope it will not take too long. I have plans." A vision of the two of them together hit her and with it, a pulse of lust.

"I love you." She broke the connection, focussed on John O'Connor and transferred. There was a moment of sliding through thickness, then a quick pop and she was standing in the other man's loungeroom.

He nodded. "Greetings, Sabhamir, and welcome to my home."

"Thank you, John. Do you have a copy of the newspaper?"

"Certainly." He handed it to her.

The article was titled 'The Search for the Black Star Killer'. Sinéad's eyes were drawn to the accompanying pictures. In one, a police officer was holding up a black card. The picture was not clear enough to see the star, as John had suggested.

She quickly read the article. Over the past month, five people had been killed—three men, two women, of varying ages. All had been taken from a speakeasy within an hour of a police raid. All were intoxicated. All had been strangled.

There was nothing to suggest that gadda power was being used. Except for the description of the card—a white, six pointed star with a heart in the centre printed on black.

Black was her colour. The colour of the Sabhamir, the protector of the gadda. The card was a message to her.

"Do you mind if I take this?" She waved the newspaper at O'Connor.

He shook his head. "Not at all. Is it important?"

"I do not know, but thank you for bringing it to my attention."

O'Connor smiled. "Always happy to serve the guardians."

Sinéad transferred back to her office. She sat down at her desk and stared at the newspaper. If a gadda was killing humans, why not use power? It would make their chances of being captured by the human authorities much less likely.

It would also make it easier for her to catch them.

A pulse of power came from the apartment. A shiver ran through her and a smile burst across her face. She put the paper down and ran across the room, throwing open the door.

"Dylan."

He spun around, grinning. Sinéad rushed into his arms and as his lips pressed against hers, power rushed through her body, igniting the passion.

Dylan's power responded with a roar and within seconds, she was wishing both their clothing away and groaning at the exquisite sensation of his skin against hers.

After two weeks apart, there was not time for finesse—they sated the first flush of lust on the loungeroom carpet.

Sinéad curled her body around Dylan's and kissed his chin. "Welcome home."

"Lovely to be back."

"You have been out in the sun." She traced the line on his waist where he had kept trunks on while swimming or sunbathing.

"I am not going to waste the opportunity to brown up where I can. It will die soon enough in the Irish drizzle."

Sinéad lifted herself onto her elbow to look down at him. It had been three years since they first met and still, the sight of him sizzled. His face was strong, with harsh lines and a hooked nose:

overwhelmingly masculine. His brown hair now had blond streaks that made his pale blue eyes sparkle, although the tan detracted from the redness of his luscious lips.

"I thought you spent all your time indoors, talking to gadda."

"I cannot work all the time, Nady. That would make me sick myself." He pushed a strand of hair back behind her ear. "I am glad the call did not keep you away for too long."

Sinéad frowned. Although she was still aroused, and could also feel Dylan's mix of contentment and desire thanks to the sharing of their power, her mind flipped back to the mystery of the newspaper. "I have a feeling that it has potential to in the future."

"What do you mean?"

"I will show you." She got up, ignoring his groan and went into the office. She came back with the newspaper. "What do you think of this?"

Dylan sat up and read it quickly. "You have not felt anyone using power incorrectly in Chicago?"

"No, and there is nothing in this report to suggest power is being used." She sat next to him. "What do you think of the card?"

"Hard to tell, from either the picture or the description."

Sinéad took the paper back. "I have to get hold of one of those cards. Perhaps there will be an essence there that I can trace."

"It is still late afternoon in Chicago. We can go visit the police."

Sinéad nodded. "Find out which officer is handling the case, where his desk is, then at night, transfer in and get hold of the card."

• • •

That was exactly what she did, only to discover there was no essence on it. It felt as clean as though it belonged to a human.

"So is it a gadda, or is it just a human who has coincidentally devised the Star of Gulagh as their sign?" Sinéad paced up and down the loungeroom, tapping the card against her chin.

"It has to be gadda," Dylan said, lounging on the floral sofa. "It cannot be coincidence that they have used the colour of the protector. They have purposely designed it so black is prominent."

"Then we are going to have to flush him or her out somehow," Sinéad said. She stopped pacing and grinned at Dylan. "How would you like to run an illegal bar?"

. . .

The smooth sounds of the band floated around Sinéad's head as she stepped from her office onto the floor of her club. She stopped and watched the quartet—trumpet, piano, double bass and a sultry singer whose voice rippled through the air like the fine whiskey Sinéad sold.

Finding them was just one reason that the Lucky Clover had become one of the hottest gin joints in Chicago in just a couple of weeks. The other reason was the high quality alcohol that Sinéad transferred in directly from Ireland.

Right now, she did not have time to indulge in pride for her achievement. In a few moments, the police would arrive. She needed to make sure the Clover was still operating in an hour's time.

The speakeasy had to stay open, if she was to have any chance of catching the murderer.

She walked over to the bar, the beads at the bottom of her black dress snapping against her stockinged legs. She leant on the mahogany top and smiled at her barman.

"Now, John," she said.

He nodded, turned and pressed a button on the wall. The pockets of alcohol behind the bar spun around—a dozen small compartments—and on the other side were displayed sodas, cordials and juices.

The waiters started to move around the patrons, guiding them to finish the drinks in their glasses and fill them with the water provided in cut glass bottles. The band did not miss a beat.

A new song was beginning as the front door slammed open and a chill wind blew into the club, fluttering the candles that gave the tables a sought-after intimacy. Sinéad lifted her own glass of ginger beer and sipped at it while she watched a dozen men in dark suits and hats storm into the room.

She nodded at the band and the music stopped as the lead officer called out, "This is a raid! Everyone stay where they are."

Sinéad put her glass down and walked forward, the sound of the clacking beads on her gown drawing everyone's attention in the sudden silence. "Can I help you, officers?"

The lead man narrowed his eyes. "I am District Attorney Daryll Smith and I am here because of reports that this establishment sells liquor." He looked over his shoulder, nodded and the men started to move around the room. He turned back to Sinéad. "I want to speak to the manager."

"I am Sinéad Brennan. I own the Lucky Clover." She smiled.

"You are Irish."

"Yes, I am."

"Then perhaps you do not know the laws here, Ms Brennan."

"The eighteenth amendment? I am well aware of it, District Attorney Smith. It is one of the reasons that I came to America."

"Then you support prohibition?"

"I have seen alcohol cause great distress, sir. I think people should be encouraged to have a healthy lifestyle." All of which was true, although she did not support the laws—Sinéad believed people deserved freedom to make their own mistakes. But she would not tell Smith that.

The search was conducted and as expected, nothing was found. Sinéad struggled to hide a smile at the disappointment on DA Smith's face.

"Can I offer you and your hard working men a soda or cordial?" she crooned.

"No, thank you. We have other premises to visit." He spun around, gesturing for his men to follow as he exited.

"Half an hour," Sinéad said to the barman. "I do not want to be surprised by a sudden return."

She started to make her way through the crowded bar. This was the second time she had been raided—she hoped that this time the murderer would strike.

She loosened control on her power a little so she could feel if someone was human or gadda without touching them. She had an incantation resting on the door that should alert her if a gadda walked in, but she wanted to check herself.

It made sense that the murderer would not be here now—would be outside, waiting for the police to leave before he or she came in, but Sinéad was not prepared to assume anything.

Two weeks, and there had not been a sign of her quarry. Sinéad used the excuse of toying with the string of pearls to send a pulse of power across her shoulders to ease the tension. What would she do if the mystery gadda did not show up?

She stopped from time to time to chat with customers who had become regulars, stopping by every night for a drink or two and to listen to the music.

Dylan's voice slipped into her mind. "Sinéad?"

She rolled her eyes and headed back to the office. She was not going to speak mentally to Dylan in front of all these humans.

He was sitting in her chair, his feet up on the desk. He had taken off his sports jacket and rolled his sleeves up, revealing muscled forearms.

"I am bored," he said.

Sinéad shook her head. She did not want Dylan out in the club proper—his face was too recognisable. If their quarry saw him, they could be scared away. She, on the other hand, was not as well-known in the general gadda population. With her red curls cut off, her robe replaced by a fabulous beaded dress and her face painted, she felt she was disguised enough. "Then get a book to read. Better yet, go home and get some sleep. If I need you, I will call."

He smiled, his eyes twinkled and Sinéad's skin tingled. "I have got a better idea."

"If you are not going to behave yourself, I will make you go home."

"Oh, I will be very good. I promise." He held his hand out to her.

Sinéad gave the temptation half a moment's thought, but was forestalled by a rippling sensation in her power. Someone had triggered the incantation over the door. Dylan dropped his hand and she knew he had felt it, too.

"I think I need to check the club," she said.

Dylan nodded. "Keep in contact with me."

Sinéad slipped back into the main bar, now so packed with people it was hard to walk around. She started to wind her way toward the door.

As she skirted past a table where two men sat, her senses tingled. She glanced down as she walked behind them. One of the men was too drunk to sit straight, let alone stand. Sinéad frowned. She had directed John not to serve anyone obviously drunk—she did not believe a person's choice to drink should be taken from them, but she did not think overconsumption was a good thing either.

The other seemed unaffected by alcohol. He was leaning forward, talking earnestly while the drunken man nodded his head.

"I can help you with that," the sober man was saying. "Come with me, and I will give you a hand."

The drunk smiled and tried to stand, but fell back into his seat. His companion leapt up to help him and Sinéad also moved forward.

"Hello, can I help?" She put a hand on the drunk's shoulder. No power. She smiled at the gadda and her heart sank as she recognised him.

Ronan O'Sullivan. Second-order oman; he had been working as an odd-jobs man around Sclossin until he left a year earlier. She had briefly dated him during the terrible time that she and Dylan had separated.

Damn.

O'Sullivan smiled. "Oh yes, you can help, Sinéad." He turned and started to walk out of the club.

Sinéad signalled to John to look after the drunken patron, then followed O'Sullivan.

She lost sight of him in the crush and pushed her way through to the door, running up the three steps to street level.

O'Sullivan stood in the middle of the street. He looked at her, smiled, then disappeared.

Sinéad swore and strode forward to find his essence and follow it. She gathered her power to transfer, but a group of people came out of the club. They stood on the sidewalk, laughing and looking up and down the street.

She could not transfer in front of them, nor could she still them and do what she needed to—she did not know how long she would be gone, and someone else would be sure to notice a group of people frozen to the sidewalk. "Dylan?"

"Yes?"

She waved a hand and stilled the crowd. The silence was deep. "Come to me. Transfer."

He appeared in front of her. "What?"

"Feel this essence?" She took hold of the flimsy sensation and pressed it to Dylan's palm. He nodded. "Follow it. I will be with you as soon as I can."

He nodded and transferred. Sinéad released the crowd and walked toward them, hoping they had not noticed the few seconds that had passed. They laughed and jostled each other, and she breathed a sigh of relief.

A cut-off scream echoed through her mind and she swore. Dylan. Why had she thought it a good idea to send a healer to do the protector's job?

It took far too long to get through the club to her office, where she would have privacy to transfer. All the while, she hoped Dylan was all right. He was powerful, but he was not the Sabhamir.

Finally in the office, she reached for her husband's essence to transfer to his side. Nothing. Her heart skipped a beat as she tightened her grip on her power and sent more of it out, looking for the pulse that she knew so well.

Dylan was gone. Her first thought was that he was dead, but she pushed that aside. If he was, she would feel the spirit of the Heasimir, looking for its new home.

No, he was still alive—just hidden from her. How was that possible?

"Sinéad?" It took her a moment to place the originator of the mental message.

"O'Sullivan."

"Why did you send him after me? You know it is you I want."

"I am on my way." She focussed on him and transferred.

She was in the middle of a regular loungeroom—sofas, armchairs, bookcases, radio in one corner, bar in the other. O'Sullivan stood in the middle of the room, clad in the most ridiculous thing she had ever seen. His body was covered in stockings—he had pulled a pair on over his legs, another pair over his arms and a third over his face. His torso was wrapped in a patterned material that looked like silk and he wore shorts in the same material.

"O'Sullivan, what is going on here?"

"You took your time in finding me, Sinéad. I guess it just goes to show that you are not all that clever, are you?"

Star, he was not going to start with that again, was he? That had been his refrain when she had ended things with him—that she thought she was so much better than him, so much cleverer, just because she wore the black.

Sinéad decided the conversation was a waste of time. She lifted her hands and fired a stillness resolution at him. His body shuddered, and then he shook it off.

Beneath the stocking that flattened his facial features into a horrible rictus, he smiled. "Nice try. Now, here is what I can do." He lifted his hands and Sinéad saw the stockings had been cut away from his palms.

She threw up a shield to hold off his incantation. O'Sullivan's power, a pale blue, slammed into her shield and fizzled away quickly.

Only second-order, she remembered. She should be able to deal with him easily. Except—how had he managed to repulse her stillness resolution?

He put his hands down, hiding the hole in the stockings and sneered. "You think you are so good, Ms Sabhamir, so powerful; too good for the rest of us. Well, try this."

He whipped his hands up and fired another burst of power at her. Again, it exploded against her shield without causing her any concern.

His hands flipped back down. "You have got power, but I have got the smarts. I will get you. I can outlast you. There is nothing you can do."

After his next attack—each one just a quick pulse, not a sustained flurry—Sinéad realised he was hiding the break in the stockings over his hands from her.

She sent a flash pulse at him and it bounced off the silky material and sizzled into the floor by his feet. She nodded. There was something about what O'Sullivan was wearing that was repulsing power. He needed the cut at his hands to form his own incantations.

Sinéad noted there were some plants on the bar, and one of them was trailing across the floor and around O'Sullivan's ankle. She guessed the plant was replenishing his power, as the material that was protecting him from her power would also stop him replenishing his own from the world around him.

O'Sullivan laughed. "You see? Admit it—I have outsmarted you. I am better than you."

Sinéad recalled the other reason why she had ended things with O'Sullivan after a few dates—he had been determined to master her. He had told her that what she thought was wrong, what she ate was wrong, how she dressed was wrong. The one time they had kissed, his aggressiveness had turned her off.

After another disastrous attempt at a relationship, she had decided that men in general could not handle her being the Sabhamir. It was why Dylan had left her, soon after her elevation. She had put aside all thoughts of romantic happiness and had committed herself fully to her duty of protecting the gadda.

Then Dylan had come back, begged her forgiveness and castigated himself for feeling his masculinity threatened by her power. Over the next few months, he had proven he was more than able to be a supportive partner.

She had seen his elevation to the role of Heasimir—almost her equal—as the reward for his turn-around.

"Women should not be Sabhamir."

O'Sullivan's sneer pulled Sinéad back to the present.

"That is where you are wrong, O'Sullivan." She dropped her shield and gathered her power into a small, thin line. She watched him raise his hands and took her chance, firing her power out. It passed through the incantation racing toward her and struck O'Sullivan's palm.

His incantation hit—a power punch. She reeled backward, her head snapping to the rear with the force of the blow. She put a foot behind her to re-balance. Star, even from a second-order, there was enough there to hurt. But she was not going to let him know that. She straightened, checked that the pulse she had fired at him was still connected and smiled.

"Is that all?"

"No, not at all." He smiled, then frowned, his eyes darting to his hands.

"What is wrong? Can you not move your hands?" Slowly, Sinéad fed the stillness resolution along the thin strand of power between her and O'Sullivan's palm. "I wager that there is a lot more of your body that you cannot move now."

His body jerked and he gasped. "How are you doing that?"

"I am outsmarting you, O'Sullivan. That is how." She cut off her power and walked towards him. She touched his palm and nodded. It felt as though he would be able to talk and move his head, but the rest of his body was frozen. "Where is the Heasimir?"

O'Sullivan sneered. "You will never find him."

"We will see." Sinéad started to search the house.

In the front bedroom, a woman was sleeping. Sinéad touched her—she was human. There was a small child sleeping in another room—also human.

The third bedroom was just a storeroom and there was nothing in the kitchen or bathroom either. She came to another door and the moment she touched it, felt a curious deadness there.

She tried the handle—the door was locked. She called on her power and blasted it forward, but it bounced off the metal and she had to jump out of the way so it slammed into the wall behind her.

So this was impervious to power as well. She went back into the loungeroom, pleased to see that O'Sullivan had not moved.

"I guess you have got the key on you." Sinéad pulled at the stockings. She noted the material felt slippery, almost oily under her fingers. She found the key in one of O'Sullivan's shorts' pockets and opened the door with apprehension.

It was dark and still. She reached to flick the light switch but paused when she heard something like a moan. She turned the light on and gasped.

Dylan lay on the floor, at the bottom of a flight of stairs. One of his legs was twisted at an unnatural angle and blood seeped from a wound on his forehead.

"Darling." Sinéad rushed down the stairs and knelt by him, feeling the floor give spongily beneath her weight. A quick glance around showed the walls and floor had been covered in some sort of material—that must have been why she had not been able to feel Dylan and why her power had rebounded against the door.

She brushed her fingers across her husband's forehead. "Dylan?"

He moaned again. Alive, but badly hurt. She mentally connected with the healer on duty in Sclossin and after putting her hand on Dylan's shoulder, transferred him there, settling him on the bed.

The healer, a young woman with an overbite and stringy blonde hair, motioned Sinéad aside and bent over Dylan. She clicked her tongue.

"The leg is easily dealt with, the head wound less so. Power will not work to heal a brain injury. I will put him under the stillness resolution and we must hope he can heal himself."

Sinéad looked at Dylan, the colour of his tan leached from his skin, and tears pricked her eyes. "Please save him," she whispered.

"I will do what I can, Sabhamir." The healer pushed her away.

Sinéad stood in the corridor, fighting the fear. *Star above*, she thought. *Do not take him from me.* Please.

Slowly, the fear coalesced into anger and with rage flooding her system she transferred back to O'Sullivan.

The human woman was kneeling by his feet, taking the stockings off him. She looked at Sinéad, shock written on her face. "Who are you?" She jumped to her feet. "How did you get in here?"

Sinéad froze her and then stormed forward and slapped O'Sullivan across the face. The man screamed with more ferocity than her blow deserved.

"Coward," she sneered. "You killed all those people, have put the Heasimir in danger and for what? To pay me back for dumping you? Why not face me like a man?"

"You hide behind the black," he shouted. "Take off your robe and face me, woman to man. But you will not, because you know I am better than you."

"I have known rats that were better than you." She leant close. "You had better hope he lives, because I swear that if he does not, you will wish you were dead."

. . .

"Dyl?"

He groaned and opened his eyes. "What the hell happened?"

Sinéad squeezed his hand. Star, she wanted to dance and scream out her joy. "You seem to have taken a frying pan to the head, my darling. O'Sullivan's way of saying 'Welcome to my humble abode'."

Dylan closed his eyes. "Nice."

"You are going to be fine. There does not appear to be any major damage. You are going to feel a bit sore and sorry for yourself for a few days but otherwise, you will be fine." Thank the Star.

"So, did we defeat the bad guy?"

"I defeated the bad guy. He will face the bardria tomorrow and be banished, never to bother us again."

"Never doubted you would win, Nady."

She kissed his forehead. "You need to rest."

"I tried to reach you." His voice was hoarse. "I could not. My power would not leave the room."

She could hear frustration and fear in his tone. She touched his cheek. "It was covered in a man-made substance. So was O'Sullivan when I got there. It seems the humans have developed fibres and materials that appear to repel power. I have yet to work out how."

"Great. Just what we needed."

"Yet another reason to keep the secret of the gadda safe."

"So long as my failure does not repel you."

Sinéad smiled and pressed her lips to her husband's. "Not at all, my darling. Now, sleep."

The Sabhamir held the Heasimir's hand and watched over him until he slept.

HARD BOILED

Brian G. Ross

My name is Isaac Power.

I used to run a two-bit detective agency in Del Santos, somewhere between the rats and the bums, back when a lot of my black brothers were either being lynched or shot.

My *raison d'être* was infidelity—wives trying to pin a tail on their donkey husbands; men playing away when they should have been playing golf, that kind of thing. It was real bottom of the barrel stuff—not nearly as glamorous as the movies would have you believe—but there was nothing surer than a man and his mistress; except maybe the wife who wanted to keep tabs on him.

The money was good but never great, and watching sweaty sex between strangers, behind the steamy windows of a '61 Buick Skylark—while temporarily gratifying—wasn't all strawberries and marshmallows.

Sometimes I'd found myself squeezed into crud-covered doorways, or behind dumpsters that smelled worse than my apartment, and I'd snap bosses giving their secretaries the kind of raise nobody mentioned at the interview. It was a hell of a way to get your kicks on a Friday night, but I just kept reminding myself that if it wasn't me, it would have been someone else.

The trick was not to ask too many questions. Just take the pictures, take the *money*, and walk away.

But trust me, even a tongue in the wrong ear could be comfortably explained away if you took it out of context. If you didn't start at the beginning, sometimes you missed the smoking gun.

But all of that was a lifetime ago.

Most of the windows were boarded up now, and the ones that weren't have long since been smashed. These days you could barely see the sign above the door for all the grime and the graffiti.

Yeah, this town belonged to the dogs.

Nowadays, wives would sooner take a gun to their husband's head or a pinch of poison to their steak braciole, than throw their hard-earned dollars at mugs like me. Women weren't afraid to get their hands dirty anymore, and my kind was going out of business faster than a pig farmer in a synagogue.

So when the mysterious broad swept into my office that wet evening not so long ago like the Santa Ana wind, and the first words out of her perfect mouth were—

"I'll give you ten grand."

—I almost choked on my cigar.

I finished coughing into the broadsheet I had been pretending to read, and our eyes met across the faux Persian rug in front of my desk.

The dame—surprisingly dry for such a sodden night—smiled through the nicotine haze that belonged to both of us. She clutched an obsidian black briefcase in her left hand and a cigarette holder between two elegant fingers of her right.

She had my attention, that's for sure. Leading with the money never failed. I had been working this patch since before the war— long enough to forget more than I remembered—and I knew most of the angles. I looked her up and down and hoped she would give me a chance to get to know most of hers.

I cleared my throat, reacquainted myself with my cigar, and asked her to take a load off. While she did, I dropped the paper open at the financials on my desk. My stock had just taken a sharp turn north.

She was a looker, for sure—all lipstick and legs—and I had to question what a killer body like hers was doing in this part of town all alone. To her place or mine, I wasn't certain, but I knew then that one way or the other I'd have to take her home: a girl with that shape wouldn't last long on a night like this.

I watched her cross and uncross her gams, like a kid who couldn't keep still. She was young enough to be my daughter, but still old enough to shake it if the mood struck.

Ten thousand berries was a lot of change. It would mean my ex-wife would take her alimony claws out of my back long enough for me catch my breath, and I could finally afford to start thinking about that T-bird I had been promising myself since the fifth grade.

"You know, the last time a broad offered me that kind of money," I said. "I came up light at the end of the day."

She smiled like she knew what I meant. "Everyone pays their debts eventually. Some just take longer to cash in than others."

"You look familiar," I spoke around my cigar, but I still didn't know where to put my eyes. She knew I was giving her the once over, but she didn't care. "I know you?"

"If you did, you wouldn't need to ask."

I nodded, but I knew that staring at those legs for long enough could probably give a guy amnesia. "Do we have an appointment?"

"Do I need one?"

I hated people who answered a question with a question, so I threw one back at her. "How'd you get past my secretary?"

Betty was taking a letter in her methodical two-fingered way. I didn't know who to or what for—business was light these days—but the typewriter arms smacked the paper like firecrackers anyway.

"She's not the best guard dog I've met," the mysterious woman said. "I threw her a treat and she rolled right over."

We both smiled as we watched Betty through the glass door.

The secretary pulled a sheet of paper from the roller, cranked another one in, and carried on right where she had left off.

"All right, let me straighten this out for you." I leaned forward in my seat. "I don't take cheques and I don't like credit. I want cash. Clean, crisp bills. Large notes if you got them; small ones if you don't. You dig?"

She nodded. "You can take it all now, if you want." With that, she bent down to the briefcase, but I stayed her with one hand.

"Slow down there, Tonto," I said. "I ain't jumping into bed with you just yet."

"You will."

"That's as may be."

The undercurrent wasn't lost on me, but I shifted it to one side, at least until this business was out of the way. It was easy to get lost with those kind of diversions; but just as easy to be suspicious of someone willing to give away that kind of money that fast.

She may not have had any questions for me, but I had a few I wanted to throw at her.

"The only people I know with that kind of money are crooks, cons, and my ex-wife's attorney," I said. "And he ain't half the woman you are. So which is it?"

She looked at me as if that was the worst opening gambit she had ever heard.

I dipped my cigar into the ashtray and tapped. "If you're looking to make a confession lady, there's a church two blocks away."

"Tell me, Mr Powers: you think if someone says sorry enough times, if they pray forgiveness enough nights on their knees by their bed, that maybe it'll all even up when they get to the other side?"

I didn't know what the hell she was talking about, but sometimes it was better just to buy the ticket and jump on the train anyway.

"Why? You looking for someone to turn the other cheek?"

"I haven't done anything wrong," she said. "Unless you consider getting married at twenty-one a crime."

But with the kind of meat she was offering, I had to wonder if she knew the difference between right and wrong.

"How'd you find out about me?" I asked.

"Through a friend."

"Most of my friends are dead. You hang about in graveyards a lot?"

"A friend of *mine*."

She had a little girl's smile and a big girl's body. That kind of combination had been getting men into trouble for generations. She was carrying a scent that took me back to a long time ago, but good times or bad, I couldn't remember who it belonged to.

I was hungry, so I picked up the phone to dial this great little pizza joint I knew on the corner of Bellevue and Park while I watched her.

I didn't say she could, but she stood up and slid her red-skirted keister onto the corner of my desk. She took her perfume with her, and it settled around my shoulders like an aromatic blanket.

"Let's rewind, lady—"

"It's Davina."

"Davina's my ex-wife's name."

"That's not what I heard."

"Yeah? What'd you hear?"

"Never mind."

She was right—it wasn't the ex-wife's, but what the hell, this broad couldn't have known that. That name took me back thirty years, to a bad relationship that had soured, and some things were just best left in the past. "How about . . . Clementine?" I asked.

"You like that one?"

"I like the song."

She put the cigarette holder between her lips like she did it for a living, and puffed purple rings in my direction. I made a mental note to ask her later how she did that.

I got the engaged tone from the pizza place on Bellevue and dropped the phone into the cradle. My stomach churned.

I poured myself a stiff hooker, iced the glass, then added some more juice. I asked my new friend if she wanted to have a sniff from the barrel, but she turned me down with a smile and a flick of her hair.

"So Clementine," I said. "You want me to follow your old man, feed him a few words? What's the score? If you've got the goods, I can do most anything."

"I need to pass on a message."

I smiled reflectively.

Bunch of fives. Lead sandwich. Concrete slippers.

In the early days, if the price was right, and the risk relatively low, people had been known to disappear. There was a time when that kind of thing was the easiest way to make a buck in this deadbeat town, but those days were so many bridges back it was easy to think they belonged to someone else.

The world spun a little differently now, and thankfully, I didn't roll like that anymore. But it looked like all she had to do was say the word and I'd be right back in that despicable world I had spent so long climbing out of.

"I'm strictly hands-off now," I said finally. "It's been a long time. I've put all that behind me."

And I had.

"It's not what you think," she said.

"You show up with a briefcase full of clams, say you want me to pass on a message, and you're telling me it's *not* what I think?"

She looked at me blankly.

Maybe she was right and I'd just been playing this game for too long, but I had the feeling she was hiding something nonetheless. Perhaps it was her calm, self-assured posture, or the perfectly formed smoke circles that she blew towards me; or perhaps it was nothing more than just how damned familiar she looked. Whatever the case, in this business every fish smelled bad—even this fine looking catch perched on the end of my desk.

I swung round in my chair and looked out the window. The world beyond the glass was deserted: even a broken town like mine had its quiet moments.

Rain came down in heavy, grey sheets.

In this weather, and at this time of night, the roads were fairly clear. There was nothing out there except the fast approach of tomorrow, and Del Santos could be a frightening place at midnight. We were both much better off in here.

I knocked back the rest of my glass, slammed it on the window sill, and broke the cruel silence. "How big's this chief of yours, anyways?"

Clementine gave me a *not sure* with her shoulders.

"Bigger'n me?"

I stood up, puffed out my chest, and spread my arms like Jesus waiting for a cross. I was six-three in my socks.

She jerked a nod and I got a whiff of her hair. It was like a spring afternoon. "I guess he was about your size."

I sucked my cigar dry and stubbed it out in the ashtray. "Was?"

"Is," she corrected.

I was all right with that. I didn't like approaching guys who had too many inches on me. I bruised easily if the fists were much bigger than mine.

"Your husband carry a piece?" I asked.

"Lance doesn't like guns."

That name rang all kinds of bells. "I don't like them either, babe, but I got a dozen of 'em, just in case it hits the fan." I took another cigar from the case on my desk and flicked it into my mouth. I'd been practising that.

"We didn't have any weapons in the house," she clarified.

"Didn't?"

"Sorry. Don't."

I should've known right there that this job was coming at me a little lop-sided, but I was getting old and rusty, and it took me longer to see the signs these days. I just thought she was nervous.

She offered me a light. I said I was good, I had my own, but the truth of it was I knew never to trust a broad with a naked flame that close to my face, even one who seemed like she'd been poured out of a lingerie catalogue and dipped in perfume. I pulled a match from my breast pocket and struck it sharply with my thumbnail. Clementine looked impressed: I tried not to.

I dragged deep. "You think he's got a broad on the side?" They always did. The guys who didn't, they were the ones you had to worry about.

Clementine slid off my desk and I had to wonder why any man would need more woman than that. She shrugged and blew another couple of smoke rings my way. The ghostly haze clogged the office.

"He comes home late every night, says he's trying to land a big fish." Her red lips formed each word like she was giving birth to them.

"What's he do?"

"Encyclopaedia salesman. He went door-to-door."

The dame had a real problem with tense, but again, I let it slide. Sometimes answers came more quickly if you didn't ask questions.

"Has he got 'N'?" I asked.

"I'm sorry?" She looked confused.

"The letter 'N'." I gestured towards my bookshelf.

If there was one thing I knew about women it was that intelligence—or, at least, the perception of it—was high up on their list of desirable male qualities; right up there with a sense of humour. With that in mind, guys had been cracking jokes and feigning smarts for years. Of course, I'd hardly split a spine on any of those books, but Clementine didn't know that.

"I used to have them delivered every month, but for some reason the guy didn't show for 'N'." I moved close. "Maybe it was your bull, who knows. It's a shame; I was really looking forward to *nachos*."

"That's cute."

She smiled like she thought it was part of the script, and I stopped trying to over-egg the pudding. Mixing business with pleasure was a dangerous game, especially in this business and with those legs.

"So, who's the broad?" I asked, bringing the conversation back around to where she didn't want it. "She his book-keeper, childhood sweetheart? She work the corner?"

"How'd you know there's a girl?"

"Lady, in my world it's only ever about money or sex—or both. You sashay in here with enough green to take a bite out of Wall Street: I'm guessing you ain't concerned where your next meal is coming from."

Clementine's face softened. She swept past me and picked up a copy of something I'd never seen before from the bookshelf. She blew a blanket of dust from the top, and with it, the lid off my intellectual cover.

I coughed.

"You're a clever man, Mr Powers."

"Books'll do that." I smiled around my cigar. I had known a girl once who kept slipping an 's' onto the end of my name—same one who had soured on me. Clementine reminded me a lot of her. "Call me Isaac."

"For ten grand I think names should be my shout, don't you? I'm thinking Mickey; you've got the ears for it."

I tugged on a lobe. The girl was as sharp as a blade to the kidneys, and she moved like Niagara Falls. "So, you get a look at this girl?" I asked.

"I can do you better than that."

Clementine slid the book back onto the shelf, and I caught the title *Moby Dick* in the stark light. Good movie; I didn't know they'd turned it into a book.

She started to open her clutch bag. I quickly put my hand on hers, because too many times it wasn't gum they came back out with.

"I have photographs," she said. "But you can keep your hand there if you like."

"Allow me." I reached into her bag and pulled out a small brown envelope. It wasn't sealed. "These?"

Clementine nodded. It looked like she was about to call on the waterworks, but she'd find out fast that I didn't play those kind of games.

I pulled the prints from the envelope. They'd just been developed, so the ink was still tacky.

"That's some kind of woman." I nodded my approval. If a guy was going to cut loose, here was the girl to do it with. "She's cute." Blonde hair, long legs: everything's where it should be and then some. "Your husband has fine taste in mistresses."

"I'm so pleased."

Sarcasm didn't suit her, but I let her have that one for free.

I walked around the room with the pictures. Six of them. Each one more compromising than the last. I flicked through them like a pack of oversized playing cards.

The top photograph showed a tall, dark man, and a mysterious girl, walking hand in hand along the beach. A calm, summer night. They were smiling, licking vanilla. It was kind of sweet, in a sleazy, bit-on-the-side kind of way, but I didn't say that to Clementine.

"Very professional," I said. "Nice composition, good light, great exposure. The kind of work I did back when all that clients wanted was a nice set of prints."

Clementine would've looked pretty good in front of the lens, for sure, but I somehow knew it wasn't her behind it.

"Who's your snapper?" I asked.

"Someone you don't remember." She smirked. "Or, at least, someone you're trying hard to forget."

"What's that supposed to mean?"

Clementine breathed a stream of purple smoke out slowly. "You're the detective. You figure it out."

I didn't know whether it was the drink or not, but this dame was talking just the right amount of crazy to keep the meter ticking over.

"That your man in the picture with her?"

"Yes, that's Lance."

She was right—he looked about my height, although I'd probably take him on the scales.

Like Clementine, he had one of those faces I thought I'd seen before, but then again, if you hung around Del Santos for long enough, pretty soon even strangers begun to look like family.

Clementine dabbed at her big brown eyes with a tissue. I started to worry again that she was going to start up with those tears, but maybe it was just my particular brand of cigar. I dragged long and hard then crushed it out in the ashtray.

"You know anything about her?" I slapped the photographs down on my desk. "Her name? Where she lives? Favourite perfume?"

"Who cares about perfume?"

The air around her tasted like strawberries and kisses. "You never know what kind of information will be valuable," I said. I sat at my desk and flipped open a notepad. Now seemed as good a time as any to start using it. "All right then, let me take down what we know so far."

"I'm not here to talk about her." Clementine reached into her bottomless clutch bag and this time she did come back with gum. Two sticks. I thought she was going to offer me one, but instead, she unwrapped them and stuck them both in her mouth.

"He was messing me around." She spoke softly, into her chest.

"*You're* messing *me* around, baby."

She wiped her eyes like she meant it this time, but I knew that not even a broad who could afford it threw ten thousand dollars into the wind just so I could chase a guy and his tail. There was always more to it than that.

Something in her demeanour seemed a little sticky, and I didn't just mean the way she kept moving from one heel to the other like she was dancing on hot coals.

Clementine swayed away from me. "He's dead," she said finally.

And there was the rub. Even with all my years of experience, that one surprised me. "You sure?"

"I know a stiff when I see one."

I bet she did.

I cleared my throat. "I'm afraid, darling, a toe-tag puts your husband a little outside my jurisdiction. The only spirits I chase are Jack and Jim." I jerked my head towards the bar and smiled. "Of course, this detective business would be a whole lot easier if more of my clients were like your Lance. No offence."

"None taken."

She sat there chewing away the silence, and I worked her with my eyes. Despite the way this conversation had tipped—I wondered whether she would consider dinner and a movie after all this was dusted.

"So tell me, Clementine," I began. "Why you showing me pictures of your dead husband?"

She nodded towards one of the pictures. "He wasn't dead when these shots were taken, Mr Powers."

"Touché."

"I thought they may ring a few bells. The pictures, I mean."

If she had a drift, I didn't catch it.

She tapped her red nails against my desk and shook her scent at me again. Her deliberation was like summer rain, and it was getting pretty wet in here. She rubbed those sticks of hers together like she was trying to start a fire. Suddenly, the words tumbled out of her mouth, her voice cracked and brittle. "He used to hit me; hard enough to hurt, but not enough so it left a mark. He was always careful where he put his hands." She smiled, but there was a sadness behind it.

I hated men who smacked women about. They bottomed out the food chain, right there rubbing shoulders with the monkeys who mugged old ladies in the street, or the jerks who ripped off the homeless.

Clementine cleared her throat. "One day I decided I wasn't going to take it any longer, so I paid a guy—you know, someone like you—to take him out of the frame."

She made it sound like the kind of crowbar job I used to pull, back in the early days, when times were too tight to hang about for the clean ones.

"It was a long time ago," she finished, just loud enough for me to hear.

She kept her eyes away from mine, which made things a little awkward. It was difficult to trust a broad when you didn't know where she was looking.

"A guy like me?" I asked. "You mean a shamus?"

"I mean a negro."

I nodded as I caught my watery reflection in the window. Some attitudes would never change.

"There ain't no excuse for a man to do that, but that don't give you the right to have him knocked off. Ain't neither the two of us God." I swallowed my hypocrisy, but it went down hard.

"I know," Clementine replied.

I could tell by the way the words almost failed to reach her lips, that she had regretted it ever since. She hung her head, and I thought I may never see those pretty eyes again.

"Turns out, guilt isn't such a great nightcap after all, no matter how many pills you take." When she found the strength to lift her head back up, her face was ashen and grim, and glass tears did—finally—embroider her eyes. "Maybe you're right: maybe I am chasing ghosts, after all."

I grabbed the pictures from my desk and dragged my eyes across them again with renewed interest. I still couldn't shake the feeling that I knew this guy from somewhere.

"You said you hadn't committed a crime." I threw the pictures at her and they fluttered to the floor silently. "So what the hell do you call this?"

"Revenge isn't a crime." She closed her eyes for a thoughtful moment, and when she opened them again the tears were gone. "At least, it shouldn't be."

"No?" I doodled a picture of a house in my notepad; put bars on the windows. "I reckon the cops would say different. There are jail cells all across the country, filled with jealous wives just like you."

She smirked. "Not like me."

I went back to the bar and poured myself another. I had a feeling that tonight was going to be a long one.

Clementine said she would take a drink this time even though I hadn't put the offer out there. I threw together a martini for her and went heavy on the olives. I had seen someone do that in a movie once. She took it and thanked me with a nod.

"I'm a detective, baby, and a damn good one at that, but I ain't no priest and I certainly can't work miracles. Not even on a Sunday. Sounds to me like you need a lawyer." I took a heavy drag from my cigar and dusted it into the ashtray. "Sit down, I'll point you in the right direction."

"Don't tell me what I need, Mr Powers."

"There's no 's', lady. Name's on the door." I hooked a thumb towards the corridor. "Check it on your way out. Anyways, I told you to call me Isaac."

"I find it difficult to be on first name terms with someone who wants to send me down."

She seemed to stare right through me with those deep brown pools. You'd need to be a strong swimmer to get away from those eyes.

"And besides," she continued. "If you were half as clever as you think you are, you'd have figured this whole thing out by now."

"Yeah?"

"Yeah."

She wasn't a bad girl—I knew that—just a regular jane who had taken a few wrong turns somewhere along the way and been caught in the headlights.

But hell, we were all guilty of that sometimes.

In a town like Del Santos you soon figured out that the heroes didn't always wear white ten-gallons, and the villains rarely announced themselves as such. The world wasn't simply a swathe of black and white: far from it. There were a thousand differentials in between.

Like Clementine.

Like me.

We were all just shades of grey, blurred at the edges.

Still, the law was the law. Without it—and guys like me to turn the screws—the world would just be a cesspool of filth and grime, and bullets would be the only currency worth having. So I wasn't about to throw out the rule book, no matter how fine her legs were.

"I want to make it right," she said finally. "I want to say sorry."

"That's sweet, but next time you bag yourself a husband you should maybe try getting your apologies in *before* you have him whacked." My voice was frayed. "Besides, last I checked I wasn't a message-boy for the recently departed."

Clementine was the calm to my storm. She pulled a brush from her clutch and stroked her hair slowly like she was making love. "It happened a long time ago, Isaac. I guess this moment has been coming ever since. Redemption, I mean. I think, in a way, we've both been waiting for tonight, don't you?"

I squeezed the bridge of my nose and closed my eyes tightly. I hoped it was the booze I was listening to because, between the alcohol, those legs, and the way this conversation had taken its last corner, I was finding it difficult to concentrate. I felt like the world had been knocked off its axis and was spinning slower than it should, like every thought I had was covered in treacle.

"Right, lady, I don't know what kind of guy you think I am, what kind of voodoo magic you think I can pull, or what your friends have told you, but here's how this is going down: I'm going to look out the window here and start to count. Now, if I don't see your pretty little hourglass running across the street by the time I get to ten, I'm calling in a black'n'white to come pick you up and we'll be talking about this downtown. You get the sketch?"

Clementine tried to stare me down, but I wasn't about to budge. Life was too short to play these kind of games once the flavour had disappeared.

"Just take your goddamn pictures and go." I bent down, picked up the photographs, and held them out to her. "Speak to Betty on your way out; she'll give you an umbrella. On the house."

She took the pictures and placed them on my desk again. "I'm not crazy, you know."

But you only ever heard the whackos say that.

I blinked long and hard, opened my eyes, but she was still there. "That's funny," I said. "Because the way I figure it, *sane* people don't ask you to meet *dead* people."

Clementine smirked and sipped her martini. Either it was the greatest drink in the world, and she was taking her sweet time with it, or she didn't like it much at all and was just being polite. I couldn't tell which.

"I loved him, you know." She spoke slowly, as if the words and the thoughts behind them frightened her. "Despite everything he did to me over the years, and what I ultimately did to him, there was a time when he was my world."

"So what changed?"

"Everything and nothing all at once." Clementine shrugged, her shoulders trying to find their own answer. "But in the end it was mostly time. I guess sometimes everlasting love isn't really what it says on the tin." She made a sound as if the memory itself exhausted her. "Nothing lasts forever, you know?"

"Your heart moved quicker than your feet." I figured she didn't need me to answer that, but I took a stab at a dose of shotgun sympathy anyway.

Clementine nodded, finding a question in my words where there wasn't one. She looked past me, out the window, and into the turbulent night, while she fired up a fresh cigarette.

I looked down at the photographs; tried to place the man's face again but couldn't. It was like a taste at the back of my throat that I couldn't quite swallow.

"Lance deserved *what* he got, *when* he got it. I don't have any regrets about that." Her voice was unflinching. She blew smoke across the room. This time it kinda looked like a heart. "But it's not him I want to say sorry to; it's you."

"If you mean for wasting my Saturday night, don't worry Clementine; I'm writing this little diversion off as a bad hangover," I raised my glass. "Which I plan to have in the morning."

"It's Davina."

I shrugged. The name still rankled with me. "You can be whoever you wanna be now, darling. We're done here."

"You really don't remember me at all, do you?"

"I really don't."

But yet, when she smiled, there was something in the slant of her lips and the sparkle in her eyes that did take me back to something, *somewhere*, although I'll be damned if I knew then what the hook was.

Probably Jack. Jack was the reason for most things.

I felt a headache coming on. "Go on, get the hell out of here." I nodded towards the door. "Don't forget your briefcase."

"Keep it. It'll explain everything."

"You've had the last thirty minutes to do that," I said. "Ain't nothing worth knowing that can't be explained in half an hour."

"And you've had thirty years, Isaac." She smiled. "Combination is zero-five-zero-seven."

"My birthday."

"Yeah, it is."

"You know what lady; forget what I said about the cops. You need to be shrink-wrapped."

Clementine threw the rest of the martini down her neck and slid the empty glass across my desk.

"Closure is the only thing I need right now," she said. "That, and maybe for you to forgive yourself. None of this was your fault. It would've happened anyway. You were just in the wrong place at the right time, or the right place at the wrong time." She smiled like she had forgotten how to do it. "I don't really know anymore."

I still didn't know what the hell she was talking about. I crunched a block of ice and fixed her a look I usually reserved for my ex-wife. While I sucked down the last of my drink I turned around to face the window and started counting. My breath fogged the glass and I wiped it away with my fist. Clementine re-appeared, and in the watery reflection it looked like she was crying.

"You ever get over her?" she asked.

"Over who?"

"The girl who broke your heart all those years ago."

"Who says there was a girl?"

"A guy your age, with all your worldly experience, there's bound to be one who got in and couldn't find her way back out."

I nodded and continued to stare out the window. "I guess that's one way of putting it."

Clementine had helped me lose my thread. I started counting again, but my anger had already evaporated like so much hot water.

An old beat-up Pontiac inched from port to starboard, its wipers stuttering breathlessly across the windshield as the driver crawled kerb to kerb with his lights low and his seat pushed back. His head bobbed back and forth, to the beat of a thumping bass line that I could only just hear but didn't recognise. It sounded like thunder in a can.

Even in this weather, some things never changed.

Behind the Pontiac, a middle-aged man splashed out of the horizon. He had been caught without a hood, umbrella, or even a newspaper to fight the rain, but he didn't seem to mind. He ran for cover beneath a tree that sported a coat of leaves to shield him from the elements.

But they were lone spikes in the static night.

I watched the rain-blurred world outside my window for at least five minutes—long after I had stopped counting—and although I didn't see her leave the building nor hear her leave my office, by the time I turned around, she was gone.

She had left the photographs scattered across my desk, like confetti at a wedding that had gone wrong. The briefcase stood at the foot of my desk, unopened, and her scent hung in the air, an afterthought.

I bent down, ticked the digits on the locks over to July the fifth, and sure enough, the briefcase snapped open. It was empty, except for a narrow, white envelope that looked lost in the leather blackness.

I took out the envelope and turned it over. It was crumpled and creased—like it had spent a long time in somebody's pocket—but the gum along its edge was still fresh. I knew Clementine had changed her mind about it plenty before she had gotten around to sealing it up and dropping it into the case.

Davina.

The name was like a rash crawling across my skin.

My own name was scrawled across the front of the envelope in nervous, black print. I rubbed a thumb across it, like I was trying to arouse a memory from sleep, but it was as vague and indistinct as a light in the fog.

Sliding my thumb underneath the flap, I tore it open. Inside was a cheque—from a bank no longer trading—for the sum of ten thousand dollars. I looked at the calendar on my wall: the cheque was dated thirty years ago, to the day.

I turned it over. Scrawled across the back was a clutch of words in an old-fashioned hand that I hadn't seen since before the war.

Everyone pays their debts eventually,
Clementine

"I told you, honey," I said, shaking my head. "I don't take goddamn cheques."

Betty was keeping herself busy, still typing something to someone. As I opened my door and approached her, she stopped, and gave me one of those smiles my grandmother used to find for me when she hadn't seen me for a while.

"Betty, you see a woman come past here just now? Short skirt, red lips, all the trimmings?"

"Nobody in here 'cept me and you, Isaac." Betty's fingers didn't miss a beat as she smiled at him. "And in a few minutes, it'll just be you."

I shook my head. "You sure you didn't see anyone?"

"My eyes and my mind may not be what they once were, Isaac, but I'm damn sure if a cute little number swanned past my desk, I'd remember it." Betty dropped her glasses onto the end of her nose. "And let's be honest: it's been a long time since anyone like *that* came through here."

As she finished, all of a sudden, like dirty water in a ditch, the holes in my memory began to fill in: the name, why Clementine had looked so familiar, the scent that had eluded me, and the guilt I had never quite let go.

The jigsaw was complete.

I stared at the signature on the cheque for what seemed like hours, wondering why the hell it had taken me so long to put the pieces together. I was right: I was getting old, and I was playing a young man's game.

"You feeling all right, Isaac? You've gone all white, and that's not easy for a black man."

I smiled into the middle-distance. "That's cute."

"You thinking about her again?"

"Who?"

Betty twisted her brow and peered at me over her bifocals. "That girl you fell for a long time ago. It kinda sounds like her; the way I remember her, at least. She chewed up her husband then you spat him out for her. You remember? Charlemagne. I forget her first name."

"Davina."

"That's her. A tough little firecracker, she was. She had you wrapped around her finger so tight I think she cut off the oxygen to your brain for a while. Too bad you let those legs of hers talk you out of calling in her bill." Betty stopped typing, long enough to cast her mind back. "I wonder what happened to her."

"Something tells me she didn't go all that far." I smiled, crumpled the cheque, and threw it for two points. Betty followed it with her eyes into the wastepaper basket by her desk.

"Everything all right, Isaac?"

I nodded.

And deep down, where the weeds grow and the dust settles, I guess, for the first time in a long while, everything finally was.

SILVER COMES THE NIGHT

M.L.D. Curelas

In most cities, the criminals rule the night. Not in Fairhaven. In Fairhaven, the rich and powerful operate during the night, and the unsavoury denizens conduct business in the bright light of day. So when the door squeaked open at high noon, the *Closed* sign ignored, I slapped a smile on my face and moved my right foot to the special pedal I have installed below my counter.

A dame stood in the doorway. I focused immediately on her hands, checking for weapons. She carried a small metal box, almost like a kid's lunch box, minus the brightly coloured cartoon characters. I calculated the odds that there was a bomb in the box, relaxed, and took in other details. The dame wore a tailored suit, but the jacket bulged under her left armpit.

My eyes drifted to her face, and my welcoming smile curdled. "How can I help you, Detective?"

Detective Dolores Talon plunked the metal box on my counter.

"City payroll gettin' you down, Detective?" I whined in my best Good Fellas accent. "Got your ma's jewels in there? I can give you a good price."

Talon's lips peeled back, revealing teeth. She might have called it a smile; I called it a snarl. "Cut the comedy, Branson. I'm here on official business." She flipped the latches on the box and lifted the lid.

Nestled in black velveteen were six silver bullets. I smirked. "I thought you'd hired a new special forensic expert for these sort of cases?"

"She quit," Talon snapped. "Now, could you take a look?"

I widened my eyes. "Are you asking me, a lowly *human*, to help with your investigation?"

"You're a disgrace," she hissed. "To the badge you once wore."

Nowadays, I run a pawn shop. That wasn't the "disgrace" though. The big sin in the Detective's books was my real occupation, the one that doesn't go on my income tax form. I liked to call myself an information expert. The police said I was an unlicensed PI. Tomatoes, tomahtoes. What really jerked Talon's chain, however, was that the police needed my services every now and then, so I couldn't be shut down.

After a beat of silence, the detective swore. "Nobody on my squad can touch these things," she said, jabbing a finger at the bullets. "And being this close is making *my* skin crawl."

It wasn't an apology, but it was something. 'Sides, I could needle the detective a little and escape with my hide intact, but I couldn't push too far. I was fond of my hide. I scratched my chin, considering the bullets, and slid a glance at Talon. Fine red lines webbed the whites of her eyes, and purple crescents shaded the skin beneath. Her face looked gaunt. Fatigued. Small welts dotted her hands and jawline. Silver exposure.

Seems she'd been on the case for hours, trying to unravel the mystery of the bullets, before coming to me. Desperation smells a lot like money.

"What's the case?" I asked, pulling out a pair of latex gloves.

"A shooting."

I snorted. "That's some help, Detective. Anything in particular I should look for?"

"You'll do it then?"

I cleared my throat.

"Fingerprints," Talon said. "Ballistics. Clues that may identify the shooter."

"Thanks," I said. "Standard fee." I picked up one of the bullets. Flecks of blood spotted the surface, and a strange herbal scent tainted the air.

Oddly, it had lost little of its shape passing through the detective's unnamed victim. Silver was such a soft metal it was nearly impossible to cast bullets in the traditional fashion, and the bullets you did manage to cast collapsed in on themselves after one use. Abnormal structural integrity and weird herbs? Magic. I wrinkled my nose. Witches were a few rungs lower on the ladder than me in the eyes of the police. Humans trying to play on the same level as the supernaturals, witches were about as safe and predictable as rabid dogs.

"Scratch that, Detective. Double fee for tracking a witch."

"Agreed."

I dropped the bullet back into the case like it was a hot potato. Police budgets are never large enough to okay impulse spending. "Who died?"

Talon drummed her fingers on the counter. "Prostitute," she said after a long pause.

I cocked a sceptical brow. Fairhaven has well-defined social castes. There might be a few supernatural call-girls, but those would be high-class, expensive women, hosting rich, pampered vampires and werewolves. A mere prostitute would be human. "Magicked silver bullets weren't wasted on a human. Who was the john?"

Talon's mouth tightened.

"Gimme a break, Talon," I said, rolling my eyes. "A kid could figure that out. I assume he survived, whoever he is?"

"The Alpha of Sherwood Pack," she said. "He's at Evernight Clinic. The bullets hit him first, passed through, and then hit the woman. She bled out, had too many wounds." She leaned over the counter, close enough that I could smell stale tobacco and raw meat on her breath. "We're keeping this out of the press, Branson. You got that?" A low growl threaded her words, wrapping them with violence.

I kept very still. Werewolves get their kicks from dominance games. Talon was bigger, faster, and stronger than me, and would receive nothing but praise for ripping out the throat of a "disgrace to the badge" like myself. "Sure thing, Detective. No press."

She nodded, pushing away from the counter. "Call me at the station when you have something."

"Hey, Talon," I called as she walked towards the door. "Why come to me?"

Talon stopped. She didn't turn around. "The Alpha is unconscious, may not recover at all. If he dies, we'll have a succession battle to deal with. I want this plot uncovered before that. Fairhaven doesn't need a coward taking over as Alpha of Sherwood. Those bullets are the only lead we have, and I need the best." She left without another word.

That admission must have hurt. I almost felt bad for holding a gun on her. I removed my foot from the pedal underneath the counter. Strapped to the underside of the counter, the shotgun would have fired through the designed gap between counter-top and counter-side and blown a silver-seared hole through the detective.

I picked up the box, tucking it under my arm as I locked the front door and went to my office-cum-apartment-cum-laboratory.

Neat freaks and most dames would despair at the sight of my living quarters, but since I don't entertain much, it seemed silly to change my filing system to suit the neatniks of the world. My lab equipment, however, would bring a blush of shame to those same people.

I peeled a sheet off my lab table, releasing the odour of ammonia into the room. I set the box on the table and then prepped my microscope and equipment. Flipping on the intense overhead light and recording equipment were the last things I did before settling into my chair. I hummed as I scraped blood and metal shavings off one of the bullets.

Because of their predilection for blood and raw flesh, the supernaturals—even the Fae—make terrible doctors, which is funny considering how frequently they need medical services, especially the werewolves with their short tempers and dominance struggles.

I had had my choice of jobs at supernatural hospitals, but I had chosen to work as a forensic pathologist with the police. The dead don't lie, and neither does the science. My truth had put away a killer, a vampire called George Polidori. His victims had been a couple of squeaky clean university students, so their deaths were ruled as murders, not accidents as they might have been for willing drones or fangbangers.

A few nights after Polidori's sunrise staking, Internal Affairs had discovered large sums of money deposited into my bank account. I could have insisted on an investigation, but Talon had pulled me aside, advising me not to. Polidori's hive would be satisfied with my dismissal; if I was found innocent of charges, the hive would have me killed. They blamed me for the scandal of Polidori's conviction, and they wanted me out of the lab.

Deciding that my life was worth more than my job, I had resigned from the force, and in exchange for my buttoned lip, IA had dropped my case to the bottom of their list. I never found out how Talon had discovered the hive's involvement.

...

Using my equipment was like slipping on a pair of comfortable shoes. I spent several blissful minutes recording blood types and species, one human and one werewolf as expected, and examining the bullets for fingerprints. They were clean. I entered the results in my laptop, reading the text aloud into the mic as I typed. I also snapped a few pictures with the microscope's camera. Vampires have had centuries to study law; if the evidence isn't recorded properly, the DA will murder you under cross-examination.

I studied the bullets in their snug case, deciding on my next move. Shakespeare's witches used all sorts of nasty ingredients in their spells: eye of newt and other appetising fare. The playwright wasn't that far off base. Witches practise magic like it's gourmet cooking: exotic herbs are mixed in with oils and liquids, they in turn can be burnt, boiled, scattered, ingested, or otherwise deployed while the witch chants fake Latin.

I could run tests to discover what had been added to the silver bullets, and then track the witch through the purchase of the ingredients, but it would take too long. Werewolf succession fights happened immediately on the death of the Alpha. And since werewolves couldn't reproduce biologically, there wasn't an obvious heir to the position. A succession battle was unavoidable.

There was a quick way to find the witch, but it left a sour taste in my mouth. Dealing with the Fae was a tricky business. I dropped one bullet into an evidence bag and slid a street map of Fairhaven into my back pocket.

As salt works well to nullify malevolent spells, I strung a pouch of sea salt to my belt, strapped my handgun with its ordinary lead bullets into my shoulder holster, and slid a sheathed silver-bladed knife onto my belt. The sheath lay flat against my hip, so I could draw it and slash in one motion. The last weapon I grabbed was a silver cross that I hung around my neck. The chain was short, so that the cross nestled in the hollow right at the base of my throat. I could get into trouble for wearing it, since the symbol had been illegal for decades, but if it reached the point where I needed a cross to protect myself from an angry vampire, then I was already in trouble.

I shrugged into the only suit jacket I had that was tailored to fit over the shoulder holster, and went out my back door into the alley. It was time to go hunting.

• • •

I stuck to the back ways for a while. I knew the dirty veins of Fairhaven better than most people, and had discovered that I could usually get places faster if I avoided the main roads. I stopped at the back entrance to a bar sandwiched between a Fae delicatessen and a dingy hotel where room rates were listed by the half-hour.

The bar door was never locked. I walked in like I owned the joint, navigating the cramped kitchen aisles with ease. Nobody talked to me, although a few kids tossed me curious glances from their stations at the sinks. I grimaced. What a suck-arse job, washing tankards at a dwarf drinking house.

Once in the public area, I had to hunch my shoulders and tuck my chin into my chest. The ceilings here were much lower. I wove between squat, heavy oak tables, making my way towards a table at the far wall, where a one-eyed dwarf sat. Humans weren't supposed to be out here. Several dwarves looked up from their drinks, staring at me balefully as they tried to determine if I was a sex toy or an employee. I pulled out a chair and sat at Dutch's table. My knees came up practically to my chin.

"Hey, Dutch," I said. Dutch wasn't his real name. He refused to tell me his true name, as they have power, but he hadn't given me an everyday use name either. I had once called him Rat—most of the city dwelling dwarves worked in the sewers—and he had tapped me gently on the side, breaking a few of my ribs. So I called him Dutch and he didn't seem to mind it too much.

I grabbed a handful of peanuts and popped a few into my mouth.

"Go away." He slurped at his dark lager.

"Now, Dutch, I know you don't mean that, not for an old friend like me."

Dutch snorted. "Old friend. Ha. What do you want, Branson?"

"I'm looking for somebody. Figured you could help." I tossed the bagged silver bullet onto the table. "I need a magic trace."

Dutch scowled. "A witch." He spat on the floor. "Why do you come to me about such filthy persons?"

I gave him my best innocent look. "I was under the impression that you needed extra money. If that's not the case, I'll leave. I'm sure Frances will want a piece of the fee my client is paying."

"That half-breed, weed-smoking pixie? He knows nothing!" Dutch stabbed a finger at me. "He knows only the creatures from his hallucinations."

I shrugged. Munched on a few more peanuts.

"Huh." Dutch stroked his beard. "It is possible that I can assist you." His one eye gleamed. "How large is this fee?"

Got him. I braced my elbows on the table, and we haggled over percentages for a few minutes. When we had settled on the amount, and when payment would be rendered, we settled back into our chairs.

Dutch up-ended the evidence bag and dumped the bullet into his palm. I pulled the street map from my back pocket and spread it over the table.

Dutch closed his hand around the bullet and murmured a few words. Fae magic is different from human witch magic—it doesn't require all the gewgaws and lengthy incantations. Dutch uncurled his fist. The bullet glowed a soft green. A matching ball of light floated over the map, then dropped onto a particular spot.

I leaned forward. Blackwood Avenue. I looked up at Dutch. "Well?"

Dutch's mouth twitched. "Trinity," he said, lips writhing as if the very word burned them. It might have. The witch's parents had a pair of brass ones, saddling a Christian word on their daughter. A name like that would make her unemployable at any decent job, those businesses owned by Fae and vampires. No wonder she was a witch; it was the only way for her to earn a wage.

I held out my hand. Dutch passed over the bullet, which I returned to its bag.

I stood up. "See you soon, old friend," I said, choosing my words with care. It wasn't wise to thank the Fae: they would interpret it as a sign of obligation, and would demand all manner of things to meet that obligation. "You'll see your money when I get mine." I stuffed the map and evidence bag back into my pocket.

Dutch nodded, turning his attention back to his lager.

I resisted the urge to run as I left the bar. Some Fae considered human flesh a delicacy and the unfriendly gazes aimed at me were making me nervous. Although dwarves didn't eat people, they weren't above peddling flesh to make some extra dough. Once out the door I heaved a breath of relief, then turned north towards Blackwood Avenue.

Blackwood Avenue was a human neighbourhood. Brick tenements lined the street, small stores wedged between them. From a distance, Blackwood Avenue looked like the rotting grin of a pix dust addict.

A few discreet inquiries brought me to a blackened red building. The front steps were crumbling, and gunshot holes riddled the door. A few crumpled bills passed to a blissed-out addict got me an apartment number.

The inside of the building wasn't much better. Graffiti lay so thick on the walls I couldn't tell what the original colour had been. Stained, cheap linoleum curled at the juncture where floor and wall met; cigarette burns pocked the surface. The faint, sickly sweet odour of weed hung in the air.

I trotted up three flights of stairs and stopped in front of 312. I knocked three times on the faded green door.

A woman poked her head out the door, the glass beads and tiny bells in her braided blonde hair chiming.

"Trinity?" I asked.

She didn't answer at first, large green eyes taking me in from top to toe. "Yes," she said finally. "What do you want?"

I pushed my foot against the door, sliding it inwards several centimetres so that I could step into her apartment. She ceded the ground as I entered.

A pungent mix of scents assaulted me as I crossed the threshold. Sweat, blood, something spicy—cloves? Cinnamon?—smoke, and chocolate. The blinds were shut and the lights were off. The only source of illumination was the sun peeping through the cracks between the slats of the blinds.

"Who are you? What do you want?"

I didn't know how to answer, so I walked farther into the apartment, examining the bundles of herbs, flowers, and vegetables affixed to the walls. In addition to the standard roses and willow bark, I recognised mugwort, tansy, rue and wormwood. I stared at the bundles, trying to organise my thoughts. I hadn't questioned suspects very often. I swung around to face the witch. She was tiny, with delicate, pointed features. Pretty, but too much like bone china for my taste.

"I'm investigating a shooting incident. The victims were a werewolf and a human," I said. "The human died."

Trinity paled and leaned against a side table. "Died?" She picked up a bowl and turned it around and around in her hands. Her shoulders jerked up in a stilted shrug. "Werewolves are so violent. It's risky hanging around them."

I didn't have time to finesse the investigation like some nosy old woman in a cosy mystery novel. "Yeah. Look, Trinity," I said, placing a hand on the pouch that hung from my belt, "I did a trace on the bullets and your magic fingerprints are all over them. How do you suppose that happened?"

Trinity flung the bowl at me, pink glittery particles spewing from its innards. The pink glitz collided with a spray of salt from my pouch. Flashes of white light popped around the room. Narrowing my eyes against the brilliance, I darted forward and grabbed Trinity's hands, yanking them behind her back. I pulled her close to my body and wrapped my arms around her, trapping her arms against her sides. She yelped. Balls of light danced across our hands as the remnants of the salt on mine reacted with the pink sand on hers.

My hands felt like they were being pricked by dozens of needles, and I pressed my lips together, suppressing a cry of pain.

"That answers that question," I said. "Who hired you?"

"She'll kill me!" Trinity wriggled in my grasp. "I'm sorry that woman died, that wasn't supposed to happen. The spell wasn't for her."

The significance of her statement didn't click at first. When it did, I squeezed her hands. "A targeted spell? You mean there was more than just a strengthening spell for the bullets?"

Her head turned to the wall of herbs. I gave the dried plants another look. There wasn't any wolfsbane, the number one plant used in spellcasting against werewolves.

Trinity twisted in my grasp. I could have drowned in those sea green eyes. "She'll know that you found me. She'll be so angry. But you could help me, couldn't you? Please? You're Corvid Branson, right? You stood up to them and lived. You could help me." Her eyes widened and a single tear trickled from the corner of one eye.

Her bones were birdlike. It would have been easy for me to crush her wrists. An angry supernatural would pulverise her. Maybe I could hide Trinity for a few days, until Talon solved the case. She wiggled again, her hips brushing against my thighs. I smiled, just a little. Maybe we could become better acquainted while she was in hiding.

My hands burned. Absently, I raised them to my mouth and sucked at the hot spots. Tangy salt dissolved on my tongue.

I blinked. "Holy shit. You're not quite human, are you?"

Trinity skipped out of my reach. "No. The Fae blood is thin, not enough to have my status changed, but enough for me to be . . . persuasive." She spread out her hands in an apologetic, non-threatening gesture. "What I said was true. I'm more valuable dead than I am alive."

My fingers itched to draw my gun. I settled on grabbing another handful of salt. "Then it doesn't matter if you give me a name. I know Detective Talon. She'll protect you."

The witch laughed bitterly. "Protect me? The police?" Trinity shook her head. "You don't know who you're dealing with. I'm better off dealing with her myself." The last words were a throaty purr, full of promises, and I pinched myself to keep from being glamoured again.

"Yeah, 'cause that worked so well on me, a mundane." I was suddenly angry. Her excuse might be self-preservation, but it boiled down to protecting some supernatural, probably a vampire. Those leeches, with their magnetism and brainwashing, they got away with everything. I pounced on Trinity and shook her. "You silly bitch. Tell me who."

She laughed, a high-pitched giggle that signalled hysteria, and her sea foam eyes filled with fear. Fear of *me*. My anger melted. "I'm . . . sorry," I said.

Trinity clutched my forearms. "She's powerful. Her name—"

She slumped, hands slipping from my arms. I caught hold of her waist, not understanding what had happened until the sharp copper scent of blood filled my nostrils. A small bee whizzed past my head and a lamp exploded.

I hit the ground, Trinity falling beside me. Her head lolled, exposing a dime-sized hole just under her ear. Blood flowed from the wound. Knowing it was hopeless, I checked for a pulse.

There was nothing I could do. I snapped a picture of Trinity with my cell phone. I had to leave before the shooter decided to settle things in person. Talon would hear about the murder, but there was a high possibility that there wouldn't be a body here by the time Talon and her squad arrived.

I crawled to the door, phone nested in one fist. In one smooth motion, I jumped to my feet and opened the door. I bounded down the steps, leaping over three at a time, and rushed onto the street. With the sun sinking low on the horizon, there were a few humans out—probably going to work—but I didn't see any supernaturals.

Sliding the cell phone into my pocket, I slunk into the shadows of the apartment building and disappeared into the alley.

Returning to my place was out of the question. The shooter didn't know that Trinity hadn't spilled the beans. She'd be looking for me.

I called in Trinity's death as I headed in the general direction of the police station. If I couldn't go home, I'd use their lab. But my near-death experience had made me thirsty. As my feet passed The Stiff, I found myself entering the gloomy bar instead of continuing to the station.

A few shadowy forms scuttled in the dark corners. Nice people don't drink in the evening, the start of the working day. But that was OK. Nice people didn't go to The Stiff.

I ordered a scotch and settled at a table. Trinity's death bothered me, an itch in my head that I couldn't scratch. I hoped to numb it.

The scotch scorched a trail down my throat and I signalled for another, swallowing a cough. When the haggard waitress plopped the second on my table, I mumbled my thanks.

The drink honed my thoughts, instead of dulling them. There hadn't been any wolfsbane in Trinity's apartment. There had been mugwort, rue, tansy, and wormwood. Trinity said the spell wasn't meant for the human, and the lack of wolfsbane made it unlikely that the Alpha was the target, either. So who . . . ?

An impossible solution presented itself. I stared into the depths of the scotch. Impossible, but it fit the information I had.

My cell phone rang, its jangle an obnoxiously cheerful sound in the dim bar. Talon's name and number lit up the screen. Frowning, I downed the scotch in one neat swallow, and then picked up the phone. "Yeah?"

"Branson?" Talon sounded tired. "The witch's building's on fire. I think most of the tenants have made it out, but the fire trucks have been . . . delayed." When a good deal of the movers and shakers of a city are afraid of fire, the fire department becomes a well-funded organisation. There were too many stations for all of the trucks to be "delayed".

"Sure they have." I barked a sharp, unamused laugh. "A human wouldn't have that much pull, Talon."

"Yeah." Talon sighed. "Where are you, Branson?"

"The Stiff."

"I'll come get you; I'll need a statement about your interview with the presumed deceased."

"Fine." The itch in my brain intensified, a niggling idea. "Scratch that, Talon. Meet me at the Evernight Clinic instead."

There was a lengthy pause, filled with the quiet roar of static and the faint shouts of police officers.

"Talon?"

"I heard you. I'll be there."

Dial tone.

Talon had wheels, so I hailed a cab.

The Evernight Clinic catered to werewolves and other shapeshifters. In deference to the law, my cross was tucked under my shirt, but I caressed the silver knife at my waist more than once as I navigated the hallways to the Intensive Care Unit.

Talon hadn't shown up yet, but a patrol officer kept vigilance outside the Alpha's room. When I introduced myself, he nodded and ushered me into the room. Talon must have called ahead.

Three werewolves were stuffed into the room, one female and

two males. Probably the Alpha's mate and his higher ranking wolves. Although the furniture had been chosen with werewolves in mind, the chairs seemed too small. Maybe it was their feral eyes; it had that effect on the contraptions of civilisation.

The wolves, who had all been staring at the still figure on the bed, turned to glare at me when I entered.

"Good evening, I'm Corvid Branson."

One of the males growled. "You used to work for the police." He stood up. "I'm Will Hunter, Second of the Sherwood Pack." He nodded at the other male. "That's Jack Springer, pack Third. Why are you here?"

"Detective Talon hired me as a consultant for this case," I said, edging towards the bed. I knew that the werewolves could smell my anxiety, but I kept my face empty of expression. "I have some questions for the Alpha's mate."

I gazed down on the unconscious Alpha, my medical training decoding his chart, the style and amount of bandages swathed around his torso, the position of his bed. He stank of burnt fur and pus. I'd never seen such a severe case of silver poisoning on a living werewolf.

"I'm Farrah Sherwood."

She was tall, her height boosted by black high heels, and she wore a simple midnight blue dress that screamed money. Short, unruly curls framed her face. She didn't seem like the sort who went for the deliberately mussy look. Her unblinking yellow eyes examined me, and I could tell from the faint curl of her lip, she found me wanting.

"Where were you this afternoon?" I asked.

"At home, sleeping. My doctor sedated me last morning after . . ." Farrah waved a hand at her unconscious mate. "I was very upset."

She didn't look that upset to me.

"And that can be corroborated?"

"I don't like your tone, Mr Branson," she said softly, showing teeth.

I bowed my head. No way was I leaving my throat exposed in front of a pissed-off werewolf. My eyes flicked to the door. Where was Talon?

Sensing my unease, Farrah sneered. Will and Jack tensed, readying for a pounce. Werewolves and their dominance games. Dealing with them often meant using balls instead of brains. I narrowed my eyes at Farrah. "Your mate, did he consort with human prostitutes often?"

Farrah snarled and leaped. I stumbled backwards, bumping into the hospital bed, and drew my gun. Will also jumped forward, catching the arms of his Alpha's mate and pinning them to her sides.

"Second," I said, training the gun on the female. "Did your Alpha—"

"You better have a good reason for asking that," Will said. The female werewolf struggled in his grasp. The gun didn't waver. Not that it would do me a lot of good if she came after me: I hadn't switched out the lead bullets for silver. Lead wouldn't do shit to a werewolf.

I didn't answer. I held the gun steady, and waited.

Will sighed. "He didn't visit prostitutes. That girl, Helen, she was his mistress. He saw only her."

Bingo. "I see. It truly is regrettable that your Alpha is wounded, but he wasn't the intended victim. The bullets killed the right person."

The werewolves exchanged glances.

"Impossible." Ferrah snorted. "The. Bullets. Were. Silver."

"Yes, but they were a decoy." I paused, letting that sink into their thick skulls. "And although Helen died, she wasn't the intended victim, either. She bled out from several wounds—none of them were fatal on their own. The bullets were magicked with an abortion spell."

Farrah snorted again. "Useless."

"Ordinarily," I agreed. "We all know that werewolves increase their population by converting humans. You can't reproduce biologically. But a spell like that would be worthless for a male of any species, right, Second?"

Will's eyes drifted from my face. He looked uncomfortable.

"Will?" I prompted.

"Doug," Will jerked his chin at the unconscious Alpha, "had entered a drug trial. The pills boosted his, uh, well, you know." Will waggled his hand like a fish, a flush staining his cheeks. "Helen got pregnant."

"Thank you, Will." I licked my lips. I was in a room full of werewolves armed with a gun loaded with lead bullets and a sheathed silver knife. What I was about to do was either stupid or brave. Possibly both. "So I ask you again, Mrs Sherwood. Where were you this afternoon? And yesternight?"

The Third jumped to his feet. Growls reverberated around the small room. I couldn't afford to watch the males, however. I kept my gaze fixed on the Alpha's mate.

"Were you afraid that he'd divorce you? That he'd tear away your status, because he wanted a half-breed brat?"

"I've had enough of your insults and accusations, you filthy *human*." Farrah's eyes, molten gold with anger, belied the calmness of her words. "Where's your proof?"

Fantastic. A werewolf able to think clearly while in a temper. Farrah was right, I didn't have proof and I didn't have the authority to arrest her for questioning.

"It was a good plan," I said, glancing at the clock. Where in the *hell* was Talon? I couldn't stall forever . . . but I could push buttons. It was one of my endearing traits.

"Give the bullets a little extra zip so that they pass through your mate and hit the woman, and then the spell triggers, attacking the foetus." I forced a laugh out of my dry mouth, patting my jacket pocket. "Too bad you were so *stupid* and left fingerprints on the bullets."

Farrah screamed. She rammed an elbow in Will's solar plexus, stomped on the instep of his foot, and lunged at me.

I fired the gun even as she bowled me over, crashing into the bed. When the gun clicked empty, I threw up my arms to keep her head away from me. My strength was no match for hers, and my arms bowed under her pressure. Her face elongated, jaw thrusting out and down to accommodate larger, longer teeth.

I was vaguely aware of the door slamming open, of the other werewolves jumping towards us, but my entire world was focused on keeping those teeth from rending my flesh.

A thunderous *pop pop pop* snapped through the room. Farrah whined. Scarlet blood gushed from her mouth onto my arms and face. She collapsed against me.

"Thank God you got her to attack you," a voice rumbled above me. "Pretending to be asleep was killing me."

I spat foul werewolf blood. "Great. Happy to oblige. Were you going to let her rip out my throat?"

"Dolores had that taken care of," said Doug Sherwood, swinging his legs over the side of the bed. "I wouldn't have been much help. I'm as weak as a kitten."

He was pale, nearly as pale as a vampire, the red welts characteristic of silver poisoning mottling his jaw and cheeks. His breath was shallow and uneven. Shrewd brown eyes scanned my face. "Doesn't look like she bit you. That's good. You wouldn't be a popular werewolf."

"That's not a surprise. I'm not a popular human."

He laughed and shoved the body of his mate off me. Weak as a kitten, my arse.

"Branson, you okay?" Talon asked. She held a gun in one hand and her badge in the other.

"Yeah, fine." I ignored Sherwood's outstretched hand and heaved myself to my feet. "Just ducky. What took you so long?"

Giving the other werewolves a wary look, Talon holstered her gun. "You were doing so well, I didn't see a need to interrupt. Of course, I hadn't realised you went up against a murderous werewolf with *lead bullets*."

I picked up my gun and holstered it. "You know, Talon," I said, spitting more of Farrah Sherwood's blood onto the floor, "that I'm going to charge you triple because I almost ended up as werewolf chow? Or, even worse, a werewolf?"

"Christ, Branson," Talon said. "Can't you be serious for once?"

One thing I have learned over the years is to never show the monsters how you feel, so I made myself grin. "Always am, Detective."

Talon sighed and turned away from me to deal with the panicked medical personnel hovering in the doorway. I brushed the cross beneath my shirt and sent a silent prayer skyward for the humans Helen and Trinity, victims of the system and dead because of it. I should have been dead, too. If I continued to meddle in supernatural affairs, I *would* be dead. Or inhuman. I didn't like either option, so I said a prayer for myself too.

OUTLINES

Dirk Flinthart

The chimes above the wired glass door tinkled, and a woman came in. I wish I could say she was beautiful, but the black dress made her look dumpy, and her face was blotched from crying. Someone must have thought her beautiful, though, judging from the fine, fat diamond on her left hand. She stood in the doorway, blinking and looking around at the tat and gimcrackery which makes up my stock. No doubt she was looking for me. I keep the inside of the shop dark enough to make that difficult.

"Can I help you?" I asked when I figured she'd waited long enough.

She jumped a little, and blinked again. "Are you—do they call you Doubting Thomas?"

Ah. One of *those*.

"Thomas Donovan," I said. "Proprietor. Can I sell you a charm? A grimoire of your very own? Potions, lotions, bindings, findings—name your pleasure." The sign above the shop says 'Witchcraft'. I would add *caveat emptor*, but it still wouldn't help the rubes. They *want* to believe.

"My husband," she said. "He's dead. Murdered." Her chin trembled, and even in the dim light, I saw her eyes fill with tears. She let the door swing shut and took a hesitant step forward. I stood up, offered her a box of tissues. Black ones, naturally.

She blew her nose wetly. I waited until she was done before I gave her a reply. "Murder is a police matter," I said. "I sell magical items and appurtenances. I am not responsible for what my customers do with those. What is it you think I can do for you?" I had an idea already, of course. Nobody calls me Doubting Thomas outside of . . . certain circles.

"The police don't believe Charles was murdered," she said. "They say he had a heart attack."

I clucked sympathetically. "And the coroner? The autopsy?"

"They didn't see the marks on the sidewalk," she said. "They said the outlines were some kind of kid's game. Here—" she reached into a black purse and pulled out a smartphone. A wave or two of her fingers, and I was looking at a photograph.

"Chalk lines," I said. "On a sidewalk. I can see that much." And that was all. The lines, in pale blue and green, were smudged and indistinct. If it had ever been some kind of sign or sigil, there was no telling it from the photo.

"Charles brushed them away with his shoe," she said. "He told me not to worry about it, and made me go inside, but I took a photo. Is it voodoo?"

"I don't believe in voodoo," I said reflexively, and pushed the phone back into her sweaty hands. "Magic is nonsense. New Age fairytales for girls who wear crushed velvet and skinny boys who can't play football."

"You are him, aren't you?" she said, looking at me wide-eyed. "*Doubting Thomas.* That's what she called you. She said you didn't believe in anything, and nobody could make you. She said that's why it had to be you."

"Who said?" There were very few people who knew enough about me to provide that kind of description. Most of them were very close friends. A few were not.

"My friend, Kelly. She's a rights about this sort of thing. That's why I told her. And she said you would help."

"Kelly Sternanko?"

"Yes," said the widow, with increasing certainty. "And she said to tell you about the tape."

Telling about the tape proved complicated, but the widow—Hannah Fordyce—had invoked Kelly's name. Kelly is smart, and Kelly is my friend. She sent this Fordyce my way. The least I could do was listen.

I slid the bolt across the door and made the widow a cup of tea while she spoke. Real tea; none of the bogwater herbal potions I sold through Witchcraft. I don't believe in the damned things, anyway.

Charles Fordyce had been a cop: a plainclothes guy, already high on a career path arcing upwards. According to Hannah, he'd been one of the youngest DIs on the force, and the shiny-pants types in Roma Street had their eye on him. She'd been visiting her mother in Sydney the week before he died, but she'd come home a day early due to a flight change. Charles had picked her up at the airport, but he'd seemed agitated. Distracted. When he'd found the chalk sketches on the sidewalk outside their house, he'd sworn and scuffed them away. Stick men, she'd thought they'd been. She took the photo because he'd seemed so upset by the things.

In the house, she'd put down her bags and gone to clean up in the shower, like you do after a flight. When she came out, Charles was sprawled on the floor of the bedroom. Unable to rouse him, she called the emergency services, but they pronounced him dead almost immediately. The cops swept the place and photographed everything, while the ambos took away the corpse and Hannah gave her statement. Because Fordyce was a cop, the autopsy got priority; before the day was done, the verdict of heart failure was in.

There it would have stayed, but for Hannah. "His heart was in perfect condition," she told me tearfully. "He was proud of his fitness, and he'd only just had his regular check-up."

"It can happen like that," I said. "Even in a man in his early forties. Not often, but if there's a family predisposition . . . ?"

"Nothing like that," she said. "And anyway, there was the tape. You know that stuff they put around a body to mark its position?"

Ah, yes. The tape. I nodded. Who hasn't seen it on the TV shows?

"It was already there on the floor around him when I found him," she said. "I didn't notice it right away, because I was so upset. Then, when the paramedics and the police came in, there was so much going on that I forgot. I remembered about it when I gave my statement, but the officer who took it down told me he was sure forensics did it, and maybe I'd imagined it because I was distraught. And I thought then maybe he was right, because I really was upset and frightened and confused. But later, after they told me the results of the autopsy, I pulled the tape off the bedroom floor." She shuddered. "I couldn't stand it there anymore."

"I can understand that," I said. "What makes you so sure it was there when he fell, though? You said yourself you were frightened and upset. Maybe you just didn't notice the technicians doing that part."

She shook her head vehemently. "Charles had a Coke in his hand when he collapsed. It spilled, and left a big, sticky stain. When I pulled up the tape, I saw the Coke was on top, not underneath. Lifting the tape left a bare line right through the middle of the stain."

I leaned back from the table, rocking on two legs of my old bentwood chair. "You told the police?"

"They didn't want to know," she said. "They had the autopsy results. They said I must have been mistaken. That the Coke got spilled later, or it flowed over the tape while they were taking photos, or when the paramedics were trying to resuscitate Charles."

"What about the ambos? They'd remember a thing like that."

Hannah shook her head again. "I asked. They were too busy working on Charles. Nobody but me noticed anything. And when I asked to see the photographs, they told me they were destroyed."

"What?" That didn't sound right.

"The prints were shredded," she said. "And the digital copies wiped off the computer. Since Charles' death wasn't actually a crime, the photographs weren't evidence, and they were destroyed. I even made my lawyer ask, but it was no good. There's nothing left."

"There's the stain," I said. "If you haven't cleaned it up, it should still show the line, right?"

"I took photos to show the police. Here," she said, and fumbled out her smartphone again. "It's not easy to see on this little screen, but—"

I waved her hand away. "I'll come and take a look," I told her.

Her puffy, reddened eyes widened. "You will? Then you believe me?"

"I don't know," I replied. "But I'm beginning to have doubts about the story from the police."

• • •

The Fordyces had a sizeable Hamilton apartment with river views, very white and chic inside. The floors were polished wood, and in the bedroom, the Coke stain showed up dark and sticky against the golden wood grain. I took a minute to check the clean line that went right through the middle, like Hannah had said. I swiped my finger along it just to be sure. No stickiness: if somebody had cleaned a path there, they'd done a damned good job of it.

So what did it mean? If the tape was there first, how did Charles Fordyce come to lie in the exact position of the outline? Or if somebody arranged his body after his death, how did Hannah not discover them?

An inconsistent, inconvenient stain. Not much to go on. But why weren't the police interested? Heart attack or not, Fordyce had been one of their own. Weren't they supposed to be extra diligent because of that?

Then there was Kelly. She thought I could help, somehow, and she had a way of being right about things like that. Not that I believed in any sort of sixth sense or witchy intuition, but she had good instincts. If she wanted me to look into this, there was probably a damned good reason, if only I could find it.

I left the widow Fordyce alone in that cold, white flat with its impossible stain. It was time to catch up with an old acquaintance and ask some questions.

• • •

I'm not an investigator. I'm not a detective. I sell gimcracks and gewgaws from a store in West End. I'm not an occultist. I'm not a magician. I don't even believe in that shit. I can't afford to.

On the other hand, there are people I like and respect who do believe. And sometimes, they call me up and ask for help. When that happens, I do what I can, because that's what you do for your friends, right?

Anyway, the world's not what it was. You don't even need a trench coat and a fedora any more. Any fool with an Internet connection and a car can be a detective now. Or an occultist, for that matter.

...

"James? James Finch? No, he doesn't work here anymore." The girl behind the reception desk at the *Courier-Mail* shot me a Barbie smile, and touched her expensively streaked blonde hair. I might have been flattered if I thought there was anyone home behind those blue contacts.

"Police beat," I said, shifting my heavy bag to the other shoulder. The run from Hamilton to Bowen Hills wasn't far, but the inevitable roadworks around Breakfast Creek had screwed up traffic and put me in a foul mood. "Crime desk. He's probably just on holiday. He'd have told me if he'd quit." We weren't exactly BFFs, me and Finch, but he owed me a favour or three and he was an honourable man, for a journalist with a drinking habit the size of Finland.

"Oh, no, Mr Donovan," said Barbie, batting her eyelash extensions at me. "Mr Finch died last month. He had a heart attack."

"Huh," I said. "I guess the booze finally caught up with him." I thought about it for a moment. "Do you think I could talk to whoever's in his shoes now?"

"That would be Danny Ridgeway," Barbie said, after consulting her monitor. "I'll see if he's available."

Ridgeway turned out to be a whippet-thin guy with a badly receding hairline, which he hid under a second-rate transplant. He shook my hand, and bemoaned Finch's fate with poorly-concealed satisfaction. "Dropped dead on the sidewalk right outside after work one night," he stated. "Massive coronary, they said." He shook his head. "We'd all warned him, but he was a lost cause. I found four different bottles in his cubicle, when I got his desk."

"Did you find anything interesting? I'm following up on a case for someone," I said. Someday I'd have to print up cards that said I was an investigator. Meantime, I'd settle for not offering any details if I could help it. "Was Finch chasing anything good?"

Ridgeway turned up his palms. "Search me," he said. "I couldn't read his handwritten notes, mostly, but there was nothing much in his computer files. Anything in particular you're after?"

"Tape outlines," I said, on a whim. "Like they put on the ground, around a corpse."

"Huh," said Ridgeway. He ran a hand over that ugly hair-weave, jerked it quickly away like a boy caught fiddling with his dick. His eyes narrowed. "Well. That's a funny thing, isn't it?"

"I don't get the joke," I said.

"He had a whole file of those. Photos, I mean," said Ridgeway.

"You still got it?"

He lifted his chin, and the light caught on his spectacles, made them flat and opaque. "What's it to you?"

"I'm not sure," I said. "But I'd make it worth your while."

"Yeah, see, I had my own ideas on that." He paused. "They're good shots. Clean. And when you see 'em all together like that, they're kind of weird. There's a feeling to them. I think Finch was working on some sort of coffee-table book, you know? Lots of corpse-tape crime scenes, a little gritty commentary from a journalist who's seen it all—it could sell."

"It could," I said, though I had my doubts. "It still could. I've got no plans to go to press myself, if that's what you're worried about. Tell you what: I'll give you fifty bucks for the file, and I'll sign whatever non-disclosure form you want. Deal?"

Ridgeway held out for a hundred, and the bottle of Absolut I'd brought for Finch. He loaded the files onto a memory stick for me. I left him crowing over his new bottle and putting his best moves on a spectacularly uninterested Barbie.

Journalists, eh?

...

The universe is a strange place. Ask someone who knows serious physics: there's a good case for arguing that nothing actually exists until somebody observes it.

Schrödinger. Heisenberg. Bell. Planck. Einstein. They all knew the truth; the act of understanding the universe changes it.

No-one knows how that works. The mechanism is unfathomable. And yet it's true, and we don't even know the limits. In fact, science says that by definition, we *can't* know.

Maybe the world really was flat, once. Maybe the sun went around the Earth. Maybe witches could fly, Moses could part the Red Sea and the Midgard Serpent could encircle the world. Maybe all these things were true until somebody decided differently and investigated them in just the right way.

The right observer, influencing the universe in just the right way: that would be magic.

• • •

The photos were interesting, in a grim sort of way. What was more interesting was the cause-of-death list Finch had put together. Cardiac arrest. Embolism. Stroke. It took me a couple days to follow up and confirm enough of the list to satisfy me that the rest were likely to be accurate. Transient Ischaemic Incident. Myocardial Infarction. How many different forms of sudden, relentlessly natural death were there, anyway? Why wasn't Finch interested in murders?

And had there been an outline around him on the pavement when he fell?

The photo-set became a slideshow on my computer at the back of the shop. I slumped in my seat and watched with my fingers steepled in the slow hours of the morning, when all my witchy Goth customers were snoozing in their black satin sheets. Dead men, dead women, sprawled shamelessly in the final sleep. All with their haloes of chalk or tape, following the contours of their bodies across carpet and lino, wood and concrete, even grass and dirt and mulch.

How do you get tape to stick on mulch, anyway?

I was staring at the slideshow, watching corpses fade into one another, when Hannah Fordyce came looking for me.

She looked better this time, in a sensible cream sundress rather than widow's weeds, with her hair and make-up intact and her eyes shielded behind fashionable sunglasses. "It's me," she said unnecessarily. "You weren't answering your phone. I wondered . . ."

"Nothing useful to report," I said, clicking the morbid slideshow away before she could see. "Charles wasn't the only one, though. I can tell you that much."

A wan hint of a smile touched her too-red lips. "Really? I—I can't imagine what you mean. I've had time to think about it now, and honestly, I think I was over-reacting. Don't you?"

I managed to keep the surprise off my face. "I might have thought so, except I did some checking with the Bureau of Statistics. There's been a rise in sudden death by natural causes in the greater Brisbane area over the last fifteen years. It's not much, but it's mathematically significant. Enough that there are at least two medical scientists doing research on it."

Dark as it was inside the shop, Hannah Fordyce wasn't taking off her sunglasses today. Her eyes were flat, black rectangles, reflecting the corpse-candle light of my monitor. "So it's a natural event?" she said. "Charles is just part of . . . of some phenomenon?"

"I'd agree with you on that except for one thing," I replied, watching her carefully. "The outlines. I've got a source who says there have been nearly a hundred of them. And the police aren't talking about it."

She brought her hands together, a cream linen purse clutched in her fingers. "Why should they?" she said. "Natural causes. That's not police business, is it?"

I smiled. I imagine it wasn't pleasant. I didn't mean it to be. "I did get one cop to answer my calls. I told him I was a horror writer, doing research. You know what they told me about corpse outlines?"

Her head went back and forth, very slowly.

"The police don't use them. Not for about twenty years," I said. Reaching up, I gently pulled the glasses off her face. She didn't stop me. Her eyes were wide, staring. "Are you sure there's nothing more you can tell me about Charles and his work?"

"Please," she said, her voice a whisper. "Please don't." She fumbled her purse open, and pulled out a sheaf of notes. "Here. A thousand dollars. That's more than we agreed. Just forget about it, all right? You've done enough."

I tried to give back the cash, but she snatched her sunglasses and put them back over her eyes with shaking hands. Then she turned and ran, heels *click-clack, click-clacking* across the faded shopfloor lino until the door tinkled shut behind her.

Curiouser and curiouser.

• • •

There's a place upstairs in one of the older buildings in the Valley. It's been a brothel, and an illegal casino, and lately, a gay bar. If you stray far enough past the first door on the narrow wooden landing, you may see another door at the back in the dark, under a light that doesn't work. It looks like a supply cupboard, or maybe a utilities closet. It isn't. If you try to approach it, the man on the door of the bar will warn you off.

If you ignore him, there will be consequences. Don't say I didn't warn you.

The night was sultry, distant lightning in the west holding out the teasing chance of a storm. Music thumped from inside the bar. People glared at me as I edged my way up the stairs, alongside the line of pretty, hungry young men waiting to be let in. When I got to the landing and turned past the entrance to the bar, Ricardo—the big man at the door—put his hand on my shoulder.

"Nothing down there," he growled. "Back of the line." I let him turn me around, and gave him a flat stare, eye for an eye. His eyebrows went up. "Sorry, Mr Donovan," he said. "Didn't recognise you in this light."

I waited.

He dropped his hand, and I smiled. "Thanks, Ricardo," I said. "Keep up the good work." I don't believe in magic, but I know people who do. Some of them seem to believe there's something special about me. Occasionally, that's useful.

The old wooden door with its cracked blue paint was only for show. Behind it lay a tiny room that really *had* once been a utility closet. Now there was a steel door at the back, with a one-way glass panel.

A squawk box beside the door crackled. "What do you want?"

"Thomas Donovan," I said, then: "*Doubting Thomas.*"

The door opened, and I went in.

Call it a club. In the sense that it's a meeting place for persons of a certain like-minded nature, it *is* a club. It's also a restaurant, and a bar, and a truly remarkable library, if you favour a very peculiar kind of fiction. Most importantly, it's regarded as neutral ground by those who patronise it, which makes it valuable to me at certain times.

A sleek, dark woman in a white jacket gave me a gin and tonic even before I reached the bar. It was fresh, with a thick slice of lemon and big chunks of ice that tinkled musically against the glass. I took a long, cool swallow and nodded to her. "Is La Contessa in?" I asked, though I was sure she would be. She almost never leaves the place.

"I'll find out for you, sir," said the woman, and she slid away into the dark.

The place had no name that I knew. Members simply referred to it as 'The Club'. The lights were low as a good number of the patrons preferred darkness; the booths along the exposed brick walls were anonymous wells of shadow. You could make them even more private if you chose to draw the velvet curtains, and the soft, piped music—classical, restrained—was just loud enough to blur conversation past a certain distance.

The girl came back. "La Contessa will see you now," she said, and I followed her swaying hips into the shadows.

"Good evening, Thomas," said La Contessa after the girl left us. "To what do I owe this pleasure?" She leaned back on an antique chaise longue, a fashionably slim and pale figure with a shock of unkempt black hair.

La Contessa is beautiful: very beautiful in a very particular way. Black velvet frock coat, black lace gloves, black Dead Lennon sunglasses perched on the end of her nose; if you see a certain theme developing here, you're probably correct. On the other hand, if you mistook La Contessa for one of those skinny, witchy girls who didn't play sport, the error would probably kill you.

We are polite with one another, she and I. It was not always so. But time passes, and people change, and politeness is the easy road. And if sometimes I wish we'd found another, I keep such feelings to myself. That's simply how it has to be.

"I won't keep you long, Contessa," I said. "I know how busy you are these days."

She inclined her head, and took a sip from a goblet full of dark liquid. I smelled something musty and sharp, like wet iron. La Contessa does not like wine.

"I would like a message delivered," I said. "If you would be so kind . . . ?"

She looked up at me. "You can't deliver it for yourself? Is all well with you, my friend?"

"Well enough," I said. "I don't know where to deliver this message. But I know this much: there is someone in this city who is killing tracelessly, on demand. The person in question is in the habit of leaving a calling card in the form of an outline around the fallen body of the victim." I waited, but La Contessa said nothing, her face a marble mask. "I would be grateful if this person was told that Hannah Fordyce belongs to me. She is under my protection, and I would be . . . upset if something were to happen to her."

One sculpted eyebrow lifted, a black swallow's wing against skin pale as the moon. "How upset?" inquired La Contessa. "And with whom?"

"Extremely upset. With the killer, and anyone who helps him," I said, meeting her gaze evenly. Most people can't do that, but I am who I am, and I like to look at her, though there is a certain hurt in doing so.

She glanced away, covering the action by sipping from her goblet again. "I see," she said, after an uncomfortably long moment. "Suppose I know something about this, Thomas. Suppose I were to say you are making a dangerous enemy."

"Should I suppose you care?"

She smiled. "What do you think?"

I let the deeper implications ride. "I think he operates with, at very least, the tacit co-operation of the police. I think he does them 'favours' from time to time, and they leave him alone in exchange. I also think he must have the goodwill of The Club, or he wouldn't have license to work in this city." I glanced around. "The police don't concern me. Should I be concerned by The Club?"

Her gaze was unreadable.

"*Quid pro quo*," I offered. "There is a group of young women meeting in the Toowong Cemetery at regular intervals, in the dark of the moon. Unless I miss my guess, they are being organised by a person of interest to you."

Her gaze narrowed. Then she inclined her head. "I'll see what I can do about your message," she said.

I breathed out.

La Contessa uncrossed her legs and sat up. "Nothing else?" Without waiting for an answer, she went on, "I won't keep you then, Thomas. I do love our conversations, but I know your time is valuable."

We made no farewells. I opened the door and went back to the clubroom. The slender girl had a fresh gin and tonic waiting for me there. I drank it gratefully and left through a back exit.

• • •

Say there was something you can call magic. Say there are ways for skilled practitioners to use their privileged relationship with the universe to force changes in accordance with their will. Quantum physics is a ridiculously complex topic, understood fully by—at most—a couple of hundred people the world over. How much more so, then, the rules for changing the universe itself?

If magic was real, true magicians would be rare. They would be disciplined, dedicated, and deeply learned. Of course, there might be sports, peculiar talents capable of embracing certain aspects of the art through their individual nature, as autistic savants sometimes do with mathematics—but true magicians would be extraordinary people. Their mastery would make them both fearsome, and yet infinitely cautious. How could you hope to guess at all the possible consequences of even the smallest change to the shared universe? Magic is peril.

For decades the Soviets and the Americans kept the peace by maintaining nuclear arsenals too great to be overwhelmed by an unexpected attack. They called this policy MAD, for Mutually Assured Destruction. If magic was real, and true magicians lived, this would be a nice analogy for their co-existence.

Of course, there is no such thing as magic. And even if there was, there is an aspect which could be exploited if you knew enough, and had a certain kind of mind.

Maybe I should write a book.

...

La Contessa's people were efficient. The night after our meeting, just on closing time, a man entered my store. He was not young, nor pale, and he did not wear dramatic clothing. His silver hair was immaculately coiffed. His dark, tailored suit fit his bulky frame exquisitely; the rings on his fingers were understated, elegant.

I knew who he had to be even before he bolted the door closed behind him.

He entered with an air of nonchalance and looked casually around the shop. His glance took me in, but he showed as much interest in a rack of prints from Crowley as he did in me: none at all.

When he was satisfied with his examination of the place, he reached into his breast pocket and brought out a large stick of white chalk, then rolled aside a turntable of dried herbs to make a larger space on the floor. When he settled to his knees and began to draw, I decided to speak.

"Can I help you?" I said. "Is the stock not to your taste?"

He eyed me critically. "You're about a hundred and ninety centimetres, aren't you?"

"One-eighty-nine," I replied. "And you are?"

"Roger Entwhistle," he said and returned to his sketch. A crude, human outline began to take shape.

"Mr Entwhistle," I said. "Don't draw on my lino."

He didn't look up. "Don't worry. It's only chalk."

I rubbed my forehead. "I'm not stupid, Mr Entwhistle. You're here because I'm in your way. You didn't like Hannah Fordyce chasing up her husband's investigation into your murder business, so you threatened her. Then you got warned off, so now you've come to settle with me. I had to know you were coming, right? So don't you think I've got protection?"

He paused then, and rocked back on his knees. He frowned. "There's nothing here. I checked. You're a phony."

I reached under the counter and pulled out my baseball bat. Entwhistle's eyes widened and then he laughed. Reaching into his jacket, he brought out a large, automatic handgun.

Carefully, I replaced the bat. Entwhistle laughed again and put away his pistol. "I'm licensed," he said. "I could shoot you in self-defence, if I had to. I'd rather you just had a heart attack, though."

"That isn't going to happen," I said. "I don't believe in magic."

"Well then," he said brightly. "Who cares? It's only a sketch on the floor, right?" He looked down again and drew a rough, blocky arm. The figure sprawled, apparently on its side. There was no head yet. "I used to do this when I worked for the police," he said, looking back at me. "It was a hell of a job. Draw around corpses. Take photos. Gather bits of filth and human detritus. Wade in the muck, see the worst of everything, let other people take the credit. I did it for years."

"What happened?" I was curious. And it would be good to have a story for Hannah, or even Kelly, should she ask.

Entwhistle sighed and looked away into the middle distance. "One day, just for fun, I put a tape outline around someone important to me. While she slept." His hands tightened into fists on his knees. "She didn't wake up. I didn't really believe I'd done it. Not straight away. It seemed like some kind of evil joke that the universe was playing on me. But eventually I tried again. On a cat, you understand. And then another cat, and then a dog. Finally—

there was a man I didn't like, in the service. We got drunk together. I outlined him. He choked on vomit in his sleep." He looked back at me and shrugged, almost apologetically. "I don't know how it works. Maybe it's something that just came from all those years of death and murder. Maybe it was always in me. I just know that it *does* work, it's untraceable, and it pays very well. I don't even have to draw around the target anymore," he said, bringing out a paper envelope from under his jacket. Opening it, he pinched something between his fingers. Something small, invisible to me in the dimness.

"Is that hair?" I guessed.

"Yours," he said. "From your brush. In your bathroom, in your flat. I could have used something else but hair is easy to find." With the chalk, he sketched a sweeping arc to crown the clumsy figure's head, and it was done. Entwhistle smiled. "So, there it is. I put this hair in place; you feel a pain, maybe. You get up, stagger a couple of paces in the hope of destroying the link. Then you die, and you fall right here." He gestured at the outline.

I shrugged. "I doubt that."

His smile widened. His pink tongue protruded momentarily and he swiped it with a forefinger. Carefully, he dabbed the moistened finger onto the lino inside the head of the chalk silhouette. With no great ceremony, he pushed the hair down into the little dab of spittle and sat back, watching me.

"No incantations? No abracadabra?"

He shook his head. "Would you like some?"

I didn't answer. Instead, I rose to my feet and took a few uncertain paces across the room. Entwhistle moved back as I approached.

I looked down into the chalk outline.

• • •

Observe, and the universe changes. But which observer? And what changes?

My secret is simple. I have already told it. They call me Doubting Thomas, and I do *not* believe in magic.

• • •

I looked up again. Entwhistle looked back at me. A line appeared between his neatly trimmed eyebrows, and he glanced down at his Rolex.

I shook my head.

Entwhistle looked at his watch again, then back at me. "It's your hair," he said, but I could hear doubt in his voice. "I know it is. You'll feel it soon."

"I won't," I said, with absolute clarity. "I told you: I don't believe in magic. But—*you* believe, don't you?"

He glared. "Hell with you," he said and clawed out his gun. "I can afford lawyers. I'll do this the hard way."

"I doubt that, too," I said. He paused, watching me cautiously. I pointed to the outline. "I know you believe. *And that's your spit in the middle of the drawing.*"

Entwhistle's face went white. The gun fell with a clatter, and he lunged for the drawing, his hand extended. "Bastard," he snarled, but that was all he could get out, because the blood rushed back into his face and he went red, then a terrible, congested purple. His breath came in tortured gasps and his eyes rolled up and back, like boiled eggs in a bowl of tomato soup.

I took a half-step backwards. Entwhistle lurched forward again. He staggered. Blood dripped from his nose and he slumped, fell.

Yes. His corpse settled precisely into the chalk outline on my linoleum. It was uncanny.

Nothing more than a coincidence, of course.

I let him lie while I went out the back to fetch a damp cloth. A few minutes delay calling the ambulance wouldn't matter, and in the meantime, I could clean up the chalk. Then Entwhistle would just be a customer, dead of natural causes.

When I returned, La Contessa was there. Where she came from, I can't say. She does that, when she wants to. She stood easily in a patch of shadow by a tall bookshelf, her arms folded.

"That was interesting, Thomas," she said.

"Watching over me?" I said, kneeling to mop at the chalk. The blood from Entwhistle's nose had stopped and was already congealing on his face. Only a little had landed on the lino, and with care, I could remove the chalk without disturbing it. "I can look after myself."

"So I see," she said, her tone thoughtful. Like a big, pale cat, she sauntered out of the shadow until she loomed over me and the corpse. With the ceiling lights behind her, all I could see of her face was a menacing silhouette. "I think you may be a very dangerous man, Thomas."

Possibly the room got colder then, and the shadows deeper. More likely it was an illusion. I was under stress, after all. I went on cleaning up the chalk.

"Do you ever miss me, Thomas?"

My hand stopped. I did not look up.

"They say love is a kind of magic. It's strange," she went on. "I find I don't miss you, though I feel I should. There's something . . . lacking."

Unbidden, my hands knotted into fists, knuckles digging into the linoleum. Still, I did not look up. She knelt and raised my chin until I met her dark, sad gaze. Her hand was very strong.

"Tell me," she said, "Did you ever believe in us?"

I pushed her hand away and sat back on my haunches, facing her. "I *tried*," I said. "I wanted to."

La Contessa studied my face, then reached out and stroked my cheek, just once, with a cool, velvet fingertip. "Lonely little man," she said. "I believe you." Then she turned and walked out of my shop.

I waited until the cold, heavy thing in my chest gave way and I could breathe again.

Life goes on.

I had a corpse to report. I should probably come up with some kind of explanation for Hannah Fordyce, as well. She deserved that much. And who knows? Maybe Kelly could make something of the story. She'd have fun with it, anyhow: she likes all that dark and mystical shit. I think she even believes in it, a little.

Sometimes, I wish I could, too.

SANGUE DELLA NOTTE

Donna Maree Hanson

Murky light and the stale smell of leftover booze enveloped Dela Luxman as she descended the stairs into the depths of Sangue della Notte. As the lights lowered, the peeling wallpaper and suspicious stains in the blood-red carpet of the nightclub faded from view.

Dela was conscious of all eyes being on her, being unfashionably early. Her drop-waisted dress exposed her arms and most of her legs, the beads brushing the skin of her knees. The urge to pull down a sleeve and adjust her collar made her fidget as she strode across the empty dance floor to the bar. Gazing into the bevelled mirror that served as a backdrop to the drinking glasses, she paused to smooth her dark bob and check her makeup, adding a touch of oxblood-coloured lipstick.

Seating herself on a stool, she tried to contain her excitement and fear. She was at the notorious Sangue della Notte, right smack in the middle of the blue-light district—the eerie gas lit district of Chicago. Perching on a stool, her slinky dress revealed her thighs and enhanced the turn of her ankles.

Lowering her lashes, she tried not to think of the risks she was taking to prove herself, as she chanced a look around the place. There were about twenty people in the club, mostly staff. Waiters in dark pants, suspenders and white shirts wore their hair slick and had identical moustaches. The swanky waitresses wore short dresses, dark stockings and bobbed hair. Blondes, red heads and brunettes all looked pale and wan as they lounged on sofas waiting for business to pick up. Dela wondered how the waitresses had the energy to serve drinks or bring the cocaine pipes to the tables; they looked so sickly and tired.

A burly bouncer in a dark suit suddenly loomed in front of her. Dela caught sight of a holster when the movement of his arm shifted the lapel of his jacket. "New around here, huh?"

Dela tried to strike a pose and felt a blush steal up her cheeks. How could he tell she wasn't an experienced flapper?

He glowered at her. "Don't make trouble, puss." The bouncer snickered at her and walked off, heading upstairs to guard the door. Dela repressed a shudder. Posing as a flapper had her treading on dangerous ground.

After a half hour or so, as if by an unseen signal, the blood crowd appeared from the shadows, their clothing richly tailored and their expressions jaded. The band began to play, a mellow-voiced girl singing about love and death. Dela arranged her herself on the stool, draping her skirt so that the beads caught the dim light and glittered when she breathed. She crossed her legs as a handsome guy in a tuxedo walked up to the bar.

"Would you like some nuts?" she asked him, holding out a bowl. He turned his gaze toward her. She felt her skin chill. This was it. He was one of the blood crowd.

"No, thank you. Nuts do not agree with me." He had a neutral expression as if nothing in the room mattered to him—a high and mighty one. He walked away, pipe in hand and went to nestle in the sofas with two waitresses. Dela let out a breath. First encounter survived. She was ready for the next.

The bartender appeared in front of her and used a dirty cloth to wipe the clean bar. "What will it be, honey?" He stopped to stare at her, measuring her up. "Water or water with ice?"

A smile helped ease her tension. "Ice, but go easy, okay?" She watched as he sloshed water into a glass from the tap, chipped some ice from a grimy bucket and dropped it in. How had he had picked her as a fraud like the bouncer had? She had studied so hard to pass unnoticed in the club scene. She wondered what gave her away.

The bartender chuckled as he threw in a slice of lemon and slid the glass across to her. "God you're a looker," he said, then leaned in close only to draw back suddenly. "Geez, you stink. What kind of perfume you call that?"

Dela lifted an eyebrow. "A private blend. Very effective in controlling sleaze." She had liberally applied garlic to her skin.

"You betcha," he commented as he began wiping the bar down again. She took a sip, and he made eye contact. With a nod, he said, "Be careful, I can tell you're goin' to be trouble." He turned his back, talking to himself, but she could hear every word. "A teetotalling flapper? What next? Wonders will never cease. The thrill-seekers are getting younger and stupider every night."

She banged her glass down, and he turned, a look of surprise on his face. "Ha. I'm no thrill-seeker." She was not here for the booze or the drugs or the sex. She knew the risks when you let the blood crowd take you. She'd witnessed the harm, when the thrill-seeker doesn't come home.

Tossing the rag to the side, he placed both hands on the bar and leaned toward her. "What are you then? A pushover? Why don't you scram; go home where it is safe? Blue-light is no place for a baby doll face like you."

Why did he have to call her that? She hated how she looked with her new hairdo. Leaning in until they were almost nose-to-nose, she said calmly, "Listen. I'm doing fine. Bring me that bucket of ice, will you? I can help you out, chip some and offer your patrons a few morsels now and then."

She slid five cents across the bar. He sniffed at it, but threw it into his tip jar. Next, he slid the grimy bucket with its solid piece of ice next to her.

Dela repressed a frown when she realised her tip was not quite the thing. She was new to this game. "Thanks. What's your name?"

"Larry."

"Thanks, Larry." She grinned at him, slipped a nut between her lips and chewed ever so slowly.

The joint was filling up quickly. The noise levels rose, as music and voices and laughter combined. A tall man with dark hair stalked in her direction. Dela grabbed her handbag and fished out her lipstick. She retouched it quickly, smiling without showing her teeth as the man approached. She had to hold herself still, so she didn't tremble in her stockings. The man had black, mesmerising eyes—eyes that made her feel all warm inside when she gazed into them. She sighed as he leaned in close. Her heart beat slowly and loudly in her chest. The sounds of the room dimmed and the smoke wafting around slowed and stilled to hover like clouds. Within seconds, there was only this man and that gaze. He did not move, but she felt him like a caress, as if his fingers were sliding up her inner thigh. Intimate.

Raising his hand, he silently gestured for her to lift her face. His lips lowered and she opened her mouth slightly. Blood thumped in her neck as if summoned there. He placed a forefinger on the pulse point as his cold lips touched hers. Dela wanted to surrender to the kiss, but the man fell back, a look of pain twisting his features as he moaned.

Shaking her head, Dela came back to herself, cursing under her breath. So that's what a glamour feels like, she thought. How easily he had mastered her. That had not been part of the plan. Fear crashed through her body, her pulse pounding faster than before.

The man swayed before her, palm covering his mouth. When he dropped the hand, she saw that his lips had blistered and bled. "What have you done to me? What are you?" he hissed. A few heads turned in their direction, but the crowd soon lost interest when the man straightened his shoulders, cast his gaze around and acted if nothing had happened. Only the intensity of his eyes betrayed how angry he was.

With a sense of wonderment, Dela touched her lips with the tips of her fingers. It had worked. When her own strength of will had failed, the lipstick had saved her. She arched her eyebrow, amazed by her own brilliance. Her fear quieted; her pulse eased. Confidently, she squared her shoulders and kept her expression calm. After glaring at her for a few moments more, he merged back into the blood crowd.

Tall, thin women in long satin dresses ogled her departing companion—and then her—before they turned away to continue their slow dance. Their gem-encrusted headdresses with their tall feathers winked in the light. The music mingled with voices and the chink of glasses. Dela thought she heard moans. The sound disturbed her and she looked around for the source. Was that a waitress sprawled in a booth, her body undulating strangely? Before she could shift around on her seat to get a better look, the bartender intruded, scrubbing the bar with vigorous and angry movements.

He caught her eye and she leaned in to hear what he had to say. "Nice work. I don't know what game you're playing. You've got sass, I'll tell you that much, but you're lucky the boss doesn't toss you. He don't like it when you offend the crowd. Thrill-seekers are here to keep the crowd happy."

"I'm no thrill-seeker. He didn't have the right."

The bartender looked her slowly up and down. "Yeah, sure. You with your gams catching the light and your low-cut dress. Look like a thrill-seeker to me. Invitin' you are, invitin' trouble."

Smiling to herself, Dela drew out her lipstick. It was clear and stung a bit when she applied it; she had made it from petroleum jelly and raw, pulverised garlic. Placing a layer over her oxblood lipstick, it had proven effective against drying lips and the mesmerising kiss from one of the blood crowd

The delicate hairs on the back of her neck prickled, like someone was staring at her. Turning her head slightly, she saw a guy standing off to the side of the dance floor, perfectly immobile, his gaze locked on her. He was dressed in a confederate style white frock coat and dark tie. Dixie, she nicknamed him. Dela feigned disinterest and observed the bartender mix cocaine into homebrewed alcohol, then pour it into five glasses. Her gaze flicked around, wondering who was going for the power juice. The mixture could make a cowardly person brave, the shyest person eloquent, even dull pain. Handy if one of the crowd was feeding from you, she supposed. There, in the corner booth were five young bucks, swaying to the music, their eyes alight with excitement. Definitely thrill-seekers.

From her seat by the bar, Dela's gaze continued to roam, passing over Dixie, who still watched her, and continued on. A gap opened on the dance floor and she could see through to the booth with the waitress who had been moaning and undulating before. A male and a female of the blood crowd were stroking up the inside of her legs, disturbing her dress to reveal the tops of her rolled-up stockings.

The couple sucked greedily on the girl's neck, tongues lapping the oozing blood. Instead of struggling against her attackers, the girl's expression was one of delight and heightened desire as she spread her legs wider, giving the groping hands easier access. Dela gulped, realising that the girl was feeling pleasure from the feeding.

Had her mother felt like that when the blood crowd fed off her? Feeling unsteady, Dela went to slide from her stool and make a retreat to the powder room. Her feelings were disordered; she needed time to calm herself. She reached out for her handbag, but a pale, hairless hand was there before her. "Can I buy you a drink?" Dixie asked. He had a southern twang and longish, blond hair tied back over his collar. His eyes were the palest blue she had ever seen. "Thank you. I'll take my usual. You?"

"A house special."

The bartender pushed a glass of water at her and then strained red fluid into a glass. She smelt the metallic tang of blood and gulped. He was blood crowd, but he looked so human. "Would you like ice with that?" she asked, not quite sure she was up to another encounter with one of the blood crowd, right then.

His gaze never left her as she took a sip of water. The glass of dark red liquid sat on the bar. He inclined his head toward the glass. "Couldn't hurt."

Dela put her glass down and dropped her hand to her knee, sliding her skirt up until she felt the edge of her garter. His pale eyes followed her movement, his breath shortening, nostrils flaring. She drew out an ice pick, a slender silver blade with a short handle that fit nicely into the palm of her hand. His eyes dilated and he stepped back reflexively. She clutched the pick and thumped down on the bucket, sending shards of ice over the bar. Carefully, she picked up two chunks and dropped them in his glass.

"Is that—?" Dixie asked.

"Silver?" She nodded and slid the cool pick back into place, before dropping her hem to cover it. He took his glass, nodded to her and slipped into the crowd. What a shame he was blood crowd, she thought; he looked rather swell.

Slipping off the bar stool, she squeezed through the clientele until she reached the powder room. She found an empty cubicle and shut the door. Drawing out her watch, she saw that it was midnight. She had two more hours to go. She wasn't sure she could make it.

Besides her general garlic odour, she had little else to fight off the crowd. Two of her weapons had been revealed already. There was little else she could do for surprises. Staying in the powder room was out of the question, the recruiters and the blood crowd would sense her fear and her effort would all be for naught.

Leaving the cubicle, she walked to the mirror where she checked her reflection. Smoothing her hair with her fingers, she arranged her bangs and then touched up her face powder. From her handbag, she drew out her scent bottle. She lavished the liquid over her neck and then checked that her crucifix was still nestled between her small breasts. As she put away her things, she felt someone come up next to her. There was no reflection in the mirror. Turning, she saw a willowy woman with pale skin and brown eyes loom over her. The cloth of her dark red dress hung in luxurious layers, giving a sense of movement even though she was still. Dela stepped away to make room, but the other woman grabbed her arm, holding her in place.

"Stop there," her voice was commanding.

Dela wanted to leave, yet couldn't get her legs to move. Thoughts whirled, trapped by the icy bars of one of the blood crowd's commands. She had not expected to be prey to the crowd's females. How stupid. Surely by what she had witnessed, she should have realised. Foolish, foolish girl. The woman's arm shot around her waist and drew her close. Dela was forced to lean backwards over the sink, her heart beating furiously, her breathing rapid. The lip-sticked mouth loomed closer.

"Pretty, young virginal thing." The woman purred. "You may look like a flapper, kitten, but you aren't." She ran a finger along Dela's chin. "You belong to Darlene now."

Darlene was strong. Dela stood stiffly, unable to shift out of the creature's embrace. Darlene ran her hand from Dela's crotch to her collar bone. "Yes, no scent of man on you. Just pulsing hot blood and rich life beneath the surface."

Darlene's fingertips lingered between Dela's breasts, caressing slightly above where the crucifix lay. Dela wished the woman would expose the cross. Just tug her dress down an inch, maybe more. It would be enough to startle her, allowing Dela a brief chance to escape. The creature's lips lowered, tongue tracing over the contours of Dela's chin. Dela's breathing was laboured as the creature grabbed a handful of her short hair and tilted her head back, exposing her neck. Dela felt the strain on her spine, wanted to cry out and fight back, but she was paralysed from the command. Darlene's fangs extended and touched her skin.

There was a piercing scream.

Dela was abruptly released and slid to the floor bonelessly. Quickly as she could, she scrambled away from the writhing Darlene, her body shaking. The anger in the other woman's expression chilled her. She darted out the door and into the throng, panting with effort.

Dela gulped down breaths and hid in a nook, hoping to avoid another encounter with Darlene. It had been sheer luck that she had refreshed the holy water from her perfume bottle minutes before the attack. She'd brought it as a last resort. Good to know that it worked. Dela did not see Darlene emerge from the powder room. Young women went in. Some did not come out again. Dela hoped that Darlene had found other distractions.

Dela's heart rate slowed as her calm and confidence returned. Not long now and she'd be finished the test. She decided to return to her place by the bar.

Gazes appeared glued to her. She could feel the cold, hard stares, the resentment of the crowd building. She was supposed to be easy meat, a cheap floozy drunk on cocaine or alcohol or both, ready to be sucked on and used, but she was Dela and she would fight this crowd. She hoped the recruiters were watching and taking notes.

More men hovered near the bar. Rather than waiting for them to approach, Dela removed both ice picks from her garters and chipped diligently at the ice in the bucket, twirling the picks with practiced flair, even tossing them like pizza dough and catching them in smooth movements. When she had finished her display and the supply of ice, she asked the bar tender for more. It helped to pass the time and her skill with the picks kept her would-be admirers at bay. After she chipped the second bucket, she slid the picks back into her garters, shivering at the cool kiss of the metal on her skin, and took a sip of water. Swaying to the music, she glanced around the room before checking the time. It was one A.M. The clock was ticking down to her success.

The Duke played the piano along with his band, enlivening the crowd to his catchy tune. A joint could charge for entry and afford to give out free booze to its clients with a band like that. The booze attracted the thrill-seekers and then the blood crowd could drink for free, too. Did they drink from her mother? Is that why she never came back?

Dela decided to mingle with the throng, as she could no longer brave it out in full view of the crowd at the bar. Hands groped for a free feel as she wormed her way through the closely packed bodies. There was little she could do; there were too many people to find the culprits. She squeezed her thighs together, limiting the range of the questing hands. Considering the other fates that had almost claimed her that night, there was not much harm done, except to her dignity. She walked along the back wall, past the booths full of unseeing eyes and pale limbs. She found a spot against the wall at the back and took in the scene. Finally, she was away from the groping hands and the leering eyes. Nearing two A.M., the place was full. The air filled up with smoke haze and it became difficult to breathe.

Recovering from a short fit of coughing, she felt large hands surround her waist and shove. Next thing she knew, she was pressed up against a wall with a well built man leaning against her. Power seemed to emanate from him. Once over the surprise, she struggled, pushing against his wide shoulders and when that didn't work, she tried reaching for her ice picks.

"So, Miss Luxman, you have managed to repel the elegant blood crowd for an evening." He inhaled her scent, taking in a lungful of garlic. "Not bad. Effective against the creatures, but not me."

"Leave me alone." She punched his shoulders, and he grinned at her efforts.

His tongue shot out and lathed her lips. "Garlic there, too. Tasty."

She spat the taste of him off out of her mouth. It made his grin wider. There was something in his expression that stilled her. He was clearly not of the blood crowd. But he was not human, either. What was he?

His hands slid up her thighs, finding both her ice picks. "These are very nasty. There's enough silver in them to hurt me if you chose to use them." His hands continued on their upward path, past her hips, her waist, under her arms. He had not groped her, but there was something very sensual in his touch. A kind of reverence. It held her spellbound. A finger traced her bottom lip.

Their gazes locked, snapping her free of the sensual trance. "What are you doing? Leave me alone." She pushed again, tried to kick. But she could not break free.

He leant down and nuzzled her neck. "Holy water has a salty taste, don't you think? Still, it's no protection from me." He bit her gently, not breaking the skin.

A thrill passed through her body at the feel of his mouth on her neck, his warm breath setting her blood on fire. There was so much muscle to him, so much of him surrounding her. Her senses succumbed to his strength, his power, as easily as if he had cast a glamour over her. Yet she could still think and act, so it couldn't be like the blood crowd trick that had mesmerised her. His warmth radiated over her, and she had the odd desire to run her hands over his chest and up his arms. He growled low in his throat. It made her shudder with desire. Dela's eyes widened. How could that be?

"How old are you?" His mouth was close to her ear.

"Twenty-one."

"Born in 1900? A naughty girl. Interesting and so young, so fresh. Not a flapper, either. Just a pose. It's effective, but you can't fool me. I can taste you, smell you . . . " He grinned at her, his eyes sparkling with amusement and something else. Satisfaction.

"What are you?" she finally managed to ask. The heat radiating from him sank into her flesh; she liked the feel of it, the feel of him.

"Don't you know?" The grin hadn't left his face. "Your research wasn't so informative, was it? Ask your friends, your recruiters, and if they can puzzle it out, they'll tell you. There is more in the blue-light district than the blood crowd."

Dela frowned. How did he know about the recruiters?

"Who *are* you?" *Wait*, she thought . . . "How do you know my name?"

He eased away from her, not quite freeing her. He inclined his head, as if he was being introduced. "My name is Alf. Alf Zimmerman."

"Alf?"

"The *pleasure* is mutual, I assure you."

"Pleasure?" her voice hardened. "I assure you—" she renewed her struggles. *Of all the arrogant, pieces of* . . .

His finger hushed her lips. "You can't hide it, sweets. You want me, want me bad."

She thrashed, trying to push him away. "You've got some nerve."

He laughed softly. "I have a lot of nerve. So do you. You've lasted the night here, holding your own against your known foe."

With a ghost of a smile, Dela lifted an eyebrow, softening at his praise. His lips came down and she met his kiss. His hand grabbed her head and his kiss deepened, savaging her mouth. Straight away she panicked. She'd never been kissed like that before. It was dangerous, tantalising. The strength of the kiss bruised her lips and his tongue invaded her mouth. And then he released her. She panted. *God what was that?* Heart thumping, she swallowed hard, trying to get a grip.

Alf was less smug she noticed. His grin was replaced with a serious expression. The kiss had affected him, too. "I like you. Tasty, that's what you are. Untainted, too."

The look on his face gave her pause. "Untainted by what? The blood crowd?"

Alf nodded. "Untainted, untouched, unclaimed."

With his arms either side of her, he bent into a crouch. As he slowly rose up, pressing his face to her as he breathed deeply. "I know your scent now, sweets. You will be mine."

Surprised by his actions, she stared dumbly at him. He stepped back, an eyebrow cocked in a mocking salute.

Dela slapped him, hard, across the face. He laughed at her, dark eyes searching her expression. "Is that the best you can do? No clever tricks for the likes of me?"

"What are you?"

"You'll find out soon enough. I'll not harm you. I want you, sweets, like you lots too. You will enjoy being mine . . . eventually."

Before she had time to respond, he darted away into the shadows and milling people. Frowning, she tried to follow his retreating figure. Given his height, she should have been able to pick him out, but it was as if he'd disappeared.

Leaning against the wall, she let the swirl of feelings he'd aroused in her sort themselves out. Was she attracted to him because he was dangerous, or was it something else, something more basic than that? He made her feel sexy, desirable. Worst of all, he made her want him. Whatever he was, he had rattled her. She had come prepared to deal with the blood crowd, not something else entirely. There was more to the blue-light district than she first supposed.

Back at the bar, she retrieved her handbag from the bartender. He looked concerned. "What's wrong, honey? The crowd scare you off?"

She took out her watch. She had five minutes left. She leaned over the bar and stared at the bartender. "Hey, Larry, do you know someone called Alf? Tall, muscle-bound guy with dark eyes?"

The bartender's eyes widened and his gaze shot around the crowd. "You met the Alpha here?"

"Alpha? He said his name was Alf. Do you know him?"

"I've seen him from a distance. You be careful. He's top dog around here; you know, the big cheese an' all that." The bartender turned away and began to polish glasses with his grimy cloth. Dela glowered at him.

"I've had several complaints about you," a wet voice said from behind her. She swung around. A fat man with a bald patch—barely disguised by the sparse, greased strands of hair scraped over it—stared at her, anger in his eyes.

"Really? Complaints about me?" She pouted, hoping to distract him.

"Yes. I don't like hearing complaints, particularly when they involve injuring or insulting the crowd."

"So, don't listen to them. It's none of your beeswax anyhow." She turned away, wondering if she would have to use her picks again.

"I'm the manager, Hugo, you dumb dame. It's exactly my business."

Her gaze dropped to the badge on his lapel and frowned. "*Oops!*"

"Don't get all pussy on me, kitten. Just get out and don't come back." He signalled someone with a sharp flick of his hand. The bouncer she met on arrival appeared by her side. Hugo said, "Escort her out and don't let her back in."

"Told you not to make trouble. Now I won't get to see your pretty face again," the bouncer said as he led her up the stairs. "Pity really."

"Gee aren't you swell," she said sarcastically as he shoved her out the door.

Out on the street, the gas lights flickered with a blue tinge. She hadn't brought a wrap, so the air was cool against her exposed arms. Even after surviving Sangue della Notte for four hours, she felt vulnerable making her way home. If what Alf had alluded to was true, then other dangers lurked in the dark streets and alleyways. Dangers her holy water and garlic would do nothing to stop. She stepped off the kerb and a voice calling her name stopped her. "Miss Luxman?"

A man slid out of the shadows, his facial features obscured by a low brimmed hat. A light overcoat hid his size well. Her body filled with tension. "What do you want?" Her hands hovered by her right thigh, her fingers resting on the handle of her ice pick. A pick worked on humans as well as the blood crowd. And from what Alf had said, him too.

"You did well tonight." The man handed her an envelope.

"What is it?" She took it.

"An invitation to enrol at the academy. It's what you wanted, isn't it?"

Dela felt her tension release as she smiled. "Yes. Thank you." She gaped at the letter, not quite believing she had succeeded. There were so many questions, she wanted to ask. She glanced up.

Too late, the shadowed man had stepped back into the darkness. "Wait . . . "

He was gone. She didn't even hear him leave. Next time, she'd ask him about Alf, about what he was, but she didn't want to let on that she was ignorant. Darn that brute—why did he have to appear and unnerve her—undermine her confidence, when she'd been doing so well.

Dela strode through the lonely night, clutching the envelope to her chest. The echoes of her steps drove away the unease she felt about traversing such dangerous terrain. Nothing, though, could dim her happiness. She had done it! She'd gained entry into the academy. Throwing her head back, she laughed at the night sky. She would be a part of blood crowd control. She would finally be able to fight back and maybe, just maybe, she would find her mother.

A howl sounded when she crossed the mouth of a dark alley. With a hitch in her stride, she hurried along, looking back over her shoulder. Was there a shadow there, something moving? It made her think of the man who had kissed her and who had tasted her scent. Was he following her home?

When she walked into a part of the city lit by yellow electric bulbs, she relaxed. After that, it didn't take long for her to reach the boarding house. She slipped the key out of her purse and pushed the old door open slowly, cringing when it creaked. She didn't want to wake the landlady. By the porch light, she lit a candle to light the way to her room. The squeaky stairs made her heart race, her eyes on the landlady's door. She didn't want a scene with the old crone now. She opened the door to her room. Her roommate, Esther, lay fast asleep and snoring softly on her bed. Her friend was as poor as she was, so they shared the room to halve the cost of the cheap dump they lived in. Placing the candle on her bedside, Dela opened the envelope, taking out the letter, her eyes and mind devouring the cursive script.

She was to enter the academy the following morning. So soon! But it was a good thing. She'd spent the last of her grandmother's inheritance on getting to the city. If she'd failed tonight, it would have meant contemplating other avenues of employment, and none of those options would have been pleasant. Now, with a place in the academy, she would have the chance to search for her mother, to save her if she could.

Dela slipped off her dress, blew out the candle and slid into bed. As she drifted off to sleep, she wondered if she would cross paths with that intriguing creature, Alf, again.

THE AWAKENED ADVENTURE OF RICK CANDLE

Joseph L. Kellogg

The gravel crunched like breakfast cereal outside my trailer, and the engine I hadn't noticed creeping up on me suddenly cut off. I pushed aside the blinds to take a look and saw a black car with tinted windows just outside. Damn. Without thinking, my hand slid down to the heater I wore on my hip. Even though they'd been nothing but helpful since the Awakening, I still couldn't make myself trust the feds. Old habits die hard, I guess.

Forcing myself to relax a bit, I flicked open the latch on the door before heading to the mini-fridge and grabbing a cold beer. Sinking into the cheap recliner along the wall, I cracked open the beer. When the footsteps stopped at the front door, I yelled "It's open!" and squinted against the slanted sunlight that poured in through the newly-open door.

"You're a hard man to find, Candle." The fed was still just a silhouette as he shut the door and my eyes adjusted back to the dim lighting of the trailer.

"Did you try the library?" I asked, taking a swig.

He chuckled. "How's the circus life?"

I could see his face now, boyish and clean-shaven, and he held a manila folder in one hand. I didn't recognise him; probably a new guy. They came and went at the BAI like kids on a carnival ride. They expect the thrill of getting to meet all their heroes, but when they learn it's little more than glorified babysitting and job placement, they leave disillusioned and beat it to some other assignment where they might find some real action.

"It's a living," I replied. "But you're not here to shoot the breeze. I'm not due for another check-in 'til January. What gives?"

He ignored my question, one of the things I hate about the feds. "You live with another Awakened, don't you? Raven, no last name?"

"Yeah, but that's not news."

"Is she around?"

"She's out."

The fed peered at me suspiciously. "Nothing's happened to her, has it?"

I straightened up in the chair. "You accusing me of something?" The way he just stood in the doorway was creepy, and I wished like hell he would sit down. But I wasn't going to offer him a chair, or else he might start thinking he was welcome.

"Not accusing," he said. "Warning." He opened the folder that was clenched in his hand, and flipped through the papers inside. "You remember Reginald McCoy?"

"That British cowboy fella?"

"He went missing three days ago," the fed said, pulling out a paper and shoving it in front of my nose. The picture of smashed furniture showed a smaller inset of bullet casings littering the ground, both peppered by the evidence markers that cops use these days.

"Looks like he put up a fight," I said, sinking back into the chair and taking a sip.

"A lot more than the others."

"Others?"

"Four other Awakened have been abducted in the last couple of days," he said, "and several more have just vanished."

"So someone's coming after us? Thanks for the tip; don't let the door hit ya."

"You're not worried, then?"

"If you stick around to see mine and Raven's act tonight, you'd see why. I could out-shoot McCoy with my hands behind my back and piss in my eye."

"Well, I can't bring you into protective custody against your will. You have your rights, after all."

That was something else I didn't miss about the Flat life. The only justice I ever found there was at the end of a gun. Here, even though we had to keep our existence a secret, the courts did a halfway decent job most of the time. "But you didn't need to drive all the way out to the middle of nowhere to warn me," I said. "A phone call would have worked."

"Not for someone who refuses to buy a cell phone."

"Okay, not me directly, but you could have called the circus manager or something. Instead, you came out to see me in person and flashed pictures of a crime scene in front of my face. You want my help, don't you?"

"You're supposed to be one of the best detectives in the world," he said with a grin. Definitely a new guy.

"You ever read one of my books?" I asked. "I solved all my cases through a string of random coincidences, sheer dumb luck. If you'd read my file, you'd know that I tried the private eye thing in Chicago for two months right off the bat. Couldn't crack a single damn case."

"And now that you're Awakened, you want to spend your life doing a sharpshooting act in a second-rate circus?"

"I've got a steady paycheque, a girl, and no one's trying to kill me: three things I never had in the Flat life for more than a hundred pages." I didn't tell him that I liked seeing the mountains in the window every morning, liked feeling wind that wasn't blown from the back of taxi cabs, liked knowing that people and their problems were just vapours that appeared and then faded back into the landscape. I didn't like waxing philosophical with government employees. "Could be a lot worse."

"Well," the fed said, "two out of three isn't bad, anyway." He fished around in his pocket for a few seconds, eventually pulling out a small white card. "Call me if you change your mind."

I took the card from his hand and glanced at the name, if only to see who I was going to ask the Bureau of Awakened Individuals to take off of my case. Agent Danver. But he wasn't BAI; he was

FBI. The flimsy screen door creaked and bounced as it slammed closed, leaving me reclining in the dark again. I tossed the card onto the pile of papers I never look at, and polished off my beer to the sound of the retreating car. From across the room, I stared at the uncreased spine of the lone book on my shelf: *Snuff the Candle*. One of these days, when I was beyond bored and filled with morbid curiosity, I would read it. But not today. With a grunt, I heaved myself off the couch and began to change into my costume. Show time was in an hour.

...

Raven disappeared after our act, like most nights. The supers had it pretty rough after the Awakening. In the Flat life, she had been a half-vampire warrior, running around Los Angeles killing demons, or something like that. I'd tried to read one of her books once, but couldn't get through it. While I was spending half of my Flat life trying to stay out of trouble, she hungered for it. She'd spend hours perched on top of the highest building she could find, scanning the horizon for a portal to Hell that needed closing. That kind of stuff didn't happen in the Real world, but old habits die hard. So she kept strange hours, but when a dame's got a body like hers, you're willing to put up with a lot.

I lay out on the bed alone, but sleep didn't come, despite the rhythmic chirping of crickets. Aside from the initial commotion after the Awakening—when a couple hundred fictional characters had woken up in the smoking crater of a small Montana library—life had been pleasantly safe. But if what Danver said was true, that might all be over. Someone was hunting us down. The difference was that this time, I could say no. Unlike my books, there were competent people around me, and I could let them handle it. All the same, my hands drifted up behind my head, and reassuringly touched the gun I kept there. For the first time in months, it was loaded.

The cry of some prairie animal echoed in the distance. But something about it sounded... off. Before I could consider it further, the silence was torn open by the raucous shattering of glass and splintering of wood as a dark figure hurtled through the trailer window and crashed into the flimsy dresser. By pure reflex, my hand seized on the gun, and I jumped to my feet. The sound I thought was an animal was louder now, and definitely human.

I tip-toed around the broken glass and peered cautiously out the shattered window. Two silhouetted figures danced on top of the animal cages, weaving and dodging each other's fists and knives.

Raven.

I turned back to the hapless fellow that had been tossed into the trailer. That girl might not have any magical powers, but the muscle in those legs was as real as anything. The unlucky guy was big, looked mean and ugly as a bulldog, and had a blue dragon tattooed on one side of his face. It writhed around as he winced and groaned. I didn't have time to deal with him properly, so I cold-cocked him with my pistol and went back to the window. The two of them were still at it, and they were moving too fast for me to get a good shot. I needed to get closer.

I jumped through the freshly-broken window and landed with bare feet on the gravel outside. I dashed across the camp in just my boxers, the cool night air biting into my skin almost as much as the gravel. When I reached the animal cages, the grunts and cries of close combat were even louder. I clambered up the first set of hand-holds I saw, flecks of ancient paint sticking to my sweaty palms. Below me, a tiger paced anxiously, woken up by the sounds of battle nearby and he roared, inquisitive.

"Don't ask me, pal," I mumbled.

I reached the top of the cage next to the fighting figures, balancing on two of the crossbars that held me out of the carnivore's reach. It boggled my mind how the two of them could jump around like that, but some people were just written with better training. I was now close enough to make out their faces in the moonlight; Raven was on one side, her pale stomach peeking out from between her black clothes, while a heavily tanned man, his face wrinkled and worn, moved opposite her. He wore a black eye-patch. His sword flashed in the night, moonlight glinting off the blade as it parried Raven's strikes, and thrust forward with its own. I levelled my gun.

"Raven, get down!"

Without even looking, she dropped on all fours, catching herself on the bars that separated her from a sleeping bear. I fired off a shot at her attacker, but he'd also heard my warning. He dove from the top of his cage, his hands catching the bar on the top corner of mine. Like some kind of gymnast, he twisted his legs sideways, flung his body through the side of the cage and up through the gaps in the roof, and kicked my feet out from under me. I tumbled, my legs slipping down into the cage, and caught myself by my armpits. With a snarl, the tiger pounced up at the tasty midnight snack that had dropped into his home, and I felt the side of his paw graze my ankle as I frantically pulled my legs out of reach.

While I was busy trying to keep myself off the tiger's menu, the one-eyed man pulled himself gracefully on top of the cage. He swung his sword at my left hand, but I pulled it away, the cold iron of the bars slamming into the tendons under my right arm as I dropped back down. I struggled to pull my body up again, but with my gun still clutched in my hand, I couldn't get a good grip. As the man drew back to swing again, I heard the rip of fabric, followed immediately by a cry of pain. A warm drop of blood set loose by one of Raven's knives landed on my cheek. I took advantage of his distraction by grabbing one of his feet, yanking it hard and sending him tumbling down, bouncing between the top bars of the cage until he was dangling like me. I grabbed the nearest bar with my left hand, freeing the hand with the pistol in it.

Our uninvited guest tried to kick me, but I pulled my legs up and wrapped them around his waist, hoisting myself out of reach. He let go with his sword arm and tried to swing it down, but I was faster. With the roar of gunpowder, I sent a slug of hot lead through the top of his chest. He went limp, his arms sliding from their grip, and dropped into the cage with the waiting tiger.

"*Bon appétit*," I groaned, pulling myself up through the bars. The only response I heard was a rush of wind above my head, then Raven's scream. As soon as I was out of the cage, I looked at where she had been seconds ago. There, silhouetted in the moonlight was the Bird-Man, Raven struggling futilely in the grasp of his talons. Damn.

They were too far away for me to shoot at, and even if I hit him, she'd probably die from the fall. So instead, I climbed down and jogged back to the trailer. The other attacker was still out cold and bathed in moonlight from the window. I wasn't sure what to do, but whatever I did, I'd need to get dressed first. I opened the tiny closet and pushed past the costumes and civilian threads, then pulled out my first clothes, the ones I'd been wearing when I Awoke: a cheap suit that didn't seem to ever lose its wrinkles, a weather-beaten trench coat, and a faded black fedora. I didn't want to be involved in all this, but they brought the fight to my doorstep, and I was sure as hell going to bring it right back to them. Isn't that how it always goes?

...

There were two basic theories about what happened that night at the library, and neither of them were very good. One camp said it was space aliens, using some fancy ray-gun or something like that. The other thought it was magic or an act of God. They had both scientists and occultists studying the site, and the scientists seemed to be on the losing side. Last I'd heard, some of the occult researchers had made some interesting progress regarding summoning rituals, but I didn't pay much attention. I'd never been religious, but on the other hand, I doubted any god who could get his wires crossed and bring a few hundred fictional characters to life was the type to have any churches built for him.

I leaned against a tent pole with my arms crossed while the cops took pictures of the scene. They were small town and hadn't seen the things I had back in my Flat days. One of them threw up when he saw what was left of the guy in the tiger cage. I bounced my foot on the gravel, as much from impatience as from the cold. I itched to do something, but the police wouldn't let me go. There was a lot more red tape these days.

I caught sight of Danver weaving his way through the chaos, flashing his badge at cops who turned and pointed to me. He approached me with a frown on his face and his hands shoved in his pockets, like a bread-line bum in Humboldt Park.

"What happened?" he asked.

"Some punk came in and tried to steal the tiger from his cage. He pulled a knife on me, and I shot him."

Danver got closer, leaned in and whispered. "What really happened?"

I moved over to the shadow of the elephant enclosure. "You were right; they came for us. We killed one of the pirates, but the Bird-Man snatched Raven and flew off somewhere with her. There's some other guy I don't recognise tied up and unconscious in my trailer. Got a dragon tattooed on his face. Know him?"

"Yeah," Danver said, nodding. "*Battle for Chinatown*. He's a Triad henchman, one of the Awakened we weren't able to track down."

"I've managed to keep the cops away from him. So far they think this is all there is to the crime scene, but it's only a matter of time before they smell something rotten behind that broken window. But I guess the feds are taking over now?"

"Right. When Awakened started going missing, the BAI thought it would be a good idea to bring some FBI people up to speed on the situation."

"I figured you were new at this. So what's the plan?"

"I can't discuss ongoing investigations with civilians," Danver said with a wry grin.

I sighed, dreading what I was about to say. "You can count me in. This is personal now, and it feels like one of the cases from my Flat days, anyway. I might just be able to help you out."

"So what do you think we should do?"

"We'll need to question that goon," I said, glancing around to make sure nobody was too close. "Someplace nobody can hear us."

• • •

I was one of the lucky ones; I had a whole fourteen-book series—fifteen, actually, but I don't like to count the last one—full of habits, dreams, history. Others had just one book to make them, but for the most part, they were still rounded out enough to function. The goons were the ones that had it really bad. They showed up for a page or two, waving a gun around, but didn't have the brains to piss on their own shoes. The BAI tried to help them out, set them up with social workers and get them jobs digging ditches. It didn't work for most of them; all they knew was violence, sometimes just five minutes of it.

"You really think we can trust what he told us?"

Danver glanced over at me as we followed the orderly down the hallway to the special wing of the asylum. Our shoes beat rhythmically on the grimy linoleum, and broken light shone through the barred windows.

"He doesn't have the sense to make up a lie," I said.

"How can you be sure?"

"We may not be from the same book, but I've dealt with goons before. Just rough them up a little bit and they spill the beans like a short-order cook who's been hitting the bottle."

Mind you, while it was easy to get him to tell us what he knew, it wasn't much. He just kept muttering gibberish, random words that didn't add up to anything, except for one name: Dr Maniac. I didn't know what kind of hold Maniac had on him, but he couldn't shut up about the guy. And, as it turned out, Dr Maniac had escaped from the crazy house over a week ago.

Anyone who's read a book knows that not everybody is a good guy. But a well-written villain has motivations, most of which don't apply when he's been pulled into the Real world. For the most part, they're able to move on with a little counselling and become halfway-decent fellows. Others weren't so lucky. Some were written as psychopaths, doing evil for evil's sake and couldn't be trusted as far as you could throw them. Still, others weren't all checked-in; if one of their books was missing from the library, it left a gap in his memory. Dr Maniac's comic books were hard to come by and the library's collection had been spotty. So when he woke up, his memory jumped around like a barefoot kid on a July sidewalk. Some of those bits didn't quite fit together, and the strain broke him.

"I don't know what you expect to find," the orderly said, leading us into the empty patient room. She wore baggy scrubs and her blonde hair was pulled back into a simple ponytail. They sure didn't make nurses like they used to. "The police finished up here a week ago."

"Did they figure out how he escaped?" I asked.

"Well, no."

"Then that's what we expect to find."

She gave us an annoyed glance and closed the door behind us. The entire room was stripped clean except for the essentials: a bed frame with a bare mattress, a toilet and sink stained orange with rusting metal bits, and a polished steel mirror hanging on the wall. Sunlight glinted off specks of dust floating lazily in front of the window. Danver and I scanned the walls and floor, looking for anything that seemed out of place. Given how small the room was, it didn't take long.

"I think she may have been right," Danver said. "I'm not seeing anything."

"Me neither," I said. "I never was actually good at this. What was I thinking coming out here with you, anyway?" I plopped down on the mattress, and it sank pitifully under my weight. My mind wandered and visions of soaring mountains floated in front of my eyes, covered with misty evergreen forests. I was never quite sure why I was fascinated with the mountains; it wasn't written into me like the rest of my personality. It wasn't dictated by a guy who'd spent the last fifteen years rotting in a Hoboken cemetery, and so I had seized on it, followed it, travelled with the circus up and down the Rockies. I closed my eyes and almost felt myself drifting there in the lush greenery, dripping with fresh water.

Then I snapped my eyes open and jumped off the bed. The feeling stopped. I had been getting carried away there, even for me. Something about that feeling wasn't natural. I crouched down and examined the bed. Scratched into the metal were barely discernible lines and curves, circling the entire frame. Lines and curves that made letters. Not English letters, but something that I almost recognised.

"What does the police report say about the bed?" I asked Danver. He squinted at me in curiosity, but flipped open his manila folder and scanned the papers.

"Nothing about the bed itself," he said. "But the mattress—"

"The mattress was missing," I said, cutting him off and standing up.

"Yeah. Why?"

"Just sit on the bed."

Danver eyed me warily, but he went along with it. I could see his eyes glaze over a bit, looking at something that wasn't there.

"You see another place, don't you?" I asked. "A place you love, that you wish you could be right now?"

He nodded slowly. "My girlfriend's house."

"There's some kind of writing all over that thing, carved into the frame. Some kind of . . . spell, or something. He turned that bed into a portal and just zapped himself out of here."

"I thought the Awakened lost all their supernatural powers when they came over."

"They did. Dr Maniac must have picked up some new tricks on this side. Real, honest-to-God magic."

"That seems a bit out there," Danver said as he stood up.

"Hey, remember who you're talking to. We both know there's some kind of power out there that can do this kind of thing. Maniac must have found it."

"How do you know that's magical writing, and not just the meaningless scribblings of a mental patient?"

I paused, my stomach churning at the thought of what I was about to say. "Because Raven's got stuff just like that tattooed all over her back."

"You think she'd know about this?" Danver asked.

"Yeah, maybe. She wasn't content to just move on, like I was. She missed the power, always looking for the real deal. If it's out there, I'm sure she's heard of it."

"Wouldn't she have told you?"

I sighed. "Yes. Unless she's behind this."

"You can't possibly think Raven helped break out Dr Maniac, can you?"

"Why not?" I asked. "You know how many times a dame I was seeing turned out to be one of the bad guys in the case I was working on?"

"Seven," Danver replied quietly.

"I thought I was done with all that, with the Flat life, but now it looks like it's all starting again. I can't seem to get away from it."

"She can't be involved," Danver said. "She was with you this whole time, right? Plus, you saw her get kidnapped."

"Hey, I've seen my share of staged abductions. And Raven had a bad habit of disappearing between towns, sometimes for days at a time. I never knew where she went, and I didn't much care, as long as she always came back. I thought I was finally in a place where I could trust the people around me, but it's starting to look like I was wrong."

"Don't worry. She may have had her quirks, but she wasn't crazy. She wouldn't help someone like Dr Maniac."

"Well, somebody had to do it. They don't exactly keep spell books in the library around here. Someone had to smuggle in the information he used."

"He did have some henchmen come through with him," Danver said. "A couple of them among the missing. Probably one of them."

"I doubt any of them knew as much about this magic stuff as Raven. She always tried to keep up with the occult research on the Awakening."

"They must have been good students, then. We're not going to start jumping to conclusions about Raven. Let's start tracking Maniac's former henchmen down."

"No," I said. "If this involves Awakened and magic together, there's one guy who can tell us what's going on."

...

Butte, Montana, was my kind of city. When it rained there, it didn't drip down like grease on the wall of a small-town diner. Not like in the Flat Chicago I remembered. No, the rain here meant business, and you could see it rolling in over the mountains, lightning flashing like the headlights of a subway train. You could always see the mountains, even from downtown, so you never felt trapped, never felt like you could take a taxi and drive your whole life and still never see the end of the skyscrapers. Not like Chicago at all.

The BAI kept a small office there, the closest they could be stationed to the site without drawing suspicion. It was really just a single room carved out of the local Forest Service district station on the outskirts of town, masquerading as a Department of Energy project monitoring the "dangerous natural gas pockets" they had blamed the explosion on. It was only a few blocks from downtown, but far enough away that the smell of coming rain could beat out the restaurants and car exhaust.

Danver and I strolled inside, trying not to look out of place in our cheap suits, surrounded by uniformed forest rangers. The walls were all wood-panelled, covered with topographical charts, informational plaques, and a clock made from a polished slice of tree trunk. A couple of the rangers glanced up at us from some paperwork behind the front desk, but they didn't react. They must have been used to strange characters stopping by to visit the DOE suits.

I knocked on the slightly open door to the BAI's annex, and it creaked open a bit wider. A single man sat inside at a computer, hair just barely hanging on in a ring around the edges of his head. He jerked at the sound, then got up and rushed to let us in. His eyes opened wide when he got a better look at me.

"You're Rick Candle," he said. "You must be with the BAI, then."

Danver closed the door quietly behind him. "Sort of. I'm Agent Danver with the FBI. Candle and I have been looking into the kidnappings."

"And you're Eli Pickens," I said, extending my hand. "A pleasure to finally meet you. Raven's told me a lot about you."

"You too," he said, shaking my hand in a vice-like grip. "She and I certainly had some interesting discussions." He turned to Danver. "The FBI, you say? They're looking into this now?"

"They took Raven," I said. I decided not to say all the other things I was thinking.

Pickens lowered his head sombrely. "I'm really sorry to hear about that," he said. He wandered back to his desk and sat down like a sack of potatoes, rubbing his temples in slow circles. The office around him was in disarray, papers strewn across the desk and part of the floor. Books littered the work area, most of them open to diagrams of runes and pentagrams.

"Dr Maniac's behind this," Danver said. "He escaped from the psychiatric hospital, and now he's rounding up Awakened. Do you have any idea why? What does he stand to gain?"

"I . . . I really don't know. Dr Maniac was always crazy, wasn't he? He probably doesn't have a good reason; it's just crime for the sake of crime."

"But he's not just going on a rampage," I said. "He's specifically targeting Awakened. That has to mean something. You're looking into rituals, right? What could he do with a few dozen Awakened?"

"I've run into a dead end," Pickens said, shaking his head. "I'm afraid I can't help you."

He was a terrible liar. All that nervous energy, the sweating, the wringing of the hands; it just screamed that he was hiding something. He reached up with a shaking hand to adjust his tie, and I caught a glimpse of a fresh wound poking up past his collar. A wound that looked about a week old.

"What did he do to you?" I asked, gesturing to the scar.

"I told you," he said, unbuttoning his shirt. His entire chest was covered with the same arcane script we'd seen on the bed. But this time it was carved into flesh, stitched together but still red with new skin. His eyes were wide with fear and warning. "I don't. Know. Anything."

"Hell." I instinctively took a step back and reached for my revolver, but that wasn't going help. "He can't talk. Maniac's got him muted or something."

Pickens gestured with his head to one of the open books. I picked it up and scanned the ancient writing, with Danver looking over my shoulder. The script cut into his skin seemed to match the one on drawn on the human figure on the page. Underneath it was a Latin translation. I didn't know much Latin, but I could make out one word: *mortis*. Death.

"Damn, it's a booby trap, right? If you talk, you die?"

Pickens nodded his head slowly, fear dripping from his face like melting ice cream. He sat back down in his chair, breathing heavy, fingernails digging into the armrests.

"How much can you tell us?" Danver asked.

Pickens strained against his fear for a moment, then began to speak, his words broken by heavy, nervous breathing. "That night, in the library. Somebody was summoning a demon. But there was a gas leak. A candle set it off, apparently. Whoever was attempting the summoning was killed, a sacrifice in flames." Pickens wiped his forehead with his sleeve, soaking it dark with sweat, but spoke a bit easier. "But there was no one to give the name of the demon. So whatever being accepted the sacrifice took the next best thing."

"The books," I said.

Pickens nodded. "The detailed descriptions must have been sufficient substitutes for true names, so instead of a demon, fictional characters were summoned."

"How does that help us?" I asked. "What is Dr Maniac trying to do?"

Pickens took in a deep breath before finally speaking through clenched teeth. "Back." Nothing happened, and he let some of the breath out.

"Back where?" I demanded. "To the crazy house?"

"Books," Pickens managed to squeeze out.

"He's going back to his books? Back to the Flat life?"

Pickens nodded.

He shouldn't have.

With a cry, his back arched, and he slipped down to the floor, writhing in pain. The script carved into his chest glowed with a sinister red energy. Danver and I both crouched down. I tried to pull Pickens back up, but his skin was like fire.

"How is Maniac doing it?" I demanded, pulling him up by his unbuttoned shirt. "Why is he kidnapping us?"

"Sacrifices..." Pickens thrashed about, his head snapping from side to side. "He needs sacrifices from the other side to—"

Pickens was interrupted by his own primal scream that tore through the building. Two of the forest rangers rushed in through the door a few seconds later.

"Call an ambulance!" I shouted. I didn't think it would help much, but it got them out of the room. "Where can we find him?" I asked. "How can we stop him?"

"He has to perform the ritual in the same place. You'll . . . you'll find him at the library. I don't know how much time you have. But . . . not much."

"Was Raven involved?" I asked, grabbing him by the hair to keep him facing me. "Tell me!" His screams were deafening; the smell of burning flesh stung my nose. He just kept flailing around in pain, no longer able to speak. By the time the ambulance got there, he was still. When the ambulance left, it didn't use the siren.

. . .

The rain tore into our car like a Tommy gun as we crept along the streets of Carson, Montana, buffeted by the hellish storm. Most of this part of town had been abandoned after the explosion, and only occasional flashes of lightning lit the pine trees that lined the road. Danver pulled into the gravel driveway of an empty house a few hundred feet away. The windows were dark and the yard was full of sun-bleached toys half-buried in weeds.

"See anything?" Danver asked.

"Just a lot of rain," I said. "How long until back-up gets here?"

"It's an hour and a half drive from the field office in Bozeman, so I'd guess about an hour. Then they can set up surveillance and spring the trap whenever Maniac shows up."

A flash of lightning speared through the sky, split in half by the dark silhouette of a gigantic pair of bird wings. "Unless he's already here." Before I could explain what I saw, a ring of tiny lights flared up on the ground surrounding the bare foundation of the former library. "Damn. Looks like we're just in time for the party."

I checked the chambers of my revolver to make sure they were fully loaded, then shoved it into the inside pocket of my trench coat, next to a couple of speedloaders. I pulled my hat down tight onto my head, and Danver and I stepped out into the torrent. As we slowly approached the empty lot, more flashes of lightning turned vague dark shapes into human and mostly-human forms. Candle flames, undisturbed by the wind and rain, glinted off a trio of dark vans parked just inside a cluster of trees. Bound and gagged people, other Awakened, were being herded single-file toward the centre of the occult circle.

"So, what's the plan?" I asked Danver as we both huddled behind trees on the edge of the clearing.

"Not sure yet. We can't take them all by ourselves. We need to keep them busy for an hour until reinforcements show up."

"I don't exactly have an hour's worth of bullets, and I don't think you do, either."

"I know. But maybe if we—"

I didn't hear the rest of his plan, because I was distracted by the talons that plunged like fire into my shoulders. Skin and muscle tore as I was picked up off the ground, and dragged through the ice-cold rain toward the circle.

It hurt like hell, but I was able to reach my arm inside my coat, feel the cool metal of my heater on my hand. I pointed it up and fired blindly, but there wasn't much room to miss. The barrel roared louder than the thunder. The rain on my face washed some of the blood into my mouth as I plummeted to the ground. I tried to roll as I hit the sodden earth, but the lifeless body of the Bird-Man followed me down and pinned me to the gravel, which bit into my skin and tore at my clothes like sandpaper.

The subtle approach was blown to hell. Two more goons rushed at me, but I pulled the body of the Bird-Man close to me for cover. I could feel the bullets thud into it; I lifted my head up just enough to see my attackers, and fire a few rounds their way. One got caught in the throat and toppled backward, while the other clutched at his chest and fell, as if in slow motion. I heard a couple of shots ring out from the trees where Danver was, followed by a scream farther back among the prisoners. I glanced up, around the winged corpse, and a small blade gleamed red in the hand of Raven as she sliced off the plastic zip tie that held her hands together. She grabbed the gun from the man she'd just killed. Damn. She really wasn't working with them.

The whole scene collapsed into chaos. After I threw off the Bird-Man, I saw Reginald McCoy throw some good punches before he took a bullet in the head. Cera managed to gore a couple of goons with her three horns before a sword pierced her over-sized dinosaur heart, and she toppled to the ground with a heavy grunt. The smell of sweat, blood and gunpowder filled the air, along with scores of shouts and cries. I thought I heard Raven's voice scream behind me in the chaos, but I was too busy trying to stay alive to look for her. There was no way we could win this fight straight out; we had to find another way to end it. I figured Dr Maniac was the only one that knew the ritual involved, but I didn't see him anywhere, and I couldn't look much harder while fighting for my life.

Finally, I spotted him. He wasn't fighting, but instead slunk around in the chaos like a shadow, grabbing panicking prisoners and henchmen alike from behind, slitting their throats, and dragging them to the centre of the circle, muttering in a low voice. I dug into my pocket for a speedloader, flipped open the cylinder of my revolver, and slammed six new rounds into it. With my arm outstretched, I took aim at Dr Maniac's head and fired. But he didn't fall. The bullet fizzled in the air with a bright flash, and Maniac just smiled at me. The ground began to shake and a hazy barrier began to form around him. The din of combat slowly died down as everyone watched the magic swirl around Dr Maniac with a macabre glow.

"It seems we're at a stalemate," he cried with glee. "You can't touch me inside the summoning circle, but I can't complete the ritual without leaving the circle to collect a final sacrifice. Perhaps you'd like to volunteer?"

"You're crazy!" I yelled. "You want to go back to the Flat life? You might as well just kill yourself."

"I used to be a god among men; people cowered at my name. Now I can barely think straight." His voice cracked a bit. "My mind is a maze now, always changing, and sometimes I can't find my way out. I want to be who I was."

"You'll never be him again," I said. "You were just ink on a page. You were nothing, and that's what you'll be again, a figment of someone's imagination!"

"If you're so certain this will be my end," Dr Maniac said with a smile. "Then come help me."

"Or I could just wait here," I replied. "You're the one that's trapped."

"I only said that I couldn't complete the ritual," he said. The shield began to grow protrusions that slowly moulded themselves into limbs and a head. "That doesn't mean I am completely without power." The sinister form shimmered as it grew in size, almost reaching the tops of the trees. A translucent hand swung down and clutched at a goon scrambling to get away, smashing his body into tiny, bloody bits.

"That won't do at all," Maniac said, his own voice nearly drowned out by the booming echo from the demonic head that floated above him, repeating his words. "I'm afraid I lack the gentle touch necessary for a proper sacrifice." None of his goons moved to help him; they were too dumb to understand that the big scary thing was being controlled by their boss.

I backed up until I hit a tree and a hand grabbed my arm. I whipped around, prepared to punch someone between the eyes, but it was Danver.

"What are we going to do?" he asked.

"What makes you think I know?" I cried. "I don't even understand what's going on!"

I scanned the area, looking desperately for some clue as to what could stop Maniac. I didn't know much about the occult; all I knew was that the ghostly figure continued to grow. A few yards away, I saw Raven. She was slumped against a tree, covered in blood, and crumpled in a heap of shattered limbs. She'd been fighting along with the rest of us, not with Dr Maniac's goons. Someone else must have helped Maniac break out, but I didn't know who. Hell, I didn't much care. I was no detective. All I knew was that Raven was innocent. And now she was dead.

I didn't have much time to mourn, because the thing reached down to one of the vans and tore back the metal of the roof like tin foil from a casserole, and clamped one of its hands down over it.

"Well," Maniac cried in his new demon's voice. "It looks like we have some cowards that thought they could hide from me. Do you want me to crush them, or will I get my sacrifice?"

"To hell with it," I said, pulling off my trench coat and jacket. The rain soaked me to the bone, stinging the wounds on my shoulders, but grit and adrenaline kept back the pain and the chill. "I'm going in."

"You'll be killed," Danver said weakly. I could see right then that he was just a kid, scared for his life. He didn't want to watch his childhood hero die.

"I should be dead already," I replied. "I'm only alive because someone didn't return his library book on time."

Danver looked up at me with pained eyes. "You didn't die in *Snuff the Candle*," he finally said. "You faked your death and ran off with the girl from the first book."

"Where to?"

"To Colorado," he said with a smile. "To the mountains."

I paused for a second.

"Hell."

I shoved my hat firmly down onto my head, readied my revolver, and charged forward. Dr Maniac waited inside the barrier, crouching down and holding a long, curved knife. I leapt at him and as I crossed the ghostly wall, everything went black.

. . .

Late the next day, after the survivors were taken to the hospital, witnesses were instructed not to talk, and all the reports had been written and filed, Danver sank into the chair in front of his desk at home. The same tired thought ran endlessly through his mind: Rick Candle, the legendary detective, was gone.

Danver opened a blank white page on the computer and began to type.

"The gravel crunched like breakfast cereal outside my trailer . . ."

THIRD CIRCLE

Lindsy Anderson

I leaned up against the wall in a narrow, no-name street in the wrong part of town and lit a cigarette. The taste of the tobacco hitting my lungs clawed out the foul miasma of the garbage from the alley behind me. It was nearly midnight and the glowing end of my cigarette was the only light around. Way behind me, the frenetic nightlife of the city was buzzing like a wasp trapped under a glass. But I had walked a long way from those streets. My clients belonged back there, sipping champagne in Manhattan. Not here where even the rats travelled in packs.

My clients had stepped into my office earlier that day on the back of a harsh September breeze that rattled at the shutters. He introduced himself as Fredrick Withingforth and her as his wife, Annabel. We didn't shake hands. She was a looker and he matched her. They were as English as King George himself. Him in his tweed suit and hundred dollar shoes, hair so blond it looked white. Her with her cloche hat protecting brown hair that bounced around her chin. Ice flashing above the gold band on her finger. Both blue-eyed with accents that could cut glass. She kept twisting the ring as if it was new and she wasn't used to wearing it. My guess was that they were newlyweds not long arrived in New York. How they ended up in my office was another question.

I sat the wife down on the wooden chair that I kept for visitors. It wasn't comfortable: that way clients never stayed long. He took up position behind her. If I had known how much trouble they were going to be, I would have thrown them out, but I didn't. That was my first mistake. I asked them to explain what their problem was. I knew that they had one. No one came to see me who didn't.

It was the woman who started talking.

"We were hoping you could help us, Mr Rafe."

"Just Rafe," I interrupted her. "No Mister."

"Oh." I could tell she wasn't used to being interrupted. But it didn't hold her back for long.

"We are on our honeymoon you see, and I said that seeing New York would be absolutely the cat's whiskers and get us out of the country until Daddy gets over that whole misunderstanding with the policeman. So Freddie was sweet and got us tickets on the next boat over. But we had to call in on Aunt Louisa while we were in Southampton, otherwise she would complain to Mother, and she asked us to look in on Betsy while we were over here, as she hasn't written this last month. Which is most unlike Betsy."

I put my notebook down. There was no way I was writing down everything she said. I had noted the name, Betsy, and ignored the rest. I lit a cigarette as she kept talking.

"Anyway, Betsy is my Aunt Lousia's great niece and my second cousin once removed on my father's side and to be perfectly honest, I can understand not writing to Aunt Louisa. But Betsy is very conscientious about letter writing and Aunt Louisa said she wrote every week. I think Aunt Louisa was sending her money. Betsy was with me when there was the misunderstanding with the policeman and she had to pay half the fine. Her father wasn't as understanding as mine, so she came to New York. We told Aunt Louisa we would take Betsy out to dinner. Only she's not here." She paused and peered up at me through long brown eyelashes. She had a funny way of talking, like a flock of small birds chirping.

"We'd like you to find her," she added.

I stubbed my cigarette out in the glass ashtray on my desk. I didn't like missing person cases. Either the missing person wanted to stay missing and you got in trouble for finding them, or they were missing for a reason—which was always bad. Either way, the client was unhappy. Unhappy clients didn't pay well. I preferred missing property, but the rent was due that week and I was more than a few dollars short.

"Why me?" I asked. I didn't move in the same social circles as them and I didn't advertise. My clients were usually wives looking for cheating husbands or cheating husbands looking for a way out from blackmail. A rich English woman was a step up.

"My man Williams came up with your name." Freddie said. "Evidently, he knew you from the War, and he came up with your name when we were looking for a private detective. I am unaware as to how he knew you were in New York, though."

"We met up while I was hunting a murderer in Ypres. He helped me out of a jam and I told him if he was ever in New York to look me up," I replied.

"I saw a large number of dead bodies in Ypres. I am pretty sure no one hunted down all their killers." Freddie reached down and held on to his wife's shoulder as if she was a good luck charm against bad memories. She reached up and covered his hand with her white gloves. Perhaps she wasn't as cloudheaded as her speech suggested. I shrugged and picked up my notebook again. I wasn't about to start discussing the War with them.

"Where was Betsy staying in New York?" I asked, making quick notes with my pencil.

"At a tiny boarding house over by the river." Annabel said, pulling a piece of paper out of her small handbag and handing me the address. It was considerably more downmarket than the couple in front of me. I raised an eyebrow.

"Oh, it's so stupid," Annabel rolled her eyes. "Her father cut her allowance due to that whole affair with the policeman and the fine and the newspapers. She came over here to get away from it all. And all she could afford was that stupid little room. In her last letter, she was even talking about getting a job. But she's not at the boarding house and no one there knows where she could have gone."

It struck me that the last place you would want to send a wayward daughter was New York, not unless you wanted her to get in more trouble. It didn't seem the moment to mention that, though.

"The landlady said her behaviour changed about a month ago," Freddie said. "She started going out every night and not coming back until dawn. Prior to that, she had only gone out during the day—mostly to the museum and library. Her rent was paid up until the end of the month, but the landlady says she hasn't been around at all for the last two weeks."

"Any men in the picture?" I asked.

Freddie shook his head. "The landlady doesn't allow men in."

"There are none mentioned in her diary," Annabel added.

"You took her diary?" Freddie sounded shocked. I would have thought he knew his wife better. She nodded and pulled it out of her handbag. I took the slim leather journal from her and flicked through to the last few entries.

On the last page, there was an address copied out neatly, with the words *Friday 9pm* written beneath. It was in the wrong part of town for a girl who wrote with purple ink and decorated the page with stars when she was happy. The address was for a club called The Third Circle. I didn't know it, but I knew the area. Full of speakeasies and illegal nightclubs. As fast as the police shut them down, another six sprang up. Half the time the police didn't bother, especially when they got a cut of the profits. I told the Withingforths that I would check it out later that night and let them know tomorrow if I'd heard anything about Betsy.

But Annabel didn't like that plan. She said she was going to the club as well, as I wouldn't recognise Betsy. Freddie wasn't so sure about the idea, but wasn't about to let her go off on her own. I told 'em both no. They wouldn't listen to me about the dangers. Thought they were invincible, strong enough to beat the world.

Upshot of it all was that we agreed to go to the club together. My second mistake.

I was willing to bet ten large they would have changed their minds by morning. I would have lost. Still, they had a better chance with me than wandering off like two little sheep putting their noses into the wolf's den. We arranged to meet at midnight, a block down from the address in Betsy's diary.

After they left, I reached out to a couple of contacts but no one was willing to talk. I gave up shortly after sun down and headed downtown.

I arrived an hour before midnight and took up a position on a street corner, trying to suck in warmth from a cigarette. This place hadn't changed since the last time I had been paid to come down here. It was the kind of place you only went if you wanted to make a profit, or lose one. One street to my left, women stood ready to distract a man while their accomplices stole his wallet. Two streets to my right, losing your wallet was a less pleasurable experience: eyes watched from shadows; hands ready with knuckledusters.

All around, whispers moved in the shadows as beggars shuffled from doorway to gutter. But not on this street. There was just one door, halfway down, watched over by two faceless walls. The cold wind whistled through it empty-handed. A few people were dropped off in expensive looking cabs at the top of the road before clattering their way towards the door. They all disappeared inside after a short conversation with the doorman. None of them came back out.

A distant clock struck midnight and I lit my fourth cigarette of the evening. I hadn't taken more than a drag from it when the low grumble of a Cadillac engine pulled up beside me. The driver was the man I had known as Corporal Williams. He was still wearing a uniform, but no longer the khaki of the British Army. He had replaced it with the black and white of an English Gentleman's Gentleman. It suited him better than the green. Williams jumped out of the driver's seat and held open the back doors for the Withingforths to step out.

I cursed when I saw them all dolled up in their glad rags. She had on a short drape of white that stopped dead above her knees, decorated with a long curl of pearls around her neck. She had feathers in her hair that sparkled with the shine of expensive rocks. Every man and most of the women within four blocks would kill their grandmother for that much sparkle, let alone a woman stupid enough to take a walk in the wrong part of town. He wasn't much better. Every inch of his clothes screamed money, from the banding on his top hat to the shine on his shoes. And I was willing to bet the stick he was waving around was solid silver at the top. At least they matched the others going into the building. I was a little shabbier. My suit was out of date when it was new.

"Sir, it's good to see you again," Williams said as he came up to shake my hand. He leaned forward and lowered his voice. "Look out for them, will you? They're good people, but no common sense. He knows how to handle himself in a fight, but keep an eye on her? I'll be in the car nearby if you need me."

He opened his jacket slightly so I could see the dull gleam of a Webley Mk IV revolver tucked into his waistband. He spoke normally. "A lot less mud than the last time I saw you, although it's still cold."

"Thank you, Williams," Freddie said. "No need to loiter, we'll get a taxi back." Williams nodded at me and got back into the car.

I led them down the street to the doorway and knocked against the thick wooden panel. Three times quick, twice slow. The door opened a crack. A surly face glared out at me.

"I'm a friend of Joe's," I said, dropping some coins into his hand. He grunted and heaved the door fully open, allowing us to pass.

"What is this place?" Annabel asked as we walked down a narrow, grey corridor. It was an old industrial building with pipes running above our heads. Faint music hummed along the metal tubes. As we descended a corkscrew staircase, the music got louder until it settled into the slow croon of a jazz beat.

"Welcome to The Third Circle," a cheerful, too-young waitress said, leading us to a table. As speakeasies go, this was one of the better ones I had been to. It had a high vaulted roof, walls panelled in wood, sealed with black and decorated with white geometric patterns. Round wooden tables and high-backed chairs surrounded a small dance floor, half-full of butterfly girls dancing too close to men they didn't know. On the stage next to the dance floor was a four-piece jazz band, with a man making a saxophone cry.

My clients were slumming it, but my cheap suit had never sinned in such a classy joint. The waitress came back with our drinks. She was wearing a man's suit that was cut tight in all the right places. As she leant over to serve our drinks, I could see that she hadn't bothered with all the buttons on the shirt. I tipped her extra for the view. It was what she was expecting and I wanted to blend in.

It looked like we had got the last free table in the place. All the others were full with a mix of people; from young girls from the best parts of town looking for a little danger, to women with faces painted to hide time's ravages, holding cigarettes in long thin holders so they could blow smoke in the eyes of the men they were flirting with. Drunken boys mixed with gangsters' molls, risking broken legs or worse in the pursuit of fun. At the tables in the back of the room were some faces I recognised from wanted posters, sitting by the door so they could make a sharp exit. They all had one thing in common.

Money.

Some of them wanted it and would do anything to get it; some of them had it and didn't care what they did with it. A pickpocket was working the room. Dressed as a waitress, she dipped into pockets, taking purses and wallets with the empty glasses as she cleared the tables. She returned them with the next round of drinks, considerably lighter. Most of the people were too drunk to notice the difference. As she headed over to our table, I lifted Freddie's wallet before she could. I figured it would be safer with me.

There were some who didn't fit in, pale-faced, sober compared to the rest. They were standing alone, hiding in the shadows. Occasionally, one of them would slip over to a dark doorway, hidden in a corner where the light from the chandeliers didn't reach. The door was guarded by a shadowy figure. Once a drunk couple made their way over to him and he steered them back into the club. For a second, he stood in the light, a tall drain-pole figure with a suit that had been fashionable three decades ago. The kind of suit a man was buried in. I knew; I had been the one who had buried him in it.

Freddie had been questioning the waitress about Betsy to no avail. She didn't recognise the description and no promise of money seemed to jog her memory.

"What do we do now?" Annabel asked.

"Now, you dance," I said.

They were a bit reluctant, but I persuaded them that it would add to our cover. Freddie spun her out onto the dance floor, where the other dancers cleared them a space. I didn't recognise the dance, but they were good at it. All kinds of fancy twists and dips. It certainly wasn't a foxtrot. Soon, they were the centre of attention, and out of my way. Out of danger, as well. I wanted to see what was behind the door that was guarded by a dead man. The sentry had carried a particularly nasty shiv the last time I'd met him. As he'd kept the suit for thirty years, I was willing to bet he had kept the knife, as well.

I tapped Freddie's wallet against my leg. It was thick with notes, certainly enough to buy my way into the back room. I was willing to bet that the entrance fee would be higher than I could otherwise afford. I glanced back at the dancing couple. The music had slowed to a sultry croon and they were swaying gently in each other's arms, close enough that not even a draft could sneak between them. They wouldn't even notice I was gone.

. . .

I downed the last of my rye and strolled over to the dead man at the doorway. That was my third mistake of the day. I should have stayed and watched the dancing. As I got closer, the dusty smell of decay got stronger, grabbing the back of my throat and forcing its way down my lungs. The doorman smiled at me politely, glinting white fangs against his blood red lips.

"I'm sorry, sir; these rooms are for members only." For a vampire, he was pretty polite. Most of the ones I'd met didn't bother with manners. Not to humans, anyway. One of them once told me it was like humans talking to cows or chickens. But these vampires had learnt to blend in. I was pretty sure that made them more dangerous.

"I'm sure we could come to some arrangement," I said, flashing Freddie's wallet and a hint of fang. The fangs were an illusion, but he wasn't able to tell the difference. One of the few tricks left to me. He opened the door and ushered me into another corridor, half a world away from the black and white of the club. A thick red carpet muffled my footsteps. The walls were draped with old-fashioned tapestries, probably imported from Europe. Small wooden tables were dotted along the hallway, each supporting a marble statue. I was no art expert, but I had once taken a girl up to the Met. They had similar statues there, only guards and ropes and alarms stopped you getting this near to them.

"What is this place?" I heard Annabel's voice behind me. I turned around. My clients were standing hand-in-hand behind me.

I cursed softly.

"Steady on old chap, we're only trying to help," Freddie said.

"Freddie saw you leave and we couldn't let you go in alone. So we told the doorman that we were with you and he let us in," added Annabel, a proud smile on her face.

"Do not say a word to anyone but me," I warned. "And do everything I say. Exactly as I tell you to." I could only hope that they would follow my instructions. If I made them leave now, it would only arouse suspicion.

The door ahead opened as we approached and we were met by a young waiter. "Welcome to the Seventh Circle."

He showed us to a corner booth. It was further from the exit than I would have liked, but at least it meant no one could get behind us. The room had about ten booths, all with low, cushioned seats on either side. It was dark enough that it was hard to make out other people, but I could hear the low muttering of voices. The European theme extended into this secondary club: oak panelling and gold painted fixtures surrounded us.

"Can I get you a drink, sir?" the waiter asked me, ignoring Freddie and Annabel.

"Looks like you spilt yours," I replied, looking at the red drops that marred his otherwise pristine white shirt cuffs. He raised his arm to his lips and slowly licked them off. His eyelashes fluttered at the taste. Out of the corner of my eye, I could see Annabel moving restlessly. I hoped she wouldn't do anything stupid.

"My apologies, sir. What can I get you?"

"What do you recommend?" I asked. I could guess what I was about to order, but I didn't want to get it wrong. They would kill us all if my illusion failed.

"We have a fresh young French white, with a twist."

I nodded. "Sounds good to me." I pulled out Freddie's wallet again and paid the waiter, who left to prepare my drink.

"What is going on? Why is the waiter ignoring us?" Annabel demanded, glaring at me. "What is the deal with Freddie's wallet? Are you a thief? Are you planning on robbing us of all our money? Because let me tell you now—"

"Give the man a chance to answer," Freddie cut her off. "Although what drink are you buying for ten times the price of champagne?"

"The drinks are bottled differently here," I said. "Makes them a little more expensive." The waiter returned with a very drunk blonde woman, dressed in a simple black dress and deposited her on the seat next to me.

"This is what you ordered?" Annabel hissed.

"Hello," the woman slurred, a hint of a French accent smothered by alcohol. "Fancy a drink?"

Freddie looked at her and then around at the other booths. I could see the traces of the genial fool he played draining away. He sat upright, a military bearing taking over.

"Is this a brothel?" Annabel asked. She tried to fake a nonchalant air, but her voice cracked.

"No," replied Freddie. "It's worse. Isn't it?" He looked at me.

I nodded and pulled the drunk girl across my lap. Annabel looked around and I could see the dawning realisation in her eyes. She had a face that would lose a packet in poker. In the booth beside us, a young girl licked the blood off the neck of an old soldier, his eyes burnt out some time ago by phosphorus. In the next booth, a slim young man in a chauffeur's uniform gnawed on the neck of a heavily pregnant woman. It was a pattern repeated in every corner of the club. The faint, sweet smell of blood spread throughout the room.

"What is this place?" Annabel asked.

"Vampire bar," I replied, pulling the girl's head back until I had easy access to her neck. She had passed out, making the task more difficult. "Vampires can't get drunk from drinking alcohol. It doesn't affect them at all. But drinking the blood of a drunk person? That gives them all the buzz and none of the hangover. Usually the victims survive the first few times, but eventually someone takes too much blood. It's why they're using people they think no one will miss. Like your cousin. No one to ask questions when they don't turn up." I pushed the hair away from the girl's neck and leant over her.

"What the hell do you think you are doing?" Freddie demanded. There was a metallic *snick* and I looked up into the dark barrel of a Webley MK IV Revolver. I didn't know he was heeled, otherwise I'd have taken it off him earlier. He held the gun with the easy confidence of a man who had pulled the trigger before and would easily pull it again. Luckily, he had the sense to hold it under the table, so no one else could see it.

"Shall I get my gun out, too?" Annabel asked calmly, as if she was talking about another round of drinks.

"No. Just stay behind me for now," Freddie said. From the flick of his eyes when Annabel spoke, he hadn't known she was carrying, either. I had no idea where she was hiding a gun. But if he was just as ignorant, I was willing to bet it was in her handbag. Freddie had had his hands almost everywhere else.

"Explain." Freddie glared at me.

"I'm trying to not get us killed," I replied. "They believe I'm a vampire and that you two humans belong to me. I'd like to keep that belief going long enough for us to get out of here. Which means I have to make it look like I'm drinking her blood. Now, are you going to put that away or are you going to shoot me?"

"Okay." The gun disappeared back inside his jacket and Freddie leant back against the wall of the booth, as if he was sitting in front of the fire at home. Only the flicking of his eyes betrayed him. Annabel curled in next to him like she was cold, one hand resting on her handbag. I eyed them both suspiciously. I had expected more of a reaction to the vampires. Not that I was complaining: screaming would have only drawn unnecessary attention. But I'd seen dead bodies react with more emotion to the news that vampires were real.

"You're taking the whole vampires idea very calmly," I said.

"Well, after Great Uncle George got bitten by a werewolf while exploring some jungle somewhere, the family made sure that we were all educated properly about the dangers that are out there. It was all very embarrassing. He had to live in Scotland, you see. He kept frightening the horses. And then there was the incident with the sheep on the home farm. Mother insisted he move out, after that. Still, it is a very nice island he moved to. No rabbits anymore, though," Annabel said.

I looked at Freddie. He shrugged. "He is also my Great Uncle by marriage, so I got the warning lecture, too. Although I have to admit, I wish I had paid more attention. They didn't really discuss the killing aspect of the whole business."

"It's all very exciting, though. Imagine what Daddy will say when we tell him."

"Let's not mention it," Freddie winced.

"You do realise they will kill you in heartbeat," I said. This prospect shut them up for a while. I flicked the knife out of my sleeve and made a couple of pinpricks in the girl's neck, a fangs' width apart. A trickle of blood ran across her skin and I wiped it up with the sleeve of my jacket.

"We need to get out of here," I said when the bleeding stopped.

"But what about Betsy?" Annabel asked. "What if she's been captured? We need to make sure she's not being held prisoner here."

"We can't do anything except leave," I said. I wasn't about to risk getting them killed. If I had been on my own it would have been different. But they had no idea of the risks involved. I looked at Annabel. Soft tears were forming at the side of her big blue eyes. I cursed softly. I was a sucker for a woman's tears: always had been.

"I'll come back tomorrow in the daylight. Pass some money around while the vamps are sleeping; see what I can dig up. If she's here, I'll find her," I promised. "But we can't fight all these vampires tonight. Not if we want to come out of it in one piece."

"Thank you," Freddie said. I leant the drunken woman up against the corner of the booth, brushing her hair back of her face. There was nothing more I could do for her tonight.

As we stood to leave, a woman came out into the centre of the room. She had dressed to get attention and I couldn't help but stare at her. She looked like she was important and leaving now would just draw attention to Annabel and Freddie, so I motioned for them to take their seats again.

The woman was wearing a red dress, with a swirl of beads around her hips that chimed as she sashayed from side to side with every step. The dress stopped short enough at the top and the bottom to give a glimpse of what it was concealing, but hiding enough that a man would ask all the right questions about what was underneath.

She glad-handed her way around the room, stopping at every booth, sipping a little from the pregnant woman and the soldier. The soldier dropped to the floor after she had finished. The way none of the other vampires were complaining about her snacking on their food meant she was pretty high up on the ladder in this particular group of vamps. Perfect.

"Let me handle this," I said. Annabel nodded, her lips pressed into a thin line.

"Good evening," the vision in red said as she walked up to our booth. "I don't believe we've met. I'm Lily. Welcome to the Seventh Circle." She reached out her hand for me to kiss. Even through the glove, it was cold under my fingers. She sat down next to me, ignoring everyone else in the booth.

"I hope you have found my establishment to your liking," Lily said. She had a soft, throaty voice with the slightest hint of a foreign accent, and I found myself leaning towards her to catch what she was saying.

"It's ritzy enough," I said. She laughed, a low chuckle that set the hairs on the back of my neck dancing. It was the kind of laugh that a tiger in the jungle would give once it had cornered its prey.

"I'm surprised that a man of your resources would need to visit us," Lily said, gesturing to Freddie and Annabel. They had moved closer to each other. Annabel was trembling gently, like a leaf at the first sign of winter, but her hand was still over her handbag.

"I like to try new things every now and then, but nothing can beat home-brewed," I said. She nodded and cocked her head on one side, staring at Freddie and Annabel as if she was choosing the best cut at the butchers.

"I do believe I have something very similar in my store, if you were ever thinking of completing the set," Lily said. "If you are interested . . ."

"It's worth a look," I said. She clapped her hands and the waiter from earlier ran up. Lily whispered in his ear and he effortlessly picked up the drunk girl from the side of the booth and left. Lily leant back in her seat and crossed her legs with a brush of silk and a jangle of beads. She reeked of death and decay in the same way other women smelt of perfume.

"You sound like you have lived in New York a while, Mr . . . ?" she asked.

"Rafe," I replied. "Just Rafe."

"I thought I knew everyone worth knowing in New York, and here you are proving me wrong. Tell me where you've been hiding, Just Rafe." Lily said. My name had never sounded more exotic as she dragged it out into a caress. I could feel a pull of command in her words, the vampire's hypnotic powers demanding a reply. She was good. But I had learnt to refuse a much stronger command and her seductive voice was no more than a cheap parlour trick.

I smiled at her. "Who says I've been hiding?"

The waiter returned with another girl. This one was in a much worse state than the first. Barely able to stand, she was wearing what had once been a fashionable dress. Now all that could be said about it was that it covered her where it needed to. Her hair fell around her face in clumps like dead ivy clinging to the side of an empty building. I looked across at Freddie. He nodded slightly.

It was Betsy.

"What's the price?" I asked as I pulled her towards me.

"An hour with that English gentlemen," Lily said. She stood and reached towards him, slicing her nails across the line of his jaw, leaving beads of red where she touched.

"No," Annabel said. She spoke calmly, like a teacher drilling facts into a class of school kids. Just as calmly, she pulled a pistol out of her handbag and put two rounds in Lily's chest before we could stop her. Lily fell backwards and when she hit the carpet she didn't move. Annabel dropped the gun at my feet and fell back on to the sofa.

There was a silence in the room that seemed to last for eternity. No one seemed to believe what their eyes were telling them. Then everything sped up again. Freddie stood, pulling Annabel behind him while he withdrew his gun in one swift movement. I was impressed. He made it look easy. I wasn't as smooth as I stood, sheltering Betsy behind me. The pregnant woman was cowering underneath the seats as best she could. The vampires were a bit slower, the liquored-up blood or the surprise dulling their reactions. But too soon they surrounded us and had blocked off all the exits.

Lily stood up. Annabel had put a couple of neat holes in her dress, but that was it. That's the problem with vampires. Filling them full of lead doesn't kill something that is already dead. It didn't stop Freddie from pointing his gun at the blood-drinkers, though.

"Now don't get sore," I said. "She's a little protective, but no harm done. We can still agree on a price. I'll throw in the cost of a new dress."

Lily fingered the holes in her gown and stepped slowly towards me. If she had been breathing, I could have tasted her exhalations, we were standing that close. She crouched down slowly, never moving her eyes away from mine, and picked up Annabel's gun. It was a pretty little thing: mother of pearl handle, light enough to carry around in a handbag, heavy enough to get rid of most dangers. But vampires aren't the usual problem ladies meet in dark alleyways.

Lily turned the gun over in her hands, and then handed it back to me with an air of disdain. "You are not a vampire. But you are not exactly human, either. Who are you? What are you doing in my club?" She put an edge of command in her voice again, but it still wasn't strong enough to compel me to talk. I stepped away from Lily and turned to Annabel. I wiped a tear from her face and dropped the gun in her lap. Her hands were shaking as she picked it up. I rested my palm on the gun and whispered a prayer.

"We came here looking for a woman," I said as I turned back to face Lily. "We've found her. How about we leave, before anyone else gets a hole in them, or worse?"

"You think I am going to let you go after this?" Lily asked, hatred twisting her face into an ugly mask. "I will drain you dry. But not until I have taken those two and bled them until they beg to die."

"You will not touch her!" Freddie said, aiming his gun directly at her head. Annabel stood next to him, her gun pointing in the same direction.

"Touching, the devotion they have to each other," Lily said. "I wonder if they will be as devoted when I get them to slice into each other, when every touch that the other brings is nothing but pain."

"Don't," I said. I could feel my power, locked away beyond my reach, burning as I tried to get at it.

"How are you going to stop me?" she taunted. "You have no power to hurt me, or you would have done so by now. Nothing you can do will harm me."

"You want to bet on that?" I asked. "Annabel, shoot her again."

Annabel didn't hesitate, putting two more rounds in Lily. I was impressed by that girl. There was a long pause and Lily coughed, all the blood she had stolen running out of her, dripping down onto the floor. She collapsed slowly, falling away into dust. The blood soaked into the carpet, staining it darker in a perfect circle.

For the first time, I saw fear on the faces of the vampires surrounding us. They had thought themselves invulnerable. We had just shown them they weren't. It was a young one at the back that broke first, running for the exit without even picking up his coat. He was soon followed by the rest, until we were alone in the club.

"What just happened?" Freddie asked, pulling Annabel tight against him.

"I blessed the bullets in the gun," I said. "I had to be touching the gun to do it, which is why the first set of bullets didn't work."

He opened his mouth a couple of times like a goldfish, but couldn't spit out a sentence. Finally he shook his head and returned his attention to Annabel.

Around the room the vampires' victims were slowly getting to their feet. I helped the pregnant woman out from under the seats. She led me to a back room with a large padlock on the door. I picked the lock. Inside there were more captives.

"Don't worry—I'm not going to hurt you," I said as I stepped into the dark room but they drew back away from me, further into the shadows, fear filling their eyes. There were too many of them, nothing I could do but call for help. I propped the door open as I left. Once I would have been able to heal them with less than a thought, but that power had been taken from me a long time ago now.

I kicked open the next door along. It looked like Lily's office, a large wooden desk dominating the room. I used her phone to call the police, telling them to bring some medical help. They would shut down the club for a while. Another would spring up somewhere else soon, but I would take any victories I could these days.

"Come on, we need to leave now," I said, as I returned to the main room. Annabel was fussing over Betsy and had managed to wake her up a bit. Between Freddie and I, we got Betsy standing and headed in the direction of the door.

"Wait, we have to help these people," Annabel said.

"The police are on their way, with ambulances. With your record, you may not wish to get arrested again," I said.

"He's right; let's go," Freddie said.

Freddie led the way back into the main club. It was chaos after the vampire exodus. We made it out without any further trouble and Williams was waiting with the car, gun in hand. I helped Betsy into the back seat and held the door for Annabel. She hugged me briefly, whispering her thanks into my ear. Freddie shook my hand and I gave him his wallet back.

"Thank you," he said. "I don't know what would have happened if you hadn't been there. Can we give you a lift?" I shook my head and he got into the car.

I slammed the door shut behind him. Before they drove off, a window wound down. Annabel's head poked out.

"Rafe," she said. "That isn't your proper name is it?"

I shook my head.

"Then what is it?" she asked.

I turned and walked away from her, down the long, dark street towards the dawn.

"Raphael," I said, but there was no one left to hear.

THREE QUESTIONS AND ONE TROLL

Chris Bauer

Mrs K perched atop the crumbling stoop leading into the building she collected rent on. Rent that I'd been trying to avoid paying for a few months now. The old harpy had staked the place out, and like a rube, I'd walked right into it. Her eyes narrowed when she saw me. She pointed a twisted finger at me and beckoned me forward. I adjusted my fedora and summoned my most charming smile as I approached. This was not going to be pleasant.

"Mrs Kriminey. What can I do for you?" I knew damn well she wanted nothing more than to rip my still beating heart from my chest.

"It's Krimides, Mr Steele. You're late with your rent. Three months I've been waiting for it. Pay up or out you go." Her voice had the allure of fingers on a chalkboard. Thin strands of saliva bridged the gap between her lips and a rank carrion stench surrounded her.

I've been stabbed, sliced, bludgeoned, poked and shot by every weapon under the sun without wincing. I've sunk my teeth into the rancid underbelly of undead merfolk during battle. Once, I even kissed a morbidly obese demoness on a drunken dare.

Mrs K's breath made me gag.

A bony finger prodded my chest. "Look at me, Mr Steele. I want you to *see* me when I'm talking to you." I met her gaze directly. The crowd on the street faded to vague, grey shapes. The blazing sun dimmed and shadows grew long. Even the building grew hazy, insubstantial, like a mirage in the distance.

I *saw* her true form.

Her wings were a mottled cloak of grey and black feathers raised behind her. She stood hunched atop two spindly legs that were covered with yellow-brown scales ending in wicked, curved talons, black as obsidian. Her arms were plumed in filthy ochre and a single, gleaming claw traced the outline of my heart. Dull orbs of black marble glared at me. Her misshapen beak bobbed up and down with each word for emphasis and chunks of rotting meat clung to her cheeks.

"You owe me seventy-five dollars. Not promises or excuses. I expected a little more from a scion of the Summer Sept. I see that even a courtly upbringing can't change your base nature, Mr Steele. I don't care if you and your red cap tribe were the terror of the Twilight Realms. You're stuck in the Mortal Maze. I want that money by Friday. You will promise me that I'll get it, or I will toss all of your junk on the kerb. Understand?"

I grimaced. The old bird had me over a barrel. If I didn't promise her the cash, I would be on the street. If I did make the oath, I'd be beholden to her for the full amount in four days. Double-crossing her was out of the question. Nobody ever broke a promise. There were a few similar laws: the obligation of hospitality, the sanctity of holy ground and mercy debts. But those were by consensus and tradition. Like agreeing not to break wind in polite company.

A promise was different. There was no out.

"I, Brendan Sharpshanks Steele of clan Skullsmasher, son of Braken Heartrender, Ward of Lord Oberon the Illuminated, do so swear upon my word to pay in full all debts owed to you by sunrise four days hence. So mote it be." I grumbled the last part under my breath.

"So mote it be," she echoed in satisfaction. The deal was done.

My vision returned to normal. The office building shimmered into sharp resolution, passers-by gained definition and the sun beat upon me once more. Unfortunately, Mrs K didn't look that much better.

"I'll see you on Friday, Mr Steele." She hopped off the stairs and bullied her way through the crowd up Fremont Street with an ungainly swagger.

I tipped the brim of my fedora, taking some solace in its familiar creases. I'd been in worse jams before and gotten out unscathed. Scarred, yes. But never scathed.

I trudged up the stairs into the faded, red brick building where Steele Investigations Inc. was based.

For now. Until Friday, at least.

. . .

My office is a lot like my personal life: small, cluttered, and in serious need of a cleaning.

I draped the trench coat on the rack next to the door and placed my red fedora atop it. Yeah, I sometimes get looks for wearing a red hat. Most gentlemen prefer dun or black. But with my kind, tradition is hard to break. Impossible, in some cases, as Mrs K had proved earlier. I was between jobs at the moment, and had spent all the money from my last one keeping a roof over my thick skull at a cheap tenement eight blocks away.

"Come on, Bren. Seventy-five dollars? That's not even the dowry for a goblin princess, for crying out loud." I muttered to myself.

Before my exile from the Twilight Realms twenty years ago, I 'acquired' some trinkets from the Summer Palace of Titania and Oberon, undisputed rulers of the Dawn Court. Mithril dining ware, crystal goblets, a few precious stones and a dozen napkins crafted from the golden rays of the setting sun. I figured my uncle, the sanctimonious buffoon, owed me at least that much for throwing me into the Mortal Maze. I'd be set financially once I got here.

What a chump I was.

Upon arrival, the napkins turned to worthless straw and the priceless plates sublimated into moonlight, evaporating in a silvery mist. I was able to pawn the crystal and jewels for a couple of hundred bucks. I've never been good with money.

I checked the contents of my pockets: seven dollars and thirty-seven cents; an enchanted penknife that never lost its edge; a Zippo ensorcelled to always light on the first try; an onyx carving of a bird the size of my thumb, which would parrot back fifteen seconds of conversation; a dog-eared notepad and the stub of a pencil. There were also a few crumpled receipts, last week's grocery list and a lot of lint. Nothing important.

Unfortunately, there were no outstanding bills from deadbeats. Nobody was stupid enough to welsh on my fees. Never whistle in a graveyard, never accept a drink from an infernal and never, ever hold out on a red cap. We tended to take that whole 'pound of flesh' thing literally.

I stood and gazed out the dusty window of my office. My reflection offered no advice; just an average looking Joe staring back. He had a swarthy complexion, specks of dark stubble dotted upon a slightly overlarge jaw, gunmetal grey eyes and a shock of unruly black hair. He also had broad shoulders, and was about five foot eight in height. You'd walk right by him—me—without a second glance. Which is the way our glamours are designed to work.

Your taxi driver? A cigar-chomping goblin. The Oriental lady down the street who does your laundry? Humans don't see her bushy foxtail. We're everywhere. You just can't see us, not the way we really are. Of course, every so often one of us will slip up and the glamour fades for a second or two. In the best case, you pull a double take and swear off java for the week. Worst case? Well, that depends. Catching a glimpse of a blue-scaled nixie diving into the local community pool is just startling. Stumbling across a drunk minotaur in some dark alley at two in the morning is frequently fatal.

We try to be on our best behaviour while in the Maze, but accidents happen.

A precise set of three knocks on my office door interrupted my thoughts. I saw a slender silhouette framed in the frosted glass. I slid into my chair, did my best to smooth the wrinkles out of my shirt, and answered in my most professional demeanour. "Yeah. Come in."

A tall, distinguished gentleman of obvious means and middle age strode into my office like he owned the place. The three-piece suit he wore was custom tailored and probably cost more than I made in a whole year. Immaculate white gloves with mother-of-pearl buttons hid his hands. His face was strong and proud, dominated by a hawkish nose. Streaks of grey hair in the black gave him a patrician bearing. Inscrutable green eyes met my gaze evenly.

"Greetings, Brendan. You're looking well." His voice was soft, cultured and British.

I whipped the .45 semi automatic pistol out of my shoulder rig in a flash and showed my visitor the business end.

"Valdonicus Tonguebinder. The Regus Sinestra of Oberon himself. What the hell are you doing in Vegas, and more importantly, why shouldn't I blow a hole in your chest right now? You have five seconds to answer the second question. One . . . "

The head of Oberon's secret police didn't even blink.

"Come now, Brendan. Is that anyway to greet an old friend?"

I pulled back the hammer and slid the safety off. "A friend? Naw. But you? Absolutely. Two."

"Very well. His Majesty has need of your . . . services." He spat the last word out like a foul tasting morsel. "A situation has arisen in the realm which requires your unique insights and talents, loathe as I am to admit it. His Lordship was quite adamant about your participation, despite my protests. Are you willing to listen further, or shall you continue to menace me with that ridiculous trinket?"

It took a lot of juice to fuel a jaunt into the Mortal Maze, something Oberon wouldn't do without good reason. And to send somebody like Valdonicus to speak with me meant that the stakes were high. Too high for a double-cross. My curiosity finally trumped my thirst for revenge.

I raised the barrel of the pistol away from Val, released the hammer and set the gun on my side of the desk, within easy reach.

"The safety is still off. But you've got my attention, Valdonicus. What does my dear old uncle want? I haven't heard from him in decades. Why now and why here?" Oberon wasn't really my uncle by blood. I suppose it would be more accurate to call him my former warden.

The air spirit across the desk placed his fingertips together, steepled against them his chin and smiled. If I had a nickel for every time he had done that to me in the courts while I was a Ward of the King, I'd never have to worry about money again. I was sorely tempted to grab the .45 and end this little reunion right now.

"Yes, well. As you might imagine this is awkward for His Lordship. But these are dire times, which call for extreme measures. Such as yourself. The particulars of the situation are somewhat delicate, you see. A myriad of existing political alliances, extensions, fiats and highly born personages are rather impacted in a negative fashion . . . "

"Valdonicus."

His silky, smooth cadence collapsed like a hind felled by an arrow to the heart. "Yes?"

"I'm going to start counting again if you don't get to the point." I put my hand on the gun. His eyes narrowed and tiny sparks danced within them. I heard the distant rumble of thunder echoing in the cloudless Nevada sky and the hair on my arms stood at attention. He wasn't the High King's number two guy for nothing. I'd seen him smash a hilltop into a broken pile of smoking sod and white-hot rocks with conjured lightning. But I figured he was under strict orders from Oberon to play nice.

I wanted to twist his nose a bit.

"As you wish. One of Titania's handmaidens has been kidnapped and spirited away to the Mortal Maze. To Las Vegas. The Lord of the Hunt tracked her through a moongate to an establishment called Virgil's Path. The Huntsman is a peerless tracker, but would have . . . difficulty blending in."

The Lord of the Hunt is an eleven foot tall hairy giant with deer antlers sticking out of his head, not to mention the glowing orange eyes, boar tusks and cloven hooves. There was a limit to what even glamour could hide. Nice guy, though. I once made him laugh in court by commenting on his spectacular rack.

"Yeah, I can imagine that would be problematic. So you want me to find this handmaiden. What the Balefires is so important about her, anyways?"

"She is a Ward of the Court, as you were. But unlike you, she is of value. His Majesty provides for her in return for continued cooperation from her clan. She is betrothed to Reginald, the King's nephew. They are to be wed in two full moon's time. Should this marriage fail to occur, there would be significant anxiety in the realm. His Lordship wishes to avoid that; ergo, your assistance is required."

I knew Reginald. He was a carrot-topped idiot with no lands to his name, no victories in battle and no ambition to earn either. But he didn't need them—he was fourth in Oberon's line and that was priceless.

Now it was all becoming clear. Oberon needed this job done without perking any unfriendly ears. If it was common knowledge that she was gone, it would cause all kinds of political problems for him. If somebody was intent on causing him grief, this was a great way to do it. No conflict, no blood and no proof.

"Okay, my 'assistance' requires payment. My normal fee is twenty bucks a day plus expenses. But for old time's sake, I'll charge you an even one hundred. Payment in full when I find the princess."

He nodded and started to rise from the chair, eager to return home.

"Not so fast. We ain't done negotiating yet."

He glared at me but dropped back into the seat.

"I also get three answers from you when I rescue the broad."

His face contorted and he hissed through clenched teeth. Information is power to the Fair Folk, and nobody was privy to more secrets than this weasel.

"Three. No less, no more. Otherwise, you'd better start looking for that missing dame yourself, 'cause I sure ain't."

We both knew damned well I had him between a rock and a hard place.

"Done, Brendan Steele."

. . .

I entered the smoky haze inside Virgil's Path. A gnome tossed his losing poker hand on green felt and stumbled off while a swarm of pixies hovered over a Coca Cola with a dozen straws protruding from the bottle at another table. In the corner, a clutch of pale-skinned banshees cackled, enjoying their ladies' night out while a crestfallen guardian angel with drooping wings was taking sips of white wine, shaking his head and mumbling to himself. That happened a lot in Vegas.

Yeah, we were exiles. But like the expatriates in Paris, we could carve out an oasis of familiarity to congregate in. The place was neutral ground, where you could get drunk without looking over your shoulder for a flashing blade to the back. It was also the newest place to go for non-human company.

The hostess was a knockout with tight black curly hair in a fashionable bob and not much makeup except the vivid swatch of scarlet on her full lips. She was wearing a short little floral number accented with a string of pearls looped a couple of times around her slender neck and she had more curves than a Brooklyn Dodgers' no-hitter.

"Hiya. Welcome to Virgil's Path. Table for one?"

"No thanks, could I talk to your boss? Have some business to discuss with him."

"He's not around at the moment. I can see if the owner is available. Who should I say is asking?"

"I'm Brendan Steele. Just have a couple of questions for him."

"Sure. I'm Lily, by the way. Have a seat over there and I'll bring you a drink. What's your poison?"

Around here, that question was sometimes a literal one.

"I'll take a gin. Neat, please."

"Gin it is. Back in a flash." Lily moved with jaw-dropping grace and melted into the crowd without jostling a single elbow.

Within twenty seconds, a drink appeared on the table and Lily glided into the chair across from me.

"Okay, Mr Steele. What can I do for you?" She reached behind her ear and produced an expensive ivory cigarette holder.

"Like I said, I'd like to speak with somebody in charge here. Got some questions."

"Start talking. I'm the owner." A smirk pulled the corners of her sensuous lips. She glanced at the tip of her cigarette. A flash of orange-red made me blink, and grey-blue smoke uncoiled into the air.

"Sorry for the ruse. I get all kinds in here, asking for this, demanding that. Had to make sure you were on the up and up."

I almost smacked myself in the thick head. Some PI, huh? She was an infernal. And not a minor leaguer, either.

"Virgil's Path. I guess *Dante's* was already taken? Why not *Beatrice's*?" I asked.

She chuckled. "Doesn't have the same ring, does it? My first club was a little place serving fermented goat milk to shepherds, soldiers and slaves with a great view of the Tigris River. One thing

I've learned is that you gotta have a good name. There's power in names, you know."

Infernals were just what they sounded like. Denizens of Hell. They were immortal and spent most of that time figuring out how to screw the competition, leapfrog up the ranks and gather the most souls.

"How much do I owe you for the drink, Lily? Or should I just call you Lili—"

"Careful, Mr Steele. Remember there's power in names. Lily is fine. And the drink is on the house. It's not every day that I get to meet an exiled Prince of the Seelie Courts."

Now it was my turn to smile. "Nice try. Here's a buck for the drink. We're square."

"Can't blame a girl for trying. So, you said something about some questions?"

"Yesterday, a visitor was brought here in the dead of night. Would've had a few escorts with her. She's one of Titania's handmaidens and is betrothed to some pointy-eared lordling." I took a sip of the gin and was impressed. Top-shelf stuff.

Lily leaned in across the table. I'd be lying if I said my heart didn't beat just a bit faster.

"I appreciate your candour, Mr Steele. So I'll save you some trouble by replying in kind. I'm not playing host to kidnappers. I run a classy joint, not some seedy riverfront warehouse. I'm not involved in your folks' politics. Your kind have no soul, thus no profit for me." Her voice was single malt whisky—smooth, smoky, and it sent shivers down my spine.

"The problem is, I don't believe you. You are a demo—"

"I swear upon my name that I have no knowledge of this plot." An angry wisp of smoke escaped the side of her mouth. "But I'd be willing to share what I do know." The spark in her eye was back and she was ready to deal.

"For what? I don't have two nickels to rub together and like you said, no soul to trade."

"How about the truth? I want to know what really happened the day you were banished from the Twilight Realm. I know you're oathbound to not speak of it, but I have ways to get around that. All I need is your okay. I promise my lips are sealed." She placed her index finger lightly against her luscious lips.

"Deal."

The effect was electrifying. Jumbled images from my past flashed before me. Battles, conversations, desires, secrets, fears and everything in between. All the tiny details accumulated over a lifetime were played like a high-speed newsreel. She found what she was looking for and paused. After an eternity of *déjà vu*, she was done.

And now she knew.

"Jeepers. So that's it, huh?" she asked.

"Yep. Not my fondest memory."

"So you didn't murder your father. Oberon and Tonguebinder knew, but still banished you? Why play the patsy?"

"If I didn't agree to his terms, Oberon would have had no choice but to declare war on the red cap clans. Somebody had to be the fall guy, otherwise it woulda undermined his authority. We're a tough lot, but against the combined might of the Summer Court? Not a chance. The cost of victory for the Seelie Court would be high. But in the end my people—my family—would fall."

"So if you didn't kill your old man, who did? Your brother?"

I shook my head. "Naw. He had nothing to do with it. He was campaigning in the Far Reaches, putting down a centaur rebellion. No way Brand was involved. Everybody knows atrocities and senseless bloodshed are the cost of war. The price of peace is lots higher. The Dawn Court will do what it needs to for stability. That includes cover-ups, double-crosses, executions and outright lies. Once my father was dead, why keep me around? Oberon received my brother's oath of fealty so his Highness could keep using red caps as shock troops—his rabid wolves in Mithril chains. He made the smart play and sent me here."

"But who murdered your father?"

"Dunno. Been trying to figure that for twenty years. Your turn."

Lily grinned and bit her lower lip pensively. "Fair enough. Last night I did receive some guests. They paid gold coin, in advance. Six of them, including your princess. But she isn't here against her will, I can promise you that. She fancies herself a singer. Her manager, some twisted little imp named Gristlepick, set up the deal. He's sitting at the corner table nearest the stage."

I glanced over. The imp looked like a diminutive, rich old guy, with fancy threads. I'm no expert at demonology, but one picks things up here and there. Lily has probably been harvesting souls for four thousand years; my guess is she does as she pleases as long as she doesn't ruffle any major powers. Guys like Gristlepick? They have to be more careful. One busted scheme and back to Hell you go. He had two human bodyguards with him at the table. I needed to have a private conversation with the demonling.

Lily was still reading my thoughts.

"I got some girls I can introduce the humans to. It'll cost you, though. A future favour?" She removed the swizzle stick from my drink and twirled it between her soft red lips. Her gaze never left mine and gleamed with a thousand delightful promises.

"Done," I stammered without a second thought. By the Balefires, she was good.

She smiled a predatory grin and pushed away from the table. "See you round, Brendan Steele. It's been a pleasure. Maybe I'll ring you sometime." She sauntered over to Gristlepick's table and bent low enough to display her abundant cleavage. After ten seconds, both humans left the table and followed her upstairs.

Yep. She was *beyond* good.

Before Gristlepick could object, I slid into a chair vacated by one of his human gorillas and smiled, dropping my glamour for him.

What he saw wasn't pretty. Corpse-white skin marred by red scars across muscular arms and thick, broken knuckles and narrow, slit-like nostrils. My grin was over-wide and needle-sharp. The battered trench coat became a suit of ring mail comprised of links of bone and other trophies from fallen foes, but the imp's eyes were fixated on my crimson cap—the red cap trademark. Gone were the sharp, crisp angles of my hat. Gristlepick saw the lumpy, sodden headgear which gave my clan its name, dripping with fresh blood.

"Let's chat. My name is Brendan and I think you might know something about a kidnapped princess."

I took a sip of his Tom Collins and watched his eyes narrow.

"I'm going to ask you some questions. You answer them. If I think you're lying, I'll remember. Not tonight, not tomorrow night, but sometime after, I'll pay you a visit. Late at night when you're alone." I set his glass back on the table. "For every lie I think you've told me, I'm gonna take a nibble, starting with your nose, which I gotta say reminds a lot of Jimmy Durante. After that, we work our way down. Did you steal the princess from the Summer Court?"

Gristlepick reached into his vest pocket, removed a silk handkerchief and wiped the lip of his glass before taking a drink. Tough little bastard.

"No, I did not. I was told to be at a certain place, at a certain time, and make certain arrangements. I met the dame, sweet talked her a little, and set things up. She's going on stage right now—her debut. As her manager, I have a professional obligation to critique her performance. So why don't you keep the empty threats silent while we both listen to this broad warble, okay?"

I raised an eyebrow. So much for the direct approach. The imp must have a serious patron to face me down.

The house lights dimmed and a blazing spotlight illuminated a spot on stage. The myriad conversations died down, the curtains rustled, and a figure appeared on stage. She was a real looker. Tall, at least six feet. A flow of crimson curls spilled down her shoulders and her pale skin reflected the light's glare. She was wearing a classy green cocktail dress, which highlighted her verdant eyes. Shapely, muscular arms protruded from the outfit and she clutched the standing microphone like it owed her money. She was a big girl, but she wore it well. The bassist in the jazz ensemble struck a mellow tune with his instrument and the other players joined in. It was 'And the Angels Sing' by Benny Goodman. Unfortunately, she was no Martha Tilton.

Her notes were all over the place, never quite finding the right scale. Her gravelly voice strained with every high only to fall short each time. It was a shame. She had the looks, the moves, and the passion. The only thing missing was the talent. She was oblivious to the pained expressions of her listeners, lost in her butchery of the song.

Gristlepick was smiling and nodding his head to the beat of the music.

Something was screwy here.

I rummaged around my pockets, fished out a bent Pall Mall and lit up the nail.

"Listen. She's not very good, is she?" I asked. I tapped the black head in my pocket.

"Nope. She ain't. She's horrible. Couldn't carry a tune if you strapped it over her back. She's got no clue as to how bad she really is. But as her manager, it's my job to keep her motivated. We've already got a tour set up. Pearl is going to be one busy lady. What she really wants is to get into movies. I told her this was the first step to bigger stardom."

"But won't you have a hard time booking her at clubs if . . . " I had to wait for Pearl to finish screeching a particularly shrill note before continuing, " . . . if she sounds like this?"

The imp laughed. "Not a problem. I already booked a couple of dozen joints. The owners don't care how good their singers are; they just want to sell booze and make a profit. Hell, don't you think she might drive some people to drink even more?"

She finished her first number and smiled to the crowd. "Thank you so much. Next I'd like to sing a song by a little lady you've all heard on the radio." She proceeded to massacre Judy Garland's latest hit, 'Somewhere Over the Rainbow'.

"So if you've already paid in advance, where's your profit? You've gotta be losing money every time she opens her mouth."

"Pearl has a very generous and wealthy benefactor. I just make the arrangements and pass on the cash. I don't know anything about a kidnapping. Pearl is having the time of her life, chasing down a lifelong dream." The little jerk was as smug as cat in cream.

The audience suffered through another three numbers from Pearl before she took a break. The house lights grew bright and she vanished behind the curtain. I'm sure she would've been shocked at the number of empty tables in the once-teeming establishment. The only patrons not scared away by her performance were a pack of goblins. I think they might've actually enjoyed it, but everybody knows goblins are a few cards short of a full deck.

• • •

Gristlepick escorted me backstage. "She'll tell you the score herself."

We stopped in front of a dressing room. A yellow star cut from construction paper was taped on it. Beautiful calligraphic script declared, "Pearl Mercedes".

"Mercedes? That the best you could come up with?"

He shrugged. "Wasn't my call. Her dream; her name." He rapped on the door.

"Come on in." The voice on the other side of the door sounded cheerful and carefree. "I'm decent."

I removed my hat and entered. The place was a wreck, with piles of abandoned clothing, old makeup containers and faded playbills strewn across the floor. Pearl was seated in front of a mirror brushing her hair. A cheap vase with a dozen wilting roses was on the on table in front of her, as well as a candy dish filled with brightly coloured sweets. She saw my reflection and smiled.

"My first fan. You enjoyed my performance?" She was radiant, caught up in the excitement of her debut.

"Ms Mercedes, I can honestly tell you that I've never heard anything like it before."

She clasped a hand to her chest and turned a bright crimson. "You just made my night. You gotta name?"

"Brendan Sharpshanks Steele, at your service." I did a low bow and clicked my heels together once.

"Oh! I've heard of you. For years it was all they talked about at the Summer Court. You were banished before I was sent to attend Her Majesty, but your story lives on, Sir Steele." She winked at me. "A whole lotta stories, if you catch my drift."

Gristlepick cleared his throat. "You were wonderful, darling. I've matters to attend, but shall see you shortly. Brava, my dear. Brava." He vanished into the hallway, closing the door behind him.

"What can I do for you, Sir Steele? I don't have much time before the second act."

Now or never, I figured.

"First off, just call me Brendan. Next, I gotta ask you a kinda funny question. Are you being kept here against your will?"

She looked puzzled for a moment and then guffawed. It sounded a lot like her singing—strangled snorts of air escaping a blacksmith's bellows.

"Whatever gave you that crazy idea? Titania's got plenty of other handmaidens to take care of her. I'm gonna be a star." She laughed and grabbed a fistful of candy from the dish and tossed it into her mouth. From all the cracking and crunching, they must have been industrial strength butterscotches.

I looked at the colourful assortment in the dish and did a double take. Those weren't Werthers. They were rocks. A dazzling array of different sizes, shapes and . . . flavours? No time for social niceties. I willed my vision to pierce her glamour.

Her true form loomed over me, at least seven feet tall. Her alabaster skin was literally stone, pale white marble with mottled veins of granite. Braids of shiny copper hair spilled down her broad shoulders and twin emeralds stared back at me, set above a wide mouth and chisel-like teeth. Her hands were like manhole covers. Oh, Puck. I was right.

She was a troll.

Trolls were earth elementals and stonemasons without peer, capable of creating works of breathtaking beauty and skill. None could match their affinity for stone. Queen Mab of the Dusk Court had been the first to discover their darker talents. What wall could withstand an assault by soldiers capable of eating right through it? There was also the matter of their stone skin and terrible strength. Oberon's father had emptied the royal coffers thrice to buy their loyalty. They ate rocks and minerals, along with the occasional goat.

"Sir . . . Brendan! I'm aghast at your manners! How dare you . . ."

My brain was struggling to keep up with all the moving parts this case had grown and the last thing I needed was to calm down a walking, talking, and ticked-off flying buttress.

"I don't have a lot of time left. The imp is sure to come barging in here with some backup."

She started to protest until I snapped at her.

"Stuff it, sister. Like I said, time is short. I don't know who's the bigger sucker. You, for taking an infernal at his word, or me for not getting more details from Oberon's Left Hand. Do you know that you've been kidnapped from the Twilight Realms?"

She opened her cavernous mouth, but I stopped her. "Nod or shake."

Pearl shook her head.

"Do you know that you're supposed to marry Prince Reginald in two months?"

Her eyes bulged out of her head and she shook her head. It sounded like two boulders rubbing against each other.

I took a deep breath. This could be very painful for her pride. And my health.

"You've been conned. I don't know by who, for sure, but I've got an idea. You're a great entertainer, but I gotta be honest. Your unique skills might be better appreciated in the Twilight Realms. You don't want to go to LA. For every Judy Garland, there's a thousand more waiting for the big break that never comes."

I felt, rather than heard, a low grumble in my direction. Either she was getting really heated or very hungry. I figured it was the former.

She cleared her throat. It sounded like a landslide.

"Brendan, are you saying I ain't star material?"

"I'm just saying you can't . . . "

The door burst open and Gristlepick barged in with five armed humans on his tail.

The imp had a triumphant look on his wrinkled face. "So sorry, my dear. I didn't recognise this criminal until just moments ago. I've done my best to keep your true identity secret, but your parents are quite influential. I was afraid you'd become a target, which is why I've hired bodyguards for you."

There were twenty-seven ways I could take out three of the gunmen. None to drop all five. Not a chance in Hell.

Time to gamble.

"Let me guess. You want me to lose the iron and empty my pockets?" I removed my pistol and tossed it to the ground. I spilled the contents of my pockets on the makeup table. Six dollars and sixty cents in change, the penknife, my Zippo and the obsidian raven.

Gristlepick grinned. "Boys, let's take Mr Steele on a tour. I hear they started pouring concrete for that new casino on Fremont Street. Three months ahead of schedule. Lucky for us, huh?"

Pearl was still struggling to take it all in. She stammered, "But Mr Gristlepick . . . Sir Steele . . . he's a knight of the King's Guard . . . "

"Was. He's nothing more than a kinslayer now. Don't worry. We've got a busy schedule ahead of us and as I've told you many times before you can't—"

I tapped the head of the onyx crow on the table and muttered a word to activate the magic: "Sing."

The infernal's recorded voice echoed in the small room as the trinket spoke word for word what it earlier heard.

"Nope. She ain't. She's horrible. Couldn't carry a tune if you strapped it over her back. She's got no clue as to how bad she really is. But as her manager, it's my job to keep her motivated. We've already got a tour set up. Pearl is going to be one busy lady. What she really wants is to get into movies. I told her this was the first step to bigger stardom . . . Not a problem. I already paid out to a couple of dozen joints. The owners don't care how good their singers are; they just want to sell booze and make a profit. Hell, don't you think that having her on stage might drive some people to drink even more? . . . Pearl has a very generous benefactor. Generous and very wealthy. I just make the arrangements and pass the cash."

Gristlepick turned pale and grimaced; his hoods looked confused. I waited while Pearl simply listened.

Balefires, I would've rather done this more gently, but my options had been limited. Sometimes the truth hurts worse than a rusty, twisted blade to the gut. But one usually recovers from the truth. Most of the time.

The troll princess bellowed an ancient war cry and ripped the mirror free from the table. She hurled the looking glass into the midst of the armed men. Two of the hapless humans were crushed against the concrete wall amidst the sharp crack of breaking bones and shattering glass. I grabbed the barrel of a tommy gun and yanked hard.

The thug was too stupid to let go of the stock and so I rewarded him with a knee to the bread-basket. He grabbed his midsection and bent over, sucking air and giving me a clear shot at the idiot behind him. I swung the submachine gun like a Louisville Slugger and cracked the guy across the face. Babe Ruth would have been proud. He spun to the ground, unconscious. I didn't forget about my gasping friend. I ploughed my knee into his face. He flew against the wall to fall atop his unconscious co-workers in a heap.

Pearl still had some hurt feelings to work through. The remaining thug was dangling three feet off the ground, held aloft by the lapels of his cheap suit. In his right hand, he clutched a dainty-looking ivory-handled .25 calibre semi-automatic pistol. He pointed the weapon at her and pulled the trigger three times. The reports were crisp and sharp in the confined space.

Each bullet sparked off her white marble skin without leaving a mark. She smashed her forehead into his face, flattening his nose and dislocating his jaw. He was lucky to still be breathing when he hit the floor.

Gristlepick was cowering in a corner when the enraged troll grabbed him by the throat and slammed him against the wall to get his undivided attention.

"Who is my 'benefactor', you little worm? Tell me now."

"I swear by all that's unholy, I don't know. I've tried to be a mentor, a teacher, dare I say, a friend to you—"

Pearl roared an unladylike curse and smashed her left fist into the wall, creating an imp-sized depression in the concrete.

He sang like a canary.

"It was the King's nephew, Reginald. Paid a fortune to keep you hidden until things died down. Said he'd rather be banished than marry a rock-eater. If things didn't work out, he'd pay extra for you to vanish. It was all his plan, I swear upon my name. You gotta believe me. Please don't squash me."

I put a hand on her shoulder. "Let him go."

Pearl dropped him and Gristlejaw fell to the ground in a gibbering jumble. He vanished into the twisting corridors.

She was still as a statue. Which is natural when you're a troll. But statues don't have tears rolling down their cheeks, leaving runny smudges of dark mascara in their wake.

I'd rather face a squad of angry ogres than a single weepy-eyed broad. Especially if she could benchpress a tractor.

She turned to face me and the waterworks burst. "What am I gonna do now, Brendan? All my dreams. Gone like faerie gold at sunrise."

"Look, the way I see it, you have two options. One, you stay here in the Maze. Find another manager to run things. Heck, you could probably still show up at the places Gristlepick booked for you. They're paid for. See what happens."

She smiled through the tears. "Yeah, but I hear I don't have the greatest singing voice." She brushed away a lava flow of pebbly mucus with a tissue.

"Option two. Tonguebender will be at my office tomorrow. If you want to go home, he'll give you a lift. If not, I'll tell him you left town. Want my opinion?"

She nodded.

"Reginald is a white elf. You're a troll. Two of the longest-lived folk in all of the realms. I can't think of better payback than a thousand years of marriage. Imagine what you could do to the poor bastard in that time?"

She laughed through her tears and I shuddered. I *almost* felt sorry for Reginald.

. . .

The next morning, Valdonicus Tonguebinder breezed into my office and hovered over my desk while I put the finishing touches on his bill.

I enjoyed making him wait. I circled the final figure with a black ballpoint pen, pulled the sheet free of the pad and handed it to him. His eyes danced over the figures before arriving at the final tally. Val reached into the vest pocket of his expensive suit and tossed the cash down on my desk. I leaned back in my chair and steepled my fingers under my chin, mimicking his favourite pose.

The subtle mockery of the gesture was not lost on him.

"And the princess?"

"Waiting for you in Los Angeles. She wanted to do some sightseeing before she goes back. I told her you'd send the royal coach to pick her up at the Biltmore around midnight on Saturday. She is royalty, after all."

A trip to the Maze for one person was taxing enough, but sending an enchanted stagecoach pulled by at team of nine jet black unicorns was exorbitant.

Tonguebinder clenched his teeth. "Wonderful. I can't wait to see her."

"Yeah. She can't wait to get hitched to Reginald. Won't stop talking about it. He's a very lucky guy."

"Of course. And did you unravel who the miscreant was behind this foul deed?"

"Nope. Never got around to it. Besides, I'm confident that the architect of this scam will suffer for quite some time to come."

His eyebrow rose at the veiled reference, but he let it slide.

I drummed the fingers of my right hand on the desk and stared into his shifty eyes. "We're almost done, your Lordship. There is still the matter of my questions to resolve."

"Very well. Ask your questions and I shall answer to the best of my ability."

"No riddles, free verse or double-talk allowed, right?"

"Just get on with it. I don't have all day."

"Were you directly or indirectly responsible for my father's death?"

The smile vanished and he was suddenly all business. I don't think he expected such a blunt query out of the gate. Truth is, I kind of surprised myself. He was oathbound to answer as honestly as possible and he seemed to realise that my questions might get very uncomfortable.

Good.

"No. To either charge. Next question."

"Was Oberon in any way responsible for my father's murder?"

"Don't be stupid. No. Last question."

I took out a bottle of gin and poured myself a glass. I offered Tonguebinder a tumbler, but he was firm in his refusal. I downed my drink in a single gulp.

"What do you know of my father's murder?"

He stared at his feet for a moment before answering. I can only imagine how many pacts, promises, vows and secrets he was on the verge of breaking to answer my final question.

"Very well. Your father was slain by a human. For what reason, we've never been able to determine. Vincent Wylde is what he called himself and his last known address was in San Francisco. Will that be all, Brendan?"

I let the gin warm my belly before answering the regal messenger boy. "That's it. Now get the hell out of my office. I've got real work to do."

BE GOOD, SWEET MAID

Penelope Love

Be good, sweet maid, and let who will be clever;
Do noble things, not dream them, all day long:
And so make life, death, and that vast for-ever
One grand, sweet song.
　　　　　　　—From 'A Farewell' by Charles Kingsley

George Dooley was out of breath. It was a one-storey climb to my office but it was straight up. I got the room cheap on account of the stairs, and that it was above a butcher's shop.

"Come in," I called, and gestured for him to sit. There wasn't a lot of choice in chairs. I only had two and I was sitting in one of them. The office was stinking hot. The window was open to catch a breath of breeze from the dusty street.

Dooley was a fat, worried-looking, balding man in his mid-thirties. He was wearing a beautifully pressed grey suit. A teetotaller pin shone on his lapel. He took a folded handkerchief from his pocket and wiped the sweat from his forehead.

I rattled away on my typewriter as I took him in. It was all for show. I called myself a typist, but truth was I hadn't had a job for a week. The typewriter was an Underwood 5, "black metal, front striking movement, cylindrical paper carriage, circular arrangement of type bars striking at common centre, and individual types on rod". That's a quote from the catalogue.

Heavy black beast of a thing. That's my opinion.

Dooley was freshly shaved with a double chin and tired, grey eyes behind black-framed spectacles. His wedding ring was a thick gold band. He looked like a solid, prosperous citizen. He took off his hat and held it in his lap, with a *Truth* newspaper tucked underneath. The date on the newspaper was 6 February, 1922.

I finished my typing with a racketing return carriage ring. "Betting man?" I asked.

He looked startled.

"The *Truth* is a Sunday paper. It's two day's out. Only reason you'd carry that around during the week is the racing news."

He looked relieved that I didn't actually have psychic powers. "I work as a clerk in a bookmaking firm," he said. Posh accent, too.

"Robbie sent you," I guessed.

"I beg your pardon?"

"Mr Harrison," I clarified.

"Correct." He looked pleased.

Robbie worked for a big professional firm on Spencer Street. They specialised in insurance and shipping fraud. He sometimes sent me jobs too small for them.

I hauled open the desk drawer, found my cigarettes, lit one on the penny gas ring in the wall, then perched on the window sill. Along with the smoke, I inhaled the smell of hot, rotten, bloody sawdust straight up from the butcher's shop.

Dooley looked gratifyingly shocked. I was wearing my most modern outfit, a shapeless grey dress with no waist, the skirt cut almost to the knee. I had my black hair cut in that new shingle style, full around the face, shaped short and close to the head at the back. His eyes darted to the hat stand, saw the rusty red, bell shaped, cloche hat. I read *flapper* in his panic-stricken gaze.

"How can I help?" I asked.

"Mr Harrison explained that you were, er, female," he started, cautiously.

"That's nice," I followed his train of thought: *He didn't say you were fast.* "I'm perfectly capable," I said.

"He said you were married."

I flashed the ring.

That shred of respectability comforted him. He drew a deep breath. "I've been having this, er, dream," he said. "Over and over. For years. Since before the war. It's greatly worrying. The fact is, I, er . . . " He shot another look at me, screwed his eyes shut and blabbed it out. "I dream that I'm dead."

"You look pretty alive to me." He'd gone white. I didn't want him fainting on me; I'd have to share my medicinal whisky.

"I dream that I'm lying on a bed, a brass bed frame with a red, yellow and green check quilt. I'm in a horrible room," he shuddered and his mouth screwed with disgust. "It's a cheap rooming house. I'm on my back, with my head turned. I can't move. All I can see is the mantelpiece. It has a, ugh, a carved emu egg and one of those nodding china dogs, brown and white." Horror infused his tone. "I can see a calendar on the wall. One of those agricultural machinery ones you get at the Show. All the dates are crossed off until the date, Friday, February 10, 1922." He shuddered. "And that's when I realise why I can't move. I'm dead. Then I wake up."

"I don't like nodding dogs and the emu eggs, either," I said. They were a sure sign of defeat. They meant you were trapped in a cheap room paying rent by the week, and you were never going to claw your way back up. I had a room like that myself. "You realise that's not a lot of help. We've got two days. You left it a bit late."

"I started seeking help some time ago. I've been to see all the, er, professional detectives. None of them would help. I believe they thought I was, er, not perfectly sensible."

"They thought you were as mad as a cut snake."

He took that on the chin. Didn't get flustered or angry. Under the flab, Dooley had backbone. "You're my last hope," he said, quietly. He took out his handkerchief and pressed it to his forehead again. "Please don't tell me to see a doctor. I assure you, I've seen a specialist already. He tells me my nerves are perfectly in order."

I stood there looking at him through my cigarette smoke; a fat, middle aged, middle class gent scared by a bad dream. But you know, I liked him. "Do you know how you died?" I asked.

"I'm afraid not. I can't move," he explained.

"Do you have any enemies?" He shook his head, after just a trace of hesitation. "We're not going to get anywhere if you not honest with me," I said.

He stiffened. "I know no one who would want to, er, kill me," he said.

"Have you told your wife?"

He looked shocked. "How did you—"

"Wedding ring."

"No. I haven't told her, and I'm not going to," he said, firmly. "I couldn't bear it if she thought—" His resolve wobbled. So did his chins.

I came back to sit at the desk, the black bulk of the Underwood looming between us. "Mr Dooley, I really think you should tell your wife."

"Absolutely not," he said.

"All right. My rates are a pound a day."

"I'll give you two pounds in advance," he said. He opened his wallet and pulled out two crisp notes. I hadn't seen one of those in years. "I'll give you two more on February 11."

He really was mad as a cut snake.

"I'll dig around and see what I can find. I'll meet you again tomorrow. Where do you work?"

He named a well-known firm of bookmakers. "But you're not going to meet me there," he said.

"Naw," I agreed. He would want his employer to know about this even less than his wife. "Give me your home address." He started to protest, but I shot him my best exasperated look. "I'll keep an eye on you on the quiet. Meet me here tomorrow evening."

He let himself out, while I perched on the windowsill and engaged in some serious thought.

Was Dooley having me on? I thought not. The look on his face reminded me of an old Irish bloke I knew up on the Murray. His son had drowned and that old bloke had held a ghost supper. He'd laid out a meal, knife, fork and plate and all, and left the door open so the ghost could come in. It was his way of saying goodbye, good luck and sorry.

• • •

'Be good, sweet maid, and let who will be clever': That was what my mother used to say when my sister or I were too smart with

her. I was brought up in Wodonga, a country town on the border, all dust and flies; the only choice was between getting married or being a shop girl. I got angry with my mother when she said *'Be good sweet maid'*, once too often. I went to the town library, and found out that the line came from a poem by Charles Kingsley. I asked her why she never went on to the next line: *'Do noble things, not dream them, all day long'*.

It was because she bloody couldn't. She'd heard only the first line from her mother and had passed it dutifully down, along with *'Mother knows best'*, and *'They that ask no questions are told no lies'*. I soon found out why girls shouldn't be clever. I got a reputation for being fast, and left Wodonga. Life was better in Melbourne. I got a job at the Cadbury chocolate factory, £3 a week, and that was where I met Wal. Wallace Wallis. Wal's dad had had a sense of humour.

Wal was an idealist, a unionist, a tub-thumping Marxist. He'd never lasted in any job. He always got fired for asserting someone's rights. But he was a hard worker and he always got hired again someplace else. We got married at the registry office in June, 1914. We had two rooms to ourselves up the back of Smith Street in Fitzroy. Wal's looks were nothing to write home about but he was grand. He was a long, lanky bloke; his legs never fit anywhere. He used to come back from work, step through the door, throw his arms out wide and give a huge yawn, then slump in his favourite chair. I'd know that yawn anywhere and the scrape of that chair. It was his signature tune.

He'd been dead against the war, was Wal. Capitalist exploitation of the workers, he'd reckoned. So I thought I was safe. Then when all his mates joined up, he did too. I could have killed him. He wanted to go overseas, he'd said. He'd never been; couldn't afford it. Might never get another chance, he'd argued. His voice had been filled with all his old enthusiasm when he talked about Paris and Rome and Cairo. I blamed his mates. They filled his heads with talk of pyramids and castles— and girls, I suppose.

I saw Wal off at the Spencer Street train station, March 1915. He was in uniform, happy as a lark amid his mates, waving from the Sydney train until it puffed out of sight.

• • •

I went down to the butcher, my landlord, to use his telephone, breathing shallow against the stink of sawdust and blood. Flies buzzed around my head.

"G'day, Robbie. What the hell have you got me in for?"

"Dooley came to you, did he?" Robbie sounded pleased. I could see his thickset form hunched over the candlestick phone, with two days' worth of stubble and a suit gone baggy at the knees, stubbing out his cigarette then lighting another. His blue eyes would be squinting against the smoke under sharp brows. "Don't worry Jane; he's harmless. I asked around. It's money in the bank."

"Then why didn't you take him on?"

"I've got my reputation to consider," Robbie said, smugly.

"And I don't—you've got bloody cheek." I hung up.

I slapped on the old cloche hat, and legged it down to Dooley's bookmakers. It was a prosperous shop on Gertrude Street: two-storey brick with a plate-glass front under a corrugated iron veranda. Men were standing around outside smoking and waiting, others crowding inside to punt. I didn't enter. I mooched around and asked a few questions. It was a nice walk, if you liked flies. I soon found out what I wanted.

The bookmaker's was one of a chain owned by Mr John Wren. Wren lived in Collingwood opposite Archbishop Mannix, a millionaire who ran pony clubs and theatres, newspapers, trots and boxing. Everyone said his funds kept the Labor party going. Everyone knew he made his money in illegal gambling—the totes. He wasn't a man to cross.

I checked on Dooley again. I could see him through the plate glass, industriously at work with sleeves rolled up and wearing a green eye-shade. I decided he was safe as long as he stayed inside. Then, despite my sincere promise to the contrary, I headed over to Dooley's house to talk to his wife.

• • •

Wal was listed as missing at Gallipoli in August 1915. Missing always means dead, people said. But they didn't know my Wal. I figured he was alive and well somewhere. I kept the two rooms in Smith Street, even when money got tight. Wal would come there, first thing, as soon as he returned. He wouldn't know where else to look for me. I kept losing jobs because I was at Spencer Street station every day at 4.15, when the Sydney troop train came in. I had to keep looking for him.

I had been standing at the railings when Robbie jumped out of the train on crutches, a cigarette dangling from his lips. He limped over, looking at me with sharp blue eyes under black brows. "Gotta light?"

I gave him one. He grinned. "These crutches are great for pulling sheilas," he confided. "They think I got wounded doing something heroic, but I got drunk during the voyage home and fell down the stairs."

We got to talking. He didn't have anywhere to go, so I let him stay the night.

...

Dooley lived in a brand new Californian bungalow in Coburg. I had to catch a tram to get there. The enclosed rear section was stifling, so I sat upfront in the dummy where the driver stood with his clamp.

A high, cypress hedge guarded a neatly trimmed lawn. The house had a roughcast yellow front, brick veranda pillars, a terracotta tile roof, and leadlight in the front door and windows. A glazed ceramic plaque by the door proclaimed its name, *Thistledome*. I didn't see how Dooley could afford such a posh place.

The door was opened by a little fluffy rabbit of a woman, with long brown hair in a bun, slippers and a calf-length floral dress. She had washed-out brown eyes, a pink tipped nose and a receding chin.

"Mrs Dooley? I'm here about your husband," I said.

Her soft face lengthened. "Is he in trouble?" she asked at once.

I stepped inside, then smiled. "Funny you should ask."

We sat down at the kitchen table with a cup of tea and slice of cake from Herbert Adams. The kitchen was so well polished I could see myself in every surface. On the mantel above the stove was a family photograph. Little James and Ethel were proudly introduced to me in miniature: ten and seven.

I found my task easier than expected. Mrs Dooley already knew about her husband's little secret. "He had rheumatic fever before the war," she explained. "I nursed him through it. I know he looks well, but his heart is weak. While he was sick, he kept babbling about his dream, and *that* room." Middle class distaste filled her voice, and steel flashed in her soft brown eyes. For a moment, she changed from rabbit to piranha. Mrs Dooley ran this home, and there was no way she would ever find herself in such a room. But she refused to tax him. "He is the man of the house. It's not my place to question him or worry him."

I could make no headway against her resolve, so I explained my plan. I'd keep an eye on him through the next few days, then we'd find somewhere public to spend the night of the ninth, probably sit tight in my office with the door open to the street. I'd look after him, I said.

She eyed me carefully and pursed her lips, then nodded. She was smart enough to see her old man wasn't my type. "Just make sure there's no scandal."

"Ta for the tea, Mrs Dooley," I said, rising and grabbing my hat.

• • •

Mrs Dooley had given me food for thought all right, sitting in the dummy on the way home. I felt uncomfortable whenever I remembered the steely glint in her eyes. Rat poison in the tea would see our Dooley out of this world, especially with a weak heart.

I stopped in a doorway opposite the bookmaker's. It was knock-off time. The younger clerks bolted out the door to drink themselves blind in the six o'clock swill before the pub closed, but Dooley took a slower pace. He locked up his desk, took off his eye-shade, unrolled his shirt sleeves, put on his coat and hat, and said his good-nights, before strolling out into the hot summer evening. He headed for the tram stop. I followed him along the other side of the street, glancing in car rear-view mirrors and reflections of shop windows, keeping a watch out.

The screech of tyres and bang of an exhaust made me jump. A mustard-coloured Ford touring car with a buggy-top shot past Dooley, then mounted the kerb in front of him blocking him off. One of the three men in the Ford jumped out; a flash-looking, dapper cove with deep-set eyes and a blinding waistcoat. He hauled Dooley off down a side street.

I recognised him. He was Mr Joseph Taylor, otherwise known as Squizzy, self-styled king of the Melbourne underworld. He made his money through sly grog trading and blackmail. I was willing to bet the other two were Richard Buckley and Angus Murray, a couple of Squizzy's best Bourke Street Rats. Murray and Buckley were thugs for hire, specialising in standover and protection rackets.

I darted across the road and jumped on the running board of the Ford. Buckley was an overweight ex-boxer, while Murray was a little, rat-like man. "Well, there I was thinking I saw Clark Gable and Harold Lloyd, and it's only you two blokes," I said, and shot a glance down the side street.

It was a dirty little dead end. Squizzy leaned against the wall, holding forth. Dooley had his wallet out. I saw a pound note.

Murray glowered at me but Buckley guffawed. "Off you go love, we're working," Buckley said.

I'd seen enough. I jumped off, scarpered round the corner and kept an eye out. A few minutes later Squizzy sauntered back to the Ford, hands in his pockets. It roared off. Then Dooley crept out of the side street. As he walked, slowly his shoulders firmed and his stride lengthened. By the time he reached the tram stop, he was once again a prosperous middle class citizen at peace with the world.

I let him go home alone.

I went back to my two rooms. It was baking, so I opened the kitchen window, which every fly in Smith Street took as an invitation. I stepped into the bedroom. It could have been my room in Dooley's description. It could have been any cheap room. I had a chequered quilt on the bed, just like he said. The mantelpiece held a brown and white china dog with a coil spring in its neck, and an emu egg with a kangaroo carved on it. The only thing missing was a calendar, although there was a nail over the sink for one. I didn't have one. I grew up in Wodonga. The last thing I wanted to look at was another tractor.

I folded the quilt up and put it away. I wouldn't need it tonight, anyway.

I sat on the bed, smoking and looking at the mantelpiece. I hated that emu egg and nodding dog. I'd wanted to smash them before, but they belonged to my landlady. They came with the room and if I broke them, I'd have to pay for them. With two pounds in my purse I felt bold. I threw the emu egg into the grate, then the china dog. They smashed to pieces with a satisfying crash.

Then I lay down on the bed, fully dressed in the sweltering heat, staring up at the ceiling. This wouldn't do. I went downstairs and I called Robbie again.

"I got rid of that emu egg and the nodding dog I had on my mantel," I said.

"Stout work," Robbie approved.

"Did you look into Dooley's story at all?" I asked.

"Naw."

"He works for Wren and he's making too much money, I reckon. Wren won't be happy if he finds out. Plus, Squizzy's putting the squeeze on him."

"You should be working for us."

"You couldn't keep up. Do you know if Dooley's wife's taken out any insurance?"

I heard him scratching on a pad. "I can find out."

"Your blood's worth bottling," I said, and hung up.

. . .

Robbie and I were good for a while. He asked me to marry him, but I was still waiting for Wal. We drifted apart. Still, Robbie had a kind heart. When I told him I was pregnant, he gave me money and an address for the abortion.

I used Robbie's money to buy the Underwood. I could charge ten pence a page, say £5 a week. That meant I could pay my way. I was my own boss. I could meet the 4.15 every day.

Besides, it was Robbie who put me onto my first job. He came around one day and told me where he'd met one of Wal's old mates. My, didn't that bloke run a mile when he saw me.

He didn't want to say what he knew about Wal, so I got him drunk. He thought he was in luck, but I got through the groping part. I got him so drunk that he told me all he knew before he passed out. Robbie was impressed when I told him what I'd done. That's when the jobs started coming in.

Turns out Wal got through the Gallipoli landing and did all right until the Lone Pine assault. The Turks were throwing bombs into the trenches. The last his mates saw of Wal, he was chucking the bombs straight back out.

I couldn't bear to think of Wal dying such a stupid death. He'd probably done a bolt, I told myself. Made his way to Egypt and seen those bloody pyramids he was always banging on about.

Gone off all over the world and forgotten his poor old wife. But he'd be back, I was certain. One day, I'd hear the door swing open and his signature tune; the scrape of the chair and that huge yawn.

Oh and the baby; I went back to Wodonga for that. My sister had done well for herself, married the local storekeeper. She could have read me a lecture. *Be good, sweet maid.* But she was beaut. She took my son on as her own. Aunty Jane, I am. As soon as I was better I headed back to Melbourne.

...

I kept an eye on Dooley all that Thursday. It was hot, thirsty work. By mid-afternoon, when the heat hit its peak, he was still hard at it in the shop. I judged he was right for a bit. I went into the local movie theatre. It was dark and cool. I took in a newsreel and Constance Talmande in *The Virtuous Vamp*. If only life was like that. I followed Dooley safely all the way home.

I waited for Dooley that evening in my office, sitting on my desk with the door open. I could hear him coming up the stairs, slower and slower. He stopped at the top to perspire.

I gestured him curtly to a chair. "You didn't tell me you were cheating Wren, or that Squizzy has the squeeze on you. Either of those could get you killed," I said.

He tried to bluff it out then collapsed. He was a trusted man at Wren's. The trust had done him in. It had started off with a pound borrowed just after little James was born. The doctor's bills had piled up when Doris was ill. He'd meant to replace the money, but no one had noticed. The con built up, little by little. Now he was too deep in to stop, taking three pounds a week. Squizzy had found him out.

It was the teetotaller angle. Dooley never touched a drop. Taylor and Buckley had recognised him in the street as one of Wren's men. They hated Wren's guts, though I doubt Wren even took notice of them. Wren was the one thing standing between Taylor and his boasts of being the underworld king. Wren would always be bigger than him. They dragged Dooley into a pub at the height of the six o'clock swill and poured beer down him. He couldn't hold the liquor; he'd blabbed. Taylor had been putting the squeeze on him ever since.

He was a pathetic sight by the time he got this off his chest: a blubbering, sweating mess sagging in his chair. His stomach was growling like a good 'un.

"Have you even eaten anything?" I asked.

He shook his woeful head. "My wife was that upset that I couldn't touch my tea." The posh accent was slipping. He must be distressed.

"Look, I'll go down and get you something. No point in being scared and starving. I'll lock the door while I'm out. Don't let anyone in," I instructed, then nicked down the street for some fish and chips.

• • •

When I came back, the door was open and the office was empty. The room was the same as before. There was no sign of a struggle. Dooley had gone, that's all.

Had this all been a trick? Had he got cold feet?

I looked for him all night.

I even went to *Thistledome* and peeped in. I saw Mrs Dooley in there, alone. She was hunched over the kitchen table, clutching a lace hankie, all pink nose and receding chin.

I went home at dawn. Dooley was lying dead on my bed, his eyes fixed on the mantel. There wasn't a mark on him.

The quilt was back on the bed, and a nodding dog and an emu egg stood on the mantelpiece. There was a calendar on the nail on the wall above the sink, with a picture of a tractor and the dates crossed out until today's; Friday, February 10.

I let out a shriek as soon as I clapped eyes on Dooley. The neighbours came crowding in, then the police. The police were hard-faced men with disbelieving eyes. They made me tell my story several times. I claimed I never met Dooley in my life. They wanted a character reference, so I gave them Robbie, hoping he had the sense to back up my story. I knew Mrs Dooley wouldn't squeal. It was too unsavoury.

The police soon worked out I hadn't been home all night. They decided that Dooley must have been visiting the house and fallen ill, then stumbled into the first room he came to. I must have left my door unlocked, silly girl.

Dooley's attempts to evade his death had just led to it, but it wasn't fate. Someone had arranged the new knick-knacks.

I took the ornaments and the quilt down to the pawn shop and got two pounds for them. Then I went back to my office. I sat down at the desk, but didn't do anything. Just stared ahead. The smell of blood was in the air. After a while, I went downstairs and rang Robbie.

"All sweet?" I asked.

"You never met the man in your life. Neither did I," he confirmed.

"Good bloke."

There was a pause. "Mrs Dooley didn't take out any life insurance," he said. "Dooley didn't have any."

Dooley dead and no insurance meant an end to Mrs Dooley's sweet life in the suburbs. "So he didn't really believe he was going to die," I said, slowly.

"Or he figured he'd be tempting fate."

"Ta for finding out."

"No worries."

. . .

I returned to my office after dark, a bundle under my arm. I left the street door and the office door open. I moved the Underwood to the floor and laid the desk with a knife, fork and plate. I set a chair before it. Then I lit the penny gas ring and put a frypan on it. I cooked eggs and steak then dished it out onto the plate and sat down opposite.

I heard a confident step on the stair, the steady, seasoned climb of someone who'd tackled them many times before. Robbie came in. His eyes lit up under the angle of his brows. "I wasn't expecting tea," he said, rubbing his hands.

"It's a ghost supper for Dooley," I said.

"I heard a ghost supper summoned the man you're going to marry," he said, hopefully.

"I heard about them from an old Irish bloke up on the Murray, his way of saying goodbye, good luck and sorry."

"Too bad for the dead; they can't enjoy it." He sat down and started to eat.

"You killed Dooley," I said.

Robbie raised his brows at me, but didn't stop chewing.

"Spit it out."

He sighed. "How did you work it out?"

"You sent Dooley to me. So you were the only one Dooley would trust enough to open the door. Besides, you knew where I lived." It was simple.

Mrs Dooley might be tougher than her old man, but she wouldn't do anything that would threaten her home or the future of little John and Edith; two sprats who knew exactly who their mum was. Old Wren would tongue lash you all right, cruel and cold, make you pay back every pence plus interest, pay back until you died, but he wasn't the murdering type. And Squizzy wouldn't kill Dooley while he was scoring a pound a week, while receiving the satisfaction of getting Wren's goat on the sly.

So it had to have been Robbie.

"All right, all right. Good thing you told me you smashed the ornaments, so I brought some over from my place." He caught my eye. "Jane, it was an accident. I was only going to give him a fright. I didn't know he'd croak like that. Fair gave me a turn, I tell you, when he went blue and keeled over."

"He had a weak heart," I said.

Robby shrugged. "Nobody told me."

"You told Wren."

"You've got to keep in good with Wren if you want to work in this town," Robbie said. "He told me to bring Dooley round, but give him a scare first."

"I told his wife I'd look after him," I said. *Do noble things, not dream them, all day long.* I didn't know how much I'd taken that phrase so much to heart.

Robbie cleaned his plate, scraped the chair back with a satisfied sigh, put a cigarette in his mouth then lit a match. "Look, I'm sorry, all right? I told you, it was an accident."

I could sure pick them. I thought Wal had ideals, but he only ever believed in something while he was saying it. He'd do anything his mates said. Robbie was smarter than Wal, but he was hollow. I looked at him sitting there, putting the match to his cigarette. He still hadn't a clue. Some things you need to do otherwise you're not living life; you're just drifting through.

I dropped four pound notes on the empty plate, the two that Dooley had given me and the two from the pawn shop. Then I set fire to them. They burned, brief and quick, flaring into curlicues of blackened, flame-edged paper.

Robbie eyed me. "Come on Jane, I said I'm sorry," he urged me. "You know I'd marry you like that. You can get our nipper back. Why don't we try?" He looked at my face and shook out his match. "Oh, I forgot; the late, lamented Wal," he said, savagely.

"He's not dead!" I shouted.

Robbie sprang to his feet, the chair hurled back to the floor. He still didn't understand. "Jane, I'm asking you to marry me."

"It'd be bigamy."

"Don't be a fool. Wal's dead. He died in the war."

I mashed the burned paper into ash.

"You've really got no heart, have you?" Now he was angry.

"If I ever did, it broke a while back."

His anger died as quickly as it had flared. He rubbed his face. "To hell with it," he said quietly.

It was a hot night, but it went cold suddenly. We both heard a step on the stair.

"Who's that?" Robbie said, irritated.

It was someone with long legs. They took the stairs two at a time. The floorboards creaked, right up to the door. The door was wide open.

There was no-one there.

The room had been stifling from the day's heat. Now it was freezing. Goosebumps rose on my arms.

"Is this a trick?" Robbie asked uncertainly.

There was a sound I'd know anywhere: a long drawn out stretch, a yawn, a sigh. My mouth went dry. "It's Wal," I said.

The footsteps creaked across the floor. The cold intensified. Robbie bolted around the noise and out the door. I heard him running down the stairs.

The footsteps stopped at the chair Robbie had thrown over. The chair hauled itself to its feet, then something sat and swung back. Long legs stretched out with a scrape.

Tears started in my eyes. "You took your time."

There was no answer. My breath smoked in the chill air.

"I didn't mean that," I said hopelessly. "Half way round the world. It'd take a bit."

The chair fell over again, clattered to the floor. Heat flooded back into the room.

Wal was gone.

He'd never stuck around long.

Tears ran down my cheeks. I'd been a fool, like Robbie said.

I picked up the Underwood. It weighed a ton. I staggered down the stairs with it. It was late by then. I caught the last tram to Coburg. The tears had dried by the time I reached *Thistledome*.

There was a light on in the kitchen. I knocked on the window. Mrs Dooley opened the door. I didn't think she'd invite me in for tea and cake this time, so I shouldered my way in. I dropped the Underwood on the kitchen table with a gasp of relief.

She confronted me, her tiny fists clenched. "What are you doing here?" Her nose was raw, her hair a mess. Her red-rimmed eyes blazed and her receding chin clenched. I never saw someone look so much like a fluffy piranha in all my life.

"Brought you this," I said.

She stared uncomprehending at the typewriter.

"You can charge ten pence a page, say £5 a week," I explained. I couldn't see her being content with my small pay. I met her steely eyes. I could see her in ten years, the boss of a typing bureau terrifying the girls.

She opened her mouth to speak; closed it again.

I didn't want to be around when she recovered her tongue. I didn't want to lug that black beast all the way back again. "I'll let myself out."

The last tram had gone, so I set out to walk until light came.

WALKING THE DEAD BEAT

Robert Hood

"What's as big as a tour bus, dead, and has a talent for urban re-development?"

Nick Grinder sucked breath through the teabag he had in his mouth. Sucking old teabags helped him think. It was a bad habit, sure, but at least it was *his* bad habit. With the phone cradled precariously on his bony shoulder and both hands hovering over the keys of his typewriter, he spat the soggy satchel back into his empty mug.

"I don't have time for your shit, Jen," he growled.

"Come on, Nick. You've always got time for my shit. What's as big as—?"

"I don't friggin' know!"

"Well, neither do I," she propelled her voice through the phone with all the vim of a veteran smartass. "But I'm looking at one right now."

"What the hell are you talking about?"

"I'm in Zuccotown. It's a low-rent border settlement. Named after—"

"I know what it is and who it's named after. But why are you there?"

She chuckled. "Told you. I'm taking snaps of a big bad monster. Rampaging."

"Oh yeah?" *Might be a story in it, I suppose*, Grinder speculated. Chaney City hadn't had a Big Monster Rampage for a while.

"I thought you might be interested," Jen remarked in a conspiratorial manner.

Even as her words drifted into silence, Grinder felt his journalistic barometer beginning to fall. *Seen one oversized thingamajig going berserk, seen 'em all.* "Reptile, I suppose?"

"Ape."

"That was my second guess. Got a name?"

"They've all got names. Dunno what it is though. That's your job. You're the hotshot reporter. You really should come look for yourself, Nick."

Grinder scanned his desk, taking in the half-empty burger wrappers and scrawled notes detailing Governor Alicia Barmer's alleged wrongdoings. Even from the inside, his eyes looked bloodshot. "I got better things to do. A monster causing trouble ain't high on the agenda, Jen. No one cares. Bit ho-hum."

She laughed.

"What?" said Grinder, detecting mockery in the *City Clarion*'s precocious camera jockey.

"Really lost your nose for this game, haven't you, Nick?" she said. "Missed the key word in my initial gag—*dead*. This is no ho-hum BMR, you useless hack."

"Dead? So the Guard's dealt with it already. All the more reason not to—"

"Dead, but not departed."

"You mean it's *undead*? You're kiddin' me." This time Grinder sat up straight and paid attention. An undead Big Rampaging Monster was more like it. He'd never heard of there being a zombie BM in Chaney City before this—or anywhere else for that matter. "I'll be there in a flash," he added.

• • •

Zuccotown was looking a tad the worse for wear. Something with size 300 stompers had been dancing a fandango up and down the main street, and not too many of the tacky shopfront emporiums were still what you'd call pristine, even by bordertown standards. Most of the residents and their 'customers' (a euphemism for 'black-marketeers') had high-tailed it long ago, but a handful of them milled about being outraged. A few more were sprawled in the middle of the road, not so much outraged as squashed. Grinder had had to carefully navigate his car around the rubble and scattered corpses; he didn't want to upset anyone by journalistically disrespecting their dead.

Jen Thule sat cross-legged on a concertinaed VW Beetle, her camera in one hand and a corndog in the other. The murky green light that bathed the area made her short, ragged hair look like a tattered beanie. She waved the dog at Grinder as he climbed out of his car.

"'Bout time you got here," she said. "Show's more or less over."

"The roads are crap this far out," he muttered. He extracted a cigarette from his pocket and lit it.

Jen regaled him with her toothily mischievous grin. "And you drive like an old maid."

"Where's the Ape?"

She gestured northward.

Grinder squinted into the haze. He thought he could see something large hunched motionless well beyond the most distant line of roofs. "Can't be it, surely," he said. "That'd be in the No-Go Zone."

"And?"

"What about the Alarm?"

She shook her head and grinned enigmatically. "Let's go look," she said, leaping down from her possie. "Corndog?"

Grinder made a face. Jen tossed the half-eaten obscenity over her shoulder and scrambled into Grinder's car.

"Mind if I finish this?" Grinder said, holding up his smouldering fag.

"Yes," she replied.

He sighed and tossed it in the wake of the corndog.

The roads were scattered with people again now, all keen to get a glimpse of the Rampaging Ape—not because they'd have any inherent interest in it, of course, but because death and destruction was a universal aphrodisiac. The Anti-Rampage Squad hadn't turned up yet, which was interesting in itself. The only authority present was the local sheriff, who looked like a cadaver and probably was, and a few gormless deputies of vaguely lupine ancestry. Policing in the bordertowns was always dodgy. The drug-traffickers and other pirates made damn sure law enforcement was pretty much a meaningless sham out here.

The sheriff had waved Grinder down as they approached the cop's improvised roadblock some 500 yards or so from the Chaney City Territory border. Even from this distance, Grinder could see that the Ape had knocked down part of the tough steel fence. The huge simian was hunched unmoving on what was left of an abandoned barrack just beyond the UN Containment Line—a dark, ragged monstrosity silhouetted against the anaemic sky. The building hadn't been manned for years and from the looks of things, the barrier it had once protected had been rendered inactive long ago. Some sort of serious shit would be hitting the fan over *that* piece of bureaucratic ineptitude.

Grinder scrolled down his window. The sheriff's gaunt corpse-face leaned close. If he had eyeballs, they were sunk so deep into his skull Grinder couldn't spot them. He shivered. The man's undead aura was like psychic BO.

"Cain't go no further, son," the sheriff drawled. His breath carried a typically undead tang of mouldy neglect.

"We're from the *City Clarion*." Grinder flashed his Press card. "Nicholas Grinder. This is my photographer."

Jen scowled at the pronoun. She hated being considered an appendage. To her mind, she was as much a lead journalist as Grinder and any of the other hacks.

"Sorry, son," the sheriff rattled from deep in his throat. "You'll hafta get ya story from back aways. Ya won't be goin' no closer. Don't want to upset the Containment Field now, do we?"

"But the Alarm's not working," Grinder replied. "Hasn't reacted to the Ape."

Sheriff Deadguy wasn't interested in such subtle distinctions. He glowered darkly. "Park yaself over there." He pointed toward an area well off the road. "And don't be getting' in the way."

In the way of what? Grinder wondered. He bumped the car over to where the sheriff had indicated, turned off the engine and sat staring at the silent, motionless hulk of the Ape.

"How d'you know it's undead?" he asked Jen.

She handed him an old spyglass she often used to set up shots.

What he saw filled him with a deep and numinous horror. As often as he'd come across zombies and other walking corpses in Chaney City, he never quite got used to the hideously uncanny aura they exuded. Seeing the signs in a creature about twenty-five feet tall was daunting.

The Ape's eyes weren't buried as deeply as the sheriff's had been, but they'd sunk into its skull and had the glazed, lifeless sheen of undeath. Its face was gaunt and skeletal, without any of the leathery vigour of a normal ape's visage; it certainly looked dead. Just when Grinder thought that maybe that's exactly what it was—straight-on, no-argument deceased—its head ground to the right so that it gazed with those weird eyes out across Zuccotown toward the heart of Chaney City.

"Shit," Grinder muttered, impressed.

Now he could smell it, too: the aroma of a vast pile of dirty socks.

"Oh yeah," he said. "It's undead alright."

"Guard'll be here in a few minutes," Jen informed him.

This wasn't merely an assumption on her part. Jen Thule had the useful ability of being able to intuitively pick up on events that were about to happen—nothing that helped predict the stock market, but the sort of thing that led her to just the right spot at just the right time to get just the right pics. No doubt that was why she'd been the only inner-city news photographer present when the Ape first stepped into the Zuccotown limelight. There were a few more around now, but all the good action was over.

"Okay, maybe I can cajole someone into commenting on why the ARG were so tardy in getting here." Grinder glanced at the rear-view mirror in time to see the first anti-rampage tank appear around a bend in the road far in the distance. Jen leapt out of the car as though she'd been jabbed by a cattle prod, no doubt wanting a good shot of the Guard as the procession approached. Her lithe form scuttled over a hill of cinders and dying grass, then disappeared down a gully well away from both the Ape and the road. Odd. No newsworthy shots over that way, Grinder would've thought. Maybe she knew something.

Nevertheless Grinder headed in the opposite direction, toward where he imagined the tanks would stop. He wanted to grab a few comments from any random officer who might emerge from the metal monstrosities. News cars were more in evidence now, including a broadcast van sprouting a spiky crown of transmitter antennae.

Grinder fended off a few hacks who recognised him and assumed he was more in the loop than they were. He didn't know a thing, of course, although he kept up an enigmatic and knowing pretence. Meanwhile, he watched with some interest as an official ARG squad car broke from the incoming traffic and headed for the broadcast van. A uniformed officer and an armed soldier bullied their way inside. Minutes later, some very disgruntled anchors and technicians emerged from the van, unencumbered by camera gear, and wandered off, muttering amongst themselves. The armed soldier stationed himself outside the door. Clearly military censorship was the order of the day. *Why would that be?* Grinder wondered.

"You!" growled a rough-faced lizard-grunt, who had crept up on Grinder unnoticed. His blue tongue flicked from beneath the snout-guard of his specially designed combat helmet.

"Me?"

"Yeah, you. ID!"

Grinder produced his Press card and the lizard-grunt studied it for a moment. Once satisfied, the grunt snarled and hissed, "The commander wants to see all you hacks when this is over. Understood? All of ya!" His tail snapped like a whip as a form of punctuation.

"Understood."

The lizard-grunt flicked his tongue again and slithered off, heading for the next gaggle of pressmen. Grinder noticed that he and his buddies were confiscating camera equipment wherever they came across it.

A vast and imposing movement, caught in his peripheral vision, made Grinder glance back toward the Ape. The air surged with undeath as it rose from its crouch on the ruins of the old barracks and leapt—or stumbled, more like—not away from the advancing Guard, but toward it. Tank turrets turned in its direction. Much shouting and confusion ensued. Some of the word-jockies pissed off quickly as the Ape advanced; it occurred to Grinder that he should do likewise. But the view was pretty good from where he was and it kept him there, feigning bravery.

Muzzle flash and a percussive boom erupted from the lead gun-car. The Ape roared as a bloodless hole exploded in its chest. Shit! They weren't mucking around. No negotiation, no half-measures. Whatever happened to Article 31B of the Non-Human Containment Act, which required at least an initial attempt at non-lethal Rampage response? Grinder glanced around. Where the hell was Jen? He needed a picture of this!

More booms, more holes in the Ape's undead flesh. The beast was coming apart—but it wasn't stopping. It reached the line of Guard vehicles, pounded shoulder-down into a gun-car and sent the metal contraption flying. Guardsmen on foot scurried to surround the Ape, took position and fired repeatedly, further adding to the damage. Bullets as such couldn't kill what was already dead, but eventually sheer structural damage would slow it down.

As though in confirmation, a heavy artillery barrage took off its left arm. The Ape crashed sidewards, stumbling, desperate to regain its balance.

With a sort of detached concern, Grinder realised that the monkey was tumbling uncontrollably toward him. He leapt aside. Swirling air-currents caused by the proximity of its tumble slammed against him and tossed him from his feet. Dust and sound smothered him, then he was being dragged up and shoved away from the turmoil by rough cold hands. "Git!" a voice snarled. "Now!"

"What's going on?"

"Go, dickhead!"

Without meaning to, Grinder ran. The air behind him exploded into holocaust and once again he lost his footing. He slammed facedown into the dirt as heat scorched his back. The bastards had firebombed the Ape! Struggling with his own fear of imminent doom, Grinder twisted around to check out the state of play. The beast was a vast ball of blood-red fury, though the only writhing was that of the flames themselves. The monster was past such activity. As he watched, Grinder saw its face and torso turn to red-hot bone then collapse under its own weight. Black-green smoke spiralled skyward. In the midst of the bonfire, Grinder spied the twisted wreckage of his car.

"Someone's gonna pay for that," he muttered.

A pair of lizard-grunts dragged him up and away from the dying flames. They dumped him somewhere relatively safe then set off looking for anyone else who'd made it through. Grinder rubbed his throbbing forehead against a patch of cool grass. For how long he lay there, he wasn't sure.

"Hey, Nick, you still with us?"

Jen?

His head felt as though the Ape was dancing on it, but he turned enough to look up at her. She was smirking.

"Where the hell were you?" he managed. "I needed pictures of that."

Her smirk widened. "What makes you think I didn't get any?"

Naturally Jen had known that the Anti-Rampage Guard was intending to confiscate cameras, which was why she'd scampered off. As a result, she'd snapped away merrily during the whole violent episode.

Too soon, though, Grinder's elation turned to despair. A grunt accosted her as they began the long trek back to town, where Jen's car was parked. He took her camera and ripped out the film. Jen swore at him—referred to him as "cold-blooded swamp trash"—and Grinder would've joined in if his skull hadn't been throbbing so furiously. They were dragged back for a meeting with the CO of the Guard—a fat, pompous Norm with a moustache that was a prime candidate for BM status. This non-freak freak told the gathered reporters that their camera and broadcast equipment would be returned eventually, but also that reportage of this incident must stick to the 'official' line—which they were supplied with, hastily mimeographed on cheap paper. Naturally enough, this piece of fiction didn't include mention of the undead status of the giant ape, the tardy arrival of the ARG or their uncompromisingly terminal response to the situation. The CO took all their names and dismissed them with threats. When Grinder asked what recompense he could expect for his car, which had been incinerated by the firebombs the ARG hadn't used, the CO growled that perhaps he should think himself lucky and just cut his losses.

Grinder whinged about the destroyed film all the way back to Jen's car and was extremely miffed by her apparent lack of concern. Once they'd left Zuccotown well behind, however, Jen pulled over to the side of the road, stuck her hand in her jeans down to the crotch of her knickers, and extracted a roll of film.

Grinder stared at it, both aroused and puzzled.

She grinned. "For God's sake, Nick, I knew what they were gonna do, so I unloaded the film and put in a new roll. Took a gamble we wouldn't be strip-searched."

Grinder grabbed the canister. "I'll keep hold of that," he said. Then he lifted it to his nose and sniffed. "Ahhh, the sweet scent of Jen's cunning."

She laughed and they hit the road back to the capital.

• • •

City Clarion's offices were not bright and cheerful. But that didn't worry Grinder. In fact, the shadowy, archaic, not to say seedy, atmosphere was so powerfully iconic, he'd fallen in love with the place as soon as he'd seen it. It carried, for Grinder, the same appeal as the monster metropolis itself. Both were baroque, dark and flat-out *weird*. In many ways, he loathed normality. Chaney City was a refuge for the Abnormal. Established as a sanctuary (or prison, depending on your perspective) through the lobbying of Lon Chaney, that great entrepreneur and advocate of Freak Rights, it had, so far—despite occasional glitches—proven to be one of Washington's few unalloyed successes. The negative impact of monsters, phantoms, mad scientists and alien invaders on the Norm world had diminished significantly since its establishment.

Originally Grinder had come to the Monster City on a not-quite-approved-of assignment for a middle-of-the-road Norm rag whose increasing conservatism had been shitting him big-time. He'd loved the place so much he'd resigned within a week and had sought out employment with the *City Clarion*. And he'd been working the Dead Beat for over three years now. One day, perhaps, he'd leave and go back to the real world, but only if his investigation of Chaney City machinations—high and low—became more boring and inconsequential than his Norm political reportage had been. So far, he'd seen no sign of that happening.

Back from their excursion to Zuccotown, Grinder set the dank, slimy lab-guys to work on Jen's roll of film, screwed up the official handout, tossed it in the bin and got to work writing up his own story. The angle he intended to take didn't focus so much on the Rampage itself as the official response to it. There were sufficient oddities involved in *that* to turn the whole thing into a diatribe against the Governor's office. Before he'd progressed much beyond an opening hook, though, the chief editor hailed him.

There was a general "no smoking" rule throughout the *Clarion* offices, and Gag Black didn't indulge either inside or outside the building. Yet the editor's enclosed cubicle always seemed to be clogged with billowing clouds of smoke. As always, Grinder could barely see Black's bulbous form through the haze and his throat felt like it was being scraped with sandpaper. But he persevered.

"What's up—" he coughed and spluttered, "—Gag?"

"You workin' on the BMR thing?"

"Yeah, there's something very—" A cough scratched up through the words. He forced it back. "—strange going on."

"Forget it!"

"What d'ya mean?" Grinder peered through the smoke, trying to pin the editor's eye while keeping the irritation in his throat at bay. Black's head was a dim grey mass without a scrap of personality to latch onto.

"There's nuthin' there. Forget it!"

"Forget it? *Forget* it! Jen got some great pics. Do you realise what went on—"

"Don't realise. Don't care. Just drop it."

Grinder manoeuvred to slam his fist on the editor's desk, but he missed in the fog and the effect was less than dramatic. "I came here from the Outside to get away from this sort of brainless political censorship," he yelled. "Didn't think you'd toady to Barmer just 'cause the goddamn bitch has her fat ass jammed into the Governor's chair!"

Despite this appeal to decency and idealism, Black proved unmoveable. Grinder stormed out and stomped up and down the corridors, ranting and screaming at anyone who wandered by. He was still doing it an hour later when stopped in his tracks by a tall elegant woman dressed in green, her manner so imperious it penetrated even Grinder's rage. She'd suddenly materialised in front of him, forcing him to throw himself against the wall in order to avoid a collision.

"Whaaa th'uck!" he blathered. He levered himself into an upright position.

"Mr Inkman wants to see you." The woman eyed him coldly. "Now."

"Wait just a—" Grinder began, but she was gone. His best and most demanding sneer was directed at an empty corridor.

He'd never been invited in to see Mr Inkman before. Mr Inkman was a legendary magnate whose wealth and power intimidated everyone—and whose lack of presence merely served to make him more mythic than ever. Grinder headed for the sole elevator that serviced the executive suite, forcing his disorientation and minimal courage into a workable state of anxiety. The elevator descended past a dozen or so floors, even though he knew the building was only six storeys high plus a basement archive.

The woman he'd already met—Mr Inkman's secretary—was waiting for him when he exited the elevator into the brightly lit, Modernist and totally upmarket executive reception area. "Go straight in," she gestured.

Grinder swallowed nervously. He couldn't believe he was being ushered into The Presence. It was unnerving.

He entered and the door slammed behind him with a worrying finality. Mr Inkman's office was made up of bare walls painted off-white, with private entrance at the rear, a few scattered cabinets and a gigantic antique desk of the so-expensive-the-profit-from-selling-it-could-feed-a-third-world-country variety. No Inkman though. Instead there was a drawing on the wall behind the desk. Grinder assumed it was a likeness of Mr Inkman, though he'd never seen the man. The image was rather cartoon-like and appeared to have been scribbled hurriedly by a kid with a set of gaudy crayons and a grotesque imagination. In this sketch, Mr Inkman—a massive, sharply proportioned man with an oversized head and wearing a suit with padded shoulders—was sitting side-on, smoking a cigar. Grinder sighed. If that caricature was anything like the real deal, he wasn't looking forward to their meeting.

Then he noticed that the smoke from the caricature's stogie was actually drifting toward the ceiling.

"What the hell?" Grinder muttered.

The line drawing turned toward him. Still flat on the wall and two-dimensional, it nevertheless fixed Grinder with its narrow, intense stare.

"Grinder, I assume," it said.

Grinder gagged.

"Well?" growled the caricature.

"Um, Mr Inkman?" he managed.

"Who else?" The caricature held out its hand. Still 2D, the drawing took on the right perspective for an outstretched limb.

Grinder stumbled close and thrust his own hand in the direction of Mr Inkman's. He felt it grasped. The sensation was strangely warm and oily.

"I've been watching you, Grinder," Mr Inkman said. He pulled the reporter closer, so that Grinder was forced to lean toward the wall. "You're a gutsy newshound."

Gutsy? Judging by his hand, which was still grasped by Mr Inkman, he'd become gut-free; he was a drawing just like the boss. He gasped and jerked away. When Mr Inkman let go, Grinder's body immediately reverted to its normal 3D self.

Mr Inkman chuckled then let the expression on his face segue into a cartoonish scowl. "But I've also taken note of the fact that you're rather wilful."

The drawing stood and paced across the room, heading along the wall to the corner then moving at right angles onto the connecting wall. When he came to a filing cabinet, he swept around its contours and rejoined the wall on the opposite side. "The thing is, Grinder, the government, in its wisdom, has requested that we refrain from publishing anything even close to the facts regarding the recent Big Monster Rampage. There was nothing in it, they say. Just a minor bordertown fracas. To engage in a beat-up would constitute a public nuisance."

Grinder huffed derisively. "It was damn suspicious, that's what it was. When did you last hear of a big monster that had become undead?"

"It wasn't undead, they insist, just sick."

"Sick? Right. And it didn't set off the border alarms either. Did they explain that one?"

"An isolated glitch in the system."

"My ass it was! We've got pictures to show—"

Mr Inkman glared at him. "The pictures are gone."

"Gone?"

"Government agents came and took them. Your claims remain unsupported. If we persist in publishing them, even as innuendo, the administration will withdraw some rather significant privileges we enjoy, the effect of which would be to make it difficult for the *Clarion* to continue. We could be prosecuted. They're quoting the national security clauses of the Act."

Grinder stared at the line drawing in utter disbelief.

"So as of right now, Grinder, I'm officially telling you that your story is as dead as Lon Chaney Jr's chances of starring in the upcoming *Barkleys of Broadway* remake."

"But—"

"No buts."

Unable to control his outrage, Grinder leapt toward Mr Inkman, flailing his arms around vigorously. "How the hell can you allow them to do this? It's unconstitutional and—"

Grinder felt himself gripped, held rigid by an invisible force. Inkman?

"I would suggest that you control yourself, Grinder," the sketch growled.

Grinder fought against the restraining pressure for a moment, but then gave up and relaxed. He became a cartoon character. "I'm disillusioned," he said. "I moved to Chaney City to get away from this sort of repressive McCarthyist shit."

"This sort of repressive McCarthyist shit is everywhere."

"Yeah, well, I thought the *City Clarion* was better than that. I won't be staying long in Monster Town if this is how things are gonna work!"

Mr Inkman laughed and released him. "Real hothead, aren't you, Grinder?"

Grinder huffed.

The drawing began to pace along the wall. "I'm going to tell you two things now, Grinder, and both are important. What you do with the information is your business. Right?"

Grinder shrugged.

"First, you won't be leaving Chaney City any time soon. As you know, only Norms can come and go as they please—*and you're no longer a Norm.*"

"What?"

"You've changed, lad, and have become less human in the process. It's a side effect of working in close proximity to the *Clarion*'s presses, I'm afraid. They're atomic powered. Didn't you read the disclaimer on your employment contract?"

Grinder simply stared at him, unable to decide whether to be outraged, horrified or disbelieving.

Inkman continued: "The non-human denizens of Chaney City can be identified genetically through certain mutations in their respective molecular structures. That's how the Containment Alarms work. Any individual of a monstrous bent sets them off, unleashing an array of deadly sub-atomic waves and alerting UN forces, who respond immediately and with terminal force. That includes mad scientists and alien species." Mr Inkman opened a cabinet and pulled out an odd-looking out-of-perspective triangular object. "This works the same way—a bit like a genetically sensitive Geiger-counter. Test yourself if you doubt my word."

He tossed the object. In his hand it was a 2D drawing; by the time it reached Grinder it had become 3D and metallic.

"Press the ON button, point the ultraviolet sensor and check the dial. Above twenty percent signals an unacceptable level of monstrosity, legally defined."

Grinder did as he was told. He registered 42%. He turned the device on Mr Inkman: 97.6%.

"Compared to you, I'm totally goddamn normal," he growled.

Mr Inkman didn't smile. "But you're well over the limit—and it never diminishes. Only gets worse with time."

"What'll happen?"

Mr Inkman shrugged. "I mention this merely to indicate that there's no going back. You're in Chaney for the long haul. Live with it. Here is the second thing I wanted to tell you." He handed Grinder a sheet of paper. On it were written the words: "Mummy treasure rumour?" and a list of contacts.

Oddly, though, the words seemed to change when Grinder blinked, becoming instead "Necrophilic Rose".

"That's—"

"Your new assignment, yes."

"Assignment?"

As Mr Inkman spoke, his voice developed a discordant echo. He said one thing, but Grinder heard something else. Rather, he heard both, one layered over the top of the other. One was external, the other vibrated in his bones.

"It's a lead."

Mr Inkman's external voice reiterated that Grinder was not under any circumstances to continue his investigation into the alleged zombie Ape or what it may or may not mean, and gave him some curiously lightweight information regarding the alternative *Mummy* story. The underlying voice, however, had something entirely different to say.

"*My sources claim that political pressure is being placed upon the Governor by someone we haven't identified. However, an informant in her Grace's office provided that scrap of information. She didn't say what it meant.*"

"The Necrophilic Rose? Whorehouse, isn't it?" For a moment, Grinder was taken aback by the double layering of his own voice. External vocalisation had him grumbling unhappily to Mr Inkman but conceding to his boss's instruction to leave the story alone.

"An undead bordello, as I understand it," Mr Inkman replied.

"So there's a certain synchronicity. But what the hell would a giant Ape have to do with a brothel?"

Mr Inkman shrugged. "Even simians have needs. Surely you know what happened to Kong."

"Bloody hell!"

"*At any rate, Grinder, keep at it. Just remember this: officially you're on your own.*"

"*Why are we talking like this, Mr Inkman? Through our bones, I mean?*"

"*Why do you think? I'm expected to bow to the Governor's authority—and my charming secretary is a mole. She'll probably be listening in.*"

"Yeah? Why don't you sack her then?"

"She's a classy tart." Mr Inkman chuckled. "Like everything I grab hold of for long enough, she becomes an ink drawing in a clinch. And in that state she's got lines to die for, Grinder. To die for."

• • •

After setting up a smokescreen composed of mummy dust and pointless phone calls, Grinder headed for the Necrophilic Rose. Situated in the classier end of the City's red light district, the undead bordello displayed an ornate art-deco façade characterised by distinctly unnerving funereal tableaux. A large skeletal gargoyle hunched high above the entrance. It watched Grinder as he strolled self-consciously all the way from the street to the main door.

"May I help you, sir?" asked the ghostly phantom who responded to the buzzer. She had long red-tinged hair that flowed over her shoulders and joined seamlessly with her translucent dress. In the light you could see right through it—and her.

"I'm a journalist," Grinder said. "Working up a feature article on the City's sex industry and wondering if I could talk to the owner."

"Owner, sir? I'm afraid the identity of the owner is privileged information. You understand the delicacy of their position, I'm sure."

"Delicacy? Whatever. How about the establishment's, um, manager?" He cursed himself for being so unprepared; he should have researched that piece of information long before blundering in like a rank amateur. Not very smart.

"Madame de Relique is busy right at the moment, sir. Perhaps if you made an appointment." Her minute smile was awash with implied scorn.

"You're right, of course," Grinder said, exuding humility, "I should have called. But the opportunity came up and will evaporate if I don't get a line on the subject today. Any chance I could see Madame de Relique if I wait? I could have a look around . . . you know, gather some background."

She bowed her head and flickered slightly. "I'll see what I can do. Please, come in."

Grinder followed her into the perfumed hallway, feeling watched by innumerable sensuous eyes. The furnishings were lush and expensive, the floors covered in immaculately groomed carpet. He expected to catch a whiff of musty undead stink but, breathing deeply, all he could detect was a rich and invigorating aroma that sent his pheromone receptors into overdrive. How did they manage to mask the zombie stench so effectively?

"All your workers *are* deceased, I suppose?" he asked.

"Yes, sir."

The phantom ushered him into a waiting room. One wall was taken up with a large viewing window, like those sometimes used in morgues to allow identification of cadavers. The room beyond was in darkness.

"Listen, can't I—?" he began, but she wasn't there anymore. The words "I'll check with Madame" lingered in the air.

He tested the door he'd entered through, but it had been locked behind him. Swearing under his breath, he idly picked up a magazine lying on a small table at the entrance—an issue of *Playdead*. Gazing at the sexily posturing corpse-models made him feel uneasy, though they looked no more dead than the girls that populated the pages of the magazine's Norm rival.

Oh, God, he thought. How long do I have to wait?

Not long, as it turned out. He was ensconced in a luxuriously comfortable chair with his feet up on a coffin-shaped coffee table when the beautiful spectre shimmered back through the wood panelling.

"Madame de Relique will see you shortly," she said. "In the meantime, she suggests that you avail yourself of the amenities. Proper house etiquette forbids voyeurism, unfortunately. Perhaps we can divert you in other ways. Do you prefer corporeal, semi-corporeal or ethereal?"

"Sorry?"

She repeated what she'd said and waited.

"Look, I—" he began.

"I see you as a man partial to the flesh. Shall we say 'semi-corporeal', then? Flesh with equal parts ectoplasm, for the added thrill? Female?"

Before he could protest she was gone. Grinder was surprised at the flush of anticipation that swept over him. He reminded himself that he was there to do a job, so availing himself of the amenities mightn't be the wisest course.

On the other hand, this way he could talk with one of the tarts in an unguarded atmosphere.

The door opened to admit a voluptuous blonde with a figure so sleek and curvaceous it made him totally doubt her reality. She was wearing a blood-red see-through chemise with a scarlet g-string underneath. Grinder's whole body tensed up.

Yeah, right, Nick. Start talking.

"My name is Glory," she said. "Glory Road."

He didn't doubt for a moment that before too long he'd be heading off down that route.

. . .

Afterwards he realised that he'd totally forgotten to ask her any pertinent questions whatsoever. The experience had been all-consuming, a mix of misty ghostliness and drifting flesh, languid transitions of her body parts from solid to airy, normal coupling moving into full physical immersion. Someone so overpoweringly alive was hard to think of as dead.

Technically, of course, he'd just committed necrophilia—an act frowned upon by Norms. He sighed at this further evidence of his being lost to the human race. Oh well, he thought, at least it was consensual.

He forced himself into full consciousness and looked around for Glory, hoping to rectify his failure to ask questions. She was standing in the corner of the room, shadowy and transparent, an expression of ineffable sadness on her face.

Seeing him watching, she said, "I'm sorry."

He dismissed her concern lightly and asked what was wrong.

"It's nothing," she sighed. "A personal matter."

The sheer vulnerability of her exquisite face reduced Grinder to a quivering mass of heroic pliancy. He pressed her to confide in him and although she hedged, he could tell she was keen to unburden herself. So he comforted her.

At last she rested her mouth against his ear, as though blowing erotically into it—which was, in fact, the effect it had. "Not here," she whispered. "Not now." She named a time and a place beyond the confines of the Necrophilic Rose—a bar well away from the bordello's powerful sexual ambiance.

After that, Grinder took the opportunity to avail himself of the amenities one more time.

• • •

Not that he felt cheated, but those delicious moments with Glory were all he got out of the Necrophilic Rose. Eventually Madame de Relique sent a message to the effect that she'd been delayed and the earliest her schedule would allow her to see him was Thursday evening, two days hence. Grinder argued, though in the end was shown politely but forcefully to the door. He wasn't too miffed; he had Glory to fall back on.

At the office, he distracted himself doing the research he'd neglected to take care of in the first place. A dozen cigarettes later, what he discovered made it all worthwhile.

He was a little late getting to the Café Freaque, due to this research and Jen's inexorable attempts to find out what he was up to. He didn't want to involve her, so he lied; her prescience didn't work in a way that could see past his deception. He was pretty sure he'd shaken her in the end.

Café Freaque was a cheery if bizarre place decorated in a carnival theme. Many of its regulars were, in fact, monsters with a background in freak shows. Glory was sitting alone among the bigheads, dogboys and two-headed trapeze artists, looking less stunning in opaque and more ordinary clothes, but just as beautiful.

Her eyes lit up when she saw him. "I was afraid you wouldn't come," she said.

"Sorry. Business." He slid in next to her. "You ordered anything?"

She shook her head. "I don't eat."

"Drink?"

"No."

"Not even spirits?"

She smiled wanly at his joke.

Grinder ordered himself a plate of spaghetti and a bourbon, straight. They talked, about general meaningless things at first, but then he gave her a lead and she opened up about why she'd been so upset. Seemed a close friend—another ghostly hooker—had "died" only that morning.

"Died?" Grinder asked. "Of what?"

"They say it was AIDS."

"AIDS?"

"Astral Integrity Deterioration Syndrome," she said. "A sexually transmitted disease that affects those of the ectoplasmic kind. It's rare, but we all take the appropriate precautions. I don't understand how Raythe could catch it."

"Well, I'm really sorry," Grinder said. "You were close?"

"Known each other since we died, over a hundred years ago."

He nodded, having trouble getting his head and hormones around these concepts.

"It's all so sad," she said. "Just yesterday a very close friend of Raythe's, someone she adored, was killed out along the border somewhere. She was so upset."

Grinder's journo nose twitched. "Border? Where exactly?"

"Some place called Zuccotown," Raythe said. "There hasn't been much on the news. Apparently they shot him."

My God, thought Grinder, awestruck. It was all starting to tie together.

"Her friend was a giant Ape, right?"

Glory jerked backwards, her image flickering in surprise. "You heard about it?"

"I was there. Are you telling me Raythe and the Ape were lovers?"

Glory sobbed. "I know it seems unlikely. But she reckoned George was really nice. It's not that uncommon—apes and women."

"How did they . . . you know . . . make love? The Ape was as big as a house. Your friend'd fit in its hand."

"She was an ethereal, fully ectoplasmic. Coupling's easy for ethereals. Size doesn't matter."

For as long as he'd been in Chaney City, Grinder still found that the place surprised him, over and over again. This giant Ape-ethereal creature conjunction was a new wrinkle to mull over—but he knew now wasn't the time.

"Did you know," he asked Glory, "that the Ape was undead: a zombie?"

She shook her head. "Impossible. Raythe didn't say anything about that. And I met George about a week ago. He wasn't dead then."

A sudden intuition hit Grinder right between the eyes; it felt a bit like a sledgehammer covered in honey vodka. He leaned toward Glory. "Tell me about this AIDS thing," he demanded. "It's sexually transmitted, you said. How would it affect the living?"

"It doesn't." She frowned. "Or at least . . . "

"At least what?"

"Recently there've been rumours about something killing our customers. Regulars have disappeared. Some are saying it's a new disease that's done it. Very hush-hush. And Dr Phrenzy, our inhouse medico, inoculated us all about a month ago. Unexpectedly."

"Against what?"

"He wouldn't say. A precaution, we were told."

Grinder's front-page news sense was screaming blue murder by now.

"Glory," he said with increased urgency, "I need you to tell me everything you know about Madame de Relique and the Necrophilic Rose. Everything."

She nodded and opened her luscious mouth to begin—but that's as far as it went. Instead of the tale of the Necrophilic Rose's

Madame, what emerged was a gasp of fear. She cringed into the shadows, thinning to a will-'o-the-wisp.

"What?" queried Grinder.

She pointed toward the main door. A huge thug had entered, sporting a familial resemblance to the acromegalic actor Rondo Hatton, but on a very bad hair day. His dark eyes scanned the crowd. "It's one of the goons from the Rose," Glory whispered. "He's looking for me, I know it."

"Can't you disappear?"

"I'm a Semi. I can thin myself, but not dematerialise. All the security staff have the Eye. They can see me, even when I'm invisible to everyone else."

"Not through me they can't." Grinder positioned himself so that his body would hide her. Rondo-man gave up after a few minutes and exited the café. Hopefully he'd been doing a random check rather than acting on information.

Grinder suggested they sneak out the back way. There was an alley there. They could stick to the shadows and keep hidden from any casual surveillance. She agreed.

As they stood and headed for the café's kitchen and external exit, a group of thugs burst in and strode straight for them.

"Run!" yelled Grinder, "I'll hold them off."

Glory thinned to near-invisibility. She was little more than a phantom smudge in the air as she made for the front door. Grinder intercepted the goon-squad.

"Hold it, boys!" He took on a threatening stance, but the first goon, whose genetic ancestry lay somewhere beyond the solar system and appeared to involve large slabs of semi-sentient space-granite, shoved the journo aside with ease. The following monstrosity clubbed Grinder across the side of his head. As he went down, Grinder glanced to where Glory's translucent form was rearing away from the Rondo Hatton look-alike. Rondo-man was threatening her with some sort of weapon.

"Don't!" Grinder yelled. A percussive roar and a bullet of sickly light spat from the weird gun's muzzle. The glowing nugget punched into Glory's torso, remained visible for a moment as it ricocheted around inside her ribcage—then exploded.

Glory screamed. Her body solidified around her cry—but only for a moment. After a few seconds of painful anticipation, her ectoplasmic flesh rushed outward like an exploding star, shredded into streaks of blue.

Grinder felt something crash against the back of his skull. Then he too was gone, following Glory into the darkness.

...

Grinder clawed his way back to consciousness, waking to a pounding headache and a foul chemical stench. He appeared to be strapped to a vertically inclined operating table. Around him, coloured liquids bubbled in test tubes and electric gadgets hissed and sparked.

"Ah, I see you're back with us, Mr Grinder."

The speaker drifted into focus. He was dressed in a large stained lab coat, a surgical mask and rubber gloves. Grinder could barely make out his face, but there were definite signs of a beard.

"Dr Phrenzy, I presume," he muttered. His lips felt swollen and unresponsive. Clearly, he'd been drugged.

"Quite right," the man said. "Yet oddly wrong. Still, I'm sure things will clarify as time goes by."

"How long was I out?"

"A little less than five hours. Now I need you awake to be sure your fate progresses as it should."

"Fate?"

Dr Phrenzy leaned toward Grinder, pressing his hand against the reporter's chest. Up close, he seemed oddly effeminate; his fingers were long and delicate, even surrounded by latex. A surgeon's hands, Grinder guessed. But there was nothing delicate about his words. "You're about to shuffle off this mortal coil, Mr Grinder. I give you perhaps two hours."

"What d'ya mean?" Grinder did an internal inventory, checking for aches, pains—any sign of mortality. There were so many he gave up. His first twinge of doubt dropped like ice into his stomach.

"Death can be our friend," the doctor pontificated. "It can free us."

"Free? What the fuckin' hell—?"

"Cussing is the resort of a moron." Dr Phrenzy clenched his hands together in front of his mouth, as though praying. "You are not a stupid man, Mr Grinder. You are here, now, because you know the answers."

The tone of his voice was strangely maternal, his words encouraging. Grinder realised that he *did* know the answers, including where he was: somewhere in the bowels of the Necrophilic Rose. The scent of the scarlet undead plying their trade in the building above them filtered down past the astringency of the doctor's brews.

Slowly the answers worked a path through his mind.

"AIDS," he said in a revelatory tone. "But not AIDS. An engineered variation, one that doesn't kill only ectoplasmic folk, but provokes undeath in the living. The monkey died of it—and came back. Others too, presumably. Now me. It was Glory, wasn't it? She was the carrier. That's why you gave her to me."

Dr Phrenzy stepped backward as though afraid of Grinder's deductions, then stopped and stared at him defiantly.

"I'm guessing Dr Phrenzy's not your name," Grinder continued. "And you ain't Madame de Relique either, though you go by that moniker." He sighed. "What sort of freak could achieve what you've achieved, eh? One that was exiled here in Chaney City with the rest of the Mad Scientists, but who wasn't to be found at the last census—assumed dead through sub-atomic disintegration in the aftermath of a failed gene-transmogrification experiment." He grinned cheekily. "You can tell I did a bit of research before I came out tonight. With a face ugly enough to pass as a man, I'm guessing your real name is Dr Skreecher La Vin—expert in viral diseases and voodoo. How are those for answers?"

Dr Phrenzy reached up and removed his surgical mask, his hair cap and his beard. His sharp Grecian nose came away, too. Underneath was a woman who wasn't exactly ugly, but was well past homely.

"You're even cleverer than I expected, Mr Grinder," she said.

"Cleverer than *I* expected, if you must know," he replied.

"Which makes my actions all the more justified." La Vin stripped off the lab coat to reveal a less-than-respectable evening gown draped over a less-than-attractive body. Grinder cringed at the self-delusion of her bared shoulders and plunging neckline. "I feared you'd discovered too much," La Vin added. "It seems I was right to do so."

"Did you kill Glory?" Grinder growled.

"She was already dead."

"You know what I mean."

La Vin replaced her flat doctor's pumps with elegant high-heels. "Of themselves, the dead are unimportant, Mr Grinder. From the moment of their passing they are an illusion, an after-thought. They only exist while the living imagine them to be useful."

"Useful?"

"I don't intend to stay in this place." Her gesture took in not simply the basement, but all of Chaney City. "A ghetto for the terminally victimised. Who has the right to class me with all those freaks and monsters out there? I am an accomplished scientist. I represent the very peak of human endeavour. I should not be here, a side-note in human history."

"And that's what the re-engineered AIDS was for, eh? Escape?"

La Vin began applying make-up in a small mirror. It didn't help. "My mutant virus creates undead nobodies, Mr Grinder. Not the ordinary walking dead that we're oh-so-familiar with, but zombies invisible to the detection devices that surround Chaney City. And these undetectable creatures answer to me!

"Only some of the Necrophilic Rose's whores are carriers, but they service, on average, about a dozen human clients a day, with an infection rate of 70 per cent. It will not take long before I command an army of undead—an army I can send out into the Norm world to undermine the fascist regime that confined me here. I will be free, Mr Grinder. I will be avenged."

"George was a mistake, right?"

She snarled. "The bitch screwing that damn Ape nearly undermined the whole scheme. My virus reacts erratically to nonhuman gene configurations. When the beast died and became undead, I couldn't control the wretched thing and it went berserk. Took all my political clout to hush it up."

"Does Governor Barmer know what sort of a nutter she's aiding and abetting?"

La Vin cackled. "Know? How long do you think I could hide this sort of enterprise without her backing? Politicians wrote the book on obfuscation. Governor Barmer sees the value of my experiments. She has *ambition*. That's why she bought the Rose."

"I knew it," grumbled Grinder. He pulled at his restraints, but there was no way they were going to give.

"If you could get on with dying, it would be much appreciated," said La Vin. "I'm attending a function in the Governor's house tonight and don't wish to be late. Your irritating penchant for sticking your nose in where it isn't wanted means I'll need to be here to establish proper control over you—once you come back—just to make sure. You're considerably more resistant than most. It's inconvenient, but having a newspaper reporter in my thrall may prove very useful."

Again, Grinder went internal, seeking reassurance he couldn't find. He could tell he was drifting inexorably toward the darkness, and vaguely wondered what the experience of dying and coming back would be like. He'd rather not find out, of course, especially if it meant being the slave of La Vin and Barmer once he did. *Shit, damn*, he muttered to himself. *What a cock-up!*

Then he heard other voices—light, ghostly voices, whispers of cemetery earth and black void and decay. He opened his eyes and glanced around, but all he could see were La Vin's arcane lab and the woman herself, as she peered grumpily into his eyes.

"For God's sake, die!" she growled.

"Sorry."

Had he just reached into the realm of spirits, touched the lost, felt their despair? A wave of anger, only partially his own, swept over him.

"I think I'll speed you along," hissed La Vin. She rummaged around on one of her more cluttered workbenches then disappeared behind him. When she came back, she waved a large hypodermic needle at him. "A booster shot. Should be safe enough."

Grinder struggled frantically. She stabbed, plunging the needle into his chest. His mind began to cloud, to pitch toward a vast, chthonian pit into which he knew he would fall and be hopelessly lost. Darkness swirled, mixed with a bloody light that leaked downward from beyond the ceiling, and coagulated into emptiness. Everything went still.

• • •

The road back was pretty rough, but Grinder fought his way through despair and utter loneliness, and eventually re-entered a world that had only changed because he was no longer part of its living matrix. He felt colder, less in touch with the currents of reality, but otherwise much the same. He had a vague memory of journeying past countless lost souls. Some had reached out to him in pity, others had burned for revenge. He was a tad concerned that one of the latter might have followed him back.

La Vin's hand pressed against his chest. "Well, your heart has stopped, Mr Grinder, though your eyes show awareness. How does it feel to be among the living dead?"

"Pretty average, actually."

"I trust you had a smooth trip?"

"There's rather a few spirits out there wanting to get their hands on you, La Vin," he said. His voice sounded hollow. "You've made a lot of enemies."

"Breaking eggs, Mr Grinder, to make omelettes."

"I'd hoped . . . "

"Hoped what?"

"I'd hoped to see Glory among them."

La Vin shrugged. "No chance of that, I'm afraid. Death isn't interested in those who die twice."

"Same with Raythe, too, I guess." When he spoke the name, something stirred in the shadows behind the Mad Scientist.

"Of course. That undead bimbo and all like her—the re-dead ones—were removed from the world by an invention of my own. You must have noticed it in Café Freaque."

"A sort of gun, right? What the hell *was* that thing?"

"Insurance. It destabilises the structure of ectoplasmic emissions. Terminally. All immaterialists it touches shuffle off into oblivion, lost forever." She undid the straps that held him down. "But they served their purpose. Just as you will, Mr Grinder, now that you are mine."

"Yours?"

"You died into undeath through my virus. Now you will obey me."

"I don't think so."

She grinned. "Kneel before me, Mr Grinder. Do it now."

Grinder stood staring at her. Behind her, the shadows shifted again and this time he made out the shape that lurked there. It was huge and simian.

"Mr Grinder! Kneel!"

Instead he spat on her nice clean shoes.

She started back. "What is this? How dare you!"

He laughed. "Didn't you say your virus was unreliable on those who aren't human? You should have done your homework better. At last count I was only 58 per cent human—and diminishing."

"What?"

"And there's more bad news."

Her face contorted into contemptuous fury.

"Seems I brought back with me one of your more recent fans." Grinder pointed over her shoulder. "A really big one, too."

She followed his gesture and turned. The shadows were seething, forming a huge skeletal ghost. Its anger burned incandescent.

"I guess firebombs aren't as effective as your Ectoplasmic Destabiliser," Grinder added. "Should've armed the ARG more appropriately."

La Vin tried to shriek, but too late to produce anything more than a whimper. The ghostly Ape grabbed her. As it did so, its massive solidity—albeit transient—pushed against the ceiling and walls. The Necrophilic Rose began to collapse around them.

Grinder closed his eyes and waited.

...

As it happened, he didn't have to dig himself out from a pile of rubble. The Ape had only dislodged about half the upper floor and one wall; the rest merely trembled and stayed put. When Grinder opened his eyes, the simian phantom had gone—he had no idea to where—and Skreecher La Vin was a bloody mess smeared across the debris.

At street level, chaos reigned. Staff and clientele of the Rose gathered in groups (or scampered into the night, seeking anonymity); fire trucks and police flashed emergency lights and encouraged their sirens to screech pointlessly; spectators gathered like excited chooks. One of them was familiar.

"Hey!" he yelled, walking toward Jen, who was busy snapping pictures. "You got here quick."

Unfazed, she nodded. "Of course. You, too, I see." Then her eyes narrowed. "You look different."

"It's a long story." Grinder found a crushed cigarette in his coat pocket and lit up. But it tasted bland and unpleasant now. He wondered if he'd have the same reaction to teabags. "I think I need to pay the Governor a visit."

"She's involved in this?"

"Oh yes indeedy."

"Proof?"

He shrugged. "Nothing worth a damn in a court of law. But I can threaten her with some nasty innuendo. At the very least, I want her to know her scheme's gone down the crapper."

Jen fumbled in her camera bag and emerged with a fist full of prints. "Take these. Might give her pause if she's inclined to be vindictive."

What Jen had handed him was a collection of excellent shots of the ARG, responding in inappropriate fashion to George the Giant Zombie Ape in Zuccotown.

Grinder raised an eyebrow. "I thought the police confiscated these from the Dark Room?"

"They did. But I got there first."

Even more interesting were a number of clear shots of Governor Barmer with Madame de Relique AKA Skreecher La Vin, *in medias res* as it were.

"Where the hell did ya get these?" Grinder asked, astonished.

Jen tapped the side of her nose with her forefinger and grinned.

"One bit of advice though," she said, leaning closer. "If I were you, I'd have a scrub-down before I went anywhere. You stink like old socks."

ONE NIGHT AT THE CHERRY

Chris Large

The doll was gorgeous: a real knockout. Her legs were toned and ended in dagger-sharp stilettos. She wore a dark leather overcoat, and maybe nothing underneath. A thin cigarette smouldered between lips that were just too perfect. God only knew what that shit was doing to her dynamic filters.

She leaned forward, giving me an eyeful of rack, and stubbed out her cigarette with long fingers and shiny, painted nails. This doll had been built for one thing, and one thing only.

"Look Miss . . . " I didn't know her name. "I can't do nothin' until you tell me what you're doing in my office."

"Mr Baum," she said in a smoky voice. "I need protection."

If she'd wanted me to watch someone, follow or kill someone, I wouldn't have been surprised. But protection? I'd never been in that racket. "Okay, for one thing, my name's Frank, no mister involved," I said. I was irritated and hungry as hell. I wanted to hit the town, find something to eat, and this doll was wasting my time.

"And for a second thing, you're a rogue screwbot, sweetheart. You ain't allowed out this late without a registered owner."

I could see it was sinking in that it didn't matter how many of her buttons were undone, I wasn't going down that road. Not tonight.

She blinked. "I'm not rogue."

"You *are* a doll," I said, jabbing at her with my good finger, the one that still had some skin on. "M70—F if I ain't mistaken, and you're here in my office on your own. Ergo, you are rogue."

"Do you smoke, Mr Baum?" she asked. She was holding out one of them thin boxes of Jarrow. I hadn't had a Jar in years, not since I was in the Land of the Living, but it'd been a tough week. Hell, it'd been a tough year. You only had to look around my office to see I was on the skids: unsolved cases spilling out of drawers, empty bottles of bourbon on every shelf. Undead detectives weren't the first choice of private dick in this town. I took a cigarette and pulled open my top drawer, looking for some matches.

The doll trumped me, taking out a shiny, oil-based lighter. After eyeballing her cleavage again, I leaned back and sucked on tar and aphrodisia. It was a kick I hadn't felt in a long time, and I liked it. Maybe I wouldn't throw her onto the street, after all.

"You're different," I said, relaxing in the haze. "I ain't never seen a doll smoke before."

She crossed her legs and settled back as though she was going to be there all night. "Like I said Mr Baum, I need protection."

"Look lady, I may be a Zommie, a private dick, even a dog catcher when I have to be, but I ain't no bodyguard. And you don't need protection 'cause you're a doll. Now be a good girl and run along home to your owner."

She lit up another Jar. "That'll be difficult," said the doll, puffing up. "She's dead."

• • •

I'm a decent guy, if nothing else, so I walked the doll home. She lived in a grimy little brownstone not far from my office. The sidewalk was slick with oily rain. It was a dirty part of town, maybe the dirtiest.

Late-night commuters, up in the Land of the Living, shot by overhead in their fancy-pants shuttle cars, darting between their towers in the clouds. They didn't even know people like us existed.

Usually that annoyed the heck out of me, but the doll had given me something else to think about.

On the way, she got to talking, said her name was Dorothy, and her owner had been one Mary Drowne.

"Who does that make you?" I asked. "Dorothy Drowne?"

The doll shrugged, like it didn't matter.

"I guess I'll call you Dee Dee."

She looked calm, perhaps the calmest murder witness I'd come across. I'd never thought about what happened to dolls when their owners died. They're bio-linked, so it must be tough. Dee Dee had no owner now, was loose in the city without anyone to take responsibility for her. Not that she was a danger. Dee Dee was built for action, sure, but not *that* kind of action. A rogue screwbot would be the least of anyone's problems in this neighbourhood.

Her arse swayed when she walked. I had to be careful. I didn't want the Jar to go to my head. Machines were machines, after all.

Dee Dee led me to her door. Like I said, it was dirty.

"You want to come in?" Dee Dee asked. "I mean, for a drink?"

"You think I should?" That was the aphrodisia talking. She opened up and took me through to the sitting room. The building still had electricity, which surprised me, and there was a fire burning in the grate. Dee Dee's owner must have been a Skin to have luxuries like power and wood. A Skin with connections.

She lit me up another Jar. The first had been a moment of weakness, the second—well, I really shouldn't have. I'd learned long ago I couldn't handle it.

The bourbon burned all the way down, and that's always something to smile about. The doll had a glass of something, too. What did screwbots drink? I didn't know. I usually kept away from the damn things as much as I could. I'd never worked out whether they were alive, dead, or something in between. Those kinds of details didn't matter to some fellas. But they mattered to me. Officially dolls weren't alive. But I'd seen a few things that had made me wonder about that.

"Do you want to see her?" Dee Dee asked, sipping from her tall glass.

"See who?" I asked, my eyes running over her body, Zommie brain not thinking much.

"Mary."

I nearly dropped my drink. "She's here?"

"Sure, upstairs on the bed," Dee Dee said, like she was giving me directions to the damn bathroom.

"Are you crazy?" I cried. "Why didn't you call the cops?"

The doll shrugged. "Mary never trusted the cops."

I couldn't argue with that. No one trusted the cops in this part of town.

"But she's dead!" I said. "You can't just leave her up there. She needs a decent burial, at least! Leave her lying around too long and something'll smell her, and you don't want a hungry Street Spawn trying to smash its way in here." It wasn't just Street Spawn she needed to worry about. I'd had three guys offer me cash for fresh meat in the last week.

Dee Dee's face was blank. "I don't know anything about decent burials, Mr Baum. That's why I need your help."

"Look, Dee Dee," I said, feeling a little hot under the collar. She was beautiful, even if she was just a doll. "I already told you, call me Frank. And you said you needed a protector, not an undertaker."

"As it happens, Frank," she said, looking me straight in the eye. "I need both."

If I thought things couldn't get any stranger than a rogue screwbot coming to my office in the middle of the night asking for protection from her owner's killer, I was wrong.

Dead wrong.

Miss Mary Drowne had been one peculiar dame. For a start, she was Skin, real flesh and blood. I smelled her as I climbed up the stairs and it near drove me crazy. She was right where Dee Dee said she'd be, lying across the bed, naked as the day she was born with a nasty length of cord around her neck and a bullet in her forehead. But that wasn't the strange part, not by a long shot. After all, murders happen every day.

Mary Drowne had been a looker. She'd had the kind of eyes that made a guy walk across the room to open a door for her. Her lips had been full and kissable, and her body—enough said. But there was something else.

"She's . . . " I muttered, staring.

Dee Dee stood behind me, holding a small gas lamp. "What is it, Frank?"

"She looks just like you!" I said.

"Yes, Mary had me customised."

I didn't know what to say. "You're a screwbot, Dee Dee."

Dee Dee nodded. "Like you said Frank, M70-F. Serial number: one-seven-five-oh-nine-jay."

"And you and Mary here, you used to . . . "

Dee Dee nodded. "Almost every night."

"So she was doin' . . . herself?"

Dee Dee cocked her head to one side, her smooth skin radiant in the glow of the lamp. This wasn't strange to her. "I suppose that's one way to look at it."

"It's the *only* way to look at it," I said. "Dammit, Dee Dee; who killed her?"

Dee Dee sat down on the edge of the bed and looked out into the night. It was raining again and big drops were spattering against the window. It was acidic, burned the skin if it rained hard enough, could melt your face right off your skull. But there would never be enough rain to wash away the stink of this town.

"You're not going to like this, Frank."

"I don't like it already," I said. "But I got to know."

What dolls thought about I never could tell, but this one looked sad and alone.

"It was Carlotta Finnegan," she said. "I saw her do it and I ran out of here. I ran to you, Frank."

Now I knew I'd be lucky to see morning, because no one messed around in Carlotta Finnegan's affairs and lived to tell the tale. Especially not freak screwbots like Dee Dee, or washed-up old Zommie dicks like me. We were the lowest of the low. Deads under the bed.

Someone would be watching this place like a hawk. Someone would know we were here. Someone would be coming with more cord, and more guns—a lot more guns.

"Go downstairs and wait, Dee Dee," I said. The smell of skin and brains was getting too much for me. "We're leaving, and there's something I got to do . . . with Mary here."

. . .

We hit the street again. I felt a lot stronger now and I bummed another Jar off Dee Dee. If I was gonna to die, I wanted to die happy, and the Jarrow was keeping me calm.

"Dee Dee," I took her hand. It was warm, like flesh. "If Carlotta wants you dead, you got to get out of town."

"Where would I go, Frank?" Her stilettos clicked against the gritty sidewalk.

I didn't have any answers. "Dee Dee, don't take this the wrong way. I think you're a great girl and all but . . . "

"Why don't I just crawl into a cupboard and switch off until this blows over?" She arched a perfect eyebrow. "They'll find me, Frank. Pull me apart. Tear out my memory chips and burn them."

There was something in her eyes that sent a shiver right the way down my crooked old spine. "I won't let 'em," I heard myself say.

"Promise me Frank, you'll take me somewhere Carlotta can't get me?"

That was a promise I knew I couldn't keep, but her big brown eyes made my gut clench. "Sure, I'll make it right."

In a side alley, two hunched shadows were grunting urgently in the slippery dark. I couldn't tell what they were, maybe Street Spawn. Well, so long as they were keeping each other occupied, that was okay with me.

"Dee Dee, why did Carlotta kill Mary?" I asked, walking faster to put some distance between the shadows and us. "I mean, was she a player?"

Dee Dee let go of my hand and wiped something off her cheek. "Mary was fooling around with Carlotta's man," she said.

"Mary was screwin' Jack Finnegan?" You could have knocked me down with a feather. "Jesus! Is he still breathing?"

I glanced behind and saw something move that shouldn't be moving. My eyes were old and half-gone, but they weren't too old to pick out a dog in a long coat at night. I caught a flash of green, deep in his eye sockets, which meant hyperspectral implants. They were expensive, but nothing was too expensive for Carlotta. She was onto us.

Ahead, the street was empty. We had to find somewhere to hide, and fast. Over on Maine there was a hotel, the Cherry. You paid by the hour, but it wasn't one of Carlotta's. If we could get there without getting ourselves killed we might be safe, at least until I ran out of credits.

I grabbed Dee Dee by the elbow and we high-tailed it down a backstreet.

"You got a gun, Frank?" the doll asked.

I pulled out my shooter and checked the barrel as we went. Two plasma caps. I didn't hold much with guns, especially on these streets, but I'd used this one a few times. Two caps would be enough so long as we didn't run into an angry Street Spawn.

• • •

The dog with the green eyes followed us the whole way. We couldn't shake him, but he didn't try to stop us. He was just a sniffer, and there was more than one of them. By the time we got to the Cherry, we had three dogs tracking us.

The place was a dirty hovel, and there was a sign above the front door: "NO BITING". The kid on the desk was a Skin. He was young, but he had some smarts.

"You guys are hot," he said, checking his street cameras. "You know that?"

I kept my mouth shut.

He looked at the doll. "Scan says she's bio-masked. Must be one of the new ones."

He didn't say it, but I could see him wondering what a slick piece of tech like Dee Dee was doing with an old Zommie bum like me.

"We need a room," I said. "I got a card."

"Who are these guys?" the kid asked, pointing at the screens. "They look like dogs. Scan says they're wired."

"Nothin' to do with us," I said.

He looked at me doubtfully, scratching his stubbly chin. "I don't want no trouble."

"Me neither," I said. "We just want a room for a couple of hours."

"You got a shooter?" he asked, eyeballing the bulge in my coat.

"Nope."

"Scan says—"

"Scan's wrong."

The kid nodded. I was right; he had a brain in that head of his. And boy, did it smell good. "If those dogs bust in here and kick down the door, it's going on your account."

I handed over the card.

"Same goes for bloodstains," he added. "And I'll keep the card."

What could I say? "Sure kid, you do that."

The card was all the little cash I had in the world, and a few hours from now it would be worthless. Even a dive like the Cherry cost a bomb by the hour.

Our room was on the third floor, north-west corner. The Cherry's crimson neon sign flickered right outside the window. The kid had cut us a break. It was almost clean, and we had a good view of the dogs. I got the feeling we were safe for a while; they were waiting for something.

I flicked off the lights, then lit some gas lamps and turned them down low. There were mirrors on the walls and on the ceiling over the bed. Dee Dee admired herself from all angles in the dim glow. She smoothed her hair, adjusted her coat, brushed off the dust.

"Are they still out there, Frank?"

I took another look and caught their green eyes staring up at us from the street. When I turned back, Dee Dee was naked and pressing herself against me. To be honest, I was taken by surprise. Then she kissed me and it was all over. An old Zommie like me ain't got no defences against something as beautiful as Dee Dee, and I had three Jar's worth of aphrodisia crawling through my system. Enough to help me get it up, and that weren't no bad thing. No bad thing at all.

Afterwards we lay together, wrapped in our sweaty sheets. Crimson light spilled through the shutters, splashing like a flickering bloodstain over the bed. Dee Dee stared up at her reflection on the ceiling.

"We can't stay here forever," I said. "Those dogs outside are waiting for someone, maybe even Carlotta."

"You'll protect me, Frank," she said.

"Dee Dee, there ain't no way I can protect you from Carlotta and all her dogs."

The doll rolled toward me and put a pale arm across my chest. Her eyes were wide and dark. "You're brave Frank," she said. "You've got courage, like a lion. You've got heart, and you wear it on the outside, like armour. If anyone can get me through this, it's you. You're my guy now."

When a girl talks to a man like that, it should make him feel like a million dollars. It should make him feel ten feet tall. But if I had the courage of a lion, it was a cowardly one. I didn't feel like no knight in shining armour, more like a scarecrow, standing stiff and alone. And the blackbirds were circling, staring at my button eyes, waiting for me to blink.

...

Just before daybreak, the kid was hammering at the door. Dee Dee lay on her back next to me, the sheets messed up all around her. The aphrodisia had worn off, but that didn't matter. I loved her. Loved her dark hair, deep brown eyes, long legs, crooked smile—everything. She wasn't a doll to me no more. She was a real, live woman.

"Hey!" the kid shouted. "You're card's out. Time to hit the road."

"Yeah, yeah," I said. "Gimme a minute."

Dee Dee was waking up. I didn't know dolls needed sleep. Maybe it's programming.

"We gotta go, Dee Dee."

That was when they hit the hotel. The whole building shook like it was an earthquake—plaster and dust everywhere. Dee Dee fell out of bed and crawled to her coat. I was pulling on my pants when they hit the building again. This time part of the wall fell away. Through the dust and falling bricks I saw people moving down on the street.

People with big guns.

I grabbed my coat and shooter and ran for it, pushing Dee Dee along in front of me. Laser sights cut through the clouds of powdered masonry, followed by plasma rounds and bullets. I slammed the door shut and we bolted down the hall as fast as my tired old muscles and rickety joints would go. We hadn't gone far before the door to our room was blown to splinters. Gunfire peppered the walls all along our floor, followed us to the stairwell.

"Which way?" Dee Dee cried.

I had to make a decision, and fast. The sound of snarling, barking and plasma fire rose up the stairwell from the ground floor. Carlotta had sent in the dogs.

"Dee Dee, you gotta tell me something. Carlotta's going to an awful lot of trouble to get to you. Sure, you saw her murder Mary, but Carlotta ain't scared of the cops, so why does she want to kill you so bad?"

"I don't know—honest! You won't let her get me, will you Frank? You *promised*!"

I didn't know if the doll was being straight with me, or if I was getting played, but I'd fallen hard. Downstairs it sounded crazy. Whoever owned the Cherry was prepared for a turf war. This was one of the few places Carlotta hadn't got her claws into. I didn't know how long the Cherry boys would hold out against Carlotta's dogs, but with all the howling coming from the lobby, my guess was not long.

Then there was a dog on the stairs, eyes wild and gleaming, blunt snout dripping with blood. He'd been shot in the leg and the shoulder, but he was wired and running on stims. I pulled out my shooter and aimed. It was a long barrelled Grinner, and used the old kind of caps. Blew his head clean off. I smelled burnt hair and brains. It was all I could do to stop myself from climbing down there and lapping it up.

"Frank?" Dee Dee tugged my arm, bringing me out of it.

"Up!" I shouted. There wasn't really a choice.

There were footsteps on the stairs behind us. I couldn't see who it was, so we just kept going. I knew we'd run out of real estate before long, but we didn't have a whole lot of choice. Eventually we hit the roof. I was feeling a powerful need to eat, and my legs were starting to go to jelly. The joints weren't what they used to be.

"Go check the other side," I said, leaning against the railing.

Dee Dee ran to the back of the building. "There're dogs all over, Frank. What do we do?"

I wasn't going anywhere. My knees had seized up. I staggered over to Dee Dee and we stood together, watching the sun struggle up out of the muck. From the roof of the Cherry, I could see through the curtain of woodsmoke hanging in the air, right up to the Land of the Living. It was beautiful; glittering towers of emerald jutted out of fluffy clouds, glowing bright in the morning sun. There was even a rainbow, if you can believe it, an arc of wonderful colour. I felt a stab in my chest just looking at it. We were toe jam to the people in that city up there. And now the woman I loved was gonna get shot and there wasn't a damn thing I could do to stop it.

I caught the smell of diesel and lavatory water, the stink of my town, and it brought home everything that was wrong with the world. I wanted to climb up into those clouds and start hurting people. How could they live like that, like we didn't exist, when all they had to do was look down to see us neck-deep in shit?

"It isn't fair, Frank," said the doll.

"No, Dee Dee," I replied. "It ain't."

Dee Dee was quiet for a moment. "When we get out of this mess, I'm going to get up there," she said, looking up into the clouds. "I'm going to get up there and find out why the hell they think they're so much better than us."

I looked at her then, and there was something in her eyes I hadn't seen before. It was anger, and I didn't know dolls could get mad like that.

"Someone up there built me," she went on. "Pieced me together bit by bit, and then gave me life. It's a miracle when you think about it. But this isn't the kind of life a girl would want to live, Frank—getting screwed over by anyone with the cash to buy me. *What right did they have to make me like this*? What right did they have to throw me down here in the dirt, with the dogs and the goddamn Street Spawn?"

I didn't know what to say. Almost everyone in town felt like that, but Dee Dee was a doll, and wasn't supposed to have feelings, or dreams. She wasn't supposed to love and hate, but I guess when you make a machine like Dee Dee, you can't know how the chips will fall. And now her owner was dead, she was making her own way.

It was Carlotta who kicked the door open and stepped into the dawn, her long, black coat flapping in the breeze. I shoved Dee Dee behind me and pointed my Grinner at Carlotta, holding her in my line of sight with a shaky hand, my good finger lightly squeezing the trigger.

Carlotta walked casually forward, like she wasn't worried, and pointed her shiny little laser pistol right back at me. "Get outta the way Zommie, or I'll burn a hole through both of you." Her voice was hard, no give in it at all. But she smelled good. And I was hungry.

I stood my ground. Dee Dee didn't flinch, she just put her hand on my shoulder and squeezed, like she was giving me strength.

"You think you can fool around with my man and get away with it, you dirty whore?" Carlotta spat, talking around me at Dee Dee.

"You got the wrong girl," I said. "You already killed Mary Drowne, this one's just a doll."

Carlotta laughed. It was a loud, masculine sound. It matched her square jaw and wide stance. "Is that what she said? I think the worms must have got to your brain, Zommie. You've been played. Now get outta the way. I got no beef with you, but I don't have a problem wasting your kind."

"This ain't Mary Drowne," I said again. "If she was Skin, I'd know. I'd smell it."

The door crashed open again and someone else came through.

"Drop the gun, Lotta." It was a tall guy in a pinstripe. He had real short hair and moved easy, like a sportsman. He was a Skin, too: bright and pink and soft. He was pointing a plasma rifle at Carlotta's back. I figured he must be the man of the hour.

"Jack, don't be a schmuck," Carlotta spat. "We talked about this."

"Yeah, we talked," said Jack Finnegan. "But you never listened. You never understood me, Lotta. This ain't Mary, and it was never about Mary. Now, put the gun down."

"This *is* Mary Drowne," Carlotta said, jabbing her pistol as us. "And I'm sendin' her straight to the pearly gates!"

Carlotta would have to shoot right through me to kill Dee Dee, and I could see in her eyes she was fixing to do just that.

"Don't do this, Carlotta," Jack tried again, coming closer. His eyes were red, maybe from the smoke, maybe from something else. "We've had some good times and . . . I still love you. But I won't let you kill Dorothy."

"Shut up, Jack!" Carlotta screamed. "I had you followed. I've got pictures. I know you've been screwing Mary. And I know this is her."

"Drop the gun," was all Jack said, but Carlotta's grip tightened on her pistol. She wasn't giving up her chance for revenge that easy.

Getting burned through by a laser probably wouldn't kill me, but it would sure as hell kill Dee Dee. I felt the blackbirds closing in, their sharp beaks ready to rip and tear. This was the moment when I had to decide whether I was gonna take it like a lifeless scarecrow, or whether I would roar like a lion. Carlotta's trigger finger tensed and so did mine.

Jack fired. I shielded my eyes from the plasma flare, and a moment later, the most powerful woman in town was nothing more than a smoking corpse. I never thought I'd be around to see

Carlotta Finnegan killed, but there she was, deader than most corpses I'd seen. My mouth began to water.

Dee Dee instantly let go of my shoulder and ran to Jack. He dropped his rifle, caught her in his strong, young arms and lifted her high in the air. They kissed long and hard. My old heart had been shrivelled and dead for years now, but the sight of Dee Dee and Jack together made it want to start beating at a hundred miles an hour. I thought I'd blow apart right then and there.

"Jack," she said. "I thought I'd never see you again."

"You should'a known I'd come for you, my beautiful doll."

I was still holding my shooter out, ready to fire at something. My arm was starting to shake. Dee Dee saw me and looked at Jack meaningfully.

"Hey," said Jack. "It's over. Put the gun down."

But I couldn't. There was still one cap left and I wanted to use it.

Dee Dee walked towards me. "It's okay, Frank. I'm sorry I did what I did, but I needed your help. The fact is, I love Jack. Please, give me the gun."

Her hand closed over mine and I went limp at her touch. She took the Grinner and I sank to my knees, finished. But Dee Dee had one more surprise in store. She turned, pointed the shooter at Jack and used my last cap to blow his right arm and half his chest away. The poor sap flew backwards and hit the deck with a strangled scream.

Dee Dee tossed the Grinner aside and strolled over to where he lay. Jack's blood was running all over the roof of the Cherry Hotel like shit from a sewer.

"*You screwed my Mary*," she hissed at him, and I'd never heard such venom in all my days. It was white-hot hate. "You screwed my Mary, and now I'm gonna screw you!"

"B . . . but you can't," Jack gasped. He was having trouble breathing, what with only having one lung and all. "You're just a . . . just a . . . "

"That's right, arsehole," said Dee Dee. "I'm just a doll. But even so, I got my limits. You lied to me, the same as you lied to Carlotta. It *was* about Mary. You thought you could have both of us. Hell, you thought you could have *all of us*. Well, here's a newsflash, Jack. *Fuck you!*" She turned to me. "Frank, come give me a hand with this two-timing ape."

I got to my feet. My knees felt like someone had tried to open them with a claw hammer. I took his legs, Dee Dee his arm, and we dragged him to the edge. The dogs were still milling around ten stories below. Some cops had turned up and were making a half-arsed effort to clear the area.

Dee Dee leaned over and looked into Jack's eyes. His stare was dead, but he was still in there, somewhere. "When I found out what you and Mary were doing, I shot her between the eyes. I killed her, and now I've got both of you. What have you got to say for yourself now, Jack?"

Jack spat up some blood.

"Thought so," she said, her lip curling. Then she turned to me.

"Do it, Frank," she said, and there was excitement in her voice. "Do it now. And make it hurt."

"But Dee Dee, the cops—"

"This is just another turf war to them, Frank. They won't care about us. After all, we're only a couple of deads under the bed." She gave me one of those crooked smiles that melted me inside.

This was the real Dee Dee, looking at me with those shining eyes. Dorothy Drowne. She wasn't playing me no more, and by God she was gorgeous. I didn't need telling twice, and Dorothy didn't look away neither. She watched me, and she smiled. When I was done, she shoved the corpse over the edge and walked away. I watched her go, perfect arse swaying under her long coat, and I smiled, too.

If revenge is a dish best served cold, that dame's gonna rock this town to the core, because revenge is a way of life around here, and she's as cold as ice. Folks in the Land of the Living ain't ever come across a woman like that, sitting up there, over the rainbow, in their cotton wool clouds.

But one day they will. One day Dorothy's gonna figure a way to get up there to that Emerald City and tear down the curtain, just like she said. One day Dorothy's gonna show those Skins the kind of balls it takes to make it in *my town*, and that's the kind of dream that gives a man hope.

That's the kind of dream that gives a man a reason to live.

PROHIBITION BLUES

Lisa L. Hannett and Angela Slatter

Music drifted like smoke from beneath the closed door. Slow rhythms carried a baritone's chocolate voice out the house's open windows, dripped it down the front porch and left it pooling beneath Maeve's high-heeled Mary Janes. If this song had a colour, she thought, it would be silver. Just like that dress she'd been eyeing off in Trehaine's display: the slip's fringed hemline abbreviated at mid-thigh; over that, a sheer sheath beaded with oyster fruit; and, best of all, only available in sizes 2-5. As soon as they got paid, that dress was hers. It would show off her figure and blackberry hair to perfection.

She shook her head, focussed and yelled: "Tallulah! Get the hell out here or I'm going without you."

For effect, she bent down in front of Bella's dark green Model T and rolled the crank. The jazz cut short as the jalopy sputtered to life and she could hear her cousin's heels clattering on the wooden stairs inside. It would only be a moment before the front door was flung open and Tallulah flew out, temper as hot as her bouncy red bob. Maeve grinned. It was almost as easy pushing that girl's buttons as it was getting the yokels to open their wallets at the speakeasies night after night. A crimson tornado tore out the entryway to the ivy-covered, drunk-angled house they shared. As Tallulah slammed the front door shut and powered down the steps, Maeve could have sworn she saw steam coming off her.

"Maeve Beaufort, you two bit chippy! Where are my—you are wearing my best shoes!"

"Oh, c'mon Tallulah. You know I can't find one of my strappy black ones and our outfits need to match. Don't take on. After tonight, we'll have plenty to throw around, more shoes than you can poke a stick at. Josephine Baker herself will turn green with envy."

Tallulah sighed. "But I haven't even worn those yet. You could've taken these ones."

"These fit better. Now hurry up and don't fuss. We can't afford to be late."

"Those Faerie types aren't keen on tardiness, cousin; you're quite right."

"Got everything?"

Tallulah held up a battered brown suitcase with tarnished gold locks. She shook it gently and slid one set of slender fingers along its edge. Glittering sparks shot into the night and a delicate series of clinks rang out. "Hell, yes."

"Then let the good times roll."

. . .

The parties they frequented were always two parties, not just one. Oh, most folk who went along, all gussied up in their flapper finery, their gangster chic, were there for the canapés and the occasional bootlegged liquor. More often than not, the very people promoting the prohibition laws were the first ones to break them. Yet the majority of these wheelers and dealers, these hypocritical law-keepers, didn't generally know that the real action wasn't something they controlled; that in back rooms, cellars, attics, and sometimes in hidden rooms that once sheltered those poor folk shuffling along the Underground Railroad, in those places the other parties were in full swing.

Few people knew that with the right lineage and a *bon mot* for the thugs manning the door, a girl could have a taste of the underworld and share in its riches. But as Tallulah and Maeve were only too aware, whether or not she survived to cash her cheque depended on savvy and the quality of her performance.

The girls pulled into a parking space on Clancy Robillard's front lawn. The antebellum mansion was lit up like a ship at sea, light rolling out into the night, chasing away the darkness as an unwelcome guest. They checked their hair and make-up in pretty hand-held compacts and got out of the car, adjusting their matching red dresses, shimmying so all the gleaming fringes fell just so. Maeve grabbed the suitcase from the backseat and they walked up to the portico, arm in arm.

The two doormen were muscular, squat and very, very hairy. Bitten, thought Tallulah, thankful the moon was nowhere near full. Bitten and making the best of it by working as bodyguards and security men—now that the newly morally correct police force wouldn't employ them. She wondered what happened when that unfortunate time of the month rolled around; who locked them up and kept them (and everyone else) safe while mistress moon held her sway. She notched a smile to her lips, tight as a bowstring, so the men wouldn't know what she was thinking.

Maeve did the same, tilting her head so the lustrous black of her locks lay across her high cheekbones. Tallulah played peek-a-boo through her long fringe. Born flirts the both of them, their Grandmamma used to say. And who taught us? the girls would ask and screech with laughter as Bella sent sparks shooting from her fingertips—not hot or hard enough to hurt, just to let them know she wouldn't be sassed. At least, not quite so much.

"Good evening, boys," purred Maeve.

The shorter, squatter one looked them up and down. "Y'all the entertainment?"

Tallulah didn't like his tone. Made them sound like cheap hookers.

"We're the singers, *cher*," Maeve drawled, playing out an accent she didn't actually have. "Don't you be thinking otherwise."

The hairy one relaxed visibly and stepped aside so they could go through. As Tallulah passed his companion, the man leaned in and whispered, "Dry tonight. Feds are here."

She smiled and nodded as if he'd made a joke. Maeve's grip on her arm told her she'd heard, too. They'd need to be careful. If there was no booze here because of the long arm of the law, then chances were the other party, the under party might be known or suspected. They would need to keep their wits about them. Neither girl planned on spending her youth in a federal penitentiary.

The chandelier-lit ballroom thronged with the rich, powerful and sober of Charleston. Maeve hid a smile—she'd seen more than a few of the same faces at other soirées, leaning hard against walls, bow ties loose, dress straps slipping dangerously low as alcohol fumes filled the air. This evening they were all much more... temperate... why, butter wouldn't melt in their mouths. And— wasn't that Lucille Vander-something-or-other? The last time Maeve had seen her at a shindig, that leading socialite and member of the Temperance League had been straddling Beauregard Fortescue in the back parlour of Libby Landorff's *pied-à-terre* in town. Maeve looked at her cousin and saw by her raised brows that Tallulah was remembering the same thing, or something very close to it.

They made their way through the crowd and found their host standing by the huge unlit fireplace, his elbow resting casually on the mantel, and surrounded by five or six other men, equally well-dressed and prosperous-looking. Mr Robillard tilted his head back when he spoke, perpetually looking down his nose at those around him. His voice held all the zeal of a preacher and the shoddy conviction of a snake-handler. "Why, even more invidious is its effect on our own people! I swear it won't be long before even Mickey Malone's own mother is set to join our campaign." A round of deep chuckles tore through the group. "Just imagine: young Mick, standing in his ma's parlour with a look of innocence so compelling she wouldn't have noticed the Tommy gun slung over his shoulder, the blood spattering his hands and suit. No matter how hard she looked, to her eyes his soul was so spotless it glowed! What a trick."

Chuckles developed into guffaws. "Soon as old Mrs Malone realised her son's squeaky clean image came out of a bottle of 'shine," Robillard continued. "That he hadn't earned his absolution like the rest of us, but snorted it instead, word is she whacked him so hard he couldn't keep his bookies' numbers straight for a week." His laughter subsided. Wiping a tear from his eye, his face suddenly grew serious. "Filthy stuff, that 'shine. Even filthier that felons like him can still get their hands on it—and use it to fool their own mothers, no less! Mark my words, gentlemen. She'll come to us before moon dark."

All around, grunts and nods of assent. Robillard broke off his speech when he saw the girls, and smiled fit to burst.

Tallulah thought, not for the first time, that his teeth just weren't quite right. And he was running to fat—in a year he'd be giving a French bulldog competition in the jowls department.

"And here they are, the gorgeous Misses Beaufort, honouring us with their beauty and talent tonight. Gentlemen, we are spoilt."

"Why, Clancy, you are too kind." Maeve smiled sweetly. She knew Tallulah couldn't stand the man, but she gave her cousin credit for keeping a civil tongue, and not slapping Robillard as he looked her up and down like she was a piece of meat he might buy.

Their host stopped his ogling long enough to make introductions to the men in his circle, which was all fine and dandy until he got to someone they already knew far too well.

"No introduction necessary, Clancy," said the tall blond man with a wide insincere smile and eyes as blue as his sapphire tie pin. "We're family."

"Why, Fayette, how charming to see you again." Tallulah's tone said it was anything but. Here was the reason for the complete lack of booze. She'd wondered before if the Feds knew about the other party. If cousin Marc Fayette, the renegade of their family, the white sheep if you will, was at this gathering, if he was the face of the Feds, then hell yes, someone knew something was going down. Or suspected. And it meant the girls had to be extra careful.

"Tallulah, Maeve. Didn't expect to see you here. Still living in the old place?"

"Of course. No reason to leave the legacy behind, Fayette. We know where we come from," Maeve said. She pulled at Tallulah's arm. "You'll forgive us, we have a show to do. Do drop by sometime, if you can remember the way."

The girls felt Fayette's glare long after they'd found the room Robillard kept aside for performers. As soon as the door shut behind them, Maeve began to swear.

"Shit. Shit, shit, shit."

"Can't you do better than that?"

"Double shit with a honey glaze."

Tallulah laughed in spite of herself. "Maeve, this is a bad idea. If Fayette's here, he's got an inkling. He'll be watching us."

"He'll stick to us like shit on a shoe, Tallulah. Damnit!" She wrung her hands like they were dish rags. "Maybe we shouldn't go through with it tonight?"

"Nuh-uh. We've got to stick to the plan. Feds or no, if we don't come through on this deal, they won't trust us again. It won't matter that we're the last of our kind or that our family have supplied for the last hundred years. None of that will amount to a hill of beans. The Faerie don't forgive and they sure as hell don't forget."

"Shit," said Maeve again and kicked at an elegant side-table. One of its legs snapped and the whole structure wobbled. The expensive-looking vase on top teetered dangerously, but didn't fall. "Shit."

"We go on stage. We do our thing, we muddle through." Tallulah grinned at her cousin. "Hell, we're smarter than Fayette, always were."

Maeve nodded and returned her grin.

• • •

The band was on a raised dais, playing soft, dignified tunes. The girls had worked with them many times before, so the musicians knew what to do when Maeve and Tallulah appeared.

There was a great drum roll starting out like distant thunder and then building to a vibrating crescendo; the trumpet player let loose a wailing blow as the girls mounted the stage all shimmering and shiny, before every member of the band produced an ear-splitting wolf-whistle. It had the desired effect, stopping the gathering in its tracks and bringing the attention of everyone in the enormous ballroom to the one place.

The Beaufort Girls had arrived and the tone of the evening, having no chance against their particular brand of charm, changed.

"Well, hello, good people of Charleston," Tallulah breathed, batting her lashes.

Maeve made a cupid's bow moue and sang out, "My, what a handsome group!"

With just the right amount of preliminary eyelash fluttering and pouting, they launched into a round of songs, belting out favourites like 'Ain't Misbehaving', 'Love Me or Leave Me', and 'Lovesick Blues'. Previously sedate butter and egg men took their hands off their bankrolls, and applauded wildly after each number. To keep themselves amused, before each gig the girls arbitrarily selected the audience members they'd lavish with particular attention. One night it was men without jackets, the next it was those with. Sometimes black hair would seal the deal, others it was ginger bucks who tickled their fancies. This little extra attentiveness had been known to ensure handsome gifts and cash donations from besotted admirers. So when Tallulah had declared this afternoon, "Ascots. The more outrageous the better," ascots it was.

Between sets, Maeve took a swig of water, covered her microphone. "Striped and purple, stage left. Pinned with an emerald the size of my knuckle."

Tallulah looked at the balding gent with the designated tie. "Oh, my. Gotcha. That would pay to replace the roof at home," she said. Taking her mic from its stand, she caught the gentleman's eye and held it. Sauntering to the front of the stage, the fringes of her dress swaying enticingly, she said, "Our next tune is real close to my heart." She tilted her head earnestly, trying not to laugh at the sweat beading Purple Ascot's forehead. "It's a gem, sung for a real gem of an audience."

Over her shoulder, Tallulah called out, "'Embraceable You', boys."

Purple Ascot couldn't contain himself: he whistled like he was slumming it at a barrel house.

"Easy tiger," Tallulah laughed. "We're only getting started."

The band carried the crowd through set after set of smoky blues and old-fashioned ragtime tunes; the girls by turns fluttered their fingers and swung their hips in Maroon Striped, Eggyolk Yellow and Beige Herringbone Ascots' directions. In the middle of their third encore, Tallulah spotted their final tie for the evening.

"White with a black moon clip," she whispered, while she and Maeve had their backs to the crowd, their arms and legs swinging in the frenzied dance that was making their town famous. "Caught a peek of it over near Fayette's circle of feds."

Maeve spun on her heel and scanned the room, already planning what she'd say before breaking the poor man's heart with her last chorus. Waiters holding trays of soda and lemon water negotiated the throng, taking no offense when people nipped out to steal a swig from hidden flasks. The suit-clad feds and uniformed local constabulary, secretly wishing they could join the train of revellers as they moved in and out of the ballroom, worked the crowd half-heartedly unless Fayette was nearby. Maeve spied her cousin and a couple of his deputies next to the Mayor and Charleston's Chief of Police. Standing between them, just hidden by the Chief's overly large form, was a stark white pantsuit. The type that would be topped off perfectly with an equally white ascot tie.

"Thank y'all for coming," she said, the band playing and replaying the bridge until they got Maeve's cue to wrap it up. "You're in our hearts, each and every one of you—but this last chorus is reserved for the boys in blue over there."

Judging by the noise, this crowd was as expert at feigning love for its lawmen as the Beaufort girls. Maeve whooped, twirled her finger at the pianist, and she and Tallulah turned to their mics in unison. "I love my man," they began, putting their all into it—and both faltered, just a little, when the white ascot's wearer came fully into view.

The woman's platinum blonde hair was slicked back in a bun. Her dead brown eyes were ringed with black eyeliner, and though they were directed at the men before her as she nodded in agreement to whatever they were saying, those dark orbs seemed to focus on twelve different places at once. Eugenia Laveau hadn't seemed to notice them, although Tallulah couldn't figure out how she could have avoided it. Eugenia Laveau: practising sorceress; local crime boss; distant descendant of New Orleans' witch queen, Marie. The woman who knew where the bodies were buried because she'd put them there. Once Grandmamma Bella Beaufort's sworn enemy and rival.

Tallulah signalled to the band to finish with a drum solo. Hearts pounding furiously, the girls blew kisses at their admirers, curtseyed at their detractors, then beat a hasty retreat from the stage. Quickly, they ducked into the performers' room to collect the battered brown case, before slipping along a deserted corridor until the music became nothing more than a burbling hum.

"That was too close," Maeve hissed, pushing open the door to the basement stairs. "We're lucky she didn't recognise us."

Tallulah was hot on her cousin's heels. "Don't count your chickens, doll." She knew it was only a matter of time before Eugenia caught wind of their presence. The rest would be dominoes: Beaufort girls meant moonshine; which meant there'd be Fae prowling around the joint; which meant deals were being struck beneath Laveau's nose.

Without her say-so.

On her turf.

Much to her displeasure.

The heavy wooden door swung shut behind them, muffling the demands of a crowd too fired-up to notice the girls' clumsy exit.

• • •

The tunnels beneath Clancy's house were filthy. Tallulah shied away from the spiders' webs mainly because they had spiders dangling in them. The shining steel door at the end of the tunnel was attended by two burly guards. Maeve thought they did a reasonable job of passing as human, but "Work on the aftershave, boys," she said as one of them pulled the enormous bolt on the barrier and the other pushed it open. "The peppermint's a dead giveaway."

"A rasher of bacon in your pocket will do the trick," Tallulah suggested with a wink. The men grunted before closing the door behind them.

The ante-chamber the girls stepped into was like a storm porch, a spot where you could tidy yourself up after being outside. Carefully placing the suitcase on the ground, Maeve checked her hair for spiders and webs while Tallulah rubbed her arms as if imaginary arachnids danced on her skin. Each used the other as a mirror, making sure they were clean and lovely and nothing less than they could possibly be. One thing they couldn't escape, though, was the smell of smoke in their hair. There were so many folk upstairs puffing out white clouds that the girls' locks reeked—their lavender toilet water was no match for Charleston tobacco.

This was their first solo deal. The first time they'd done anything since Grandmamma died in the accident. Since the main still she'd kept out in the swamps had somehow ruptured, frying Bella Beaufort and leaving a hole in the ground where 'gators and gars now swam quite happily. It had taken months to set up a new still, to get the recipe right, to make enough to fill the order they'd received—and when it came, it was not only an order for goods, it was an order as in there was no choice as to whether or not they supplied. They'd been the couriers before, delivering Bella's best to under parties all through Charleston, but this time they were it.

A last, slender barrier stood before them. One final breath, deep and steadying, then Tallulah picked up the case and Maeve turned the handle on the door.

...

The light was almost blinding.

The room was the white of snow and almost as cold. The furniture, what little there was of it, was pale Nordic pine, silver metal, thickly blown glass strong as a diamond. Mirrors edged with linear etchings stretched from floor to ceiling along the near and far walls, making the space look infinite as the girls entered, positioned briefly to see their own reflections. For a few seconds, hundreds of Tallulahs and Maeves stepped across the marble floor, the bright red of their lipstick, the deep berry shades of their hair, and the sparkle of their dresses almost garish against the bleached backdrop. It was a relief to move beyond the frames. The air reeked of peppermint and a haze of white smoke, almost a mist, floated near the ceiling as if the people in the room could command the clouds.

Tallulah thought they might be able to, if they wanted. If they ever troubled themselves to do anything so pointless, so frivolous. Maybe these ones would—these who snuck around on their own kind, doing things that might just get them exiled. Shoulders back, heads held high, the girls threaded their way through the crowd. The group was select: maybe thirty of the Faerie folk, mostly male. Real daisies, the lot of them. All were tall and thin to the point of emaciation, not burdened by the weight having a soul lends human frames. A handful of them reclined on elegant chaises, crystal wine flutes loosely clutched in their fingers, while the rest stood in pairs or perched on painfully slender barstools. They seemed as if they'd all been cast from the same elegant mould, inhabitants and barstools alike. Both were sculptural and looked liable to shatter at the slightest disturbance. Both, Tallulah knew, were stronger than they appeared and could break your neck if pushed the wrong way.

When they deigned to notice the girls at all, the Fae regarded the pair as if they were something less, a subspecies. Tallulah didn't think they had any right to be so high and mighty, not when they were buying what they were buying. Not when they were no better than those human addicts who hid themselves away to chase the dragon. No right to be so uppity when their own folk would hand down terrible judgment on them if it were to be discovered they were using what the Beaufort girls made; what was in the case they had with them. Tallulah felt the sweat from her palm slicking the handle.

"Miss Maeve?" A voice, feather-light, slid through the air and caught their attention. "And Miss Tallulah. Thank you for coming."

"You say that like we had a choice." Tallulah didn't feel like mincing her words. Her cousin put a gentle hand on her shoulder.

"Mr Indridi?" Maeve said and received a minimal nod in reply, unsure whether it was all her client felt was needed or all he could be bothered to give. She decided she didn't really care. Though most of the club's patrons were doing a fine job pretending the girls weren't there, Maeve knew they were being watched. From the corner of her eye, she could see heads turned to follow their progression in the mirrors. She was tempted to pivot and wink at them.

But this was business, not pleasure.

"You have the product?" Navan Indridi asked. He was dressed in a grey so pale it was nearly white. Slim-cut slacks accentuated the length of his legs; a silk shirt, buttoned up to a high collar and linked three times at the cuff, skimmed across his lean torso like water. The only suggestion of colour was the green of his narrow tie, precisely the cold hue of his eyes.

"Yes. We've got your 'shine, Mr Indridi." Tallulah noticed, with no little satisfaction, that he cringed at the word. She bit down on a smile.

"Not here." Clasping his hands behind his back, he gestured with his head to a curtained door on the far side of the room. "This way," he said. He didn't tell them twice, didn't turn to see if they followed.

The click of their heels echoed as they walked across the main room, the sound as stark as the music they could hear softly playing. A very different music to that of the upstairs party. Single piano notes seemed to drop from above; a double bass was plucked at random, its tones mournful next to the icicle clarity of the piano. Occasionally, a violin would tie the two together, its fine wail setting Maeve's teeth on edge. There was no band, no musicians to speak of, so she couldn't figure out where the sound was coming from. Goosebumps pimpled her bare arms as she hurried to keep up with the Fae.

"The curtain," he said, once they'd all crossed the threshold into a private dining room. Tallulah looked at her cousin and lifted the case as if to say, "Hands full," then waited for Indridi to invite them to sit in any one of the sixteen chairs flanking the long birch table. She was still waiting, even after Maeve had loosened the tasselled ropes from hooks embedded in the doorframe, letting the heavy fabric fall shut.

"We mustn't excite the masses," Indridi said, taking a seat in a high-backed chrome chair. He crossed his legs, folded his hands on his knees. His face, perfectly illuminated beneath a cluster of triangular chandeliers, betrayed no emotion. "If the vintage of these spirits proves less than what we've bargained for, it's best they don't get so much as a whiff of it. I'm not sure I could assure your safety in that instance." He removed his steel-framed glasses, examined the lenses for a speck of non-existent dust, then replaced them on the bridge of his sharp nose. "There's nothing worse than taking a hit of coffin varnish when what you need is something pure."

"You faekes sure have some nerve—"

Maeve cut Tallulah off before her tart tongue got them firmly on Indridi's bad side. "Bella always used to tell us," she said, silently daring her cousin to contradict her, "That your establishments are no average juice joints."

"Is that so." Indridi's tone was flat. "An insightful woman, your Greatmother."

Keeping her eyes locked on his, Maeve smiled a dimple into her cheek. "Pardon me, but it's Grand—"

Noticing the correction, and the faint flush rising up the Fae's neck, Tallulah slid the case onto the table top. She clicked the clasps, quickly opened it, deftly removed the false bottom, and displayed the contents as she would a picture book to a child. "You couldn't be righter, doll," she said to Maeve. "Beaufort Moonshine is grand. Always has been, always will be. Have a belt, Mr Indridi. You won't be disappointed."

His schooled expression transformed when he caught sight of the twenty-four cut-glass bottles, each the length of a man's hand and three of his fingers wide, topped with silver filigree caps shaped like corks and nestled into custom-fit grooves. Though its violet sateen lining was worn and dull in places and the padding flattened from years of use, the box emitted a glow so bright it made the milk-white walls look beige in comparison. The girls relaxed, seeing the flint melt from Indridi's eyes. Now this was an exoression they recognised: they'd just seen it on half their audience's faces.

Their smiles widened. Whether it was sported by man, woman or Fae, red hot hunger was unmistakeable. Longing was longing, no matter who wore it.

Tallulah plucked a phial at random, removed the lid and waved it beneath the Fae's nose. She held it there barely long enough for him to catch the moonshine's complex aroma before whisking it away, covering its mouth with her thumb. When the tension eased in her client's shoulders, and his posture slackened ever so slightly, she knew the mixture was as potent as she and Maeve had suspected. Even she could detect the lingering musk of humanity, taunting him. And she also knew, before he'd even opened his mouth, that he'd want another sample.

"Too short," he said, jaw clenched to retain his veneer of calm. "I couldn't quite catch the afterglow. No deal if it mellows too quickly."

"Do we look like the type of girls to brew up a batch of mellow?" Maeve's laugh was the throaty one she'd practised a thousand times on stage. "Give him another kick, Tallulah," she said, and was tempted to let her heels match her words, but realised that, just now, Indridi was in no state to appreciate the finer points of cabaret timing.

With a wink for Maeve, Tallulah held the bottle out for three solid seconds. Indridi inhaled deeply, drinking in the scent of starlight mixed with a dash of love, loss, hope—the essence of a human soul. The delight of such foreign emotions broke his concentration. For the briefest instant, he forgot to maintain his guise: his glasses vanished and white feathers sprouted where his eyebrows had been; cheekbones lengthened and gained an icy blue sheen; his irises, already pastel, lost all hint of colour and swirled with washes of iridescent white. The neat silver braid restraining his long hair unravelled, his tresses lifted, caught in a whirlwind no-one else could feel. Crystal dust flaked from his lashes when, almost immediately, he sneezed. With that, he regained his composure. The only evidence of the lapse was a slight reddening of his cheeks, which he masked by dabbing at his nose with a linen handkerchief.

"Right, then." Tallulah replaced the phial, closed the old brown suitcase. "Peppy enough for you?"

Maeve picked up her cousin's line of questioning. "And the soul's afterglow: tell me that's not pure as a babe on Sunday morning." She sidled over to Indridi, leaned up against the table. For the first time that evening, it felt like the Fae was exuding warmth.

"It'll do," he said, a shade louder than a whisper. The corner of his mouth twitched with the beginnings of a smile.

"Dandy," Tallulah said, placing the case on the floor behind her. "Let's talk about the twenty large this lot'll cost you."

"Bandying numbers is so crass," Indridi began.

"Then call me crass to your heart's content, Mr Indridi, but let's talk about money while you do it." Tallulah tossed her head carelessly then fixed the Fae with a stare that said she meant business.

He opened his lips to begin negotiations.

Beyond the curtain, the stark Faerie music abruptly stopped. Chairs and barstools scraped on the marble floor, then these too fell silent. Around them, the girls noticed, the dining room walls went from polished white to dingy brick. Mould and damp rotted the baseboards, stained the ceiling in an instant. The chandeliers popped like bubbles and were replaced by a single bare bulb dangling from a tattered cord. Its feeble light left the room mostly in the dark. Curtain, table and chairs vanished—mops, tin pails and spartan shelves appeared in their place. Through the door, Tallulah could now see exposed water pipes dripping condensation. Where the Faeries' chaises had lounged, now boxes with faded labels were stacked in haphazard rows. Piles of dirty linens waited to be ferried into the laundry down the hall. Whispers rose and fell in the empty basement, then rustled into the room like dry leaves.

"We've got company, *séfinn*."

Tallulah's ears popped when the Fae's disembodied voice fell away. Maeve shivered. "What's going on?"

Footsteps moving quickly struck the floorboards over their heads. Indridi's eyes focused. Once more they grew sharp, serious. Cool with disappointment.

"Tut, tut," he said, looking beyond the broom closet, through the basement to the door opposite. Yellow light traced its outline as the sound of clomping boots reached the anteroom. The door handle turned from horizontal to vertical. "Should've known you kittens would've had tails."

• • •

Tallulah and Maeve were far too pretty for jail.

"What happened to the guards?" Maeve asked as the door swung open, releasing a swarm of dark-suited Feds and blue-uniformed Charleston flatfoots into the basement, headed by their bastard of a cousin. The girls groaned at the sight of Fayette and retreated further into the shadows. Pressing their backs against the cold wall, they peered into the adjoining room, scanning the place for another way out.

"Over there," Indridi said quietly. No longer kitted out like a pair of ham-fisted bouncers, the Fae security men now wore impressive imitations of the feds' double-breasted jackets. Like the real bulls, their black Oxfords shone beneath perfectly pleated trousers. There were so many law-enforcement officers crowded into the room, in the confusion no one would question a couple of unfamiliar faces. Their batons swung menacingly as the interlopers surveyed the room, ensuring their Fae kinsmen had made a clean sneak.

"Do that voice thing y'all just did—tell them to steer the herd clear of us." When she looked back at Indridi, Maeve faced the spitting image of one of Charleston's finest. Dark, round-cheeked and sweaty, with a belly large enough to make a joke of the twin rows of brass buttons running down his front, the Fae took Maeve by the elbow. His grip was firm, its heat cooling rapidly as the effects of the 'shine he'd snuffed wore off.

"The merchandise," he muttered at Tallulah. As soon as her fingers slid around the handle, the case became a small brown evening bag, but she kept her surprise in check. Indridi locked onto her upper arm, and raised his voice:

"Call off the search, boys. Look'ee, look'ee who I found sticking their mugs where they don't belong." Indridi shuffled the girls into the other room, their protestations at being manhandled adding a nice touch of realism to the act.

"Get your paws off me, Mister—" Tallulah's voice dropped away as the crowd of coppers parted, leaving an avenue wide enough for Fayette and his smug grin to pass through.

"What have we got here, Lieutenant?" Fayette sauntered over to the trio. He stood so close, they could smell the red onions he'd had with lunch. "This what you call keeping the Beaufort name alive, ladies?"

"Want me to get on the blower, sir?" Indridi caught Maeve's eye, held it. "Give the boys down at the watchhouse time to shine the cage up for these canaries?"

Maeve understood the Fae's drift: Make tracks before the bulls sniff out the 'shine. She didn't give her holier-than-thou cousin the opportunity to reply. "Don't bother playing so high and mighty with us, Fayette. Can't nab us for something you're guilty of yourself, unless you're hankering for a family reunion down at the Big House."

Fayette cleared his throat. "Your mind's gone off the track, hasn't it?" He smirked. "Just like the old bat's did before she blew herself to kingdom come."

Tallulah ignored the gibe, although she dearly wanted to apply the toe of her shoe to Fayette's backside. For now, she picked up Maeve's thread, and improvised the way they used to for Mr Ziegfeld's show. "You're a known lurker at Clancy's séances, Marc—don't you try to deny it."

Fury turned Fayette's olive skin a shade lighter. Maeve pretended not to notice how his eyes hardened when she continued: "Keeping such fun to yourself—well, it's downright selfish. So we asked ourselves, 'Why not go downstairs and get an eyeful of the hocus pocus?'"

"'We could catch up with our old pal Fayette in the process.'"

"'And keep our friends close, but our family closer'—isn't that just what we were thinking, Tallulah?"

"Sure was." She directed her next comment to the elephant ears hanging on their every word. "See, my dumb Dora of a cousin here's lost one of her snazziest shoes." Maeve shrugged her shoulders, widened her eyes, and puckered her lips in the best Helen Kane impression this side of the Ashley River. The men chuckled despite their superior's frown. Tallulah leaned as far forward as she could without breaking Indridi's hold, and whispered conspiratorially: "We were hoping a real live witch like the ones Clancy hires for his get-togethers might be able to track it down for us. Now, is that a crime?"

"In some places." A woman's voice echoed from the back. "Yes, it is."

The subterranean temperature, already chill, dropped another few degrees as Eugenia Laveau crossed the room. Hands in her pockets, she walked unhurriedly but with purpose. Her eyebrows lifted when she spied the clutch Tallulah carried. They rose even further when she turned to the broom closet; her forehead creased to the roots of her hair as she investigated its dim interior. Stooping down, she ran her fingers along the floor where the Fae table used to stand. She sniffed the sparkling crystal dust on her fingertips. Licked it. Nodding, she plucked a single white feather from beneath the rim of an overturned bucket. Before straightening up, she tucked it in her pocket, head tilted back as though she'd been struck by an elusive thought. As though she was on the brink of a sneeze.

Fayette's gaze followed Laveau's impressive figure. Tallulah could see he wasn't happy to have her there. "Hang whatever will stick on them," he told Indridi. "Just get them out of here."

"Find anything of interest, Officer?" Laveau's gaze was still averted, focused on the floor and walls, but it was clear to whom she'd addressed her question.

"Not to my knowledge," Indridi replied, his voice suitably gruff. He tightened his grip on the girls and began to move towards the door. Laveau glided into his path, and the tension in the room ratcheted up. Maeve held her breath. From the corner of her eye she caught sight of Fayette's expression; he looked an awful lot like Bella on her lightning temper days. He stepped between Eugenia and her prey, just as she was pulling a hand from her pocket, raising it towards Indridi's chest.

Marc was brave, Tallulah would give him that. Or stupid. Or he just really didn't want anyone pissing on his patch, especially not some spell-shooting, voodoo-doll pinning, crime boss. She could see Eugenia hesitate, like she really wanted to hex him, but decided not to—like there were too many feds here even for her. She could bide her time. She would wait.

"Lieutenant, get the suspects out of here," said Fayette. "And you, Miz Laveau, have no place here. Kindly remove yourself from my investigation."

Maeve caught a smile from Eugenia that made her think of the Bitten Ones and she shivered involuntarily. Indridi nodded dutifully to Fayette, and then half-pushed, half-dragged her and Tallulah out, through the storm room, along the long corridor, then up the steps once more. As soon as the light at the top of the stairs showed, Maeve started to breathe again.

Maybe, she thought, just maybe we'll get away with this.

• • •

"Little ladies! Y'all are back at last," hooted a fat industrialist with a penchant for plaid trousers. It seemed he and quite a few others had taken the opportune disappearance of the sterner bluecoats to openly indulge. Over his shoulder Tallulah could see the Chief of Police taking a swig from a hip flask offered by Clancy Robillard's son. She laughed, and felt an overwhelming urge to kiss the boy.

"Now, when is the next set, my sweets?" continued their inebriated beau.

"Not now, darlin'," crooned Maeve. "Show's over."

"Oh," he said and his face fell like a spoilt child denied candy. Then he brightened as if a very clever thought had occurred to him. "Party's not over until I say so!"

He swung towards Tallulah to sweep her up. "Oh, enough futzing around," she said. Her right hand barely moved. Only someone watching closely would have seen it, but a stream of thin blue-gold sparks flew from the tips of her fingers and hit him in the chest and shoulders. He jumped back and did a jig, slapping himself as if to put out a fire no one but he could see or feel. It distracted him long enough for Indridi to bustle the girls past.

"Impressive, Miss Tallulah. Tell me, do you have any other tricks?"

Maeve answered, "Nope. That's pretty much the extent of our mixed blood heritage: cheap fireworks. Nothing like what Bella Beaufort had in her arsenal."

They were almost at the exit. No one was paying them any attention now: the girls had consciously dimmed their showgirl sparkle, and Indridi's magic helped to dampen their natural glamour. They slouched and imagined themselves small and nondescript as they headed to one of the house's less-employed back doors, so they made it to their goal unmolested. All three stepped out into the cool night air, breathing a mutual sigh of relief.

"Lordy, lordy, something smells out here," drawled a low rough voice. Maeve whipped around. Two stout, hirsute men stepped out of the darkness, moonlight accentuating the crags in their cheeks and around their yellow eyes. Bitten Ones, smaller and nastier than the two posted out front, noses crinkling with the smell of Fae blood. It wasn't full moon; they couldn't shift, but they were still mean and dangerous, with one hell of a bite. They moved quickly despite their stunted legs; before Maeve could blink twice the men were closing in. Indridi pushed the girls aside, spat words: two silver chains streaked from his mouth, shifting like snakes in the air, coiling around the torsos of the security men, who began to snarl and scream. Tallulah caught a whiff of burning fur and flesh as the links tightened and took hold.

"You're right, gentlemen," she said, sniffing and daintily blocking her nose with the backs of her fingers. "What a stench!"

The Bitten Ones' howls of rage intensified and were taken up all around the house's perimeter. Shadows bobbed across Robillard's manicured lawns, stretching from the direction of the side and front yards as the other guards' lupine voices drew nearer and nearer.

"Don't just stand there," hissed Indridi. "Run!"

• • •

"Told you we should have turned right," grumbled Tallulah as her foot slid in the mud and plunged into the quagmire of the bayou. "Oh, my second-best pair of shoes!"

"If you could concentrate on surviving instead of moaning about fashion, we'd all be better off, Miss Tallulah," shot back Indridi. The Fae had dropped his copper's façade, and was doing his best to ignore both the cloying humidity and the mud stains seeping up the pale fabric of his trousers.

"All well and good for you, Mr Faeke, but these pumps are Herman Delmans—the closest I'll ever get to a pair of André Perugias at this rate!"

"Not to mention Ferragamos," Maeve muttered.

Tallulah exhaled sharply, lowered her voice. "And they're my only other pair of shoes. Of course, someone as flush as you wouldn't be familiar with that problem."

As she spoke, she heard a splash and a whole lot of cursing. Maeve was struggling to get out of a knee-deep bog. When she freed herself, her left foot was unshod and the right was a high-heeled mess of mud and muck.

Tallulah sighed as she helped her cousin. "And now I have no shoes."

"Get us out of this and I will buy you all the damned shoes you want!"

Indridi, thought Maeve, was displaying rather more human emotions than one of his kind was wont to do. Of course, Tallulah could be a trial and would drive a saint to distraction—why not a Fae? She shrugged.

"Don't fuss so, Mr Indridi. We know this place like the backs of our hands." Idly, Maeve turned her left hand over and examined it with vague surprise. "Well, look at that. Of course, normally we're here in daylight. And it was a few years ago . . . " A small vertical wrinkle grew between Maeve's eyebrows as she concentrated.

Feeling the greedy mud eager to claim her right shoe, she lurched forward. Stumbling into her cousin, Maeve surveyed the shadowy landscape. "I want to say this all looks familiar, but . . . "

Everything was so dark, so similar. Hundreds of trees loomed like ghosts out of the bayou. Moonlight was dappled through the leafy canopy overhead, its reflection lost in the fog curling across the water's surface. Stray moonlight caught the eyes of watchful 'gators that languidly trailed the trio. In places, long reeds and cattails poked their heads out of the haze, marking the boundary between riverbank and solid ground. Bullfrogs hummed and croaked, the sound hemming the three in. If only they could find a point of reference, or one of Bella's markers. Maeve had heard of people gauging their position by looking at the stars—so she released Tallulah's arm, craned her neck and strained to locate the Big Dipper. She took a few steps forward, seeking the brightest star in Orion's belt, and—

"Watch out!" Tallulah warned, waiting for the splash as Maeve toppled off the path and disappeared into the murk.

Instead, there was a squeal, a thump, and the sound of timber snapping.

"Shit," Maeve hissed as she righted herself, inspecting her dress for snags and her palms for splinters. "Those railings were much sturdier when we were kids . . . "

Tallulah snorted. "There are more graceful ways of making an entrance, you know."

Maeve put on a serious face, but her relief at having found the causeway to Bella's second storehouse was irresistible. She smiled and retorted, "It's a new dance move, called the 'Told you we were going the right way' step. Nice, huh?"

Tallulah hefted the case and returned her cousin's smile. "That's enough out of you."

Water lapped the walkway's planks, which were soft and slick with algae from years of disuse. It zigzagged across the bayou, its furthest pilings invisible more than ten metres out. The trio stepped carefully, clutching the handrails only when absolutely necessary. After five minutes their legs ached from walking so unnaturally—and by the time they reached the copse of trees sheltering Bella's shack, they were stiffer than a shot of cheap whisky.

Indridi sneered at the sight of the dilapidated cabin. Its foundations were propped on a network of stilts two feet above the waterline; its walls were weathered and its red tin roof sagging. "This is where you intend for me to stay?"

"Take it or leave it," Tallulah said, casually swinging the valise. "The feds are bound to look for us at home, and they surely know where Bella's main warehouse was, given the explosion and all . . . And since you won't whisk us away to your place—"

"Not won't, Miss Tallulah. Can't."

"Like I said, since Faerieland is apparently too good for the likes of us, this is what we're left with. You want the 'shine, Mr Indridi? Then you have to help see us through 'til morning, wait 'til the heat's a little less intense."

"I'm afraid that isn't going to happen any time soon, cousin."

Fayette eased himself off the sturdy bench Bella Beaufort kept on the shack's front porch. Sore feet make a person stingy, the old woman used to say. The most profitable deals are the ones negotiated sitting down. Maeve always thought that was just a line her Grandmamma spun to teach the girls about hospitality—anyone who dealt with Bella knew she judged the weight of a man's wallet by the clink his arse made on that bench. But now, looking at Indridi's ragged appearance and thinking of the money she and Tallulah still hadn't seen from him, Maeve wondered if she shouldn't have listened closer to that piece of advice.

"Don't make things difficult," Fayette said. "We want the case. Leave now and I'll even forget you two were fraternising with twinkle-toes there—consider it a family favour."

"Bastard!" Tallulah stormed up the steps as quickly as the slippery surface would allow. "How dare you come here!" She stopped short on the landing, her momentum broken by the .38 in her cousin's hand, and the chorus of low growls coming from inside the shack. Keeping the gun steady, Fayette moved aside. The cabin door creaked open behind him.

"Get a wriggle on, ladies. That's our cue to make an exit," Indridi began, his words trailing away as three of the Bitten Ones they'd eluded back at Robillard's stepped outside, followed by their sleek-haired boss, Eugenia Laveau.

Maeve and Tallulah's faces were twin masks of disgust and anger. "What the hell are you playing at, cousin? Since when did you become the witch's lapdog?"

"It's not that simple—"

"Bullshit!"

"Watch that tongue of yours, kitten." The sorceress's outfit was miraculously pristine, all things considered. Sharp and ice-white, just like her voice. "My boys here are only too fond of chasing after waggling meat. Besides, you're too hard on your cousin."

Maeve's pulse raced; she caught sight of Fayette's sapphire tie pin placed just below Laveau's, gleaming like a trophy on her ascot. Fayette had been compelled. "Dry up, hag."

Laveau shook her head, took her hands out of her pockets. Blue fire crackled along her fingertips. "You Beaufort women are all the same. Stupid rubes, the lot of you. I should've known you'd be too thick to learn from the lesson I taught old Bella."

Tallulah retreated, overwhelmed by visions of the distillery in flames; the calm night screaming with moonshine explosions; Bella's charred skin, singed hair, lifeless eyes. She stumbled on the bottom step, but kept her balance. "It was you."

"Give the girl a hand, boys." Eugenia applauded while the men filled the air with catcalls. "She can add two plus two."

The muzzle of Fayette's gun drooped as he looked sideways at the sorceress. "Just give her the case and we'll be through here." Squinting, gaze fixed on the pure energy licking up Laveau's fingers, he growled, "Now." Maeve was gratified, just a little, to see him struggle against the witch's hex. He may have been an arse, but he was family.

"I'll pay you double to listen to him, Miss Tallulah." Indridi edged forward, keeping one eye on the pistol and the other on Eugenia. Feathers ruffled across his brow; his features stretched, hardened. Maeve thought of the white feather Laveau had pocketed and wondered if the witch's magic would work on the Fae.

"What—this case?" Tallulah said, throwing it to Maeve, just as one of the Bitten Ones taunted, "Too much a faery to fight like a man?"

"That's the kicker, isn't it?" Indridi watched Maeve open the battered suitcase and remove two bottles of 'shine. He licked his lips, and for a fleeting moment his face darkened. "I'm not a man."

In an instant, his plumage turned to white fur. His nose elongated in perfect imitation of the Bitten Ones' full-moon snouts and his mouth grew ragged with deadly teeth. His tailored suit stretched, turned to flesh and muscle, lending his slight frame a werewolf's weight. Then he smiled, and his eyes glowed with the light of a thousand fireflies.

On the porch, Laveau stretched out her arm, launched a streak of lightning at the Fae.

Before the spell hit, Indridi disappeared. Blue fire blasted a hole through the walkway where he'd been, sending Maeve flying. She scrambled to her hands and knees, slid across slimy boards, and gathered the scattered bottles of 'shine back into the case. Holding two in one hand, she pulled their stoppers, snapped her fingers until a shower of sparks cascaded into each. "Thanks, Bella," she whispered, quickly replacing the caps, and shaking them until the glass grew too hot to hold.

"Tallulah," she cried. "Duck!"

In quick succession, the phials of 'shine sailed over Tallulah's head as she crept up the stairs, crouching low to avoid the bullets Fayette was spraying in Maeve's direction. As his free will warred with Laveau's spell, the shots went wide—or his aim was particularly bad. At any rate, none, as yet, had met their target. Tallulah lunged for his legs just as the first bottle of 'shine exploded against the shack wall behind him.

A deep concussion shook the cabin. Rainbow embers flared, blindingly bright. The whole structure rocked on its stilts, tilted dangerously to the left. Fayette pitched forward, down the stairs, still shooting wildly. He collided with Tallulah, who bore the brunt of his weight on her back and shoulders. Instinctively, she straightened up and shoved him away from her. The pistol fell from his grasp, skittered down the steps and landed at her feet.

Indridi, in werewolf shape, appeared on the porch as the second bottle landed. It struck the floorboards between the sorceress and the cluster of men to her left, the explosion knocking two of them over the right-hand railing. Maeve had never met a Bitten One who could swim: these were no exception. She watched the pair flail their arms as they tried to keep afloat—then the waters around them began to churn as the 'gators' patience was rewarded. The howls were drowned out by the incredible sound of the shack's roof caving in. Windows smashed, spitting shards of glass. Indridi leapt out of harm's way, straight into the path of the third goon.

The Fae-in-wolf's-clothing and the wolf-in-man's-clothing wrestled, their strength evenly matched: Indridi bolstered by magic, his opponent hyped on adrenaline and hot blood. Oblivious to their struggle, Eugenia Laveau stared down at Maeve. Hands alive with elemental fire, the witch once more lifted her arms, took aim, and unleashed a searing bolt of light at Bella's granddaughter.

The night split with the snap of released electricity. Fayette shuddered as though struggling to wake. His body swayed, head drunkenly bobbing from side to side as he looked around him. Eyes focussing, he stepped into the path of the blast. While Maeve cowered on the ground not ten feet in front of him, Fayette's torso took the brunt of Laveau's casting. His camel-hair coat and stiff-collared shirt were instantly reduced to a pile of witch ash; the skin beneath scalded, then bubbled, then blackened. The beam of light held him upright even after his knees buckled and his body went slack.

Tallulah snatched up Fayette's lost weapon, pointed it at the sorceress, squeezed her eyes shut and pulled the trigger. The bullet lodged in Eugenia's shoulder, red blossoming on the white fabric, throwing her aim wide just long enough to release Fayette. He slumped down on the walkway and half slid into the water, one of the widely-spaced pilings the only barrier between him and complete submersion.

Still clutching the gun, now empty, Tallulah turned and ran towards Maeve. "Keep tossing those pineapples, girl!"

Maeve reached for another bottle, sparked and shook it, and threw it hard. Too low: it shattered on the steps, about a foot away from where the witch stood. Though wood erupted in a shower of splinters, Eugenia smirked, kept her feet—until the floor lurched beneath them. The platform supporting the shack rumbled, then squealed as it twisted and shuddered. Indridi, teeth clamped around the Bitten One's neck, shuffled awkwardly backwards and collided with Laveau. Maeve's shot might've missed her, but it had ruptured the last solid strut supporting Grandmamma's not-so-secret storehouse. The shack, groaning in defeat, completed its lean to the left, and collapsed into the bayou, taking both Fae and witch with it.

Tallulah and Maeve crawled over to Fayette. While they hauled their cousin's waterlogged body from the mire, they didn't speak; their attention was focused on scanning the water's black surface, waiting for Eugenia's alabaster head to emerge. Hoping as hard as they could for any grace the 'gators might bestow.

"Don't bother: she's gone." Indridi's bare skin gleamed as he hoisted himself onto the walkway beside them. "I think not dead, but gone."

The Fae offered no further explanation. The girls didn't press the issue, merely kept their eyes averted while the naked Fae shook himself like a dog. Water flew from him like diamonds in the moonlight, then he shifted himself back into his stained clothing. They turned their attention to Fayette. He smelled like something toasted too long, and he was glowing with residual magic.

"Aw, Marc. Shit," sighed Tallulah, trying to find a non-burnt spot on his head to rest her hand. But the thick blond locks were now singed beyond belief.

"Give me the case," Indridi said.

"Is that all you think about? Getting high?" Maeve yelled, disgusted, a catch in her voice.

"You want him to die, then?"

"Well, no, but what the hell can you do about it?"

"Give him the damned case, Maeve!" said Tallulah. Indridi hadn't fallen victim to Laveau's hex; he was more than a man. Maeve flung open the lid and handed him one of the phials.

Indridi uncapped it with his teeth, holding Fayette's head on one hand, then poured most of the contents into the unconscious man's mouth. When there were a couple of swallows left, the Fae held the bottle under his own nose and inhaled, several deep huffs. His form lost any semblance of humanity. The girls were aware only of a sharp-featured face and an intense white plumage that seemed to illuminate the night. Squinting, they watched as he leaned over, placed his lips on Fayette's, and exhaled. He repeated the motion again and again until he wheezed with the effort. Wisps of lavender, yellow and green mist escaped as Indridi finally broke away, taking a ragged breath.

Fayette's blackened chest heaved in spasm. His shrivelled features convulsed, then lengthened and grew calm as the charred flesh filled out. Deep blue feathers sprouted around his jaw and wrists, and along the length of his spine. As they watched, he grew taller, just a few inches, but it seemed make him thinner, as if he'd been stretched.

"Oh, my. Diluted blood plus 'shine," breathed Tallulah.

"And a modicum of magic," Indridi offered, quietly pleased.

"There is certainly more to you than meets the eye, Mr Indridi," said Maeve.

Indridi inclined his head, "I might say the very same about you both." They helped Fayette to his feet. Stunned, he blinked at them wordlessly until Tallulah burst out laughing. "Now, Marc, if we hadn't brewed that 'shine, where would you be?"

"The very least you can do is show your gratitude," added Maeve, smiling.

"God, I'm ruined." Fayette's eyes were wild as he brushed at his facial feathers like handlebar moustaches. He scowled at the girls. "I won't help you keep breaking the law, you know. Even like this."

"And who asked you to? Hell, we'll be happy to have some of those feathers though." Maeve reached out as if to pluck one away. Fayette slapped at her hands and Tallulah went back to business, barely stifling her mirth.

"As for you, Mr Indridi. Consider that bottle a freebie, but the other ones will cost you. Plus interest."

"Interest?"

"Yeah: the kind that comes in red, black, and silver," Maeve chimed in.

"Ferragamo. Patent leather with heels as long as your index finger. One pair each in all three colours. Size seven," Tallulah fairly sang.

"We'll discuss particulars in the morning, shall we?"

"Let's finish it now—talking money is too crass to dwell on. Don't you agree, Mr Faeke?" Tallulah grinned and winked at Maeve.

"I couldn't have said it better myself, cousin."

"Oh, and one more thing."

Exasperation wrinkled Indridi's face. "What?"

"Ask them to engrave our initials into the soles, will you? Let Maeve lose her own shoes for a change."

Maeve crossed her arms and huffed. "Fine idea. But make mine six-and-a-half. I've got a more delicate bone structure than the Amazon Queen over there . . . "

ABOUT THE CONTRIBUTORS

LINDSY ANDERSON is a writer and web developer. An avid reader, she started writing one day when she ran out of books to read. She lives near Hereford, UK and has just completed an MA in Creative Writing.

CHRIS BAUER lives just north of Chicago, Illinois with his wife, two children (Emma & Finn) and one remarkably aloof dog named Juno. He has worked in the software industry for over 20 years and authored dozens of technical whitepapers, but this is his first published work of fiction. His website is pwiddershins.blogspot.com.

ALAN BAXTER is a British-Australian author. He writes dark fantasy, sci-fi and horror, rides a motorcycle and loves his dog. He also teaches Kung Fu. His novels, *RealmShift* and *MageSign*, are out through Gryphonwood Press, and his short fiction has appeared in a variety of journals and anthologies in Australia, the US, the UK and France. This is Alan's first writing collaboration and he's honoured to share the page with Felicity Dowker. alanbaxteronline.com

JAY CASELBERG is an Australian author based in Europe. His work has appeared in multiple venues around the world and in several languages. His latest novel, *The Jackal Dreaming*, writing as J.A. Caselberg, a YA Fantasy, is available now. More can be found at jaycaselberg.com.

M.L.D. CURELAS lives in Calgary, Canada with two humans and three guinea pigs. Raised on a diet of Victorian fiction and Stephen King, it's unsurprising that she now writes and edits fantasy and science fiction. Recent work includes "Harvest Moon" in *Tesseracts 14*, and editing the anthology *Ride the Moon*.

KAREN DENT's latest fiction "Endless Hunger" will appear in *The Call of Lovecraft* anthology by Evil Jester Press in 2012. Her short fiction has appeared in various anthologies. A full-length play written with her sister Roxanne, was produced at the Firehouse Theatre, Newburyport, MA and won the Newbie Award that year. Her short screenplay, "The Bloated Beetle" won first prize from Screamfest Horror Film Festival. Karen is a member of EWAG, The Dramatist Guild, SAG, AFTRA and NEHW. TheSistersDent.com

Melbourne-based FELICITY DOWKER is a multiple finalist and winner of various awards for her short stories and reviews, including the Ditmar, Chronos, Aurealis, and Australian Shadows Awards. Felicity's debut story collection, *Bread and Circuses*, is due for release from Ticonderoga Publications during 2012. "Burning, Always Burning" is Felicity's first collaborative work and she couldn't think of anyone she'd rather have written it with than Alan Baxter . . . but don't tell him that.

DIRK FLINTHART lives and writes from Northern Tasmania. In his "spare time", he teaches martial arts, maintains fifty acres, is father to three dangerous children, and is studying for an MA. Despite that, he still writes stuff. Upcoming projects include a novella, a novel, a short film, and even the libretto for a bloody opera. The man is a lunatic.

PETE KEMPSHALL is a writer and editor living in Perth, Western Australia. His stories have been published internationally by the likes of Morrigan Books, Big Finish, Dark Quest Books and Apex Publications, and he has been nominated for the Australian Shadows, Aurealis and Ditmar Awards. He blogs about his various projects at tyrannyoftheblankpage.blogspot.com.

LISA L. HANNETT lives in Adelaide, South Australia. Her stories have been published in *Clarkesworld, Fantasy Magazine, Weird Tales, ChiZine, Shimmer, Electric Velocipede, Tesseracts 14* and *Steampunk II: Steampunk Reloaded*, among other places. "The February Dragon", written with Angela Slatter, won the Aurealis Award in 2010. Lisa's first collection, *Bluegrass Symphony*, was published by Ticonderoga Publications in 2011. *Midnight and Moonshine*, co-authored with Angela Slatter, will be published in 2012. You can find her online at lisahannett.com.

DONNA MAREE HANSON resides in Queanbeyan, NSW, Australia. Her short fiction appears in anthologies: *Belong, Dead Red Heart, Scary Kisses* and *More Scary Kisses* by Ticonderoga Publications. Donna usually concentrates her efforts on novel length manuscripts. Her website is at donnamareehanson.wordpress.com

ROBERT HOOD's long career in the fantasy/horror/SF/crime genres has always had a noirish tinge. With over 150 stories published, many re-printed in his three collections to date (most recently *Creeping in Reptile Flesh*), his is a significant presence in the field. His novels include *Backstreets* and the Shades series. A dark fantasy novel, *Fragments of a Broken Land: Valarl Undead*, is due out in 2012 from Borgo Press (US). His website can be found at roberthood.net.

JOSEPH L. KELLOGG is a writer and air emissions technician living in Northeast Tennessee. His stories have been published in *Ray Gun Revival, Andromeda Spaceways Inflight Magazine*, and *AE: The Canadian Science Fiction Review*, among other places. You can follow him on Twitter, @JosephLKellogg.

CHRIS LARGE lives in Tasmania with his two wonderful kids. Most days he's a director of an African mineral exploration company, and a Masters student at UTas. His writing, book collecting, running, volleyball playing, and coursework occur during stolen moments of 'free time'. His other published stories have appeared in *Andromeda Spaceways Inflight Magazine*, and *AntipodeanSF*.

PENELOPE LOVE lives in Box Hill Australia, is married and has no children or cats. Period background for this story came from three books, *The Confident Years: Australia in the Twenties* (Robert Murray), *Twenties Child* (Ivy Arney) and Les Carlyon's *Gallipoli*. She based Wal's fictional fate on the all too real death of Corporal H. Webb, an orphan from Essendon (p.368, *Gallipoli*). Remember Corporal Webb. Remember him.

NICOLE MURPHY has been a primary school teacher, bookstore owner, journalist and checkout chick. She grew up reading Tolkien, Lewis and Le Guin and lives her love of SF and fantasy through the Conflux conventions. Her urban fantasy trilogy Dream of Asarlai is published in Australia/NZ by HarperVoyager. Her publishing venture *In fabula-divinos* (thetaletellers.wordpress.com) is aimed at mentoring up-and-coming writers. Visit her website nicolermurphy.com.

BRIAN G. ROSS is a thirty-six year old Australian who lives in Scotland. He has one hundred publications—from humour (*Defenestration*) to horror (*Murky Depths*), mystery (*FMAM*) to mainstream (*Southern Ocean Review*). He appears in the first three volumes of paperback horror anthology, *Read By Dawn*, and crime collection, *The One That Got Away*, by Dark Prints Press. He runs a blog of his literary wanderings at briangrantross.blogspot.com.

ANGELA SLATTER is a Brisbane writer of dark fantasy and horror. In 2011 *The Girl with No Hands and Other Tales* won the Aurealis Award for Best Collection and *Sourdough and Other Stories* was shortlisted for the World Fantasy Award for Best Collection. *Midnight and Moonshine*, co-authored with Lisa Hannett, will be out in November 2012. She blogs at angelaslatter.com about shiny things that catch her eye.

ACKNOWLEDGEMENTS

"Third Circle" copyright © 2012 Lindsy Anderson.
"Three Questions and One Troll" copyright © 2012 Chris Bauer.
"Burning, Always Burning" copyright © 2012 Alan Baxter and Felicity Dowker.
"Blind Pig" copyright © 2012 Jay Caserberg.
"Silver Comes the Night" copyright © 2012 M.L.D. Curelas.
"A Case to Die For" copyright © 2012 Karen Dent.
"Outlines" copyright © 2012 Dirk Flinthart.
"Prohibition Blues" copyright © 2012 Lisa L. Hannett and Angela Slatter.
"Sangue Della Notte" copyright © 2012 Donna Maree Hanson.
"Walking the Dead Beat" copyright © 2012 Robert Hood.
"The Awakened Adventure of Rick Candle" copyright © 2012 Joseph L. Kellogg.
"Sound and Fury" copyright © 2012 Pete Kempshall.
"One Night at the Cherry" copyright © 2012 Chris Large.
"Be Good, Sweet Maid" copyright © 2012 Penelope Love.
"The Black Star Killer" copyright © 2012 Nicole Murphy.
"Hard Boiled" copyright © 2012 Brian G. Ross.

All stories appear here for the first time. All rights reserved.

AVAILABLE FROM TICONDEROGA PUBLICATIONS

978-0-9586856-6-5	Troy by Simon Brown (tpb)
978-0-9586856-7-2	The Workers' Paradise eds Farr & Evans (tpb)
978-0-9586856-8-9	Fantastic Wonder Stories ed Russell B Farr (tpb)
978-0-9586856-9-6	Love in Vain by Lewis Shiner (limited hc)
978-0-9803531-0-5	Love in Vain by Lewis Shiner (tpb)
978-0-9803531-1-2	Belong ed Russell B Farr (limited hc)
978-0-9803531-2-9	Belong ed Russell B Farr (tpb)
978-0-9803531-3-6	Ghost Seas by Steven Utley (hc)
978-0-9803531-4-3	Ghost Seas by Steven Utley (tpb)
978-0-9803531-5-0	Ghost Seas by Steven Utley (ebook)
978-0-9803531-6-7	Magic Dirt: the best of Sean Williams (tpb)
978-0-9803531-7-4	The Lady of Situations by Stephen Dedman (hc)
978-0-9803531-8-1	The Lady of Situations by Stephen Dedman (tpb)
978-0-9803531-9-8	Basic Black by Terry Dowling (limited hc)
978-0-9806288-2-1	Basic Black by Terry Dowling (tpb)
978-0-9806288-0-7	Make Believe by Terry Dowling (limited hc)
978-0-9806288-3-8	Make Believe by Terry Dowling (tpb)
978-0-9806288-1-4	The Infernal by Kim Wilkins (limited hc)
978-0-9806288-4-5	Scary Kisses ed Liz Grzyb (tpb)
978-0-9806288-5-2	Dead Sea Fruit by Kaaron Warren (limited hc)
978-0-9806288-6-9	Dead Sea Fruit by Kaaron Warren (tpb)
978-0-9806288-7-6	The Girl With No Hands by Angela Slatter (l/hc)
978-0-9806288-8-3	The Girl With No Hands by Angela Slatter (tpb)
978-1-921857-93-5	The Girl With No Hands by Angela Slatter (ebook)
978-0-9807813-0-4	Dead Red Heart ed Russell B Farr (limited hc)
978-0-9807813-1-1	Dead Red Heart ed Russell B Farr (tpb)
978-1-921857-99-7	Dead Red Heart ed Russell B Farr (ebook)
978-0-9807813-2-8	More Scary Kisses ed Liz Grzyb (tpb)
978-1-921857-94-2	More Scary Kisses ed Liz Grzyb (ebook)
978-0-9807813-3-5	Heliotrope by Justina Robson (limited hc)
978-0-9807813-4-2	Heliotrope by Justina Robson (tpb)
978-0-9807813-5-9	Heliotrope by Justina Robson (ebook)
978-0-9807813-6-6	Matilda Told Such Dreadful Lies by Lucy Sussex (l/hc)
978-0-9807813-7-3	Matilda Told Such Dreadful Lies by Lucy Sussex (tpb)
978-0-9807813-8-0	Year's Best Australian F&H eds Grzyb & Helene (hc)
978-0-9807813-9-7	Year's Best Australian F&H eds Grzyb & Helene (tpb)
978-1-921857-98-0	Year's Best Australian F&H eds Grzyb & Helene (ebk)
978-1-921857-00-3	Bluegrass Symphony by Lisa L Hannett (limited hc)
978-1-921857-01-0	Bluegrass Symphony by Lisa L Hannett (tpb)
978-1-921857-97-3	Bluegrass Symphony by Lisa L Hannett (ebook)
978-1-921857-05-8	The Hall of Lost Footsteps by Sara Douglass (hc)
978-1-921857-06-5	The Hall of Lost Footsteps by Sara Douglass (tpb)

WWW.TICONDEROGAPUBLICATIONS.COM

thank you

The publisher would sincerely like to thank

Elizabeth Grzyb, Amanda Pillar, Lindsy Anderson, Chris Bauer, Alan Baxter, Jay Caselberg, M.L.D. Curelas, Karen Dent, Felicity Dowker, Dirk Flinthart, Lisa L. Hannett, Donna Maree Hanson, Robert Hood, Joseph L. Kellogg, Pete Kempshall, Chris Large, Penelope Love, Nicole Murphy, Brian G. Ross, Angela Slatter, Karen Brooks, Jeremy G. Byrne, Kim Wilkins, Marianne de Pierres, Jonathan Strahan, Peter McNamara, Ellen Datlow, Grant Stone, Sean Williams, Simon Brown, Garth Nix, David Cake, Simon Oxwell, Grant Watson, Sue Manning, Steven Utley, Lewis Shiner, Bill Congreve, Jack Dann, Janeen Webb, Lucy Sussex, Stephen Dedman, the Mt Lawley Mafia, the Nedlands Yakuza, Shane Jiraiya Cummings, Angela Challis, Kate Williams, Kathryn Linge, Andrew Williams, Al Chan, Alisa and Tehani, Mel & Phil, Hayley Lane, Georgina Walpole, everyone we've missed . . .

. . . and you.

IN MEMORY OF
EVE JOHNSON (1945–2011)

CPSIA information can be obtained
at www.ICGtesting.com
Printed in the USA
LVHW051400260523
748107LV00001B/3